The First Stone

by Guido Casale

This book is dedicated to Laura and Esther
with much love

Guido Casale is hereby identified as author of this
work in accordance with Section 77 of the Copyright, Designs
and Patents Act 1988

This book is published by
Grosvenor House Publishing Ltd
28–30 High Street, Guildford, Surrey, GU1 3HY.
www.grosvenorhousepublishing.co.uk

A CIP record for this book
is available from the British Library

ISBN 978 1 905529-31-5

Chapter 1

It had felt like stepping through an invisible door which linked one world with another but how she had stumbled upon it Donna could not recall. This land in which she roamed appeared to have no boundaries and all manner of amazing creatures abounded, delighting and terrifying her by turns. For a while she stood on a small bridge gazing down at the stream which meandered underneath and only now did she realise that her fingers were gripping a packet. It was a gift intended for the one she had been sent to find and on a sudden impulse she let it drop with a splash into the water, entirely confident the contents would reach their proper destination even if she failed.

Suddenly an ogre approached, bristling yellow hair and rapacious intent, and she found herself running away up a craggy path and emerging breathless on the other side of a chasm between two rock faces which offered a panoramic view of the sea. Now her fear melted away to be replaced by a sense of wonder as she took in the vastness of the blue-green void that lay between her cliff top position and the horizon. What other enchanted land might exist beyond the line of sky and sea? How dangerous the journey to get there? And was that where she might finally find the friend who eluded her? These were the questions that lay siege to her mind when all at once she spotted a small craft bobbing faraway in the waves.

Her gaze assumed the power of a zoom lens accelerating the image right up close so that instantaneously she could peer inside the hull and appraise the raised blue cabin at the front and the water gathering in the bottom. The boat was listing badly as if about to sink and a human form lay slumped face down by the keel apparently fast asleep. She shouted at him to wake up but he did not stir. Was this the one she had been looking for? Helpless and dismayed she watched the boat go under in a gurgle of white foam and she woke up trembling.

It had been a dream and yet it had been much too real to be a dream. Donna blinked twice, pulled a pillow over her head and willed to be transported back to see if the man had escaped and was swimming for shore. But immediately an alarm went off somewhere in the house, a radio voice spluttered into life and she reopened her eyes on mundane reality. The new week, hooded and naked like a vulture, suddenly hovered over her. Footsteps creaked on the landing and the seascape memory split into a thousand ghostly remnants. Even as she pulled back the duvet and climbed down the tottery pine ladder at the end of the bunk beds these phantoms were fast evaporating until, as her feet touched the floor, nothing remained of that magical adventure except a residue of inexplicable emotion imprinted on her heart.

It was then a strangulated noise close-by, part nasal – part vocal, arrested Donna's attention. The lower bunk was occupied!

"Sarah?" she heard herself mutter in surprise, "Why, Sarah? What's this?"

In the bottom bed lay her sister, moving slightly, but oblivious to the questions. Donna gazed at the pink blue lips, the eyelids taut and fixed as drum skins. How pretty she is, considered Donna, how soft and gentle! But what was Sarah doing here? Why had she not spent the night in her own room? Quite suddenly the mouth distorted into an ugly grimace. Groans and noises like words retched out of it.

"Don't look at me! No! I told you! Don't look at me!" they demanded. "Please! Don't!"

"Sarah? Why shouldn't I look at you?" asked Donna startled by the outburst "It is my bedroom. Sarah?"

But Sarah neither offered a response nor opened her eyes and it was not until Donna lowered her head much closer to her sister's that she realised Sarah was still fast asleep, breathing heavily. The desperate request had not been directed towards her. Or so it seemed. So after a few seconds spent in the silent adoration of her older sibling Donna turned towards the door and with the stealth of a burglar padded noiselessly out of the room, enticed by the smell of frying bacon downstairs.

*

The three dog-eared photographs were a lifeline leading not just back to his past but across dark bleak territories of the mind to the sane side of reality – to a cherished oasis of innocence and contentment. Frank fingered them gently in front of his eyes. Frequently he felt if he did not have these celluloid images he might have imagined the whole experience – dreamt it. Marriage. Fatherhood. Susan.

Francesca. It was mid-morning but nobody else stirred. He lay sprawled out on his bunk in the dormitory he shared with five other residents all of whom he disliked. Three were alcoholics and the other two heroin users. He could see the bruises in their arms when they swilled out, carriers all of indolence and disease.

"Frank? Are you awake? There's a Mr Brown come to see you?"

The door had opened and the warden seemed to be speaking to him across miles of empty space. At the third attempt Frank overcame his torpor sufficiently to croak back, "Dunno any Mr Brown."

"Scottish, I think. Sixty-ish. Oh, and says to tell you he once shared a room with, er, Leppy, I think? Shall I bring him in?"

Frank lurched into a semi-upright position. "Leppy!? Your joking ain't yer?" he challenged. Above his head a body rolled over and emitted a string of incomprehensible oaths. "Tell 'im I'm comin' outside to the kitchen. Gimme a coupla minutes to get dressed."

Alex McLeod stood in the kitchen and Frank recognised him instantly even though age had wrinkled the other man's face and apparently endowed him with a new name. He was wearing a dark suit with a trilby hat and an avuncular smile that made him look like an insurance salesman following up a cold call.

"You've lost weight, Frank," observed McLeod in the measured Glaswegian brogue Frank remembered from Wandsworth Prison. "Where've you been eating?"

"Mainly in church soup kitchens. How did you find me?"

"It wasn't difficult. You've been seen sniffing around some of your old haunts. Tower Hamlets. Lewisham."

"By who?"

"It's a shrinking world, Frank. Did you find what you were looking for?"

"You tell me," snapped Frank impatiently. "You seem to know my business better than me."

"All I know is that you were let out on license six weeks ago," replied McLeod with unshaken affability, "and that I'm here to offer you a decent home and give you a leg up."

"Pull the other one, McLeod. You must want something."

"Yes. I want to put a business proposition to you."

Frank smirked. "What is it? Nickin' pensioners giros from some country post office?"

A fat resident lumbered into the kitchen and hovered unsteadily scratching his armpits by the sink.

"Look, I can't talk here, Frank. Can I buy you breakfast? I know a caff –"

But Frank was already shaking his head. "Gotta check in with my probation this morning," he explained. "And after that I'm due to turn up at some warehouse in Penge fer a job interview. This afternoon any good?"

Now it was McLeod's turn to demur. "Sorry. I've got business on the far side of town. Tomorrow morning's a possibility – about nine?"

"Where?"

McLeod scribbled the details of a caff on a scrap of paper. "You go up to the Mare Street traffic lights –" he began but Frank eyed the address and interrupted.

"I'll find it," he snapped. "See you at ten sharp. And this'd better be good."

Within moments of the Scotsman leaving, however, Frank found himself disconcerted by a vagrant impression that the entire conversation had been a product of his imagination. "Did you see anyone? In 'ere just now?" he spontaneously asked the fat resident who merely picked at a nostril with contemptuous apathy and rolled his bloodshot eyes. But when Frank peered through the window he received instant reassurance. The apparition of McLeod had rematerialised, standing beside the door of a spruce grey saloon, smug and affluent like a watermark of hope improbably surfaced on the futile texture of things.

*

Donna felt tired and anxious. It had been a long frustrating day but they were not being allowed to go home just yet. Through the classroom window she could see a red army in full retreat giggling and skipping towards the main gate. In her other school a bell used to ring very loudly in two prolonged bursts and everyone cheered and stomped their feet. St John's Church of England School was different. You never quite knew when the release was going to come. It all depended.

"We are waiting for you now, Harry Cummings," said Miss Frobisher into the silence.

"But I've stopped talking," retorted Harry, "and I'm sitting up straight with my arms folded."

Donna found herself laughing along with everyone else at the cheeky smirk on Harry's face and the exaggerated way he arched his back and sat to attention.

"But you haven't put your work tray away, have you?" countered Miss Frobisher and sank back in her chair with a sigh as if she had all the time in the world and would be happy to stay there til tomorrow morning if necessary.

The tray quickly disappeared with a clunk, clunk, clunk of plastic against wood, then somebody coughed and somebody else shushed. Eventually Miss Frobisher stood up and surveyed her minions. "You may leave the room quietly. Goodbye everyone."

Donna joined in the muted chorus of "Goodbye, Miss Frobisher" as she broke from her chair ahead of the adjacent tables but Miss Frobisher caught her arm. "Donna, can I have a word with you please?" she asked. Donna stood there next to the big desk, watching the other children leaving, nervously shuffling from one white stockinged foot to the other.

Sarah will be angry with me, she thought to herself. It isn't a games day today and she hates to be kept waiting. But she said nothing to her teacher and just hoped she had not been naughty again without realising it. "It's about the parents' consultation evening," said Miss Frobisher once they were alone together. "Remember you took a letter home inviting your mummy to come and talk to me? Well, she's the only parent who hasn't replied. Can you remind her?" Donna found herself wondering why Miss Frobisher was speaking so slowly again. She did not speak like that to the other children."This is the invitation," continued Miss Frobisher, extracting a letter from a pile of stuff all held down by a gold paperweight. "Did you remember to give it to your mummy, Donna?"

Donna looked at the official typed letter. "I can't remember," she said. "I think I gave it to Katrina."

"Well, you had better take this one just in case it's gone astray," said the teacher and handed it over. "Don't forget now will you?" Donna promised she would not forget. "It's very urgent," intoned Miss Frobisher with a frown and Donna was turning away towards the door when the teacher added, "Is everything alright at home, Donna? You seemed very distracted today?"

Donna hesitated to reply. She did not know what 'distracted' meant and she was worried that she ought to.

"Are you happy?"

"Yes," Donna nodded. "I think so."

"You're not bored are you – by the things I'm teaching you, I mean? It's not too fast? It's quite alright to say," smiled Miss Frobisher encouragingly.

Now 'bored' was a word Donna knew. Her sister Sarah used it all the time. "If I had a pound for every time you say you're bored I'd be richer than the Sheik of Kuwait by now." That's what mummy liked to say. It made her laugh to herself to think of it now. The Sheik of Kuwait! What a funny name.

"No – oh," giggled Donna. "I'm not bored."

"That's good. See you tomorrow then. Bye. And bring an umbrella with you if it's raining." Donna felt puzzled and the teacher must have noticed because she added, "We're going to the river! Remember?"

It was no more than a brisk three minute walk across the playground out onto Winchester Road and round the block to the sweetshop on the main road where she knew Katrina would be waiting in mummy's car to collect them.

"What kept you?" snarled Sarah as Donna opened the door and climbed into the back seat next to her sister.

"We were the last class out and Miss –"

"You're quarter of an hour late," interrupted Sarah. "My bum's sore. Don't do it again! Understand?"

"Sorry, Sarah."

Katrina had already pulled out into thick traffic and they were queuing at the lights. Some pedestrians crossed in front of them and stopped on the central island. "There's Harry with his Dad," began Donna and tapped eagerly on the window to catch his attention.

"Shut up," snapped Sarah. "I'm trying to listen to the radio."

Harry grinned back, screwing up his nose like a chipmunk. He was having a swimming pool birthday party at the weekend and had given invitations to most of the children in 4F including the girls, but he had not given one to her. Maybe he had forgotten? Or maybe he just did not like her? It was frequently very difficult to know if somebody liked you or not, especially boys.

Katrina turned left into Mansfield Road and immediately jerked to a halt to avoid colliding with a people carrier coming in the opposite direction. "Wait there! Wait there!" shouted Katrina at the windscreen in her funny European accent. "Can't you see it's not possible for me to back up? Impatient woman!"

As Katrina edged and manoeuvred her way past the vehicle Donna wondered why people in cars always became so angry with each other. She gazed at the Victorian terraced houses, the bricks – some painted, some not – the sash windows, the squat patio front gardens, the boxes of spring flowers, the red and yellow posters with two bold words written on them that she could not understand but wanted to.

"Sarah? What do those –" she began but Sarah frowned so ferociously that Donna thought better of completing the question. The radio was playing the latest Spice Girls single. She recognised it instantly. And you interrupted that at your peril.

They passed the garage now, went up and over the hump back bridge a bit too quickly and Donna felt her tummy lurch. Number 28 was her house. On the left. The one with the green door and two before the corner of Clifton Road. But Donna could not see it. Somebody had parked a huge truck right outside it so Katrina had no choice but to drive past and turn left into Clifton.

"Why haven't we got a red and yellow poster on our window?" Donna felt it safe to ask as Katrina backed into a space at the kerb.

"Because we're not committed," retorted Sarah and flung open the door as if she had been about to expire from asphyxiation. "We're tactical voters."

"Don't forget the bags, will you, Sarah!" ordered Katrina.

Sarah reached back inside the car impatiently and snatched the schoolbags, marching off imperiously across the street while Katrina eased Donna out and locked up. The creamy white painted house opposite instantly attracted Donna's attention. It had been uninhabited for months now. She had been inside several times. First in the row, it was prettier than the others. A concrete driveway ran along the side of the building down to a garage whose huge green doors were clearly visible. The small front patio garden, flanked by a three foot high wall that gave on to the pavement, boasted nothing special. What caught the eye was the wrought iron barrier protecting the entrance to the driveway – all spikes and swirls with a coat of arms containing the logo of a big golden sun and the words *River Bank.*. Donna liked its quaint cottage shape, architraves, alcoved casement windows and narrow roof. Mummy had once speculated that it had been the very first house built in the area when orchards would have surrounded it and the fruit taken up to the city markets by boat.

Donna gazed at the lace curtains in the unwashed windows and the darkness beyond them and she tried to remember everything about the family who once used to live there before they moved to America. The father with a dark bushy 'tash, the mother with the curly blonde hair and not least Georgia, their little girl who went to a school where you paid the teachers money just to attend! Donna had not known the family long. Shortly after their departure in January a wooden signpost had appeared in the front garden.

"What does it mean, TO LET?" Donna had asked Sarah at the time. She knew the words but put together in combination like that they did not make any sense.

"Put an i in the middle and it spells toilet," Sarah had laughed. "Maybe that's what it's going to become, Dimbo, a public toilet."

But Georgia's mummy had told her that they were going to come back in two year's time! Wouldn't they be very upset if they found their house was being used as a public toilet? Donna knew she would be. And for a while she had been totally taken in by the joke.

"Donna! Donna!"

"What is it?" answered Donna breaking out of her daydream.

"Stop dawdling, will you!" shouted Sarah from the corner where she had now been joined by Katrina. "And carry you own bag. I'm not your donkey." With which she dropped it from a disdainful height onto the pavement before disappearing into Mansfield Road.

"So when do you expect to be moving in, Mr Brown?"

Donna turned her head back to the white house, hardly believing what she saw. The front door had opened and two men were coming out, smiling and chatting politely in the way her teachers did at break times. One of them appeared much older than the other. A passing car drowned out their voices momentarily.

"And I must apologise that the gardens haven't yet been sorted out," she heard. "I'll send somebody around as soon as I can."

"Please don't trouble yourself, it's not really necessary," replied the older one.

"Well, we'll see what we can do. We've got a spare set of keys so it's no problem accessing the mower." They had come up the path and opened the garden gate. "Don't hesitate to ring if you've got the slightest problem, Mr Brown."

"I think we've covered everything," beamed Mr Brown and they shook hands. Mr Brown walked to a grey car parked right outside and was about to get in when he turned back. "Oh, just one thing," he said. "I may have a colleague staying with me for a while at some point. He's just split up with his wife. Could need a base til he sorts himself out."

"It's your place now, sir," replied the other with a polite smile. "You can have whoever you want staying."

Donna watched the grey car disappear round the corner and when she looked back the younger man had approached close to where she stood by the mouth of the driveway. His hands gripped the 'toilet' sign apparently with the purpose of uprooting it, shaking one way first then another but all to no avail. She wanted to ask him about the new owners but was too shy to speak. Then he gave up and rubbed one hand against the other to get the dirt off, suddenly noticing her for the first time. "This won't be here much longer," he smiled down and briskly walked off to another vehicle.

Chapter 2

Mrs Montgomery came bustling out of the canteen building with a frown on her face. "Is everyone ready, Vicky?" she asked Miss Frobisher and glanced up at the fleecy blue sky. "Thank God the weather has changed!"

"Just about," answered Miss Frobisher and turned on the only two children left who had not been assembled into the line now strung out to the length of five classrooms. "Abigail, pair off with Donna, will you? And join the end."

Donna did what she was told in silence. She had never spoken to Abigail before.

"Do you have to hold hands, Miss?" asked Abigail as the troop moved forward in slow orderly fashion, a phalanx of teachers and parents marshalling the flanks.

"Better had until we cross the main road and reach the embankment," replied their teacher.

As far as Donna understood it was a nature walk to finish off year 4's geography project on the local community.

"I usually walk with Laura," explained Abigail as the snake negotiated the crossing junction on the Great Chertsey Road. "She's my best friend. She's off sick this week. You don't come from round here, do you?"

"No, I – I was born in Clap –" stammered Donna shyly. "Clap – ham."

"Where's that?"

"In London."

Abigail giggled. "This is London too," she said a bit mockingly. "You know that?"

Donna nodded and fell quiet again. Then Abigail's hand tightened on her own. That's how she knew it was alright between them. "Who's your best friend?" asked Abigail.

Donna tried to think of the right answer. It felt uncomfortable and made her eyes squint up. She had no real friends like the others did. "Georgia," she answered at length

"Georgia? I don't know anybody called Georgia," said Abigail. "Which class is she in?"

"Oh, she isn't," explained Donna. "She's gone to America with her mummy and daddy –"

"I meant at St John's, not at your last school," interjected Abigail unhelpfully. "I suppose it takes time. You only came in September, didn't you?" Donna nodded. She wanted to say that Georgia was not at her last school either but did not get a chance. "What's your favourite subject? Mine's English," gabbled on Abigail.

"I like art best," considered Donna. "And geography, a bit."

They had turned out of the avenue now and into the embankment promenade. The splendid Victorian footbridge loomed suddenly in front of them, a green and cream painted ornament straddling the waterway in four symmetrical parabolas of confidence. A battery of bleach white gulls rose up from the water shrieking in fear or anticipation. Donna felt the sudden imprint of the moment like a stain on the back of her mind.

"You don't go to the church, do you?" announced Abigail. Donna shook her head. "I thought not. I'm one of Bronwyn's family service helpers. And so is Laura." Donna had no idea what family service meant but smiled as if she did and watched a trim blue launch tying up on the Old Deer Park side of the river to which she knew they were heading. "I've got a puppy called Snoop and a door mouse called Whiskers," continued Abigail. "Have you got a pet?"

"I'm not allowed," replied Donna. "But Sidney's got a cat called Chelsea and –"

"See that house over there, behind the trees?" Abigail interrupted. "A lady on the television lives there. The one who does the lottery. Big, isn't it?" Donna looked to her left but could not see much apart from the trees and the occasional slice of roof beyond them. "We live in the next road past," added Abigail proudly. "Our house is called Hammonds End. My daddy's a senior executive. He's responsible for that big factory place near Gillette Corner."

"What's a factory?" asked Donna confused by all the words.

"It's a building where you make things. Didn't you know that?!"

"Oh, yes," said Donna quickly. "I just forgot."

*

The cafe was called "The Silver Spoon." McLeod sat at a corner table next to the window nursing a large coffee. He gestured the counter assistant over with casual familiarity and Frank ordered a fry-up, tea and toast.

"You?" asked Frank "Not eatin'?"

"Finished."

McLeod talked in a relaxed understated way, mostly about old times, occasionally lowering his voice if anyone seemed to be ear-wigging. There's no point rushing him, Frank considered as the meal arrived. He'll get to the point eventually.

"So let's talk about you, Frank. How did your bird split in the end?"

Frank told him briefly the names of the prisons and the dates. "What about you, McLeod?"

"I've kept clean since I got out." Frank shot him a look of disbelief. "Honest, son. What are the conditions of your licence?"

Frank shrugged and stuffed a piece of sausage in his mouth. "Thirteen months. The usual bollocks. Report weekly to a probation. Live in that doss. No leavin' the country. Waiter! Another mug of tea over here!"

"And work?"

"Had me diggin' holes in the underground for ten days. I pretended to pull a muscle. Jacked it."

Frank felt McLeod's narrow eyes appraising him like you might appraise a racehorse in a parade ring before placing a bet. He did not much like it. "Did you hear about Leppy?" he asked to deflect them. "Diagnosed bowel cancer. Kicked the bucket three weeks after the operation. About a year after your release I think it was."

McLeod's mouth puckered up with amusement. "Bowel cancer, eh? Leppy always called his wife a pain in the arse. I didn't think he meant it literally."

Only a fresh mug of tea being placed on the table served to restrain Frank's annoyance at McLeod's apparent indifference.

"Anything for you, Mr Brown?"

"So what's with the 'Mr Brown'?" challenged Frank once the waiter had retreated.

McLeod took a couple of small cards out of his wallet and passed one across the table. Frank read the printed name Alexander G. Brown. Human Resource Consultant. Followed by a fancy company logo and an office address in Aberdeen.

"Human resource consultant? Very subtle that," smirked Frank, handing it back. "What's the scam?"

"I've been working on it for six years," smiled the other, passing over the second card. "It's my retirement scam."

Now we're getting down to it, thought Frank and read the print on an identical business card – only the name had changed. "Anthony W. Smith," said Frank. "What's the W for? Let me guess –?"

"Keep it. Get used to the name."

"Why?"

"Patience, Frank. I'm coming to all that. You seem mentally quite resilient, son. Sharp," remarked the Scotsman running his index finger along the blade of a knife. Frank made cow eyes and let his jaw sag loose like an idiot. "I'm serious. A long stretch like that can do powerful damage to a man's brain. I mean it's not just the bird. You get out and find nobody's where they should be any more. Nobody will tell you what you need to know. And you discover time on the outside can pass even slower than it did on the inside."

Frank stopped eating and stared hard into McLeod's face, struggling against the temptation to punch it. But McLeod's gaze never faltered. It was almost as if McLeod was tempting him to strike deliberately, Frank felt.

"I mean that as a sincere compliment," the older man continued eventually. "You've still got a lot of friends. You could have coughed when that building society job went wrong. Put Davenport and a few others behind bars. Fixed yourself an early release. But you didn't. You kept mutt. It isn't forgotten. Friends are important."

Frank reached for the salt cellar with an angry jerk of his hand and spilled it all over the table. "Friends?! Davenports bin in Parkhead since '93," he said instinctively tossing a pinch of the stuff over his shoulder. "Fat lot of good he can do me in there!"

"You're wrong. We're having this conversation because Davenport directly recommended you," said McLeod and relocated the salt cellar as if it were a major chess piece. "I didn't realise you were the superstitious type, Frank?"

"Oh, there is something you don't know about me then?" cracked Frank. "Trust it hasn't put a hole in Davenport's testimonial?"

*

"Where do you live?" asked Abigail

"Twenty-eight Mansfield Road," answered Donna. "There's a river near us. It's not this one though. It's little,"

"Tributary," said Abigail. "That's what they're called. I don't know any Mansfield Road. Is it far anyway?"

"Not really. There's a man who –" began Donna and then thought twice about completing the sentence. It sounded silly even to her.

"A man who what?" coaxed Abigail. "Go on!"

By this time they had marched up the stone steps and were crossing the bridge. The view along the river to Richmond Hill was breathtaking. Donna had seen it before, of course, but never on such a crystal clear day.

"My sister says there's a man in Mansfield Road who turns into a vampire at night," confessed Donna in a low watchful voice. "She saw him once."

Abigail's eyes widened incredulously then she burst out laughing as if it was the funniest thing she had ever heard. "You're a hoot," she giggled. "You really are!"

Donna liked this. She felt her face flush with pleasure like an actress in front of an appreciative audience and began to perform an encore about the crocodile who lived in the little river when Miss Frobisher called for silence and started issuing instructions on how they were to assemble around the lock, a massive self-contained tank immediately beneath them as they descended the Surrey steps.

A man in uniform called Mr Peabody was presented. He stood on an elevated part of the quay and in a hearty booming voice proceeded to tell them all sorts of things about the tides and the lock, then about the history of the Thames and its present day management by the Port of London Authority for whom he worked. Not all of it made complete sense to Donna.

"So this is a road, a reservoir and a natural habitat for many wild animals," he summarised, "all at the same time. It's height can vary by as much as 23 feet and it flows at a speed of 3 knots. In my opinion it's the most important single reason why London became such a great city and, though its function as a commercial port has greatly shrunk this century with the advent of transport technology, the river still carries over 56 million tonnes of cargo every year. Of course, very little of that comes this far up. Now then, anyone's parents own a cabin cruiser or a yacht?!"

A couple of hands went up and a murmur of interest as the P.L.A. official focussed in on their proud owners. "Been anywhere good in it?" he asked Andrew.

"Southend once," offered the boy and pointed the direction.

"Take you long?"

"Not really. I think we went with the tide."

Went with the tide? thought Donna to herself. What does that mean? And what causes the tide?

"Clever boy. Excellent," grinned the man. "Down stream on the ebb tide conserves energy. Still you must stick to a maximum 8 knots. It's a rule. But from here there are no more weirs or natural barriers to slow you down til you get to the flood barrage at Woolwich. And that's only lowered in extreme circumstances. Beyond is the estuary and open sea. Freedom. Better than a motor way, eh? You can't get to Spain and Cape Town and Australia on the M1. Most of the time you can't get to bloody Watford!"

Everybody laughed and started swapping tales of gridlock and tedious car journeys til Mrs Montgomery brought them back to order. "Mr Peabody is going to tell us what to look out for as we stroll down the river," she announced and he complied. Thistleworth Marina. The Crane Outlet. The Eyot. All Souls Church and its medieval tower. The London Apprentice.

"It's a trendy restaurant and pub now," elaborated Mr Peabody, "but in centuries past The London Apprentice used to be a favourite haunt for smugglers."

"I've been there with mummy and Sarah," whispered Donna to her companion. "For a special treat."

"Does everybody understand what a smuggler is?" intervened Mrs Montgomery and Donna joined in with the small hushed chorus of 'No'.

Mr Peabody's eyes lit up with mischief and pleasure as he told them all about prohibitive import tariffs and the ruses of old time merchant sailors to evade them.

"Nowadays the customs officers are more vigilant," he advised. "Incoming craft are carefully monitored. The main offences are committed by drug traffickers and illegal immigrants. A hundred Romanians were discovered in a giant container when a ship docked at Dartford last month."

"I think that's racist," whispered Abigail darkly but Donna did not respond. In truth she did not hear. Her imagination remained entranced by Mr Peabody's evocation of a global community of waterways. Nobody owned the water as they did the land it seemed. Water was like blood in the human body. Its purpose was to nourish and connect the major organs of the planet. The tiniest veins and thickest arteries were all connected and served the same purpose. This is roughly what Donna perceived and marvelled at as she and Abigail trekked along the towpath in the rear although she could never have put her understanding into words. Words were not her best way of communicating yet, nor might ever be. She knew that.

*

When the Scotsman left to take a leak Frank decided to declare his hand. He was fed up with the small talk. "Why am I here?" he demanded as soon as McLeod sank back into his chair.

"I need an extra man – a man who won't lose his bottle in a crisis," answered McLeod directly and brought his head indecently close. "A man who can handle a gun. Who knows how the river flows. I need you, Frank. And you'll be very well rewarded."

"The River Thames?" McLeod affirmed with a nod and was about to launch into an explanation when Frank said, "Let's get a couple of things straight before you pitch. Why did you sneer like that when I mentioned Leppy? I owed him a lot."

"Och! I shared a cell with the geezer for three years. You'd have thought his wife had poisoned him – not the other way round. Obsessed with her he was. Couldn't talk about anything else. No wonder his loathing turned into a tumour!"

"Anyway, I won't hear anything against him!" insisted Frank. "I owed him a lot. He got me interested in something. He taught me how to survive."

"Yes, I know that but –"

"He left me his gear. He knew he wasn't coming back from hospital."

"Alright. Sorry then, Frank. Let's not say another word about him. Leppy Varga – rest in peace."

"Amen."

"And what else?"

"You get out and find nobody's where they should be any more," said Frank. "What did you mean by that?" McLeod shrugged. "You meant Susan, didn't you? Susan and 'Cesca? They went to Australia didn't they? That was the rumour I heard? After the mortgage company repossessed the house? Come on, McLeod, what do you know about them?"

McLeod cleared his throat and moved around as if his seat had suddenly started to feel uncomfortable. Frank liked that. The bastard has got feelings underneath the smarm, he thought to himself.

"I know she never visited you," he said at length. "I know she never answered your letters, Frank. Nothing else. I remember how bad you were at accepting it –"

"I've got news for you, mate. I still am."

McLeod nodded and gestured as if about to make some intimate confession. "It's common place. It happened to me the first time I did a real stretch. My missus did a runner with the kids. The in-laws refused to squeal."

"Did you ever catch up with her?"

"Aye. Eventually. But by that time I'd lost interest. She was a witch and I'd found other eggs to fry. That's what you should do, Frank. You can't stay alive in the past."

McLeod angled his head towards the window where an attractive young woman was just that second walking past on the pavement. Frank felt an automatic surge of desire in his groin followed almost instantly by a knot of grief and self-disgust tightening in his chest as the idea of union with somebody who was not Susan infiltrated his mind.

"Come on now. Let's take a stroll," said McLeod dropping a ten pound note on the table as he stood up. "It's time to get down to brass tacks."

*

"Your shoelace is undone," said Abigail suddenly.

As Donna knelt down to tie it up she spotted an animal with a small pointy face and prominent bushy tail crouching on the embankment no more than twenty yards away and staring her defiantly in the face. At most it lingered three seconds but she felt intimidated, a bit like a trespasser caught red-handed on private property. The beast resented this chattering serpentine invasion of its territory.

"Did you see that dog?!" she shouted back over her shoulder but Abigail had walked on and was gazing up with the other children at a heron's nest on the island.

"Something round here smells good," remarked Abigail as Donna caught up. She began to sniff at the yellowy blossoms of a spindly plant. "Could it be this forsythia?"

Donna thought it looked nice but could detect no particular perfume. Suddenly a butterfly flitted out of the foliage, hovered in the air suspiciously for a second or two, then alighted on one of the lower stems.

"That's the first butterfly I've seen this year," exclaimed Abigail. "It's a good omen. So early, I mean. There should be a warm dry summer ahead."

Donna stopped to examine the markings on the insect's wings, circles and parallel lines in orange and white with tiny piebald patches of white and red. "It's beautiful," she said and recalled with just a tinge of regret how much she liked animals but how difficult she found them to draw.

On the walk back they stopped as prearranged aloft the pedestrian bridge and watched the great sluices mechanically lowered, the river churning and thrashing in massive white paroxysms of rage as the man made dam bit deep into its natural flow. Mrs Montgomery was standing behind Donna chatting to one of the parents. "Did you see that fox on the embankment? Beautiful, wasn't it?" Donna heard her say.

"Don't talk to me about foxes," replied the other. "They're becoming the bane of my life – scavenging the dustbin bags, terrifying the cats. And the row they make at night when they take to fighting each other! It's simply awful!"

"They're certainly becoming bolder," said the teacher. "I regularly see one prowling around my back garden in mid afternoon."

"Laura suffers from Asthma," remarked Abigail for no apparent reason. "What does your daddy do?"

"I haven't got a daddy," confessed Donna.

"Oh? Which school does your sister go to?"

Donna could not remember the name. "The big school" she said. "It's near that nice park. The park with the café in the middle."

"Does she like it?"

Donna considered for a second. "I don't really think so," she replied. "She's always in de- deten – detensh -?"

"Detention?" suggested Abigail.

"That's it," smiled Donna. "She's always in detenshun."

*

"They've all done bird except Hunter," said McLeod. "They're experienced men. Handpicked with care. They know the price of failure. And they wouldn't be in if the job was flawed."

Frank lit up a fresh cigarette. "But it can't happen again," he insisted in a cloud of exhaled smoke. "Not since Brinks Mat. The security on gold bullion's failsafe."

"I've told you. We've got someone on the inside."

"So did those mugs in 83. Someone who bent at the first bit of police pressure."

"This is different, Frank. I told you. I'm talking inside – executive class."

Frank raised his eyes towards the sky and blinked. The story that he had just been told sounded implausible – like a synopsis for a third rate gangster flick. They were sitting on a bench in a scrap of public garden outside a library. The din of passing traffic served as convenient camouflage for their voices. Frank could feel the vibrant intensity of the city like small electric shocks all over his body and the sunshine dappling his face as it strobed through the branches of a solitary cherry blossom tree. He shielded his eyes and studied the other man's inscrutable countenance. Stubborn, greedy, ruthless, calculating. These were a few of the words he would have chosen to describe what he knew about McLeod yesterday. Today he would need to add a couple more. Ambitious. Daring. And how about demented? Any second I'll wake up, he thought, and find I've been dreaming the whole bloody thing.

"Are you in then?" asked the Scotsman eventually.

"It's a big one to bite off. I need more time to chew," Frank considered aloud.

"Fair enough. Forty-eight hours. I'll come round on Friday morning." McLeod looked at his watch. "After that I'll have to let you go. You're not indispensable. Any other questions?"

"This isn't just your set up, is it? It's too big? Davenport involved?" probed Frank.

McLeod shook his head slightly. "It's mine and mine alone. Of course there's a sponsor. He supplies the readies."

"And the inside information?"

"Aye. The ship and the market contacts abroad, too. But no more. He takes the same cut of the proceeds."

"What's his name? Santa Claus?"

"Fraid you gotta trust me on that, too."

As McLeod stood up Frank said, "The Old Bill will know. You can't keep the word of something this big off the street. They'll 'ave every fence and armourer in the country under surveillance within 48 hours of the job. Not to mention the smelters."

"That's why we're taking the haul overseas," replied McLeod laconically. "We miss out the middle men. Low overheads. Low risk. Think of the time they'll waste chasing up blind alleys!"

Just for a split second the Scotsman allowed his eyes to widen and Frank realised how infatuated McLeod was by the glorious fantasy of masterminding a landmark heist.

"I reckon your –" Frank began but his attention was diverted by a sudden commotion. Across the road an open backed truck had appeared out of nowhere, bedecked with red and yellow trimming and photographs of grinning politicians. The passengers were waving to pedestrians and one of them was barking election slogans through a megaphone. For the second time within a few seconds Frank found himself fundamentally estranged from the evidence of his own senses. The noise overwhelmed him and the closer the pageant moved, the less he was able to decipher the words which began to sound like monkey gibberish. And when the barker seemed to address him directly Frank could not overcome his confusion. He just wanted to run away. This vortex of nonsense was intent on sucking him into its centre. But as he stood up Frank realised that McLeod was still talking, too, chuntering away, unabashed, as if to himself.

"What did you say?!" shouted Frank above the din.

"I said it's the end of an era, Frank! Everything's changing! We're lucky to be alive! Life's going to be beautiful from now on!"

Chapter 3

On Thursday after school Donna felt unusually restless and was unable to settle to anything. A steady drizzle had been falling outside. Sarah monopolised the living room, stretched out on the settee watching 'Home And Away', a red exercise book open on her lap.

"Sarah? Can I borrow – ?" began Donna hesitantly.

"Shut up!" snapped Sarah.

"I only want to know if –"

"I'm trying to revise my French!"

Donna dropped down onto a bean bag, her eyes flickering between the screen and her sister, wondering if she would become as grumpy as Sarah when she was old enough to go to secondary school and had to do homework every night or suffer detention. "Mummy says you're not supposed to do your homework in front of the telly," she muttered under her breath.

"Va-t-en, imbecile! Sac de mairde!"

She pretended to watch the programme for a few seconds then stood up with exaggerated indifference and walked across to the sideboard where she rummaged about in the drawers. Finally unearthing a pink floral hair band, Donna proceeded to use it in front of the mantelpiece mirror to tie her hair back into a little bunch. She tilted her head and squinted sideways, pleased with the result. Sarah's electronic gameboy had been dumped on the sideboard top next to the battery of framed family photographs. This was the real target. Donna glanced at her sister's reflection, then picked it up and casually retreated to the bean bag, settling down to play with her back towards the settee.

"That was your mummy on the phone," announced Katrina bursting into the room. "She wants me to remind you to tidy up your bedroom, Sarah."

"In a minute," replied Sarah languidly without shifting her eyes from the screen.

"She says she will be late home tonight."

"What again?! What's for dinner?"

"Well, how about I make – ?"

"Leave it!" Donna felt her heart lurch. "I said leave it!" bawled Sarah again.

Donna took her finger off the play button and the tiny angular figure on the monitor instantly froze. "Please can I borrow your gameboy?" she asked apologetically.

"No. Ask first."

"But I tried to. Please!"

"Not hard enough. Too late now. Givvit!"

Donna dropped the gadget on the carpet disconsolately and rolled over onto her stomach facing the box. "How about I make you beans on toast?" continued Katrina as if nobody had interrupted. "Or maybe spaghetti bolognaise?"

"Whatever," muttered Sarah gruffly and the pale young woman retreated back to the kitchen.

"I'm hungry now," complained Donna following her.

"Take an apple and a packet of crisps to keep you going, yes?" suggested Katrina as she removed the receiver from the phone with a little shudder of agitation and patted out a very long number.

Donna helped herself and trotted up the stairs to her bedroom, resigned to her own company. On her little desk lay a box of coloured pencils open and a couple of unfinished sketches she had been intermittently working on since yesterday's river walk. Over breakfast she had considered that they showed promise, especially the one of the seagulls exploding into the air but now as she studied it again her confidence evaporated. Her memory or technique had utterly failed. An anarchy of meaningless jagged lines and swirling blotches stared mockingly back. She scrunched the pictures between her fingers and dropped them in the bin. There was more important business to attend to – the doll family.

Donna's dolls lived in a compound between fiction and reality. They were housed in two pink plastic boxes, together with their paraphernalia of clothes and furniture, underneath the bunk beds – new recruits and veterans alike. Several had been inherited from Sarah and suffered the inconvenience in old age of dislocated or missing limbs, only seeing the light of day when a major dramatic soap opera needed to be enacted. Today was not such an occasion. Donna simply had a piece of good news to share and a little picnic, too, if any of her favourite four felt peckish.

"Have you missed me today, Sylvestra?" she asked as she propped the first of two brunettes against the radiator and prised on her tiny high heel slippers.

Sylvestra did not look as if she missed anyone. She wore a two piece green skirt and jacket and a halo of charm and self-confidence. She hosted a daytime television chat show in front of a live audience who revered her every inflection of speech.

Second out emerged Caroline in her casual weekend wardrobe consisting of blue jeans and a turquoise top. Like Donna's mummy she took the train up to town every day and worked in a Travel Agency. A long time ago she had been married and lived for a while in Australia but she preferred not to talk about the old days. "I have to focus on tomorrow," she would occasionally be overheard insisting as if it was an article of personal faith and there had been a succession of shadowy boyfriends enlisted presumably to help her succeed.

"You're very late back, Caroline?" observed Donna as she modelled the supple body into an armchair. "Did you go round to Gerry's place for supper?"

Jade was a blonde with a smiley round face and a practical nononsense manner who could deal with any sort of emergency which was just as well since she worked in the casualty ward of a hospital.

"Are you on night duty again?" asked Donna. "You'd better build up your strength." And she set out the dining room table replete with plates, cutlery, cups and slivers of crisp and apple.

The last to be extricated from the boxes was Dawn. In keeping with her status as a displaced person this doll had not yet acquired any clothes and like Katrina, her prototype in Donna's fertile imagination, she remained less than half invented. According to Caroline who had befriended her one day in the station coffee shop, Dawn had run away from one of those countries where people are always bombing and killing each other. Left to her own devices, Dawn would merely laze around in bed all day and brood.

"You need to get out more," counselled Donna in a motherly voice as she stood the doll on the window ledge, fiddling on her underwear followed by one of Sylvestra's spare outfits. "You need to buy some decent clothes. What's that? You haven't got any money? Oh, don't worry. I can lend you as much as you need."

Donna left the doll propped against the window and sneaked furtively along the landing into Sarah's room. It had the appearance of a refuse dump. Clothes, cosmetics, exercise books and an unfinished game of Monopoly littered the floor. Donna quickly scooped up a wedge of banknotes and tip-toed out, gently pulling the door closed. As she returned her attention was arrested by a sudden snarl of frustration, distinctly feline in origin, and a flutter of agitated wings. Down below in the garden a cat could be seen, poised by a gap in the privet hedge and peering skywards at its prey which spiralled to safety.

"There's Chelsea!" announced Donna. "He's been prowling around the white house again – see? He's had that big back garden all to himself for ages but somebody has moved in now. He's called Mr Brown. I don't know how many children he's got but I bet it's at least two."

She pressed Dawn's wide-eyed delicate face hard up against a pane and together they scanned the premises, no more than thirty yards away, for signs of neighbourly life. From this side angle the quaint cottage style of the architecture became diminished. A vast expanse of wall stared back at them, its severity relieved only slightly by an out of character double-glazed window and frosted glass panelled door. A portion of the rear patio and adjacent French windows were just visible too but nothing remotely suggested human habitation. No lights. No voices. And most of the garden was blocked from view by the double garage with its corrugated grey roof. At least it had stopped drizzling.

"They might be down by the river playing hide and seek," surmised Donna craning her neck to no avail. After a short while she found herself wondering why all these acres of fertile land had been so unequally apportioned to the property owners who surrounded it. The detached houses on Clifton Road enjoyed long undulating gardens like private parks with a river at the bottom, whereas the terraced ones on Mansfield Road, which formed the eastern perimeter of the estate, had badly lost out. A network of tiny, squashed together backyards, linked by an L shaped ginnel, provided barely enough space for the occupiers to hang a washing line, never mind cultivate a bush or a decent tree.

"Never mind. I wonder if the mummy and daddy need a childminder?" conjectured Donna as she counted out the banknotes onto the sill. "That would be great if you get a job like the one Katrina's got here, wouldn't it?!" Dawn nodded enthusiastically back. "I could come and visit you and make friends –"

"Have you been in my room, Div?" boomed out a voice in harsh accusation that made Donna's flesh creep with mortification. Donna swung round, her frightened fingers involuntarily tightening on a five pound note. "Well? Has the cat got your tongue?!"

"N- No," stuttered Donna, keeping her back between the banknotes and the window ledge on which they lay.

"You'd better not have been," threatened Sarah, a supercilious rash of lipstick freshly embossed on her face. "Or else!"

"You come into my room sometimes," objected Donna meekly, her eyes flickering towards the bunk beds.

"That's different. Your space is twice the size of mine, Div. And it's got a view."

"So has yours, Sarah –"

"Mines got a view of a row of poxy houses. That doesn't count. It's dreary. You've got that willow over there and ninety percent of the sun. Make sure you're wearing a garlic necklace tonight. It's approaching full moon. The vampire will be on the prowl and I may not be awake to protect you!" And with a ghoulish leer Sarah flounced off down the landing.

"There's no such thing," called Donna uncertainly after her. "Abigail told me!"

It was not until she was in the toilet a few minutes later lowering her knickers that Donna relaxed her fist and discovered the toy money scrunched up inside. "How did that get there?" she pondered to herself as she sat on the lavatory seat.

After supper she had a shallow bath, brushed her teeth unsupervised and put on her blue pyjamas and nightgown.

"Can I watch the telly now?" she asked Katrina

"For a little bit," agreed Katrina without looking up from her fashion magazine.

Donna pressed the button and the screen crackled twice then spluttered into images of angry arguing heads.

"Katrina?"

"Yeah?"

"Has mummy gone to Gerry's house for the night?"

"Not for the night. She'll be coming back."

"Are you going to sleep on the sofa again?"

"No need. I'll be round in the morning to take you to school."

"What does she do there all the time? Does she love him more than she loves us?"

A smile seemed to form on Katrina's thin lips and quickly disappear. "Course not," she replied.

"Then why doesn't she invite him here anymore?"

The phone rang and Katrina answered it expectantly on the living room extension. "Yes? Just a minute, please," she answered. "Donna? Go tell your sister Polly is on the phone."

Donna ran halfway up the staircase obligingly and shouted Sarah's name twice. A splinter of light cut open the darkness overhead instantly followed by the graceless voice of its perpetrator.

"It had better be important, bitch."

"Polly's on the phone and EastEnders has started."

One sister followed the other impatiently back down. "Oh, hullo Polly! I badly missed you today. How are your sniffles?" cooed Sarah sweetly into the mouthpiece, her tone of voice magically transformed in an instant. "You avoided a well spastic performance of netball. Yeah. Miss played Zoe up front in place of you and she wasted fifteen shots. Are you still going to the youth club tomorrow?"

Later when Donna lay in the top bunk with Caroline and Dawn and her vampire torch for company – just in case – trying to sleep, she could not help wondering why Sarah never talked to her in that kind, giggly way. It was as if Sarah had two people living inside her, one very mean and tormenting, the other all sweet and gushing who was entirely reserved for her best friends and special visitors.

Suddenly, somewhere distantly in the pitch black a latch clicked and footsteps creaked on the floor. Donna buried her head deep beneath the duvet, her ears pricked like a rabbit chased to ground listening for its predator. Was it mummy arriving home or some blood-sucking creature of her nightmares? Some entity was out there moving around on the landing. She held her breath. Then the close-up, spine- chilling whoosh of the door swinging open, the feet padding right up close, the judder and bounce of the frame as it entered the lower bed. Silence. A minute passed before a low moaning sound began, gradually at first, rising and falling at regular intervals, like a wood pigeon in distress, calling to its lost mate. The images of mummy and the vampire were extinguished in a sudden rush of intuition.

"Sarah?" Donna asked puzzled. "Is that you? Sarah? What's the matter?"

Nothing replied but the dull ebb and flow of her sister's mysterious lament.

Chapter 4

The main road was heavily congested with Friday morning traffic. After ten minutes edging and braking and sighing Katrina said, "The roundabout is playing up again."

Donna spotted Abigail walking along hand in hand with a man who manifestly must have been her father. She tapped on the window but failed to attract their attention.

"Abigail's daddy is an exec- " she announced. "An execu something?"

"An executioner?" scoffed Sarah. "I've had enough of this. I'm going to walk."

In a second she had abandoned the marooned vehicle and crept up behind a tight knit group of girls all strutting like peahens along the pavement as if they owned it. A gust of laughter and play-acted shock threw up as Sarah's surprise attack proceeded. The group split into fragments, assimilated the newcomer into its banter and instantly close ranks again.

How happy and unafraid and tall they all look, Donna considered with a twinge of envy. Their smart purple uniforms seemed like fashion statements in comparison to the red and white striped tunic she had to suffer. "Katrina?" she asked. "What does your daddy do?"

"He's in the army," said Katrina and spurted the car suddenly forward.

The morning seemed to pass very slowly. After vocabulary practice 4F filed obediently into assembly where Bronwyn led the hymn singing and then told a short story from the life of Jesus before handing over to Mr Knighton.

"I must apologise that your education has to be disrupted next week," announced the headmaster with a twinkle in his eye. "On Thursday the school will be used as a polling station in the general election. Please remind your parents. And the following Monday is a bank holiday."

A spontaneous gasp of elation rose from the congregation followed by ripples of chatter and bartering for holiday company that were quickly repelled by the supervising teachers on the flanks of the hall.

*

The wings had become detached from the proboscis. Using a pair of tweezers he carefully engineered them back into position, four minuscule grooves oozing just sufficient glue to anchor the cardboard tabs. He watched them close up at the tip of his nose. One. Two. Three. Four. Like stanchions settling into concrete coffins.

"You still doing that, Frank?"

It was the unmistakable brogue of McLeod behind him. He had wandered into the dormitory unannounced.

"Not really. This one got damaged in transit," replied Frank and replaced the insect on the lid of a matchbox to dry out close to the rest of its family.

"It's very good," remarked McLeod. "Good enough to sell."

"I don't sell them. I give them to friends. And I wear them." Frank picked up a small tortoiseshell and attached it to the epaulette of his shirt. "They make me feel positive."

"We can't talk here," said McLeod gesturing across the room to an unshaven pyjama clad body propped up on its elbows whistling the theme tune to 'Match of the Day'. "Let's take a stroll, shall we?"

"No need, McLeod. He's out of it. Couldn't tell you what year it is let alone the month."

"Well?" grunted McLeod. "Are you in?"

Frank nodded. "What happens next?" he asked

McLeod looked neither relieved nor surprised. "We get you out of here as soon as possible."

"Where to?"

"Oh. A nice house with a river at the bottom of the garden."

"A river at the bottom of the garden," mimicked the derelict with uncanny precision.

McLeod glowered angrily. "Come on," he snapped. "I'm gonna fill in the details. Later on today you'll get a chance to meet the others."

Frank picked up a Red Admiral and offered it to McLeod. "Stick this in your buttonhole," he grinned. "It might bring you luck."

McLeod turned abruptly away to the door. "No thanks," he said. "I make my own luck."

*

Donna disliked Maths more than English. At least there was a point to reading and writing but adding and subtracting numbers in your head, the main thrust of a lesson which always seemed to happen

28

after assembly, just did not make sense when you could use a calculator as Sarah always did. For one thing she did not have enough fingers to count on and as she moved laboriously from one hand to the other and back again she nearly always seemed to forget which one she had started with. Left or right? The work sheets were dense and intimidating, too, little parcels of digits, all neat and untarnished, waiting to be tied into shape and delivered back to their distributor's desk. Twenty minutes staring at them and your eyes began to sting as if someone had sliced up an onion. The digits embarked on a spontaneous jig of sedition, the columns warped and wilted in the growing heat of your frustration and you ended up scribbling down anything that came into your head just to get the whole tedious exercise over.

After that, the break in the playground engulfed Donna as refreshingly as an open air swimming pool on a scorching midsummer afternoon. Gulping in great lungfuls of west London's version of oxygen, soothing her face in the breeze and sunlight, she spent every second of her parole swinging from the climbing frame, her too long cramped body and limbs celebrating their liberty in great sinewy twists and arches.

"Your e's and s's are coming along very nicely," encouraged Miss Frobisher during the joined up writing lesson. "Take care not to go below the line."

KISSES, MISSES, HISSES, copied Donna from the board with meticulous care and attention to the shapes of the letters. But now that Miss had turned her back to take something out of the cupboard, Flora, Kay and Harry – all seated at an adjacent table – were chortling at some private joke.

"What is it?" whispered Peter to Flora and she whispered something that made him suddenly rock back in amusement, stifling his wayward mouth with his handkerchief.

Donna smiled at Peter curiously as if to say, "Tell me, too."

"Pisses," he managed, still choking with giggles.

"What?"

"Pisses!"

"Oh, I get it! " guffawed Donna a bit too loudly.

"Donna? What are you laughing at?" snapped Miss Frobisher suddenly turning around.

Donna placed the palm of her hand innocently across her mouth and smirked knowingly towards her fellow conspirators for support but they had spotted the teacher's irritation and instantly buried their faces back in their exercise books, models of earnest endeavour.

"Peter?"

"Donna was telling me a joke, miss. I tried not to listen."

Miss Frobisher marched over to Donna's desk, her features contorted and cruel, where she towered like an injured Colossus, breathing down anger and retribution. "It's one thing wasting your own time," she hissed, "it's quite another wasting your fellow pupils', Donna. And, look, you've only written the words once! I said I wanted them done three times. Can't you count?"

Donna bit her lip and tried not to cry, her throat and larynx paralysed with shame.

When lunchtime came, her body was still shivering with humiliation. In the dining room nobody appeared to want to sit next to her and the sandwiches tasted like cardboard. She took a couple of bites and left the rest in the polythene box, her appetite completely vanquished. During the afternoon lessons, Donna kept her nose to the grindstone, occasionally stealing a secret glance at Miss Frobisher's face for signs of softening and forgiveness but not once were these ardent little appeals reciprocated. The atmosphere had been irretrievably polluted and Donna knew it was all her fault. She would willingly have had the classroom floor open up and swallow her.

"Next week we shall begin a project on Australia," announced Miss Frobisher just before going home time. Donna's ears pricked up. "I want you to start collecting information. Pictures. Ornaments. Anything at all you come across to do with the country and its people. Has anyone been to Australia by any chance?" The teacher surveyed her minions but nobody responded. Donna watched on with mounting excitement. What should she do? It was a risk but probably one worth taking especially as rehabilitation might be the prize, and slowly her right arm ascended to the half-mast position.

"Yes, Donna? You've been, have you?"

"No, miss. But my mummy and sister have."

"Really! When?"

"Before I was born, I think."

"Excellent. We'll look to you next week then to be our number one authority." Donna felt her chest go warm with pleasure. She did not know what an authority was but she loved the idea of being number one. "Does anyone know the name of the people who originally lived in Australia?" asked Miss Frobisher. "I mean before the settlers and convicts came along?"

Nobody responded but Donna felt she could answer this one, too. Sarah had a couple of postcards. All sunburnt and fuzzy-haired the people pictured in them were and some even wore face paints. Ab -? Abo -? What was it now? If only she could remember and Miss Frobisher's eyes had half turned towards her in expectation. Then a hand shot up. "Yes, Harry?" she asked.

"Neighbours, miss."

A good natured end of week cackle ran around the room in pursuit of Harry's joke and taking her lead from the teacher, who deigned not to take offence this time, Donna also joined in although in truth she had no idea what everyone was laughing at.

*

It had taken forty minutes to drive there, a warehouse on the Isle of Dogs that stank of ammonia and seemed to serve a secondary purpose as a social club. At least a bar had been stuck in one corner of the building and fitted out with slot machines, plastic chairs and a television set. The area McLeod had chosen to call his 'operations centre' was situated up an open flight of stairs on the opposite side. Frank had begun to move around restlessly in his swivel chair. McLeod had been at it non-stop for several hours, explaining maps and movements, time schedules and deadlines, individual responsibilities and personalities. The walls of the office on a raised platform above the warehouse floor had been papered with evidence of McLeod's meticulousness and Frank was beginning to suffer from information overload. He found himself more frequently gazing down through the windows to see if any of his other new partners in crime had turned up yet and now a smell of cooking emanating from some nearby kitchen had begun to tease his nostrils and memory bank. Something tasty was on the menu. Something he had not eaten for a long, long time. What was it?

"And the house was the sponsor's idea. He sees it as a double insurance policy. We've been waiting for a wee while for the right property to become available," McLeod was explaining. "Firstly, the river mooring. You can load onto a small craft at night in absolute privacy. Secondly, we can disappear the getaway van in the big garage instantly – dispose of it at our leisure, months later, when the heat's off. Thirdly –" McLeod hesitated as if having second thoughts.

" Yeah? Thirdly?" prompted Frank.

"Thirdly, if there's a delay, or the movements don't synchronise as I expect them to, you can hole up safely with the bullion until it can be shifted on another day."

"Are you anticipating some sort of problem on the water then?" demanded Frank.

"Of course not. But you have to realise this corner of the operation is fluid by definition. The bullion has to reach the river by a set time or we miss the high tide. Timing is the essence. If there's any delay at the security depot end Hunter won't be able to get the boat in and out."

Frank considered this carefully. His own vulnerability was at stake. "But even so we're talkin', what? – 24 hours delay at the most? Right?"

"Right, Frank. Hunter would come back the following night. That's all."

"By which time, of course, every copper and nark in the country would be on the look out?"

"They wont be looking at the river," answered McLeod. "Remember the decoy van? Challinor's gonna leave it in Greenford close to the junction of the A40. That'll give 'em the wrong scent." And he held up a green flak jacket and a grey balaclava. "Our kit'll be dumped in the back."

Frank pursed his lips and sniffed again. It was an Italian dish Susan had learnt to cook. Fish. He was positive now. And his tongue began to salivate with hunger.

"What about the home ship? The cutter? Any delay possible there?" he prompted aloud.

"The yacht's in dock at Bordeaux. Primed. It can be up in the estuary within 24 hours max." And McLeod pointed towards a 10 by 4 colour print of the ship on the wall. "Anything else?"

Suddenly an oozing plate of pasta vongole materialised in Frank's mind's eye, the last one he had ever eaten, served by Susan all those years ago. His little brown eyed eight year old daughter beaming with delight opposite him at the table – fussing, chattering, asking impossible questions that he loved to try and answer. She was real enough to kiss.

"Like some more parm'san, daddy?" he could hear her saying. "Can I sprinkle it on for you?" His heart suddenly felt as if it was going to dissolve with grief.

"Well, Frank?" broke in McLeod gruffly. "Anything else? Or shall we eat?"

"The getaway vehicle? I take it the floor will hold the bullion?"

"Course. The van's being structurally reinforced. Both of them. Okay then –"

"One other thing. I want an assurance there won't be no violence. I mean durin' the raid."

Frank felt McLeod shoot him an old fashioned look. "There's nay point in carrying shooters if we don't mean to use them if we have to," he answered. "You know that –"

"I mean violence for the sake of it," cut in Frank. "If there's non-cooperation from the security guards I want you to promise it's me who sorts it. Okay?"

"Okay," agreed McLeod. "You'll take the lead. I'll tell the boys at the meeting."

*

At going home time Donna picked her way carefully through the bodies and buggies that thronged the play-ground expectantly, raucous reunions exploding like fireworks all around her. Katrina had parked in the usual place but stood staring glumly into the sweet shop window, studying the display of postcard messages.

"Is it sweetie day today?" beamed Donna by way of a greeting, knowing very well it was.

Katrina extracted a purse from her pocket and dropped some loose change into Donna's outstretched hands. By the time she had arrived back on the pavement with her confectionary Sarah had appeared and was being admonished by the childminder.

"You are supposed to be doing detention tonight and walking home afterwards," insisted Katrina.

"Yeah. I know," shrugged Sarah. "I couldn't be bothered."

"You will be in big trouble on Monday."

"Whatever. Give me a pastel, Div."

They all got in the car and Donna opened her packet of pastels. "Guess what?" she enthused. "I was 20p short in the shop and a man just gave me the money! Want one, Katrina?"

"No, thanks."

"You shouldn't take money from strange men," censored Sarah helping herself to three.

"He wasn't strange. He was kind."

"You shouldn't even be talking to him."

"I didn't talk to him!"

"A girl of easy virtue, eh?" sneered Sarah as the car swerved through the roundabout, overtook a red bus and accelerated up St. Margarets Road. "What else have you got in there?" And she snatched the bag out of Donna's hand.

Later when Donna was snuggled up on the bean bag sucking her pink sherbet fingers in front of the television, Sarah waltzed in already changed out of her school uniform and carefully set out a number of tiny bottles and implements on the coffee table in front of her. Without shifting the position of her body Donna watched her sister pick up a pair of silver tweezers, kneel down in front of the mirror and begin plucking her eyebrows.

"I'm going to do you a favour," said Sarah staring deep into the reflection of her purple brown eyes. "I'm going to let you watch whatever you want on the telly."

"Thanks, Sarah."

"Til five o'clock. And in return I want you to do something for me. Deal?"

"What?"

"I want you to go somewhere else to play- because Polly's coming round to get ready for the youth club and we want to practice our dance routines in here in private."

"Sarah, we're doing a project on Australia next week and –"

"Deal?"

"Yes! Alright. Can I look at your pictures of Australia please?" Sarah made a noise of affirmation in the back of her throat.

"Where are they?"

"In the bottom left hand drawer of my cabinet. In a brown envelope. Don't make a mess."

"I won't."

"Bottom left hand, okay?" reiterated Sarah stressing the words. "You understand? And don't go opening any other drawer. I've got a new demon troll in one of them and he might jump out and bite you on your snitch if you're being nosy."

It felt like receiving an open invitation to Aladdin's Cave and Donna scuttled up the stairwell and into her sister's bedroom before the privilege could be withdrawn. All around her the faces of pop stars and teen idols beamed down from their pedestals on the wall, the gay and gregarious, the mean and the moody, the limp and lascivious, – a two dimensional democracy of role models frozen in the grimace of eternal youth. Along the window ledge were paraded a row of ten fearsome trolls, painted in a variety of bold colours, each with a shock of luminous wild hair and a leer that made her shiver. Underfoot, the debris of clothes and books and bric-a-brac had spread further afield and like some gigantic unruly fungus colonised its spores in every corner. Donna picked up a bra and stretched it like a catapult to see how it mechanically worked and dropped it on the unmade bed with a giggle. To think a sister of hers could actually fit into one of those! She turned to the cheap pine veneer cabinet now, unscrewing the tops of lotions and creams and other glutinous cosmetic substances to inhale their adolescent secrets one by one. Then a wire gadget like a pair of tongs caught her attention. Sarah used it to preen her eyelashes but try as she might in front of the wardrobe mirror Donna could only succeed in blotching the rims of her eyes until they ran with tears.

She opened the target drawer now, wiped her face on the back of her sleeve and located the brown envelope at once. It was fat with cards and scraps of paper and she emptied them into a bundle on the bed. Some birthday cards announcing 'Six Today!', a couple of letters in grown up scrawl that she could not decipher, a newspaper cutting, all folded and stiff, a six by four photograph of a nice smiling man balancing a toddler on his head amongst a group of other people. She spread them out neatly before turning her attention to the Australian pictures. There were five in all, displaying different aspects of the continent and its culture in lurid colours. A long orange beach, the ocean with towering waves on which bronzed athletes were somehow able to walk. A red flat mountain against an unreal blue sky looking like a casserole pot that had been stood upside down. A building with ears sprouting crazily out of its roof and walls. And then at last the natives, wide-nosed, sunken eyed, disenchanted faces, great stripes of paint – white, yellow, red – daubed onto their bodies, and hair that had never seen the inside of a barber shop tied back with red bandannas. Donna turned the card over to its printed side, found the A word she was searching for with her index finger and slowly broke it up into pronounceable pieces.

"Ab-o-rig-ines." And again savouring the syllables like particles of exotic fruit. "Ab-o-rig-ines."

She turned to the second picture where two men with dishevelled beards appeared to be about to attack each other with sticks while a woman squatted nearby on the parched soil totally naked, her breasts swollen and unashamed. "Ab -o -rig -ines," Donna read again as she reversed the postcard. "There are 500 tribes." The text became very difficult. Her finger foraged down and along the lines. "To-tem?" she tried. Then further along something she definitely recognised, "Dream Time."

As she parcelled up the memorabilia still mouthing the name Aborigine to herself in her own unique version, trying to engrave it into her consciousness deeply enough to survive the weekend, another photograph which had been wedged in the folds of the newspaper cutting became dislodged. She picked it up curiously. It was a lot smaller than the other one, maybe an inch square like a glossy postage stamp. The face looked familiar and she checked it against the large photograph. Yes. It was the same man who was carrying the baby except in the portrait only his head and shoulders were in shot and his face looked tired and serious. Daddy? she suddenly found herself wondering. Is that my daddy?

"You took your time," muttered Sarah as Donna re-entered the living room. "Did you leave my room as you found it?"

"Yes. Ab-o-rig-ines."

"What-?"

"Children, your mummy is going to be late home again," came a disembodied voice from the kitchen. "What will you eat for supper?"

"Those funny brown people. I've got to remember. I'm the only one in the class who knows their name."

"You say it abo-ridge-annies, div. And they're not funny brown people. They are the indig- indig- they are the original natives."

"Abo-ridge-annies?" tried Donna.

"Close."

"What shall I make you for supper?" said Katrina poking her head round the door. "Beans on toast or spaghetti bolognaise?"

"Polly's coming round. Will we have enough for her?"

"Yes, no problem. Beans, then?"

"Whatever."

"I will just slip out to the corner shop and buy a couple of tins," said Katrina.

No sooner had the front door banged shut than the telephone rang. "If that's a boy for me, I'm out," instructed Sarah imperiously.

"Hullo?" asked Donna tentatively into the mouthpiece.

"Is your mummy there?" intoned a voice she thought she recognised.

"No. Sorry. She's still at work."

"Oh, is she?" The man sounded taken aback. "Are you sure? I just tried. Never mind. I'll try again."

"Who is it?"

"Sorry to trouble you. Bye." The line clicked dead.

"Who was that?" asked Sarah indifferently.

"Someone for mummy. I think it was Gerry. Do you like Gerry, Sarah?"

Sarah shook her head. "He's a creep. Anyway, I reckon his days are numbered. She's got another one on the go. Do you want to change the channel? I'm not bothered."

Donna watched the telly while her sister studiously painted her nails with lime green lacquer. It was good to have a deal with Sarah. A deal meant that life would be normal, that nothing nasty would be said and there would be no coldness inside her body. When a deal was on Sarah behaved like a different person. She could be kind and answer your questions and sometimes she would even ask you to join in her games. There were a lot of questions Donna wanted to ask Sarah but she knew from experience how carefully she had to choose her moments, how quickly Sarah's patience could snap, how terrifying her explosions of temper could be. Once Sarah had erupted the effects of the devastation lasted for ages. Life became a wasteland of silence and black, bone-chilling stares. Donna took a sidelong glance at the object of her contemplation, that impenetrable mystery of common blood and rapidly growing wisdom. It was a good moment. Sarah sat, her feet tucked up under her bottom on the sofa, nonchalant and cocooned in serenity, studying her artwork with satisfaction.

"Sarah? What was it like in Australia?"

"Hot." Silence.

"The beach looks beautiful. Did you go swimming in the sea?"

"Not much. There are sharks in the sea." Silence. Then. "Five o'clock. Remember?"

"Yes. Sarah? Did you see any ab -o -rig -ines?"

"Abo -ridge -annies, div. One or two."

More silence. But these silences were different. They contained no poison. In fact, they were not real silences at all. They were cosy little spaces in which you could watch a bit of telly or practice your difficult words in your head and compose another question.

"Sarah?"

"Yep?"

"Was daddy an abo -ridge -annie? Did you spend a lot of time on the beach with him?"

"Wha-a-t?!"

"Was daddy – ?"

"I heard you. Of course he wasn't!"

"But he was from Australia, wasn't he? Sarah?"

Sarah looked angry. "Shut up! I'm watching this!" she barked.

"What was he then?" Silence. Except for a fanfare of music issuing from the television set. A fresh-faced handsome young man welcomed children everywhere to Newsround.

"The latest opinion polls show Labour maintaining a significant lead over the Conservative Party with only six days left to polling day. But the shadow Labour leader Tony Blair visiting South Wales today reiterated that he was taking absolutely nothing for granted –"

"It's five o'clock," announced Sarah with an imperious nod towards the door. "On your way."

"But –"

"Buts are for Billy Goats. A deal is a deal. Are you leaving or what?"

Donna picked herself up from the floor and slowly walked into exile, swallowing great indigestible lumps of disappointment that wedged in her throat and chest. She found Dawn exactly where she had left her at 8:30 that morning in rigid communion with the bedroom window waiting to spy on the new neighbours.

"Did you see anyone, Dawn?" she asked peering over her head. A gusting wind was heard at work raking through trees and shrubberies as far as her eyes could see. Copper beech, firs, silver birch, holly bushes all dwarfed by that magnificent willow five or six gardens down, its mottled green tresses weaving and threshing. "Never mind. Because you've been very good all day I'm going to take you and Caroline to the Metro Centre now." She picked the other doll up from the floor and straightened its blouse. "Caroline's got another boyfriend on the go, Dawn. No wonder she's always home so late."

*

The second the meeting folded Frank got up and went to the toilet. He needed a few minutes of privacy to sort things out in his head and McLeod's boys might well need the same, he reflected, to gossip about the impression the newcomer had made on them. He sat in the solitary cubicle weighing the pros and cons. On the negative side the gang had the look of small time villains – car thieves and arsonists. The eldest must have been in his late 20s. It might be like tackling the ascent of Everest with a bunch of low level fell walkers. But on the positive side they had been tightly focussed and knowledgeable when asked to talk through their roles in the operation. They were clearly all under McLeod's thumb and in public, at least, they showed not one iota of dissent in his last minute decision to enlist a fifth member. Each man's cut of thirty-five million, which was the minimum gain expected from the haul, would be that much diminished but nobody complained. On the contrary the one called Fearon seemed to be grateful that he was no longer required to squat in the house.

Overall, Frank found himself instinctively ambivalent. Was there something a bit dodgy about the house? And why did he have to go three weeks in advance of the operation? Several other details remained unclear, he thought to himself as he sat there smoking, and he would need to take them up with McLeod in private later. This resolution firmly established he left the cubicle and was washing his hands when he became aware of Hunter buttoning his flies at the urinal, a scowling reticent type who to Frank's surprise now chose the moment to practice his conversational skills.

"I remember reading about you when I was a kid. You were big news mate. For fifteen minutes." Frank replied with the merest turn of his head, unimpressed. "One thing I never understood," continued Hunter with a thin sneer in his voice, "was why you didn't just trigger the pig in the alley when you had the chance. Did the chamber stick? Or did you just lose your bottle?"

"Got the cabin cruiser sorted?" asked Frank calmly drying his hands as if he had not heard. Hunter grunted and began preening his oily hair in the mirror. "What is it? Two birth or four? Petrol or Diesel? Will it hold the weight?"

"Yeah."

"Yeah? What's that mean?"

"It means the cabin cruiser ain't your worry, mate. It's sorted. You take care of your end of the business and I'll take care of mine."

Frank swallowed his irritation and walked out. The television set had been switched on in the lounge. McLeod stood in front of it, holding a lager bottle to his lips and watching a politician inform the nation how his party, if elected, would prioritise police recruitment and the fight against domestic crime, which had almost doubled in 18 years of Conservative government.

"I'll drop you off at the hostel," said McLeod. "Is there anything else you need from me? I mean til it's time to move you to the house?"

"My wife, Susan," retorted Frank quietly. "I need to know where she is."

"Frank, I told you already- "

"I know what you told me already," Frank broke in. "The conversation's moved on. Can you help me find out where she's gone? Yes or No?"

"You make it sound like a condition of your being on board?" observed McLeod through suddenly tightened lips.

"A down payment more like," retorted Frank. "Whatever your giving these guys as a sweetener, I'll take an address instead. Fair?"

"And what if I draw a blank?" asked McLeod drawing his face closer. "I mean six weeks plucking the grapevine hasn't got you anywhere."

Frank pulled one of the photographs out of his wallet, the one with mother and daughter aged 8, taken a couple of months before his imprisonment, and began writing a few essential details on the back. "If you draw a blank I'll take the regular sweetener too," he said as he did so. "But you won't. You've got better contacts than me. More leverage."

McLeod took the photograph. "I'll do my best," he said.

As he made to turn away Frank arrested his arm. "One other thing, McLeod," he said bringing his mouth close to the Scotsman's ear. "Hunter. I don't like him. He's flash and his attitude's cocky. Are you sure he's reliable?"

Across the other side of the room Hunter was now busy fuelling a one-armed bandit with pound coins, urging it periodically to deliver with neurotic grunts and slaps of exasperation.

"I know what you mean," replied McLeod, "but take it from me he's solid. He's done good work for......" And Frank heard a name whispered into his ear that nobody in the underworld ever mentioned in vain.

*

After supper Donna retreated quickly to her bedroom and lay down on the bottom bunk, grimacing with frustration. How long did these dance routines last? And why couldn't they let her join in? Her limbs felt stiff with prolonged immobility and desperately needed the balm of the up-tempo disco music blaring out from the living room.

"If you wanna be me lover, You gotta get with my friend.

Making love forever, Love will never end!!"

She put her hands over her ears to shut it out and kicked her feet on the pine bedposts. Monopolising the living room before tea was one thing. Monopolising it after tea was quite another. That's when all the best television programmes were on. Why should she have to be up there on her own totally excluded from everything? And anyway these singing dancers always performed in fours and fives. Two people could not possibly devise an effective routine. Her Little Mermaid slippers stamped out an impromptu tattoo of rage and incomprehension on the mattress. Why didn't mummy come home and lay down the law? And then there was Katrina. She could intervene if she really wanted. After all she had been left out too! She had to sit in the kitchen with her magazines and foreign books, or find something to tidy up. On a whim of sudden inspiration Donna launched herself out of her cocoon of self-pity and trotted downstairs to plead with her newly discovered fellow victim in exile.

"Katrina, can we go in the living room now and play a game of cards?" she began even before she had reached the dungeon door.

Katrina did not hear. The young woman sat with the phone to her ear, transfixed, her eyes wet and enflamed, tuned into some desolate galaxy of her own. Donna watched her for a few seconds, unseen, biting her long spindly fingers, babbling away in that strange foreign tongue. A thick, impervious glass partition seemed suddenly to stand between them like one of those mirrors you encounter in amusement arcades, – hideously distorting all that was safe and familiar. She turned round and crept towards the living room. It had been left a couple of inches ajar and was leaking snapshots of orgasmic energy. Closer and closer she edged, stopping every time a floorboard shifted underfoot like a prowler in the dark, slowly widening the angle of vision. The song snapped to a finish. Donna froze, her face so close to the aperture now she could smell the emulsion on its edges.

"Forward. Forward. Back. Twirl," instructed Sarah. "Follow me. Forward. Forward. Back. Twirl. See?"

The other girl strutted this way and that, waved her left arm, gyrated her bottom, tripped over the fender and collapsed on the carpet in a heap of giggles where she was quickly joined by Sarah.

Donna thrust her fingers in her mouth to stifle a laugh but not quickly enough. A mane of chestnut hair twisted and reared into the vertical.

"Go away this instant! We're rehearsing!"

"Please can I join in, Sarah?"

"No."

"Please! I'll do what I'm told."

The painted and preened faces suddenly moved out of the frame. Whispers. A snort. A cackle. Then. "Sit on the stairs for ten minutes until we've finished this bit. And then I'll make my decision."

"Okay. Thanks."

The music snapped on. Seven voices shrilled out in karaoke harmony and Donna backed away into the funnel of the house humming in time and smiling to herself knowingly. She could tell that Sarah thought she was Sporty Spice by the facial mannerisms as she danced and the way she held the banana microphone. Polly had bunched her hair and wore a pink foundation in a silly attempt to appear like Baby Spice but she was far too tall and gawky to pull it off, especially with that brace on her teeth. Polly was a bit ugly.

Time passed. The music kept snapping on and off. Donna began to feel chilly on the stairs. Eventually when silence reigned she could restrain herself no longer. Were they talking again? She approached the door boldly determined to enter but a raucous chortle of laughter served to undermine her resolve at the decisive moment. Instead she lingered outside, her shoulder against the frame, and listened as best she could to the joke in progress.

"And she hasn't got a single friend. Nobody will play with her because she's retarded. She spells her name with one N. And talk about gullible! You can tell her anything and she believes it. I told her the old man at number 32 became a vampire at night and wandered the streets looking for juicy necks to bite open. And she won't walk past his gate now!"

But the narrative was so grotesquely punctuated with guffaws and whinnies and other affectations of mirth that Donna could not properly correlate the phrases she understood into anything remotely connected to a personal slander. Sarah was always telling funny stories about people and this must be a really good one because it had Polly in stitches. She pushed open the door and felt compelled to join in the laughter as an act of solidarity. The older girls rocked and reeled and pointed at Donna and howled even louder.

This is fun, thought Donna and mimicked them as best she could, rolling around on the floor her face wet with merriment, hooting and hollering til her throat hurt.

"Whatever is going on with you!?" exclaimed Katrina suddenly appearing on the scene. "Are you fighting or what?"

Katrina's funny accent only had the effect of a tickling stick on Donna's ribs and she laughed even louder, saliva running in tiny tributaries down her chin, as the child minder looked on bewildered.

"Wipe your face on this," said Katrina, dangling a tissue above Donna's head. "And you Sarah, it's time to leave for the youth club. If you still want me to take you, that is?"

A remark which had the equivalent effect on the older girls of a full throttle hose pipe on a barbecue fire. They were sober and standing to attention in an instant.

*

The car was inching its way through the rush hour. Frank could not believe how bad the traffic congestion had become. His nerves were on edge. It must have at least tripled in volume since he first got banged up. But McLeod did not seem to mind. He sat behind the wheel, relaxed and smiling, like a fat cat that had just finished off the cream.

"You're going to fix me up with a passport, I take it?"

McLeod nodded. "Of course. I'll need a photograph. Better grow a beard first. Okay?"

"Yeah. Tell me about the house again? What if someone comes round? A neighbour wanting to borrow milk?" asked Frank stroking his chin.

"Then give it to them. Just act normal," shrugged McLeod.

"Normal?! What's that mean? I'm an ex con."

"It means not to stick out like a sore thumb. To be known and not known at the same time. Light me a cigarette, will you?" Frank did what he was asked. "I mean keep yourself to yourself but not to the extent of being unfriendly or withdrawn. You're a consultant in an upmarket provincial firm with contacts in the city. Kindly behave like one."

This amused McLeod. He cackled like a goose for a reason lost on Frank. "Why don't we just leave the house empty until we need it?" he demanded. "Once I've left the hostel and failed to contact my probation I'll have the status of an escaped prisoner. They'll be looking for me."

"That house has been empty since Christmas," said McLeod. "I need to get the neighbours used to realising it isn't any more. Used to seeing someone opening the garage, pottering around in the garden – that sort of thing – so that when it comes to the big night nobody's gonna be startled by the sight of a vehicle coming down the drive after hours. Nobody who happens to look through an upstairs window or hear voices in the back garden, whatever, is gonna think anything unusual's going off. A party or something they'll think. This is London after all. It never quite closes down." And McLeod cackled again. It was beginning to get on Frank's nerves. Suddenly the whole logic of his involvement seemed to be built on marshy ground. All he had to do was wait thirteen months. Then he would be properly free. Free to apply for a passport. Free to go in search of Susan. Free to rebuild his life. But how would the Scotsman react if he pulled out now?

The traffic began to move again. They just missed a green light. "I'm not saying you should never leave the place," continued McLeod as pedestrians flooded past the windscreen. "I'm just saying keep it to a minimum. And only at night. There's a little Paki all-purpose shop on the main road. Open all hours. And as for breaking the conditions of your license, Frank, it isn't a capital offence. Happens all the time. Takes the system thirteen months just to catch up with the paperwork." He pulled away and they were motoring smoothly now at the head of the procession. "After the operation you could just as well report back to your probation. Apologise. Tell him you'd lost it upstairs for a while. Tell him you're ready to work. Remember Kenny Mac? He pulled a stroke like that while –"

"Wouldn't it make more sense if *you* lived in the house?" Frank interrupted.

"No. I need to be within easy reach of the others. Besides my real house is in Stoke Newington. My absence would be noticed. I intend to keep living there."

"Is it the same with the others?"

"Pretty much so. It's crucial in the run up we all stick to our own patches. You know the score. You've bin there before."

Yeah, I know the score alright, thought Frank to himself. Everybody's fixing themselves an alibi except me. And as far as going back to my probation, he'd smell a rat the size of an elephant.

"Anyway, I got the impression you'd prefer to stay abroad once you get the opportunity," remarked McLeod as if reading Frank's mind. "France is a big place to blend into."

They drove the rest of the way in silence. When they arrived at the hostel McLeod turned into a side alley. "Monday evening at 7. Take a cab to the warehouse. I'll be there with the car. Okay?"

"Yeah. Have a nice weekend."

"Oh, and one last thing, Frank. The boys don't think you should wear those charm things and I agree with them."

"What?"

"The butterfly. On your shirt."

"How come?"

"It's a trade mark. Someone might twig it. You never know."

"Your jokin', ain't yer? Badges like this are ten a penny."

"Not like that, son. You were well known for making them. Even Hunter had heard. Better safe than sorry."

"Fuck Hunter!" cursed Frank under his breath as he got out of the car and slammed the door behind him.

Chapter 5

When Donna woke up on Saturday morning she became immediately aware of foreign sounds and Sarah's presence in the room, one long laborious exhalation of breath followed by another. She leant over the side of the top bunk and gazed down at the comatose figure, its face transfigured by sleep to a quality of innocence and purity that touched Donna's heart. It was the third time in a week. Why had Sarah suddenly started sneaking in like this? The question remained unanswered, even irrelevant. At that moment Donna felt her sister's unexplained intrusion as a blessing.

In the space between sighs another noise gradually asserted itself. Donna pricked up her ears and pivoted her head as if to locate the direction. An engine was running outside. It grew into a metallic brittle hum, an even line of music occasionally broken by the merest inflection of whine or splutter. She lowered herself carefully down the pine ladder so as not to wake Sarah and tip-toed to the window where she lifted the curtain and hooded it over her head. The unexpected brightness of the sunshine dazzled her eyes. Wild shapes and colours exploded like fireworks in the pane, followed by cascading stars quickly extinguishing one by one and leaving the rows of back gardens intact in their absence. The roar of the machine magically amplified now. Donna craned her neck. It was down there beneath her, growing louder by the second, relentlessly approaching. Then beyond the garage she spotted something unmistakably human, a head of hair moving in a straight line, now lost beneath the foliage of an overhanging bush, now reappearing in a different place speckled with rays of sunshine. Her eyes moved to the patio door of the white house. It was wide open and shifting slightly backwards and forwards in the breeze.

Donna negotiated the route to her mother's bedroom with nervous agility, through one door into the next, bursting to confide the revelation. "Mummy! Our new neighbour, Mr Brown! He's cutting the grass!" She gazed expectantly at the reassuring symmetry of her mother's prostrate body shaped like a range of hills beneath the blankets. It twitched slightly but steadfastly maintained its silence. "He's come out at last! Can we write him a letter and put it through the letter box, mummy? Can we? Please!"

"Go back to bed, Donna. It's early," groaned mummy.

"I'm not tired. Can we?"

"I don't think anyone's moved in yet."

"But he's cutting the grass! Just a short letter, mummy!"

"Later. I'll do it later. Leave me alone. It's my day off."

"But they might all have gone out later!"

The mountain growled once, ruffled its north peak and lapsed back into a state of monumental indifference.

For much of the morning Donna amused herself in front of the television and, when she tired of that, with her dolls in the shopping arcades of the Metro Centre, which was where the fully revived version of her mummy eventually found her.

"Do you fancy scrambled eggs and bacon?" she asked, wafting her lovely perfume into the building. "I do. I'm starving. But first I'm going to put a load of washing in the machine. So if you don't mind?"

Within a split second the vast marble hallways of the Metro Centre had shrunk back down to the size of a draughty utility room in Donna's imagination and she obediently vacated the space.

"Go and have a shower and get dressed," ordered mummy. "And wake Sarah up, will you, if she's still in bed. I don't want her lazing around half the day."

"She's in my room, mummy," said Donna.

"Whatever," muttered mummy depositing a pile of tangled laundry into the machine.

"Did you have a nice time last night?"

"Yes. Thanks."

"Somebody phoned for you."

"Did they?"

"Again this morning. Twice. The same man. I was right not to bother you, wasn't I?"

"Yes, dear."

"Who was he, mummy?"

"Stop nattering, Donna. You're a proper old chatterbox! Go and get dressed!"

After they had eaten a large cooked meal with lashings of buttered toast and sweet tea Sarah went off to rendezvous with her friends and a shopping expedition in Kingston.

"Can you write the letter now?" prompted Donna. It was not a novel idea. When they had first moved into the neighbourhood last summer mummy had duplicated an introductory letter fifty times and posted them by hand to all the homes on Mansfield and Clifton Roads in the hope of creating a network of friends for her daughter. The only reply had come from the white house and Donna still treasured the message which she frequently scanned because its sentiments gave her a warm glow inside.

"Dear Donna, we found your letter only yesterday when we got back from holiday," it had read. *"So sorry to be late in answering – you probably have dozens of friends by now! Anyway, it was very kind of you to write. We live at "River Bank", that's 2, Clifton Road with our little girl Georgia. She is two years younger than you – does that matter? I read her your letter and she said she would love to play with you. Please feel free to ring our doorbell anytime. Kind Regards. John and Bev Lewis. P.S. How about coming over for tea on Sunday?"*

In the event it had been mummy who had rung the doorbell one evening after Donna was in bed just to ensure it was a genuine invitation. At breakfast the following morning she had pronounced her judgement.

"It's a lovely house, Donna. Immaculately kept. I told them all about you."

"That was a big mistake," Sarah had sneered enviously. "Bang goes the invitation now."

"They would like you to have lunch with them on Sunday after they get back from church."

"Church? Is he a vicar or something?" Again Sarah facetiously.

"No. Actually, Mr Lewis told me he is a financial lawyer."

"Our Father which art in Money hallowed be thy name," intoned Sarah with mock solemnity.

"The only bad thing is that they might not be there after Christmas," mummy had warned. "His company are thinking of transferring him to their Los Angeles branch for a couple of years."

Donna remembered the five or six times she had played with Georgia, always at her house, as mummy dug out a writing pad now and began to compose a new letter, eagerly overlooked by her daughter.

"Are you sure their name is Brown, dear?"

"Yes, I saw him. The daddy."

"And his wife and children?"

"Not exactly."

"They'll be a very good family," mused mummy as she preened her sentences. "It's a company let. Sidney knows the estate agents. You have to put a huge deposit down. Ten thousand he told me. Just to guarantee the security."

Donna sensed that her mummy was looking forward to meeting

their new neighbours almost as much as she was: "Thank you, mummy. Thank you very much," she gushed as they walked round the corner together to post it.

Fresh white gravel had been strategically placed in the front garden, the flagstones stripped of weeds and the wooden tubs planted with pansies as if to welcome the tenants. "Can't we ring the doorbell, mummy?" asked Donna as they passed through the latch gate.

"No. That's what common people would do. Push the envelope through. If they hear us and come out, so much the better."

The metal flap creaked open at the pressure of her fingers and remained like a gaping mouth, allowing Donna to hear the hollow plop of the envelope on the floor inside and nothing else.

"Come on now," coaxed mummy turning on her heels, "I need to do a big shop at the supermarket."

Donna skipped after her. "I like it when you don't have to work on Saturday, mummy," she said.

"So do I," agreed mummy. "Pity it can't happen more often."

*

Gladiators had just finished and mouth watering smells of casserole were wafting through from the kitchen when the phone rang. "Answer that, will you, Donna!" shouted mummy. "I've got my hands full."

It was Sarah. "Tell Mum I'm staying at Jeannie's after the disco," she said. "I've been invited to sleep over."

"Who is it?!"

"Sarah!" called back Donna. "She's been invited to sleep at Jeannie's!"

Mummy instantly came bustling into the living room and snatched the receiver out of Donna's hand. "Where are you?!" she snapped. "Alright, put Jeannie's mother on the phone ... What? ... How dare you use language like that! Of course I believe you! I just want to check the arrangements – ooh!"

Donna could tell by her mummy's demeanour that Sarah had rudely hung up. They ate dinner in silence, the bantering complicity that had been established during the course of the day now totally sullied.

"Are you alright, mummy?" she asked at length.

"Mean spirited, self-centred adolescent," mummy muttered darkly. "I just hope you don't turn out..." Her voice tailed off.

"What, mummy?"

"Oh, nothing," sighed mummy, emptying her half-nibbled meal into the bin. "I'm tired, that's all. I've been working very hard. I need an early night."

48

Mummy opened a bottle of wine, poured out a large glass and collapsed on the settee, her face suddenly haggard and distracted. Donna went upstairs and played with her dolls. When she returned a bit later mummy appeared to have revived somewhat. The bottle stood less than a quarter full and mummy was talking to someone on the phone, a wide-eyed soppy expression on her face.

"Better go now," she simpered as she spotted Donna. "Yeah... And you."

"Who was that, mummy?"

"Just a friend, dear."

"Mummy?"

"Yes, dear?"

"I've been wondering something."

"What?"

Donna took a deep breath. "Was Daddy an abo-ridge-annie?" she asked cautiously.

Mummy let out a short nervous giggle and topped up her glass, spilling a bit on the carpet as she did so. "Why ever do you ask that?" she said.

"Because I asked Sarah and she said he wasn't. But I think he must have been because he came from Australia, didn't he?

"Yes. He did. But he wasn't an aborigine, for goodness sake," objected Mummy archly. "He was the son of an Englishman who emigrated there and he came back to study drama here. What did Sarah tell you?"

"Nothing. Just to shut up."

Mummy put the glass down and busied herself suddenly plumping the sofa cushions. "You must be very, very careful what you ask your sister about daddy," she warned.

"I know you've told me before."

"In fact it's probably best not to ask her anything at all. She was there. Remember? When it happened." Donna nodded, undermined by the strident inflection of her mummy's voice. "It's past your bedtime. I've put a clean pair of jimmies in the airing cupboard."

"Where was I, mummy?" Donna pushed hopefully.

"You were in your pram fast asleep."

"Six weeks old, wasn't I? Can I see my baby photos in the album? Can I?"

"Tomorrow," decreed mummy firmly. "Let's go. I'll tuck you in."

As Donna lay in bed cuddling Dawn and Caroline ardently to her chest she tried to piece together the fragments of information she had once been given about the phantom who bore the name, "Daddy". They were few and far between and seemed to emanate from a dream world that did not properly exist any more. Why were there no photographs of him on the sideboard or in the albums? She tried to remember. A reason had been given once. Whatever was it? Not a very good one she was sure. And it was so difficult to ask again. Sparks of impatience or plain evasions resulted. It felt as if daddy had been stuffed out of sight somewhere like one of her broken dolls. It felt as if he was a secret that mummy and Sarah knew but did not choose to share with her. Daddy was their private territory and she entered it at her peril.

When Sarah failed to materialise by mid-day on Sunday morning mummy began to become anxious and rang Jeannie's house, having gone to no end of trouble to track down the number. Donna watched on, a bewildered spectator of mummy's anger. Nobody had answered.

"I'm going out this evening, Donna," she remarked casually over lunch.

"Where?"

"Just to a pub."

"With Gerry?" Mummy did not seem to hear. "Can I come too?" persisted Donna.

"To a pub? Whatever next!"

"Sarah does sometimes. She told me."

Afterwards they drove to Richmond Park and walked all the way from the pen ponds to the plantation and back again. "Can we ring Mr Brown's doorbell?" asked Donna on the way home. "Please!"

"Mr Brown will reply in his own good time," said mummy.

They discovered Sarah curled up morosely in front of the television set, hollow eyed and pasty. Having neglected to take a key she had scaled the ginnel door, shinned up a rear drainpipe with the aid of a dustbin and levered open the faulty bathroom window. As Donna removed the red photograph album from where it was kept next to the starched tablecloths and boxed silver dinner service the first shots of recrimination were fired off.

"So where have you been all day?"

"At Jeannie's."

"No, you haven't! I rang!"

"Don't start!" barked Sarah so stridently that Donna felt her heart skip a beat.

Propelled by a glance from her mummy she beat it upstairs to retrieve Dawn and share the contents of the special book. She placed it on the bottom bunk like a trophy, carefully opened the soft velvet cover and stared at herself in amazement. How could she ever have been so tiny and wrinkled and black haired?

"I'll go where I want and see who I want!" screamed a voice in the distance. "You do! Why not me?!"

"You're a child- you're vulnerable!" came the staccato reply. "I have to work my fingers to the bone to keep this family together!"

Eight glorious pages of newborn baby. In pram. In cot. In plastic bath. In Sarah's arms. On mummy's breasts. Smiling. Crying. Mostly sleeping. Yellow faced. Pink faced. Naked. "This is me with gran'ma and gran'dad," explained Donna to Dawn. "They live in Durham. Maybe I'll take you to see them one day."

"You're such a fucking hypocrite, you really are! You're out drinking and bonking all week while we have to stop in here with that sour faced Serbian bitch you picked up off the street!"

"I'm doing no such thing!"

"Yes you fucking are! Yes! Yes! Don't deny it! Your gonna catch AIDS one day if you aren't careful!"

"Here I am at the nursery," said Donna turning over the pages. "And at my first school. Do you like my pigtails?" Dawn nodded obligingly. "I like these ones best," Donna continued. "This is my sister, Sarah. I really love her I do – even though she's bad tempered sometimes."

Sarah's celluloid primary school image shone with happiness. She looks so proud to have me by her side, thought Donna wistfully. She looks so cute and little girlie in her Alice and Wonderland frock with waist length ribboned hair.

"I take you for granted! That's a fucking laugh, mum! Whose baby sitting Donna when you go out tonight, eh?! Father fucking Christmas?! Hypocrite!"

"That's not much to ask. I mean you're old enough to look after Donna all through the week, too. You whinge about every au pair and childminder we've ever had but the fact is you're spoilt and bone idle and –"

"Rubbish!"

"It isn't rubbish! I've had another phone call from Mr Gray. And a letter. You can't swear at your teachers like that! You can't flounce out of their classes if they ask you to stop chattering!"

"My teachers are all thick as pig shit! They know nothing about nothing! They're like you. Control freaks. You should all be locked up in a mental asylum!"

Donna closed the book suddenly. "Let's get the others to sing some songs, shall we?" she told Dawn. "It's so hard to talk with all the shouting downstairs."

"I shudder to think – never mind!"

"What?!"

"Nothing."

"You shudder to think what? Bitch!"

"Alright! I shudder to think what your father would say if he could see what you've turned into!"

51

"Don't bring daddy into this, you bitch! Or else!"

"Or else what?!"

"How do you think he'd shudder to see the way you drool over that low life loser Gerry! Not to mention the others. No wonder you don't bring them home!"

"I don't bring them home because of you!"

"You're sick, you are, mum! You really are fucking sick!"

"You're the one who's sick, Sarah!"

A door banged shut. Then another. Silence. Terrible silence.

"Row, row, row the boat gently down the stream," Donna started to sing. "Come along now everybody! Sylvestra! No slacking! Merrily, merrily, merrily, merrily. Life is but a dream."

*

Frank's hot unshaven cheeks prickled against the pillowcase as he turned over yet again in the darkness. He could not sleep but the two-day old growth of stubble was only a small part of the reason why. His every fibre felt uncomfortable in the claustrophobic space that had become home. His head was teeming with indecision, each jagged edge of thought accompanied in the background by an impromptu orchestration of nearby body functions. Grunting. Farting. Moaning. The regular leitmotiv of gibberish. It beat anything he had come across in prison. There you shared your space with one other con and a swill bucket. Here in the hostel you shared with an extra five and received a tiled bathroom as compensation. McLeod was right. Time did pass more slowly on the outside – an undeniable fact suddenly tightening like a steel tourniquet around his temples. Squeezing. Constricting. Suddenly he felt as if he would go mad if he had to endure it just one more night after this.

Then the after-truth, the residue, as he groped for his wallet in the dark and sifted through the meagre contents with the aid of a pocket torch. Perhaps he had already gone mad? Perhaps somewhere along the line of his incarceration the desires and hopes that had been required to burn so brightly in his imagination just to keep time on the move had overheated and permanently damaged the reasoning faculty of his brain? It had happened to much tougher men than him. He knew that.

"Turn it off! Yer blindin' me, yer bastard!" somebody growled in annoyance and Frank cursed back twice as hard. If that drunken slob yelled out once more he would feel the force of Frank's fists. He waited...but nothing happened. An uneasy silence settled. Then the bunk creaked as Frank rolled onto his back and focussed the halo of his torch on the two remaining photos of Susan and Francesca.

What should he do?

McLeod was using him for sure. There was no question. And what made it worse was that right from the beginning when he had slipped him that dud business card embossed with a new identity McLeod had taken Frank's willingness to become involved for granted. Five million pounds cash and a passport. No, it was not too late to give McLeod the two fingered salute. McLeod had no real power. Okay, McLeod could get angry and threaten him. Frank had spent the whole weekend considering this. The truth was he did not care one jot for the Scotsman's promise of money, or indeed even for himself – in so far as he presently existed. What Frank cared for, what defined him, lived somewhere else on the planet, if the whispers of the glass house were to be believed. The torchlight flickered momentarily and recovered. Two faces frozen in time touched an undying nerve at the bottom of his heart. Wherever they were now that was where he wanted to be. Forgiven. Reformed. Purified. Except "wanted" was not the right word. A full night's uninterrupted sleep. A decent hot meal. Now those things were "wants." You could survive their absence with little inconvenience. Susan and Francesca were a need – like oxygen. And it was for that reason and that reason alone he was prepared to consider doing business with McLeod. He would use McLeod to find out where they were, to supply him with a passport and to get him over the first leg, if not the entire length, of the journey there. Okay, thirteen months would eventually pass but even then when he was technically free to apply for a passport there was no guarantee he would be given one or allowed entry to any foreign country of his choice. Ex cons were persona non grata. He would indeed be mad not to seize this opportunity. There was no alternative. Another might never come along.

A circuit had finally been completed. A decision made.

"I have to do it," Frank mumbled to himself. "I have to!"

"Shhharrrap, will yer!"

"Shut up yourself!" he bawled back.

Nobody answered. Faraway a police siren screamed through the night. Frank pulled the blanket right over his head and within minutes had drifted off to sleep.

Chapter 6

Today's date, Monday 28 April, 1997 resided according to the classroom custom in the top left hand corner of the board but in the central space, much to Donna's dismay as she settled into her seat, two brazen rows of digits stared back at her. There was no escape.

"Four, four, four," explained Miss Frobisher with the help of a ruler. "Now how many more fours do we need to make 16? Anyone?" The usual paddy field of arms shot up. "Yes, Sammie?"

"One, miss."

"Excellent. So how many fours make 16?"

"Four, miss."

"Excellent." The paddy field instantly wilted. The ruler now picked out a similar line of threes and immediately the paddy field flourished again. "Three, three, three," intoned the teacher. "Now then?"

"Me, miss. Me, miss!"

"Please be patient, Giles. Now how many more threes do we need to make 15? Yes, Harry?"

"Two, miss."

"Excellent."

"And five threes make 15," Harry elaborated with a superior shrug.

"So I'm going to give out the worksheets now and I want you to answer all the questions in exactly the same way. Alright? Does anyone have a question? Donna?"

Donna knew Miss Frobisher was going to say her name a long moment before she said it and could feel the snake of her anxiety coiling up inside. "No, miss," she spluttered but her cheeks felt flushed and her body seemed to be expanding in the glass house atmosphere of the teacher's lingering inquiry.

"Good – let's crack on then."

What she had really wanted to say was completely unsayable. She wanted the whole thing to be explained again, very slowly, the numbers to be written on the board as she looked and not just to magically appear there at the point of a conjuring wand. What did it mean "to make 16"? Sixteen what? Sixteen cakes, for example? And why should you need 'fours' to do it with? And why was there always a row of three of them? Three fours. Three threes. Were they telephone numbers? Like 999 which you use to phone for an ambulance or the police. Who did you speak to if you dialled 444?

A worksheet slapped down in front of her on the table. All around her heads were bent in diligent worship to the mysterious task it contained. She tried to read but the criss-crossing lattice frame of numbers and letters remained only a pattern like wallpaper in front of her eyes and defied any further comprehension. She blinked and rubbed and peered again and the pattern ghosted out a secondary parallel image which held her in a kind of unthinking listless trance.

"Donna? What are you doing?"

It was the voice of Miss Frobisher right up beside her. How had she got there?

"Nothing, Miss."

"Exactly. You haven't begun yet. Were you day-dreaming?"

"No. I was thinking about the weekend."

Somebody laughed nearby and Donna felt her face flush crimson. Why did she always say the wrong things?

"Do you understand it, Donna?"

"Not really, Miss."

"Then why-?" Miss Frobisher sighed impatiently and bent low to the table, prodding at the paper with a pencil and muttering instructions.

All Donna wanted to do now was heal the wound. "Abo-ridge-annies," she spontaneously declared.

"What?"

"Abo-ridge-annies. The people who live in Australia."

"Abo-ridge-annies," intoned Harry in the same mode of pronunciation and the people at his table tittered.

"That's excellent, Donna. Thank you very much for remembering," said Miss Frobisher with a hostile glare at the miscreants. "We'll come on to the Australia project after lunch. Then you can tell us all."

Later, as 4F filed slowly into the dining room, Abigail came strutting full of self-confidence towards Donna and said, "Can I sit next to you?"

Donna looked behind her assuming Abigail must be addressing someone else. They had not exchanged glances let alone words since the visit to the river.

"Can I?"

"Me?" Abigail's chubby cheeks split open in an affectionate smile. "Yes, if you want."

"That was hard, wasn't it?"

Donna nodded and grinned.

"I don't like sums either."

They each pulled their lunch box out of the crate and sat down opposite each other at the nearest spare table, comparing the contents, swapping bits of sandwich, commenting on the melange of sausage and custard odours emanating from the serving hatch.

After a while Abigail said, "I usually eat my lunch with Laura."

"Yes, I know," nodded Donna.

"We went to the same nursery. Her daddy plays squash with my daddy."

Donna found her eyes wandering around the room.

"Laura's not here today. Probably had an asthma attack. Do you want to be my best friend in her place?"

Donna felt so awe struck she could hardly finish chewing her apple. The pieces stuck in her throat. This was going to be the best day ever. After lunch they played hopscotch together in the playground and during afternoon break they out dared each other with back flips and tricks on the climbing frame.

"I haven't heard from your mother yet, Donna, about the parents' consultation evenings," confided Miss Frobisher to Donna at going home time. "I really would like to see her but the only appointment I've got left now is 7:20 on Wednesday. Can you make sure she reads this letter tonight?"

"Can you make sure that mummy reads this letter tonight?" said Donna handing the envelope to Katrina as she jauntily opened the car door and took her place in the rear. "Sarah?" Silence. "I played with Abigail today." Silence. "We ate our lunch together and afterwards I beat her at hopscotch." Silence. "Sarah?"

"Haven't you noticed, Div? I'm not talking to you."

"Why?"

"Because you're a grass snake. You told mum that I'd been in a pub. I'll never tell you anything again."

Donna felt her stomach lurch as the car twisted into and out of the roundabout. "Sarah? Who's your best friend?" she persisted recklessly. "Polly or Jeannie?"

"That's for me to know and you to find out."

"Is it Polly?" Silence. "I think it's Polly."

"Who's yours, Div? The invisible man? Sad case!"

The car jerked to a halt outside a row of shops. "I'm just buying meat to make a spaghetti bolognaise," announced Katrina. "Won't be a minute."

*

It had taken two hours to drive across London, Frank calculated, not counting the stopover at a hypermarket in Acton where they purchased groceries and consumed a steak meal. Darkness had already closed in when the car crossed the river just after Richmond Circus. It plunged into a warren of narrow residential streets and finally lurched to a halt inside a patio garden on the hard-standing entrance to a protected driveway. McLeod opened the door with a large bunch of keys and they swiftly shunted Frank's navy holdall and boxes of groceries inside.

Frank sniffed the air, reeking of lavender polish with just a hint of disinfectant. While the Scotsman stooped to pick up the litter of junk mail and free newspapers that lay cluttered by the door Frank gazed at the hallway, a high ceiling with straight staircase leading up to a landing. He walked across deep pile carpet to the foot of the stairs cautiously, feeling like an intruder. Then he noticed the hallway was on two levels.

"Watch the steps," continued McLeod showing the way into a small but skilfully modernised kitchen. The Scotsman lifted a pristine white bin lid and dumped the refuse of paper inside without giving any of it a second glance. "You've got everything you need, Frank. Even satellite telly. This is the hot water switch." He flicked it and a yellow light came on in the thermostat. "Three bedrooms upstairs. All made up. One's got a shower in. The bathroom's at the front. I'll show you how the keys work."

"No need, McLeod. I'll work it out for myself." Frank felt tired and wanted to get rid of the other man as quickly as possible. "Is the phone connected?" he asked pointing at the yellow wall unit.

"Yes but don't use it except to answer. There's an extension in the living room. When I come back the day after tomorrow I'll bring you a mobile. Here's sixty." McLeod peeled out three twenty-pound notes from his wallet. "Anything else?"

"Which is my bedroom?"

"Take your pick. I'll be unpacking your shopping."

Frank lugged his bag upstairs. The rooms were smaller than he had expected, only one of them being a double, but all immaculately turned out like a five star hotel. The place had the feel and proportions of a country cottage. It was cosy. The bedroom at the back of the house gave onto the garden. This one, he reckoned, would be the most private and, if his calculations were correct, ought to get the morning sunshine. Judging by the wallpaper, the soft furnishings and the teddy bear it had once been occupied by a child. No matter. He dropped the holdall on the bed and opened the sash window. Instantly a scent of freshly mown grass eclipsed the one of lavender polish. He peered outside but it was too dark to make out anything except the corrugated roof of the garage beneath and to the left of him, a few isolated rectangles of light.

"Old habits die hard? Eh, Frank?" It was McLeod in the doorway behind him, beaming with private amusement, presumably at Frank's choice of the cell-sized room.

"Only idiots and politicians laugh at their own jokes," remarked Frank snapping shut the window and closing the curtains.

"I'll see you Wednesday then – with the tool-bag and mobile. Okay?" Frank nodded and took off his shoes as he stretched out on the bed. "Three short and one long ring."

"Let yourself out, will yer? My butler's bin given the night off."

Afterwards Frank made an effort to unpack. He opened the wardrobe door and discovered a row of animated kid sized coat-hangers which he studied as if they were objets d'art. Next he made to open the drawer of the bedside table but it resisted, once, twice. A piece of crumpled paper appeared to be jamming the runners and it needed a real yank to liberate the obstruction before he could place his socks and underwear inside. He was about to throw the offending litter into a little mermaid basket when he noticed a drawing on it, all green swirly plaited lines. On closer inspection the picture appeared to represent a fairy tale tree with long drooping fronds, lit by a low sun and surrounded by gleaming rooftops. Underneath a spidery children's hand had written the words *to georgia wit lov from donna. you ar my best frend.*

Instantly the memory of a song germinated in Frank's head. A fragment of melody and a lyric with the name Donna in it. What was it? His hands automatically scrunched up the etching as his mind burrowed in search of the tune. No good. It had sunk again as quickly as it had arisen from his consciousness and he lobbed the paper ball with casual precision into the waste paper basket before unpacking the rest of his meagre belongings.

*

When she padded chirpily down to breakfast on Tuesday morning Donna found her mummy scribbling a note. "Give this to Miss Frobisher," she ordered sealing it in a brown envelope.

"Are you going to the 'pointment?"

"Yes. Suppose so."

"Is there a letter yet from Mr Brown yet?"

"Haven't seen one. Where's Katrina got to? She should have been here ten minutes ago."

"Can't you drive us to school, mummy?"

"No. I'm going to be late for work as it is."

Mummy poured a pan of bubbling hot milk over the bowls of Weetabix and shouted, "Sarah! Sarah!" through the doorway. Half a minute later Sarah glided into the room like an indolent ghost and started brushing her hair in the wall mirror as if nobody else existed.

"Take off those earrings before you go out, Sarah, please." Silence. "Sarah?"

"I don't want to."

"Then take off that necklace."

"Why should I?"

"Because you're only allowed to wear one piece of jewellery in school – you know very well."

The ghost unhinged the black and silver bevelled trinket and dropped it with a flourish of disdain on the draining board.

"And you've got a double detention tonight. Don't forget. I don't want yet another letter home."

Sarah sat down with a jarring scrape of the pine chair and picked at her cereal bowl as if it had been laced with arsenic. "What are you so cheerful about, Div?" she sneered suddenly.

"Nothing."

The first half of the school morning seemed to drag on and on. Had break time been secretly cancelled and nobody told her? Donna kept looking over her shoulder to where Abigail sat by the window trying to catch her eye and elicit a common smile. By the time Miss Frobisher did release them the mounting excitement had accumulated in the region of Donna's bladder and she needed to rush to the toilet cubicles. When she had relieved herself Abigail was nowhere to be found. Not in the classroom. Not in the corridors. Where would she be waiting, Donna wondered. Where did best friends wait for one another? Was there a special place? The playground contained all sorts of nooks and shaded crannies.

Donna set off on a circuitous journey through the milling bodies, her eyes darting this way and that like a hungry sparrow, and eventually she spotted her prey sitting on a bench under the wooden gazebo chatting to somebody she instantly recognised as Laura.

"Hullo, Abigail! I needed to go to the toilet," exclaimed Donna by way of a panted greeting. "What shall we play at?"

"Nothing," shot back Abigail blandly as if butter would not melt in her mouth. "You can't be my best friend any more. Laura's come back."

And without any further ado the two little girls skipped off hand in hand towards the climbing frame.

Frank reached out for his wristwatch and received a shock as the digits moved into focus. He had been asleep for fourteen hours unless the battery had failed in the night? He tumbled downstairs and into the kitchen where the clock on the electric cooker confirmed the time. It was already afternoon. He showered, alternating between hot and cold taps, dressed and sank two glasses of chilled orange juice in quick succession. And only now the utter disorientation of occupying an entire house alone began to set in. He wandered from room to room like a visitor in a National Trust property expecting to see people inside as he entered each one, disquieted and thrilled by turns at the vastness of his territory. A dining room with a round pine table. A study with desk and filing cabinets and bookshelves, containing well used hardbacks and tourist guides. Credo – Melvyn Bragg. The Chains of Fate – Pamela Belle. Adams Empire – Evan Green. Fat tombs for people with fat reading habits. Lastly a living room fit to entertain the queen with French windows, two opulent sofas, a patio door, and view of the back garden. Any second a screw would tap him on the shoulder and tell him to sling his hook. Suddenly the phone rang. He watched it uneasily. This, too, belonged to him. It would not bite. He picked up the receiver and a plummy woman's voice said, "Is that you, Doris?"

"No," he heard himself grunt.

"Sorry. I must have dialled the wrong number again." And the bustling personality behind the voice disappeared with a click back into the nothingness from which it had so uncannily emerged.

A bit later he began fitting keys to locks and pushing buttons on gadgets. Everything worked. Then finally with a conscious effort not to appear furtive in his demeanour, he opened the back kitchen door and stepped out onto a concrete driveway. Left he saw the fancy wrought iron gate, right the huge green door of the double garage and in front the seven-foot high panels of slat board fencing separating the property from a terraced row of neighbours. McLeod had been an excellent communicator. Everything about the layout of the garden, the garage, the patio and riverbank were exactly as he had described them. If anything the premises seemed even more secluded to Frank as he strolled about than he had expected. Not a single nosy neighbour put in an appearance. Some of the fencing and the concrete mooring had seen better days. So too had the rusty padlock which fitted the rear wooden door of the garage. It was hard to work and needed oiling. Frank found a can inside as he switched on the internal strip lighting. All manner of tools, garden furniture, barbeque equipment and a petrol mower had been stored in an annex at the rear of the garage proper, leaving the main space virtually empty. As he came out, closing the bolt of the padlock with a struggle, Frank thought he heard the miaowing of a cat above his head. He looked towards the garage roof. A huge gnarled buddleia bush dominated the side of the building, its massive branches shooting prolifically upwards and across the guttering. He stepped out from beneath its umbrella onto the lawn and was delighted to behold the high lilac sprouting plumage alive with butterflies – tortoiseshells, white cabbages and a single blue. How amazing! And it was not yet May! The sudden memory of his old friend Leppy flowered in Frank's brain, the rare Scandinavian blue found all those years ago feeding off excrement when he had been punished in solitary, and the way Leppy's eyes had lit up with wonder at the gift of the insect afterwards.

This is a lucky omen, Frank thought to himself as he re-entered the house by the patio door. This is Providence. Everything is going to work out fine. Everything.

Chapter 7

On Wednesday it rained more or less all day. A bald man with a kind if rather serious expression on his face visited the school, and spoke to the children about all the good things he was intending to do for them and their parents. He wore a large flowery yellow badge with tassels on the lapel of his suit and all the teachers seemed very excited to be able to shake his hand after assembly. It was part of his last minute tour of the constituency.

"That's Vincent Cable. He's going to be the next M.P.," said Sarah when Donna blurted it out in the car. "You were deeply honoured. He came to us last week. Here. I'm going to let you play with my eyelash curler tonight. In fact you can borrow it for a couple of days. And my green troll."

Donna guessed that Sarah must want sole possession of the living room again but it was still very pleasing to be spoken to like that and given a present. It encouraged her to ask questions about things that puzzled her. "Is he going to become Prime Minister?" she ventured.

"No- but he's going to kick that pompous Tory out on his arse. He's been around too long. Like a stale fart." Sarah exchanged a spontaneous giggle of glee with Polly who had been invited to ride in the car home with them and was scribbling notes on a jotting pad. "He's a Liberal, Div," explained Sarah to her confused sister. "The Liberal Party only exists to make up the numbers in parliament. If the opinion polls are to be believed, Labour's going to win in a landslide."

"And I'm sure they are," enjoined Polly. " 'The nightmare is over! Long live the dream! New Labour. New World!' What do you think, Sar? Should we use that slogan on the hustings?"

"Who are you going to vote for, Katrina?" asked Donna leaning into her chauffeur's neck as the girls nattered on.

"Me?! Oh, dear, no! I'm not permitted to vote!" laughed Katrina. "Whatever next?!"

It transpired that Sarah and Polly had been chosen to take part in a mock election tomorrow which meant that they were to stand up in front of the whole year group and explain why they should vote for the Labour Party. It was an enormous responsibility. They needed to be carefully rehearsed, absolutely word perfect. One slip of the tongue and the result would be another five years of sleaze and overcrowded classrooms and long hospital waiting lists. Or so Sarah protested and with such conviction that the moment they entered the house Donna willingly surrendered the territorial rights her sister required as a personal contribution to the restoration of efficient government. As an alternative distraction Donna escorted her favourite dolls to the laundry utility room next to the kitchen. It was warm and smelled of soap and instantly assumed the proportions of the Metro Centre in her mind. She asked them what the word *Sleaze* meant and who they intended to vote for. None of them really knew and the conversation quickly degenerated into more mundane matters. Dawn had kept look out on the white house estate and had nothing to report except a triad of ducks skimming low across a sodden horizon. Jade had put a broken leg in plaster and delivered a mother of twins. Sylvestra had hosted a television chat programme with men who liked to dress up as women and learnt how to grow boobies. While Caroline had sold ten package holidays to Euro Disney, gone out for a drink with her new best friend and forgotten all about the appointment she had with her daughter's school teacher.

"What's his name? Your new best friend, Caroline?" asked Dawn mischievously, knowing she was unlikely to receive a straight answer.

Caroline looked down on her interrogator from behind her inverted shoebox desk and replied, "That's for me to know and you to find out."

"Will you play upstairs now with your dollies, Donna?" interrupted Katrina suddenly and Donna's sensibility reverted with a shudder to the drab familiarity of unwashed laundry bundles and soap powders. "I need to unload the washing machine and fold up the dry clothes. Okay?"

"Okay then."

"Good."

"Katrina? Who is your best friend?"

Katrina's pallid features furrowed and pinched up momentarily in thought. "Best friend? I don't know. In this country I think it must be your mummy. She gave me this job after all."

"Did you have a best friend in your own country?"

"Oh, yes. Many." The lids of Katrina's eyes seemed to flicker wildly. "Come along now."

"Who?" persisted Donna.

"My cousin, Bobo, for a start. But he was lost in the fighting three years ago. Come along now. I'll help you collect them up. This one's very pretty. What's her name?"

Lost? thought Donna. Couldn't he find his way home again? Ever? But she was too caught up in Katrina's sudden burst of evasive energy to formulate the question. And just at that moment Sarah came into the kitchen seeking mineral refreshments from the fridge.

"What? No coke left in the bottle?" she snapped peevishly. "Thanks for guzzling it all, Div."

"I never had any, Sarah."

"And pigs fly over rooftops! Did you play with Abigail again today?" Sarah asked in revenge.

"No."

"She's blown you out already, has she? Smart kid."

"You're jealous cos I've got the day off school tomorrow."

"Fat lot of good it'll do you. There's going to be an eclipse of the sun. It'll be pitch black most of the day."

"I'm not going to let you sleep in my bedroom ever again!" retorted Donna.

And as she hurried upstairs with the dolls Sarah's defiant words rang in her ears. "You and whose army's gonna stop me, bitch!"

But whatever irritation Donna experienced at her sister's short-lived gratitude quickly became forgotten as she instructed her acolytes in the dynamics of a brand new game called 'Best Friends'. It was bound to be a lot of fun, she encouraged them. In her mind endless permutations and scenarios began to flower. The dolls could endlessly be falling out and making up with one another, confessing secrets and sharing worries. They could buy each other presents, visit disco clubs together, go to private sleep-overs and indulge in midnight feasts. And most importantly, considered Donna, if I ever get tired of supervising their lives I can leave them alone in pairs and they will never become lonely or bored.

On this occasion, however, tiredness never became an issue. With only a fifteen minute interval to eat supper the entertainment continued right through to bedtime and every single mannequin in the room was enlisted. When mummy looked in to close down the soap opera a tearful finale was already in progress, worthy of any dramatic cliffhanger. Dawn's long established friendship with the Green Troll was about to be annihilated by the unexpected home-coming of her old flame, Bobo.

"Where were you, Bobo?" cried Dawn, hugging a one-legged figurine to her ample bosom. "I've missed you very badly."

"I got lost in the fighting," explained Bobo in a husky voice. "Sorry it's taken me so long to find my way home."

Dawn put him down and turned discreetly to the Green Troll. "I can't be your best friend now," she cooed complacently. "Bobo's come back." And without any further ado off they strolled to the burger bar leaving the supernatural being speechless with disappointment.

*

Frank sat aimlessly trawling through the plethora of television stations. He had almost given up on McLeod when the doorbell suddenly rang in three short and one long burst, as promised. "Where's the car parked?" asked Frank as he let McLeod in out of the dark. The Scotsman was carrying a tatty blue canvas sports bag.

"Other side of the block," answered McLeod. "I can't stay long. I've just had a bastard of a journey from Swindon and I'm running two hours late. How's it bin going, son? Any problems?"

Frank began to tell him about the patio door that did not want to shut, the rusty padlock on the garage door and the dilapidated state of some of the boundary fencing but the Scotsman cut it short with a shrug of impatience. "Your beard's coming along nicely. Seen anyone?" he remarked.

"Not a soul. Reminds me of solitary," snapped Frank, irritated by his visitor's casual indifference.

"Solitary contentment, eh?" grinned McLeod.

"What were you doin' in Swindon?"

McLeod sank into one of the living room sofas and opened the bag. "Collecting these," he said and pushed it across to Frank. "The rest of your operation's kit."

Inside he discovered several parcels wrapped in layers of newspaper. He pulled one of them apart and examined the weapon inside, a .45 calibre pistol maybe ten inches long and weighing a bit more than a large bag of sugar. He had not seen one quite like it before. The muzzle protruded like a nipple from the slide and was threaded.

"Takes a sound suppressor," explained McLeod dipping into the bag and producing a funnel that he showed Frank how to attach. "Magazine catch. Slide lock. See? And that's the decocking lever. It'll lower the hammer silently." And he indicated how.

"What's the magazine take?"

"Twelve rounds. Better give 'em a test drive in the garage tomorrow."

Frank reached to open a second parcel.

"They're all the same," said McLeod lighting up a cigarette. "Check them later. And there's your mobile. I've put my mobile number on the base. Not that you'll need it. I'll reach you when I'm ready. It's safer to keep the communications one way. There's a copy of the Thames Tide Tables in there, too, just to familiarise you with the local cycle." The Scotsman exhaled a billow of smoke. "By the way, I've found them," he added nonchalantly. "Your family."

Frank felt his heart leap with surprise and he fumbled the mobile that he had been examining as if it were a curio. "Susan? Cesca? Already?!"

McLeod nodded and said, "You haven't got a can of beer left, I suppose. I'm parched."

"Where? Where?!"

The Scotsman gave him a tatty scrap of paper on the way out to raid the kitchen fridge. Frank's eyes ravished the black scrawl, an undistinguished suburban address in Sidney, Australia. His chest heaving with elation Frank paced up and down the room trying to batten down the massive torrent of optimism that had welled up inside him, reading and rereading the precious data as if it might at any second dissolve into thin air.

"I suggest we take a ride to the station and get your passport photos taken," said McLeod coming back into the room. "There won't be another opportunity. Frank?"

"What?"

"I said –"

"Is she still at this address?"

"No idea. It was her first port of call with the kid. That's all I found out."

"Can you get me there? Australia?"

Frank watched McLeod remove the can from his lips, his eyebrows furrow with doubt. "Bordeaux. Yes. Australia's asking too much. You're on your own after that. And anyway Frank –"

"What?!"

"Even if you get lucky and track her down how do you think she'll react? She'll cut you dead. She might even go to the police. Think about it."

"Give over. I know her better than I know myself. She's my wife, McLeod."

"She used to be your wife. It'd be a miracle if she hadn't found somebody else after all this time."

Frank shook his head with an exasperated smile. He felt as if he was dealing with a deliberately awkward child. "No chance, mate. Sue wouldn't mess around like that. She aint the type," he explained. "She's waiting for me alright. I mean probably can't admit that totally to herself – but she is. Look, I've been in a very good mood this last couple of days. Don't try and spoil it for me."

McLeod said nothing. He looked unimpressed, even disappointed and Frank felt the need to convert him – why he did not know. "Look, I know what you're thinking. I hurt her. I betrayed her. She hadn't a clue what I'd bin up to all those years, where the money came from for the house and the holidays. But she knows how sorry I am. She knows I've bin to hell and back with remorse. What we had together was special. She was sixteen when we started goin' out. I was her first and only man. Our love is like a Ginko tree, mate. It's bloody indestructible."

"Ginko tree?" repeated McLeod with distaste. "What are you on about?"

"I read about it in one of Leppy's books. This tree. Eight hundred yards from the place where one of those atom bombs fell in Japan. It got obliterated along with everythin' else. And yet in the root system it was strong enough to survive. After a very short time it put out green sprouts and began to grow again."

"She didn't answer a single letter, Frank. She never visited you, not even once. Not many a sane man would spot a green sprout in there. More like a slate wiped totally clean. Let's go. This beer tastes flat."

McLeod went out into the hallway, up the steps and had reached the front door before Frank had wrestled his frustration into a final controlled onslaught. "Not everybody grows up bein' molested in an orphanage like you and then marries a witch," he retaliated. "Blood's thicker than water. And so is love. You ought to try it out sometime, McLeod. I mean on somebody other than yerself."

"You don't need them, Frank," replied McLeod refusing to rise to the bait. "Not with five million in your pocket." He opened the door and walked out into the night quickly.

"Needs work both ways," said Frank. "Did it never occur to you how much a daughter needs her dad? No. It wouldn't. You never 'ad kids, did you?"

But McLeod's figure had already been swallowed up by the darkness and so was the question.

Chapter 8

Donna woke up with a start. The bedroom door hung wide open and angry voices were wafting through the gap.

"And why does she get to have the day off?!"

"Don't start that again! You know very well! And you've got that mock election thing to do!"

"I've changed my mind. It's crap. Can't you send in a note tomorrow saying I've had to stay home and look after her?"

"You can't afford to miss another day's school, not with your record."

"And she can, I suppose! Thick bitch!"

Donna pulled the duvet right over her head. The voices congealed into an incoherent slurry and within seconds her body plummeted again into the seamless void of slumber. Then suddenly, close up and urgent. "Donna? I'm leaving now with Sarah. Donna!"

"Hmmm? Mummy?"

"Katrina won't be here til about half past ten, so there's no need to get up if you don't want to."

"I forgot to ask you last night, mummy," yawned Donna. "What did Miss Frobisher say about me yesterday? At your 'pointment?"

"Oh, blow! I completely forgot about it. Sorry, darling. I'll ring her from work tomorrow. Definitely."

Later, when she padded downstairs in her slippers and dressing gown, Donna found cereals, toast and juice set out on the table, the radio broadcasting cheerful music and beams of sunshine slanting in through the kitchen window. It felt nice being on her own, not at all scary. After eating her fill, she opened the backdoor and stepped outside into the little garden which still bore the scars of numerous unfinished improvement projects undertaken by the previous owner. Piles of bricks, a decaying cement bag, several timber remnants, two tyres and a detritus of empty paint cans and chip board shavings – none of which mummy had yet found the time to have removed.

She squatted down on the bricks and surveyed their ramshackle kingdom. It pleased her. They had certainly moved up in the world since Clapham, she considered. Inside they might have to suffer loose floorboards, draughty window panes, wobbly electrical fittings and a sombre depressing décor consisting of dark ambers and browns but it was their own self-contained property and they all enjoyed a room each. No more did the trudging of feet and scraping of alien lives seep through the ceiling. No more did the prattle of drunks in the road, the laughter and partying of adjacent families keep her awake til the small hours. This was what mummy had called a 'spectable neighbourhood. It meant nobody stole your milk bottles off the step. People like Sidney nodded and smiled at you in recognition and they had time to chat. It was a pity that there were so few children in her own age group but you couldn't have everything. The neighbours on Mansfield Road fell into two main types. They were either very old like gran'dad and gran'ma or not yet old enough to have any. Babies in prams and really tiny toddlers did not count.

"Miaow!" A sudden feline noise interrupted her thoughts.

"Chelsea!? Is that you!? Here, pussy, pussy!" she called hopefully. The animal oozed through the space between fence and privet, his head cocked expectantly, and padded between the obstacles towards Donna. Neither did he resist as she leaned forward and reached out her hands, spreadeagling his ample body across her lap. "You're so warm!" she exclaimed. "Are you thirsty?"

Chelsea purred and widened his eyes knowingly.

"Whatever are you doing here, half-dressed, Donna?" broke in a sudden voice behind them and Katrina came bustling out through the door.

"Can we give Chelsea a bowl of milk please," pleaded Donna as she followed her minder obediently back into the house. The cat hesitated on the threshold sniffing the stony atmosphere, his tail erect and quivering with anticipation.

"Shoo!" shouted Katrina and banged the door shut. "You know your mummy doesn't allow it," answered Katrina hoovering up the breakfast debris. "He has a home of his own. He'll keep coming back for more."

"Oh, but he's thirsty- and Sidney's not there!" whined Donna. "Just a saucer?"

"Go and get dressed please. Do you have some clean clothes to put on or do you want me to iron some for you?"

Donna had never known anyone with such pale skin as Katrina. There were days when it appeared she must be made of snow or porcelain. When she was in a bad mood, and you never knew what caused it, Katrina's flesh seemed to glow with displeasure and radiate cold heat like a wax candle. At such time her features pinched up, her high forehead wrinkled and her chilly blue eyes wandered about in their sockets like frightened orphans. When they settled in Donna's direction it was never for more than a fraction of a second and gave Donna the uneasy feeling they were staring right through her. Today was just such a day. She did not dare disobey.

"Can you play Fish with me, Katrina?" she wheedled instead.

"I have too many things to do," snapped back Katrina. "Maybe later – when the housework is all finished. You can watch the telly meanwhile. After lunch I may take you out. Go now."

*

Frank was kneeling down to examine the warped curvature of the living room door, the one that gave access to the rear garden patio. It was getting on his nerves. Unless he gave the thing a really hard yank the blade resisted the frame and wafted open again. The four glass panes rattled with displeasure as his right hand snatched powerfully at the handle once more and this time it closed.

In the corner of his attention the television was spewing out images of ballot boxes and voters. A newspaper, purchased during yesterday evening's visit to the station photograph booth, lay on the coffee table as yet unread. Next to it the little red Thames Tide Tables booklet and the scrap of paper containing Sue's last known address which McLeod had given him.

He had spent most of the morning pottering around his estate, familiarising himself with every nook and cranny both inside and out and learning how to use the new-fangled tools of his trade. In obedience to McLeod's instructions he had tested all four guns with silencers attached in the privacy of the garage, using a pile of discarded reading material as targets. Each one performed beautifully, emitting a dull phut and leaving a neatly drilled bullet hole roughly ten *Harpers and Queen's* deep. The mobile, too, had behaved according to printed instructions – except that when Frank tried to ring McLeod's number nothing happened. It took the operator to explain that the phone being contacted appeared to be permanently switched off and devoid of a message leaving facility.

Now as he reclined on one of the opulent settees, his mind temporarily vacated of its practical concerns, a stream of nostalgia came washing into the void and eddies of unpolluted hope engaged in battle with the flotsam of remorse. But Frank was quickly alert to the danger and diverted the flood. Even in periods of relaxation he knew he had to remain focused on the task in hand, cold and detached from his emotions. So his right hand groped for the tide tables and he transcribed Sue's address clinically onto the inside of the front cover for safe keeping. Then he studied the intricate columns of data, noting and marking all the nocturnal high tides during May – because the operation when it was signalled would have to synchronise with one of these and readiness was crucial.

Suddenly an excited television voice asserted itself. "And now there is every reason to believe," squawked the reporter, "that the victory is going to be even more comprehensive for Tony Blair's New Labour party than any opinion poll has predicted! The optimism, not just at Labour HQ but on the streets amongst the public, feels almost tangible. Of course, no senior Labour politician is saying as much but it is difficult to escape the feeling that they are convinced this will be a historical day in British politics!"

The words passed harmlessly like a distant firework explosion over Frank's thoughts which had taken several new directions simultaneously. One of these veered towards McLeod's mysterious sponsor and the quality of the inside information he possessed, another towards the invisible team work of the gang members and yet a third towards the logistics of loading a small river craft with two tons of gold bullion in a narrow tributary. And as the nib of his pen randomly doodled through the maze of Thames tidal digits a miscreant anxiety awoke in him. The Thames was not The Crane. Logic did not preclude the possibility that there could well be a variation in the height of the flood tide as it pressed several hundred yards up the tributary from the main river? He scanned every page, footnotes and all, but the booklet had no information on this subject. It had to be McLeod's independent judgement that a heavily-laden boat must necessarily always remain buoyant in that narrow stream whatever the prevailing conditions. Suddenly Frank wondered if Hunter might have influenced that judgment and the idea disconcerted him. Surely McLeod would only use muscle like Hunter as a transport link and not for any residual brain power?.... Even so?.....Frank scratched his head, perplexed. He was probably worrying unduly. The fact remained he did not like Hunter's involvement. The personality of the crook corroded his equanimity. In any case a few practical checks on site might quickly restore it. The next high tide was due very soon – at 12.42 in fact. He monitored his watch and instantly decided to take a good hard look at the rising water. Thus resolved, he went upstairs and surrendered his body to a long refreshing shower.

*

Two hours in front of the television was more than enough, Donna decided. So as Katrina busied around upstairs she collected the

Green Troll and carried him along with her night torch out into the back garden. "Shall we go and look for Chelsea? You haven't met him yet, have you? And I bet he's never been stroked by a Troll before," she encouraged him.

The back garden had trapped the heat of the mid-day sun and made the inside of the house seem cold in comparison. It was a windless day. The cotton wool clouds hung statically in a pale blue ocean. Somewhere perhaps in the depths of the brooding willow a bird shrieked urgently, at last being answered by its mate. Then an unreal silence seemed to descend broken only by the low rumble of an airplane engine. "Miaow! Miaow!" she heard nearby.

Donna's eyes darted around for the prowler, backwards and forwards, searching through crevices and knots in the ramshackle fencing for a tell tale flash of his tortoiseshell fur. "Chelsea! Chelsea! I want you to meet my new friend! Chelsea!" she called. But nothing appeared. The proud, disappointed cat had decided to keep its own counsel. This was a feline game. It refused to surrender its warm sensual flanks to the second call of temptation and perhaps not the third or fourth either.

"Chelsea?!" Nearby an unseen door clunked and shuddered open. Donna moved forward, bent low to the ground, soothing her prey towards her now, coaxing. "Pussy, pussy, pussy, pussy..." Across the flagstones, slowly, patiently, towards the gap where a rotting gate hung on one hinge.

"Miaow!"

"Chelsea -!"

In a split second the animal was there and gone, a blur of coiled agility, catapulting beyond the slatted blades of wood and disappearing down the ginnel. Donna gave pursuit a bit too eagerly almost tripping over her own feet and dropping the Troll in the process. The floor of the ginnel path was choked with rooted ivy and bindweed and Donna had to grovel around on her knees for a few precious seconds to recover her companion. She reached the L junction where the path turned abruptly left and narrowed as it passed towards the high brick wall of the garage in the direction of the river. The cat crouched ten yards further on down the tunnel, – alert, waiting, calculating his next move.

"Pussy, pussy, pussy!"

Donna edged forward confidently. She knew the ginnel ended in a cul de sac behind number 16 and there was no way out unless Chelsea jumped. The garage wall was enormous. The game was up. But Chelsea cocked his head nonchalantly sideways as if beckoning Donna on, and at the last moment simply slid into thin air. Donna froze in amazement. It was a vanishing trick the Cheshire Cat himself would have been proud to perform. Hesitantly now she knelt down and prodded the torch like a divining rod as if expecting to locate a secret slot in the envelope of the world through which all animate matter could be dispatched to an invisible dimension. The torch quivered and waggled but failed to dematerialise.

"That's funny," said Donna and put her hand right on the point of the fence where Chelsea had last stood rubbing his fur. It gave way easily like the flap of a letter box. She pushed harder and a gaping crevice opened up in front of her where the horizontal slats of fencing had rotted and become detached from the vertical stanchion. Within seconds Donna had scrambled through the aperture and found herself on the concrete driveway right in front of the metal green garage door. What should she do now? Nobody was about.

"Miaow! Miaow!" she heard again and the decision was made for her. She groped cautiously round the outbuilding to where a tongue of pink flagstones pointed the way into the garden proper and under the limbs of a miniature tree. Suddenly her feet trod on tufty thick turf. The lawn spread out like an emerald carpet before her. She stopped and looked around, her eyes flitting the length of one border then across and back up the other. She remembered how neatly they had been kept, the plants evenly spaced, the soil finely hoed by loving hands but now it was difficult to distinguish one shrub from another. A mass of surplus vegetation had established itself and was busily knotting ever more complex patterns of anarchy. For a predatory cat it must have seemed like paradise. A rustle of leaves alerted Donna to her right. Chelsea emerged from the innards of a hibbe bush, shrugged his shoulders twice and bee lined down the lawn towards the conifers. They had been cultivated in a row of ten as a kind of windbreak at the bottom of the garden, perhaps too a shield of privacy, and groomed into a single hedge about ten feet high with a keyhole shaped arch. Donna advanced confidently now and passed through it inhaling a great lungful of aromatic pine. The scent prickled her nostrils and she sneezed twice as she emerged on the river side, wiping the resultant mucous on the back of her sleeve.

The coffin shaped channel of the river with its sheer concrete vaults lay ten yards beyond her now but the area immediately behind the conifers had been partitioned from the mooring ledge by a small brick wall and served as its own private enclosure. On the left stood a circular mulching container full to overflowing with last year's rotting garden waste and on the right a patch of white gravel in the middle of which Chelsea was applying her paws ferociously to scratch out a toilet. Donna knew there was a substance you could put down to prevent animals from doing that but judging by the variegated tapestry of deposits on display nobody had bothered for ages.

"Go back to your own home to do that, Chelsea!" chastised Donna. "That's naughty."

But it was a second too late. The cat's casual endorsement of another successful visit was already in progress. He arched and shook his haunches indecently, then scooted off low between the ankles of the trees back up the garden with a sideways glance of remorse.

"Never mind him. I'll show you the river now," Donna advised the Troll and carried him forwards to the wall. It was divided by a low hinged gate which gaped invitingly open, jogging her memory of a previous visit. The kindly, concerned voice of Georgia's mummy filtered up from the past.

"We never let Georgia come down here on her own," it said. "She must stay on this side of the wall unless me or her daddy are present to open the gate. Do you understand, Donna? It gets very slippy on the embankment shelf and at low tide the drop to the bed of the stream is as deep as those trees are tall."

So who had been so foolish to leave it like that? Donna lingered on the threshold, torn between her curiosity and her conscience, scanning the shore line and back gardens beyond the river for a neighbourly resolution of the dilemma. There was nobody about. To her right three moorings down she could see the front section of a blue cabin cruiser, anchored tight to the far wall. The stream could not have been more than a foot or two deep because the hull tipped at an angle, unmoving, and was obviously still beached on the bottom. Then in an instant the silence was ripped open by a cacophony of squawking beaks as a pair of ducks rose in unwieldy terror out of the abyss of the ground, twisted towards Donna and wheeled away upwards beyond the giant willow. Donna flinched, flung up an arm instinctively to protect her face and turned on her heels back towards the conifers.

The apparition of a man stood in the keyhole staring at her. She hesitated and uttered a little gasp of surprise unsure what to do next. The stranger filled the entire space like a missing piece in a jigsaw puzzle. Her legs were gripped with the urge to run but where could they go? There was no way past. She closed her eyes in a long drawn out blink of hope but when she opened them again the shape remained as solid as before, immobile and unmoved, scrutinising her from on high.

"Are you wanting something?" spoke the man at last.

Donna gave a little nervous judder of her head and opened her mouth. The sound that fell out was meant to be "No."

"Well? What are you doin' here?"

"We were looking for Chelsea."

The face of the interrogator seemed to relax momentarily around the jaw, and he took half a pace forwards so that an elongated slice of the white house came into view between his body and the keyhole. "It's about four or five miles up river," he said. "Turn left at the weir."

Donna's brain flushed white with confusion, simultaneously perceiving the possibility of escape from this cul de sac and amazed by the man's pronouncement.

"I-I thought cats couldn't swim," stammered Donna. "My -my sister told me –" And her tongue involuntarily stopped moving.

"What's that for?" he asked. Donna squinted her eyes uncomprehendingly. "The torch?"

He moved another pace closer. A chimney, a drainpipe and a segment of roof slid into view. "In case it gets dark," she explained. "My sister told me there's going to be an e'lipse today. The moon does something. And the night comes out in the middle of the day. Have you ever seen an e'lipse?"

The man did not answer. Nor did he seem alarmed by the possibility. Donna felt herself suddenly released from his gaze. He cut across the animal toilet and in four or five crunching strides was able to reach the wall and swing his legs over to the other side, where he settled himself down like Humpty Dumpty and gazed at the river as if suddenly losing all interest in the conversation and her.

"Bye," she said but the word seemed to fall on deaf ears. So she walked to the keyhole, shedding waves of invisible apprehension. The full force of the sun hit her directly in the face as she emerged on the other side then the frolicking animus of cat shimmered into focus against a lush backdrop of grass. She hesitated, wondering whether to turn back and tell the man that Chelsea was safe after all. How could he have made such a mistake? And yet she was still a bit intimidated by him, the mean unsmiling expression on his bearded face, the curt mode of his speech. Did he talk to his children like that?

In the end it was the premise on which this question was based that made Donna look back and risk the man's further wrath. She watched him light up a cigarette, draw three times quickly in succession at it and exhale a great billowing cloud of relief which drifted slowly away into the sprouting sentinels of reedy vegetation that crowded the lower embankments. Then he thrust his free hand deep into the lining of the navy blue pullover he was wearing and pulled out a rolled up newspaper, proceeding carefully to iron out its creases on his lap and begin to read it. As far as Donna understood in her limited experience these were more or less characteristics of normal adult behaviour and her confidence marginally increased. She took a few paces closer, quietly, cat like, building her courage an inch at a time. The man stared at the front page oblivious to her continuing existence in his world. From the angle she was approaching the contents of the paper were clearly visible now, at least the large black and white photograph. It showed that handsome man with the brown wavy hair and friendly smile who was always on television and wanted to become the leader of the country. The reader coughed and Donna felt sufficiently bold to wonder who he was. He was certainly not the man she had originally seen two weeks ago on the front doorstep shaking hands with an estate agent and being saluted as Mr Brown. This man's hair was much darker, almost black, with perhaps the occasional streak of grey. He had a rash of thin beard and thick hairy eyebrows and his mouth, unlike Mr Brown's, had entirely forgotten how to transpose itself into a smile. Or so it seemed. His whole demeanour was surly and unkempt. And yet... and yet? There was something else there, too, in his face and posture, arousing her curiosity and even perhaps her sympathy.

She shifted her left foot to avoid an antique feline deposit, crunching it down in the gravel and froze immediately like a statue hoping the man had not heard. His head did not move, his gaze imperturbably lost in the tabloid print. Donna stayed immobile, scarcely breathing, for eight, nine, ten seconds and then just when the danger had passed, as she lifted the heel of her foot to edge even nearer, he said, "I thought you'd scarpered, kid."

Donna stopped again. She did not hear the words as an accusation. They were a casual observation made to nobody in particular. She felt safe and came forward to the gate, shyly but with a commitment to the task she had steeled herself to perpetrate.

"I'm Donna," she began. The man took no notice. "Donna Atkinson?" Not even a sidelong glance of curiosity. "My mummy and me, well, we delivered a letter and –"

"What letter?" he challenged abruptly.

"I posted it myself. Didn't he tell you about it?"

"Who?"

"Your friend?"

"I don't know anything about no letter, kid." He raised his head slightly but still kept his eyes fixed to the newspaper. "Are you a bit – ?" He hesitated and tapped a finger twice against the side of his temple.

Donna did not understand. She squinted towards him waiting

for the rest of the question but it failed to arrive. Then with a deceptively quick snap of the wrist he propelled the cigarette stub through a looping arc into the river. The gate she had been leaning on simultaneously swished open causing Donna to stumble down the step and onto the concrete mooring. The man eyed her remotely now, a stern expression on his face.

"Sorry," she apologised and he shrugged. "Are there any children?"

"What?"

"Children?"

"Where?"

"In the house? With you?"

Maybe he's deaf or something, it suddenly occurred to her.

"How did you get in here anyway?" he scowled.

"The fence is broken. Next to the garage," she replied as distinctly as she could manage and watched his stony reaction.

"So where do you live?"

"Twenty-eight Mansfield Road. Just over there," she pointed. "We're almost next door neighbours."

"There's no need to shout, kid."

"Sorry. Do you have any?" she asked in a whisper.

"What?"

"Children?"

The man shook his head and Donna gulped as if trying to swallow her disappointment. "This ain't no public playground," he muttered as much to himself as her and turned the page of his newspaper.

Maybe Mr Brown will come out in a minute, she considered, and behave a bit less impatiently? She shuffled one foot, then the other along the mooring to feel how slippy it was but the crepe soles of her shoes gripped tight on the dry surface and did not so much skid forward as hiccough. It had been constructed out of three thin parallel shards of concrete, one stepping down to the next, and not very well either judging by the sprigs of cabbage shaped weed and nettles that thrived in the niches between the slabs. Donna stepped onto the middle slab now and glanced furtively back at the man to check whether the rashness of her adventure might provoke a more severe chastisement but he was taking not an iota of interest. He had fixed his attention on the blue boat. Suddenly it began to wobble and creak on its tether as if struggling to become buoyant and only now did she realise that the murky water was actually moving towards them, against the direction of natural flow, from the hump back bridge which remained hidden from sight due to a slight bend in the channel. Scanning left then right she could see a mere forty yards of the river's lugubrious reedy progress. Bits of wood and clumps of grass pitted the oblique surface, a tapestry of casual garden refuse returning home on a conveyor belt as the tide turned. The channel was still only fractionally full but clearly rising fast, even to Donna's untutored eyes.

"My sister says there's a crocodile in the river and it eats people sometimes. I don't know whether to believe her. Have you seen it?" she ventured. The man lifted his head pensively, shook it once and lowered it again to the paper. "Aren't you just a bit scared?"

"No. There's no crocodile, kid."

"How do you know if – ?"

"Because ducks always come 'ere. See?" He pointed with a pistol of two fingers towards a pair of newly arrived mallards scavenging in the slime. "A crocodile would have eaten them all up. Here. Chuck 'em this crust of bread."

He pulled a cellophane wrapper out of his trouser pocket and held it out to her.

"Can I?" she checked, unsure of her ground. He gestured emphatically and she hurried over and took it out of his hand. "Thanks." She could feel his eyes in her back as she converted the crust to bite sized pellets and peppered the water with them. The ducks were circumspect at first and watched this sudden rain of munificence with dignified restraint until a ravenous gull fell out of the sky, followed instantly by another and another, triggering a no holds-barred frenzy of gluttony. When peace was restored Donna smiled back at the man for confirmation of a job well done. It did not come. The cabin cruiser had re-engaged his attention. "Where do ducks live?" she asked anyway.

"On the banks of the Thames. They paddle up with the tide."

"At the same time every day?"

He shook his head and held out another bit of bread. "Here. Throw this."

After Donna had fed them the last scrap of bread she came back towards the man more confidently and asked, "What's your name?"

The man did not answer. He looked distracted suddenly and fingered the corner of his newspaper. "Tony," he said at last.

"Tony!" exclaimed Donna. "Isn't that man called Tony, too? The one in your paper?" She watched Tony's eyes wander along the ground, weary and unimpressed. He took out another cigarette and revolved it between his lips.

"Donna! Donna!" called a high pitched voice in the distance. "Lunch is ready! Where are you!"

"I've got to go home now," said Donna but her companion looked beyond her and continued to revolve his cigarette. "Can I come again?" She wondered whether to add his name, Tony. The excitement of the coincidence bubbled like froth on the surface of her question but the man simply responded with a matter of fact shrug of indifference. At least it would have been read like that by any objective observer. To Donna it was read as an open invitation. She skipped back up the garden and burst breathlessly into the kitchen where Katrina seemed to be over-extended trying to juggle several domestic operations simultaneously.

"Didn't you hear me calling?" she said impatiently. "Where were you, Donna? Sit down please. It's on the table."

"I went looking for Chelsea at the bottom of the ginnel and –"

"Do you want baked beans with your cheese on toast?" Katrina cut in unceremoniously. She lifted a saucepan from the oven and was holding its bubbling contents dangerously close to Donna's head.

"Alright then." They splodged onto the side of the plate. "Enough now. Thank you. And then I found a hole in the fence and –"

But Katrina had instantly discarded the pan and bolted into the Metro Centre to attend to the washing machine that had begun suddenly to rumble and whine in automated spasms of distress.

"What will you do after lunch?" asked Katrina as she returned to the sink.

"I don't know. I might do some drawing."

"That's nice. We have run out of tea bags and sugar. I'm just going down to the shops to buy some. Alright? Help yourself to more toast if you want it". She wiped her hands on a tea towel and picked up her purse all in one deft, nervous movement, and was out of the house before Donna had finished chewing her second mouthful of food.

When Sarah came home, predictably in a bad mood at having to wait for a bus and still patently jealous, Donna decided to lay low. She wanted to tell someone about the man in the white house but she was terrified of being teased ever after by her sister who was bound to find some way of distorting the details of their meeting and ridiculing the whole thing. She hung about in her room with the dolls, telling them instead and deliberately missing three of her favourite telly programmes.

"What's that big dopey smile on your face all about, Div?" snarled Sarah once when they passed on the staircase but Donna tightened her lips and hurried on her way refusing to rise to the bait.

And when mummy arrived home the temptation to spill the beans became worse.

"Nice day, girls?" she asked bursting in during the mid-evening soap.

"She keeps grinning like a chimpanzee," sniped Sarah to the screen. "She's been up to something."

Donna embraced her mummy warmly and pretended she had not heard. But the second warning had been sounded now. Any whisper to her mother, however private, might be seized on or overheard by her jealous sister and lead to hours of protracted misery. "I've been drawing and painting," exclaimed Donna astutely. "Katrina took me to the lock."

"That's nice dear," said mummy with a questioning glance towards Katrina whose tight anaemic features momentarily relaxed into a smile of affirmation.

"Have you been in my room -?" demanded Sarah suspiciously.

"No."

"If you've been touching my mascara again I'll thump you!"

"I haven't."

"That's quite enough of that, Sarah," intervened mummy abruptly and turned on her heels. "What a way to be welcomed home after a gruelling day at work. Donna? School again tomorrow. I want you in bed by 8:30."

Donna had been in bed for a long time, her mind tingling with the aphrodisiac of the secret and refusing her body's every supplication to allow it to go under, when the door clicked open and closed. She felt the footsteps, the breathing and then the rustle of bed clothes in the darkness.

"Sarah?"

"Uhh?"

"There's no crocodile in the river."

"Yes there is. And it's going to eat you up before your next birthday."

"There isn't. I found out."

No reply. Donna put her thumb in her mouth, turned onto her side contentedly and fell quickly into a deep dreamless sleep.

Chapter 9

Frank's second Monday in residence had not quite advanced into the afternoon when his operation's mobile rang for the very first time. "No names," began McLeod. "Remember the rules. Enjoying the Bank Holiday weekend – ?"

"How come your mobile's always dead?" interrupted Frank. "It's been five days now."

"It's much safer that way. Every call is a risk, however small."

"But what if I need to speak to you in an emergency?"

The Scotsman sounded amused. "Our budget doesn't allow for those," he chuckled.

"When's party day?" asked Frank barely containing his exasperation.

McLeod seemed to sense it nonetheless. "I'm sorry I haven't had a chance to phone before," he offered in a conciliatory tone. "I'm in Frogland, tying up a couple of loose ends."

"Is my passport sorted?"

"Almost. It'll be on the yacht. Been out to that Paki shop yet?"

"Yeah, a couple of times late on just to buy fags and that."

"Nowhere else?"

"No."

"Good. Keep it like that. What else have you been doing with your time?"

Frank considered telling McLeod about the calls he had been putting through to the International Directories, trawling the major Australian towns for another lead on Susan's whereabouts. "Why do you want to know?" he asked instead.

"Well you might be feeling restless, fed up with your own company."

"Well I aint," insisted Frank.

"Good. It's important to keep your mind occupied son. It isn't easy waiting around on your tod. I appreciate that."

"Look, I tried a bit of detective work on that Sydney address," Frank felt encouraged to risk. "Susan ain't known there. Don't get me wrong – but are you sure it was kosher information?"

"Yes. I told you it was just a temporary address."

"And you don't know nothin' else?"

"Sorry." McLeod's tone hardened slightly. "Look, don't start abusing that phone. Okay?"

"Okay," agreed Frank diplomatically. He was standing next to the French windows now, his fingers fidgeting up and down the thick velvet curtain.

"Has anyone been round to the house?" asked McLeod.

"Why, are you expecting someone?"

"It can happen. An over-friendly neighbour. The local vicar. Don't laugh. It's important to appear normal. A polite interest is what's called for, son. You mustn't be seen acting furtively. It might arouse suspicion. We've been through all this before."

"There's a young girl found her way into the back garden," admitted Frank, "since you ask. Fortunately she's a bit dim."

"You've spoken to her then?"

"Once. It ain't exactly a fortress here is it, mate?"

"It isn't supposed to be. That's the whole point. How did she get in?"

"Through a bit of loose fencing."

"Can't you bang some nails in to fix the slats?"

"I aint sure it would work. The wood's too rotten."

"Well let her run around a bit. Keep her sweet if all else fails. No point in becoming heavy is there?" considered the Scotsman.

Suddenly Frank spotted the object of the conversation come crawling into sight. "Speak of the devil," he rasped flinching back from the window to avoid detection. "She's here again now. She comes in looking for her cat." Frank studied the carefree lilt of Donna's body as she passed quickly around the garage and down the garden lawn. A tremor of nostalgia seemed to move in his chest. "She reminds me –" he muttered. "Oh, nothing."

"What? Reminds you of what?"

"Reminds me I used to be a father once I was gonna say."

"And will be again, son. You've got time on your side."

That's not what I meant, thought Frank as Donna disappeared behind the conifers.

"You watching much of that fancy TV?" continued McLeod. "That'll keep your mind occupied eh? Four dozen channels!'

"I prefer the radio."

"Oh? Well there's three in the house."

"Yeah. I've fixed one up next to my bed. I find those late phone-ins help me doze off. Stop playing the shrink with me, will yer? My head's in good nick and so's my morale." As he spoke Frank noticed Donna walking back up the garden. "Hold on a tick," he said and pulled both sets of curtains shut. "When are you back in town?"

"Day after tomorrow, all being well."

"You never answered my question about party night."

"The date isn't settled yet. If I haven't rung you to confirm by next Monday you can assume it'll be the week after."

"That's by Monday the 12th?"

"Correct. You can keep your head together for that long?"

"I just told yer – !"

"Just joking. I know you're solid. I'm very pleased with you," coaxed McLeod. "You're relaxed, son. I can hear it in your voice. Take care now."

Frank scribbled out the date and tacked it on the kitchen message board next to the photographs of his family. Later around mid-evening he hammered a dozen nails into the loose fence slats. The trespasser had long since cleared off but for some reason he found it difficult to shift her image out of his mind. Did she really resemble Francesca or was it just a stupid, sentimental whim? He fried a steak and stared at his daughter's photo as he ate, wondering how her appearance might have changed, what she did for a living and a thousand other things on top. No wonder McLeod had supplied him with a satellite TV and three radios, he considered. The Scotsman was a wily old fox. He knew better than Frank how vital it was to keep the mind focussed entirely on the present. The regrets of the past and the hopes of the future existed like jagged rocks all over the stream of an ex-con's consciousness. If he failed to steer well away from them he could easily end up holed beneath the water line and drown. It had happened to many before.

When he got into bed his hand automatically reached out towards the radio switch. The phone-in was already in progress. He snapped off the little lamp and allowed the voices to wash over him. It made him smile momentarily to recall how these things had been such hard-earned privileges in prison and how having eventually contrived to get one he had obsessively fed on these late night chat shows the way insomniacs feed on Mogadons and whiskey.

"It's partly about social and sensory deprivation, having so much time and nothing constructive to do with it," he heard someone say in a female voice he seemed to recognise. "It's partly about self pity, rage, remorse, etc – I mean the typical long term prisoner moves from one form of obsessive morbid behaviour to another. After all he's grieving for himself and his thwarted life. Hallucinations are very common. They are an inevitable survival mechanism. The problem is this – even if he has access to good quality counselling, or other forms of emotional support –"

"Like what?"

"Like relatives visiting him. Remember many prisoners get ditched by their families, which is why the prison visitor scheme is so important. Even so the psychological damage can become chronic."

"You mean they go 'mad'?"

"Bollocks", cursed Frank. This was the last subject he wanted to hear being discussed. It was the radio equivalent of a busman's holiday. He reached to switch off – he felt really tired – but unresolved curiosity stayed his hand.

"I prefer 'unbalanced', " the woman was saying, "and in my experience the typical long term prisoner will remain in that awful state long after his release."

"Okay, well if you're just tuning in my guest tonight is Dr Rosemary Miller....."

My God it is Rosie, thought Frank. She's made a bloody career out of it. She's become a pundit!

"Do prison's achieve anything positive in the rehabilitation of offenders or are they just society's way of taking revenge? And will New Labour get to grips with problems like crime prevention, as it has promised, and prison overcrowding? Dr Miller awaits your questions on these and any related issues. But right now we break for a news summary."

As the newscaster described the world's trouble spots Frank's drowsy brain rehearsed what it had felt like to be deprived of visitors. After three years he had applied to the prison visitors scheme, eventually receiving a letter from Rosie. For five years she had visited him meticulously, once a month, and only when he had been moved to another prison had they lost touch. In those days she had been a housewife and mother, studying in her part-time for a psychology degree.

"While we're waiting for our first call," started up the phone in presenter again, "let me pick you up Dr. Miller on what you were saying about the psychological damage suffered by long-termers – hallucinations, depressive anxiety, that sort of thing."

"Yes?"

"Firstly, you could argue that fantasies are healthy, a natural human safety valve. Take religion for example. Surely people embrace the whole Christian story because living in the full glare of a meaningless existence is just too painful to endure? And secondly, my understanding is this, that as a long term prisoner's sentence unfolds he gets moved along a continuum of rehabilitation, from category A to category B prison and so on until, in the final two years or so before release, he's put in an open prison environment geared completely to personal training and preparation for life back in the community – and this is my point – presumably purged of all forms of disturbed behaviour?"

"Well that's the theory, Brian", chuckled Rosie, "but in practice it very rarely happens".

"Why not? Inadequate resources?"

"Absolutely but that's not the only reason –"

I'll give you the reason, Brian, Frank thought to himself bitterly – but already his concentration was starting to break up and dissipate. Little islands of words receded into a vast black ocean of dwindling consciousness, moving further and further apart til they ceased to be visible.

" ......not like repairing an old banger......can't overhaul the engine........talking about human beings.....profound emotional collapse........religious conviction or mission ....more likely to survive.............beyond repair?......really?.............nobody............... unscathed.............."

Chapter 10

On Tuesday at lunchtime Donna was surprised by Miss Frobisher who wandered into the canteen as if looking for somebody then came and sat down opposite to her at the trellis table.

"Did you have a nice holiday weekend, Donna?" Miss Frobisher smiled.

"Yes, thank you."

Miss Frobisher looked to her right as if to see whether anybody else was listening then leaned forward across the table in a confidential manner. "Your mum rang me up at last. Did she tell you what we decided? About your Maths?"

"I don't remember."

"Well, from tomorrow a very nice lady called Mrs Harper is going to sit next to you during the Maths lessons and help you."

"Is she?!"

"Just you. Nobody else. It will be a special relationship."

"Won't that be cheating?"

Miss Frobisher grinned widely and patted Donna's hand reassuringly. "Not at all. She'll be there every Maths lesson and you'll be able quite privately to ask her to explain anything you don't understand on the blackboard or the worksheets. Think of her as my assistant. She'll be there to help me to help you. Understand?"

"I think so."

"Good." Miss Frobisher stood up and looked at her wristwatch. "Do you know where the computer lab is?" Donna smiled. "Of course, you do! When you've finished your lunch can you go there and I'll introduce you to her? She's very, very, nice."

Donna gave a little wave of farewell, nibbled a bit off her cheese sandwich and gazed proudly round the room to see who had noticed her special visitor.

Mrs. Harper turned out to be a chubby jolly faced lady with a double chin that wobbled when she spoke. Donna had seen her before in the school waddling down the corridor and once in assembly playing the piano but she could not have been a regular member of staff because her photograph was not on Mr Knighton's notice board outside his office.

"Did you have a nice holiday weekend?" Mrs Harper smiled after the introductions had been completed.

"Yes, thank you."

"Did you go anywhere special?"

"Not really."

"I took my little boy to Thorpe Park," confided Mrs Harper her dewlaps undulating like the folds of a concertina. "It's a wonderful place. Have you been?"

"I don't think so."

"It costs twelve pounds to get in. Twelve pounds for each person."

"Does it? That's a lot."

Mrs. Harper took a bank note out of her purse. "This is a twenty pound note, Donna. Here, take it. See the number?" Donna nodded. "Let's pretend you are the ticket seller at Thorpe Park. I want to come in. How much change will you give me back from that money?" Donna hesitated, momentarily bewildered. "Think about it. There's no need to hurry. Twenty take away twelve."

"What about your little boy?" asked Donna. "Doesn't he want to come in again?"

"He's not here now, Donna. Just me."

"Oh." Donna gazed at her fingers, running her right thumb up and down the digits and twice repeating the process. "Six, no seven, no eight -?" she stuttered at last, her brittle confidence ready to snap at any second. "No -?"

"Eight! That's' absolutely right! Well done, Donna!" interjected Mrs Harper quickly. "I'm very pleased. We're going to get on just fine together."

When the class had reassembled for afternoon lessons Miss Frobisher set them a creative writing exercise entitled "How I spent the Holiday Weekend."

"My dad spent it drowning his sorrows," called out Harry and his best friends laughed. Nobody else understood the joke.

Eventually Donna wrote in her English exercise book: *I went to the shops in hunsow one day my sister got lossed and mummy telled her of also I went to the swim pool it was grat I went on the slid ten times also I lookd for toni in the big garden but he was niver ther agan.*

*

On Wednesday they had been home from school about an hour and were what Sarah always called 'chilling out' in front of the television when Katrina came in from the kitchen and said, "It's time girls."

"Time for what?" mumbled Donna.

"Have you forgotten? Your mummy's made an appointment at Scallywags for Sarah to have her hair cut. Do you want to come with us, Donna? Or stay here?"

Donna glanced across the room at her sister who replied with an unmistakable glower of prohibition. "I want to stay here," she replied.

"Fine. We will be about an hour. Okay? Don't open the door to anyone."

"I know."

After they had left Donna went upstairs to Sarah's room idly seeking revenge, found the mascara bottle and silver nail scissors amongst the debris and was instantly inspired to carry them next door to the beauty salon where she decided to submit Dawn to a full torso make over.

"How much do you want off?" asked Donna flexing the instrument of torture. "A couple of inches?"

She propped the doll on the window ledge against the streaming light to appraise the precise angle of attack and flinched with surprise and delight. There in the bottom left corner of the window pane beyond the parting lips of her sultry, uncomplaining victim the patio door of the white house suddenly swung open. Tony walked out on the patio, surveyed the skies like a creature awaking from a wintry hibernation and dissolved into the camouflage of the garden, – a patch of navy blue, a nape of black hair, flickering twice through the bushes and then extinguished.

"Would you like to meet a friend of mine, Dawn?" asked Donna discarding the scissors with a capricious lack of professionalism. "That's good. We'd better be quick. He doesn't come out very often. Just like you."

For a few minutes in the ginnel Donna thought she was going to fail to get in. The slats of the broken fence seemed to be stuck. She pushed and tugged to no effect and it was only with a frustrated lunge of her shoulder that she finally felt the secret gateway collapse.

Tony had his back to her as she approached. She spied him through the keyhole, bent dangerously close to the edge of the bank flicking morsels of toast into the cavity. It was so peaceful. Just the faintest hum of traffic could be heard far off wafting in on the breeze. Then something snapped abruptly under Donna's shoe and the dark head turned urgently, fierce and momentarily terrifying. She stopped at the gate immediately petrified by his demeanour, feeling as if she had been caught in the middle of some shameful act.

"Are you looking for that cat again?!" he snapped.

"Not –not really," she stammered.

He looked her up and down irritably and her body seemed to shiver inwardly at the unexpected assault. "You startled me, kid," he continued. " I thought I'd fixed that fence good. Don't you ever knock before you push open the door?" Donna flushed with even greater confusion and he seemed to see it. "Just a manner of speakin'," he added less harshly. "Here. Grab a bit of this. The buggers ain't exactly scramblin' for it today."

She set Dawn down on the wall, legs akimbo, facing the river and took a piece of toast from him. It was burnt and charcoal hard. No wonder the ducks were turning their beaks up in contempt. It was like offering them splinters of wood. The channel was much fuller than it had been on her previous visit. On their side the water had reached the top of the embankment and was encroaching onto the first layer of concrete mooring within centimetres of Tony's thick brown shoes. It had subtly changed colour and texture, too. A greeny brown sheen hung onto the surface which reminded Donna of the pease puddings her grandmother invariably served up on their visits to County Durham. The embankment on the far side could now be clearly seen to enjoy a good four or five foot higher elevation than their own. It had been better maintained, too, by the adjacent householders, niched with vertical steps, landscaped with crazy paving and earthenware tubs of flowers and ornamental buoys whose dark double image shimmered eerily in the mirror of the water.

"It's nice here," said Donna eventually to break the silence between them. It had been a long silence but not an uncomfortable one. "It's quiet."

"When the planes ain't passin' over'ead," he muttered back.

"Be careful."

"What?"

Donna pointed at his feet and he took half a step back to oblige her. "I stepped in a puddle once on my way into school and had to wear wet socks all day." She giggled at the memory. "I caught a cold."

"It's just about to turn. You can tell by the floaters," he said and Donna screwed up her eyes uncertainly. "The twigs and bits of grass. See?" He pointed. "Hardly movin'."

Donna followed the line of his finger. He was right. A major change began to take place even as she watched. The flood tide was spent. Inertia had usurped its authority. For a few minutes stagnation reigned. The river had metamorphosed into a lake.

"I like this time best," he said.

"Why?"

The man shrugged. "Why not?" he said and lit up a cigarette without ever removing his eyes from the moribund water. "Does your dad know you go wanderin' alone into other peoples' gardens?"

"Course not!" chuckled Donna. "My dad's dead." She noticed Tony glance back at her now. His eyes narrowed disconcertingly, then almost immediately abandoned her again. "Is your dad dead?" she asked.

"I don't know. I ain't seen 'im in ages."

"I don't remember my dad actually. He was –"

"Who looks after you, then?" Tony cut in.

"My mummy, of course. And Katrina."

"Yeah? Whose Katrina – your sister?"

For some reason Donna found this suggestion hilarious. She gave a couple of impromptu squawks worthy of a mallard being bombarded by inedible bullets of charcoal.

"Katrina's our child minder. She isn't English, though. She comes from a country where they are always fighting. Somewhere faraway. Near China, I think. Mummy says she's a ref –a ref –a referee -?"

"Refugee?" he said and Donna nodded. "And your mum's out at work all day, is she?"

Donna nodded again enthusiastically. She loved talking about her family and its routines, partly because she very rarely got the opportunity to do so. "Mummy works in one of those shops where you look for a holiday. Sometimes she has to work on Saturdays, too. She goes on the tube. It's near Piccadilly."

"So where's this Katrina?"

"She's gone to Scallywags with my sister, Sarah. Do you ever go to Scallywags? They cut men's hair as well as ladies, you know."

For the first time Donna detected a vestige of amusement on Tony's lips. It was reluctant and distrustful and obviously much out of practice but was none the less, distinctly a smile. "I've met a few scallywags in my time," he replied, "but never one I'd trust with a sharp instrument behind my back."

"Sarah's a big girl. She's in Year Nine. She goes to the youth club."

"And she likes windin' you up. Yeah?" Donna did not understand so she nodded obligingly and hoped the explanation would follow. It did not, only something totally unexpected instead. "I used to know someone who looked just like you," he said very quietly.

She looked into his eyes with curiosity and noticed how misty they had become, almost as if on the verge of tears. "Like me? Really? Who was it?" she asked.

"Never mind, kid. It aint important," he replied with sudden ebullience. "Wanna see somethin' special? Yeah? Follow me." He led the way through the gate and into the gravel enclosure, stopping close by the mulching bins where he suddenly peered into the conifers and began burrowing with his hands just below the height of his head as if searching for buried treasure. Within seconds his arms had disappeared up to the elbows in the thick pungent foliage and his head seemed likely to follow.

"Here it is!" he exclaimed. "Take a gander. Six little beauties."

He was holding the branches apart for her to see now but quite without realising the hopeless disadvantage of her height. She jumped up and down trying to hang in the air but could barely get her eyes to reach the bottom level of Tony's aperture and certainly not for long enough to detect anything.

"I'll hold you up," he suggested and hesitated momentarily, surveying his callused outspread hands as if uncertain that they could be effective implements of leverage.

Donna had no such doubts and instantly took up her position like the filling of a sandwich between Tony and the conifers waiting to be elevated into the presence of the mystery. Then with a little wince she felt his fingers dig into her haunches, his right thumb catch on the elasticated top of her knickers before freeing itself, inexpertly foraging up the flanks of her body trying to find the best purchase until suddenly her feet left the ground and she was suspended in mid air, iron-clamped beneath the armpits.

"Woooweee!" she gasped with pleasure.

"Right in front of you, kid. That's it. Look inside. "

She pushed back one tensile resistant frond, then another, then a third and wedged her head into the hole. No sun shone here. She gazed spellbound on the fairyland forest of careering branches and chintzy brown entrails that enclosed her. It was like being resurrected suddenly inside a decaying planet, a prickly sharp underworld of dusky darkness and solitude with a distinct aroma that reminded Donna of the bathroom after her mummy had just finished cleaning it. She felt like a mole, groping, half blind.

"Where? What is it? I can't see properly."

"Right there. Deeper," exhorted Tony so close to her left ear that his breath tickled and she inserted her head even further. The menacing spindle of a trunk now shaped itself slowly out of the shadows. A secondary branch catapulted back into her eye and as she rubbed out the sting with the back of her hand she suddenly saw a nest, no more than a couple of nose lengths away, perfectly symmetrical like a coracle floating in the nape of the junction.

"Oh?! Wow! They're beautiful, Tony," she gasped as she recognised the contents – a cluster of turquoise blue eggs, like faintly glowing jewels in the pit of a mine shaft.

"Ain't they just," muttered Tony.

"Can I touch them?"

"Better not. The parents won't thank you none."

Instead she ran the tip of her finger along the wall of the nest marvelling at its dedicated patchwork texture and design. Then the vice tightened suddenly around her rib cage, her head involuntarily disengaged in a great maelstrom of particles and she landed safely back on terra firma simultaneously releasing a pent up sneeze of relief from her nostrils.

"Ah – tishoo!"

"Gesundheit."

"What?"

"Gesundheit. It's what you say after someone sneezes. Never 'eard it before?"

"No. Gazun–tight?"

"Not bad. It means 'good health'. Show over!"

Tony turned round and retrieved his cigarette from the edge of the gatepost where he had left it smouldering and sat down on the wall facing the river that had now clearly begun its prolonged lumbering retreat to the sea, oblivious to the fact that Donna had followed him.

"My mummy smokes cigarettes sometimes. She calls them the devil's weed." She waited for a response but none was forthcoming. The smoke spurted out of his nostrils in two parallel blue vapour trails. "Does that hurt?" He shook his head once. "Can they make you very ill? Or die even?"

He sighed and flicked a speck of ash from his lapel before answering. "Yeah but so can crossin' the road in the rush 'our."

Donna did not really understand this and was ready to pursue her established line of inquiry but she noticed for the first time that an insect had alighted near the shoulder of Tony's shirt and her curiosity tacked instantly in a new direction.

"What's that?"

"What?"

She moved tentatively closer. "That?"

"It's a butterfly."

"It's beautiful." Donna was scared to move, to open her mouth even in case it fluttered away. The long seconds passed. "It keeps very still," she whispered at length. "It's so tame."

"Yeah. Well, I made it that way."

"Did you?!" Donna's mouth gaped open with astonishment and reverence. She still had not caught on. For a few moments she stood as if in the presence of God. Then, as she watched, a long bony index finger descended slowly into her field of vision and gave the insect a couple of unwieldy taps on its proboscis. "You've killed it now!" cried Donna in alarm.

Tony twisted the material in her direction and revealed the metallic foundations of his secret. "It's a mascot, kid – a broach. See! I made it out of bits of wire and gauze and stuff."

"It looks real!"

"Thanks."

"Do you make anything else?" Tony shook his head. There was a name for a place where you made things. It stalled on the tip of her tongue. "In a factory?" she guessed out loud. "Is that where you make them?"

He gave a sniff of amusement. "Sort of."

"And what about Mr Brown?"

Tony bristled like a guard dog suddenly alert to the first sound of intrusion. "Mr Brown?"

"Does he make butterflies, too?"

"No. How do you know -?" began Tony and swallowed his sentence. Donna felt his eyes searching her face. They were unusual eyes, neither one distinct colour or another, shifting between green and grey and blue tinted hazel. "Where do you live anyway?"

"I told you before." Donna pointed aimlessly towards the keyhole. "Twenty eight, Mansfield Road. Katrina parks the car right outside your house sometimes." The eyes remained steadfast, unblinking, containing her inside a silent curiosity, inviting a full confession to which Donna eagerly responded.

"I'm sorry I ain't got any children for you to play with," he said when she had finished her story. "You must 'ave been sad when Georgia moved away?"

Donna nodded and smiled. It was no longer such a raw memory and at that particular moment she felt as if nothing could ever make her sad again. "What about Mr Brown?" she asked.

"He does a lot of business out of town," said Tony. "He ain't 'ere at the minute."

"I mean does he have any children I can play with?"

The eyes narrowed slightly to an imperious grey and he shook his head once. Donna half understood that Tony did not want to speak about Mr Brown but could not control the urge to blurt one further question. "Did you make friends with him in the butterfly factory?"

The eyes glistened wider now, tinged with a green affection. "Yeah. Spot on. Hadn't you better be 'eadin' 'ome? Your gonna be missed shortly."

"Okay. Can I come here and play in the garden again?"

Tony looked away towards the river as if the answer to the question lay there. Suddenly a cabin cruiser chugged into view, heading in the direction of the Thames. The skipper gave a stiff little nod of acknowledgment and Donna stretched out a hand. The keel was almost close enough to touch.

"If you must," muttered Tony. "But don't bring anyone else with you."

"Not even Dawn?"

"Who?"

"I can't leave Dawn behind," explained Donna straightening out the long arthritic legs of her doll. "She never gets out anywhere unless I take her."

She felt Tony's eyes scrutinising her intensely. "Did you tell anyone real you'd bin 'ere?" he asked.

Donna shook her had uncertainly. "Mummy's always telling me not to talk to strangers."

"Quite right," Tony grunted. "Better keep away then."

"But I want to come!" whined Donna mortified at her mistake. "You're not a stranger anymore. And you just said I could. Oh, please!"

That night in bed Donna lay awake for ages replaying every moment of her meeting with Tony back through her imagination. She could feel her stomach lurch as he hoisted her into the air, the large powerful hands probing her haunches, the tickle of his breath on the nape of her neck, the resinous manly smell of shaving soap and perspiration. What made it seem all the more exciting was that nobody else in her family knew. Part of her wanted to tell them while another part was afraid of the consequences if she did. Mummy might forbid her to go. That would be awful and totally unfair. Mummy and Sarah had plenty of friends, didn't they? Surely she was entitled to one. And yet... and yet the temptation to share her excitement, to spill the beans bubbled so close to the surface of her personality that she could hardly contain it.

"Sarah?" she spoke at last into the darkness. Silence. Had she slipped in or not? The moaning had not started yet. "Sarah? Are you down there?"

"Hmmm?" came the drowsy reply.

"I've got a friend." Silence. "Sarah? I've got a new friend".

"Who is it? Bart Simpson? I'm trying to sleep."

"I'm not telling. It's a secret."

"It's more of a secret how someone as barking as you doesn't get put in a dog's home."

"Sarah -?"

"Shut up. I'm not speaking any more."

"Sarah?" Donna felt hurt and deflated. "Why do you always have to sleep in here, anyway?" she retaliated. "I don't want you to. You wake me up".

A rustle of bedclothes answered. Then silence.

Chapter 11

Something was wrong. Donna sensed it even before she reached the car in which Katrina sat waiting, alone and expressionless. "Where's Sarah? In the sweet shop?" she asked.

"No. Get in," ordered the childminder abruptly.

Donna willingly obeyed. She felt cold. The weather had turned for the worse and a perpetually sombre sky had been threatening rain all day. The car revved up hard, pulled out in front of a bus with a minimum of ceremonies and pivoted through a tight, jerky semi-circle.

"Katrina? Where are we going?" An angry pair of headlights flashed in front of them as if they had suddenly short-circuited and a desultory pedestrian leapt backwards onto the pavement like a frightened rabbit. "Aren't we going home?"

Katrina was too preoccupied to answer. She took the second right past the station and pulled up abruptly outside the local deli. "Come inside, Donna. We have time," she said opening the rear door and ushering her ward out onto the pavement.

Donna found herself inside a narrow pine timbered room smelling of fresh coffee and spiced meats and was told to sit down at a lattice table while Katrina made her purchases.

"What would you like to drink, Donna? Cocoa or milk maybe?"

"Cocoa, please."

"And an iced finger? I am having one."

Donna's eyes lit up with pleasure. As they ate and sipped their drinks in silence Donna studied the people who passed by on the pavement. Every so often somebody would stop and peer in through the shop window, attracted by the display of rich foods. It was most peculiar the different ways people moved and held their bodies. Some slouched, some marched, some shuffled, some – mostly those in school uniforms – made nervous little pumping motions with their shoulders. Almost nobody smiled. The faces all looked bored and weary and appeared to be made of plasticine. It was evidently a very serious business patrolling this commercial link road, not at all to be enjoyed. She bit deep into her cake, leaving the generous topping of icing til the end, enclosed in a cocoon of privilege and power, beyond and above the itinerant world, queen for fifteen minutes in a royal box, surveying her subjects.

"Alright, we will go and collect your mummy now," announced Katrina suddenly puncturing the fantasy.

"Mummy?! Is she at the station?!"

"No. She's at your sister's school. She had to come home early for a meeting with the head teacher."

It took no more than a couple of minutes to arrive. The car park looked forlorn and neglected. Only two cars were marooned in it apart from their own. They sat there waiting, watching the chinks between the rectangles of the austere buildings for signs of life, the spit and spat of drizzle reviving on the windscreen, blobs swelling slowly and bursting into rivulets.

"Are you sure mummy's here, Katrina? She should be at work?"

"Yes, I'm sure. The head teacher telephoned her at work and she telephoned me."

"Oh."

Katrina sighed like a very old lady, like her grandma did sometimes, and tapped on the steering column with a couple of willowy fingers. Five minutes edged round on the dashboard clock then another five. The drizzle turned to rain. The impatient agitated fingers tapped on. Finally mummy appeared shouldering her way out of a glass door, a lime green umbrella hoisted above her head, walking quickly, elegantly across the forecourt, and Sarah several yards behind, utterly careless about the weather.

"Mummy! Mummy! We had a cake in the shop!" exclaimed Donna joyfully as the door opened and Mummy slid into the front passenger seat.

"Sorry we're late," mummy frowned at Katrina, oblivious of the greeting.

"It went on, did it?"

"And on. And on."

The rear door opened and Sarah climbed in behind her sister, damp and taciturn, her head slumping back on the seat. On the drive home through squelching streets and ever thickening traffic nobody spoke, the silence tightening like an invisible screw as if somebody had died and they were on their way to the funeral. Donna risked a sideways peek at her sister's face. It was blotched and puffy and ugly as if she had been crying. The owlish dark rings which hooded Sarah's eyes remained focussed on the beige void of the car roof, her arms folded tight across her chest, her lips suctioning spastically one way then another. Something shocking and painful had taken possession of Sarah's body, some disease of the inner being, churning and pummelling. Donna averted her gaze quickly. It was too awful. Her heart welled up in pity and fear. She felt impotent and claustrophobic as if about to drown in the avalanche of Sarah's misery. Desperately she closed her eyes and tried to wish herself somewhere else, sifting through images of holidays and countryside and happy smiling party faces, clutching at one lifeline after another, desperate to keep her head above water. And on the edge of her panic a tiny indistinct voice began to whisper instructions. "Try to remember when you were last happy," it said, "and go there as fast as you can."

In a split second Donna's brain computed the information, the kaleidoscope of memories juddered to a halt and she stood once again on the banks of the River Crane close to Tony watching the flood tide caressing the soles of his shoes.

"It's just about to turn," he was explaining. "You can tell by the floaters. I like this time best."

"Why?" she heard herself ask.

"Why not?"

It was a perfect moment and a perfect answer to her question. If only you could give answers like that to the questions they asked you at school! The river had momentarily become a lake. It hung in balance with nature and so did she and Tony as they surveyed it.

Suddenly three sharp bangs like gunshots being fired in rapid succession exploded the scene into hundreds of atoms. These flared up and danced for a few moments in her imagination before coalescing back to the interior of the drab empty vehicle now parked halfway up Mansfield Road.

"Come on, Donna!" snapped one of the departing passengers through the misty window. A door gaped open on reality suddenly and great refreshing gobbets of water swirled through it into her face and legs, forcing her into evasive action.

"Where's Sarah gone?" she asked as she entered the house.

"To her room," answered mummy abruptly. "And she can bloody well stay there!"

Donna dashed towards the stairwell. She reached the upstairs landing and tip toed across to her sister's room. The door stood tight shut, forbidding entry. She listened outside, her ear right against the keyhole but heard nothing. "Sarah? What's happened? It's me," she whispered. "Can I come in?" But the silence on the other side of the partition merely intensified. Then the whole thing shuddered violently as something heavy clumped into it and bounced twice on the floor. Donna backed away, startled, unsure what to do next, where to go, or how to revive her spirits.

Eventually she picked up a couple of dolls from her room and cradled them back down the stairs, desperate to hear an explanation but not daring to ask for it. The voices now emanating from the living room sounded unexpectedly affable and yet she hesitated to risk poisoning this incipient calm with her presence so she veered right into the kitchen and set herself down on the floor of the Metro Centre where she remained half-playing, half-listening, never quite belonging to one world or the other.

"I will see you tomorrow then, Margaret," she heard after a few minutes. "No. Not at all. I just hope it sorts itself out.....Yes. Good idea. No time like the present.....Well, good luck....Goodbye."

How loud and high-pitched was Katrina's voice compared to her mummy's. It leaked away down the hall and out through the front door, a thin drawn out whine of consolation abruptly truncated. Then footsteps approaching, a creak of wood, a cough up close, the click of the telephone receiver being lifted and faint little taps of the buttons.

"Oh, hullo? Is Dr Williamson there by any chance? I appreciate that he – Oh, he is.... Yes, it is rather urgent...... Margaret Atkinson...... That's right..... Thank you so much...... Hullo? Dr Williamson?...... It's about Sarah. I'm afraid things have taken a turn for the worse......Yes, it's started up again....Almost as bad as before, I'd say. I'm at the end of my tether. Can I make an appointment for her to see you? As soon as possible.....Yes....No....Yes. And the school have made it a condition of her not being excluded...... That's fine. See you then... Thank you. Goodbye."

By supper time Sarah had still failed to materialise but her presence hung around everywhere, sticking in the nostrils like a sour smell that it is too impolite to mention.

"Can I have it in front of the telly, mummy?" asked Donna.

"No. The table's laid."

It was omelette and chips. Donna sat down and applied a liberal helping of ketchup to her plate.

"Isn't Sarah hungry, mummy?" she risked.

"I've no idea."

"Shall I call her?"

"She knows where we are when she wants to find us."

Mummy stood up and switched on the radio, an action designed to inhibit further inquiry. A man was speaking, then a studio audience disintegrated into laughter and Donna watched her mummy stonily neglect to join in.

"Are you going to work tomorrow, mummy?" asked Donna later as she helped to load the dishwasher.

"Of course I am. Why shouldn't I be going to work. Now you've done that Donna I want you to run the bath and get ready for bed."

"But mummy – ! "

"No buts. Just do it! I need my space!"

The words fell on her unprotected head with judicial severity and she ran upstairs away from the ogre her mother had decided to become, smarting with the pain of injustice. It was not her who had been naughty, after all. It had not been her intention to further sully the already polluted atmosphere of the house with her questions. Why did nobody explain anything to her? Why did nobody ever say "sorry" to anyone else? Why did she have to lie in bed unable to sleep, aching with humiliation? In fact an hour had passed before the hubbub of self-pity in which her brain had become gridlocked began to fade away. Her body exhausted like an athlete forced to sprint endlessly around the same monotonous circuits of thought had ground to a halt and was sinking into the anodyne marshlands of sleep when something hard and abrasive halted its progress, something indistinct, intangible, for a few seconds neither material nor abstract, like a waking dream, not in one dimension or another. Donna opened her eyes. She groped out with her hand into the blackness and felt nothing. She watched the patterns of shadows writhing like serpents on the curtains. They seemed to be speaking to her in fierce distinct voices from a long, long way off but it was impossible to translate their meaning. Stopping and starting. Rising and falling. Two dragons locked in mortal combat, fighting it out to the death in the bowels of the earth with invisible weapons.

She sat up on her elbows, fully awake, pushing long strands of hair away from her ears and suddenly it was as if a badly tuned radio locked onto the correct frequency. The weapons were words! Bitter, staccato, often convoluted words but unmistakably English ones. And Donna knew that everything horrible that had happened today was merely an inflammation and swelling compared to this. Downstairs in the living room the carbuncle had finally burst open.

"I'm not going to see that shrink again!"

"Yes, you are!"

"No. I'm not! You can't make me!"

"You've got no choice! The school has given you an ultimatum. If you don't agree to see him you'll be suspended!"

"They can't make me see a shrink! I'm not crazy! He's a four-eyed geek anyway! I hate him!"

"He's not a shrink, anyway. He's a child psychologist -!"

"Same thing! It's all rubbish! I'll just sit there in silence. I won't say a word. You'll be wasting your money!"

"The school are prepared to overlook your tantrums and temper it you'll promise to seek professional help. They're bending over backwards. They don't have to. They could exclude you now. All your teachers say how bright you are – if only you knuckle down."

"I don't need professional help! I'm normal! It's half those teachers in that school who aren't! Send them to a bloody shrink!"

"Is it normal to punch your best friend in the face and pull her hair out by the roots?! Is it normal to throw a book at your science teacher when she tries to intervene?! Is it normal to call her a 'lazy fucking bitch' and expect her to want to carry on teaching you?! Is it?!"

"She is a lazy fucking bitch! She's bone-idle! She never marks our books! Never bothers to prepare her lessons properly -!"

"You can't use language like that! You're so arrogant and aggressive!"

"I stand up for myself!"

"You've got a chip on your shoulder!?"

"Who put it there!"

"What do you mean by that!"

"I mean I'm not prepared to be anybody's doormat!"

"Is that why you punched Polly? Because she was wiping her feet on you?! I don't think so -!"

"She was trying to. She was saying things."

"Things like what?"

"That's between her and me."

"You mean gossiping? Behind your back? So you'd beat her up! Just for that!"

"And I'll do it again if I have to!"

"And that's what you call normal civilised behaviour!?"

"Huhh!"

"Is it?"

"I did it for you!"

"For me? What? Beat her up? Don't kid yourself!"

"You're kidding yourself. You've got no self-respect."

"What do you mean?"

"You know."

"I don't."

"Huhh!"

"What did Polly say, anyway?"

"That's between her and me. You can bet she won't say it again!"

"Tell me!"

"Alright. She's been telling anyone who cared to listen that my dad was a convict and that you were a slag."

"She what?!"

"Happy now?"

"And why should she say that!"

" 'Cos she's a thick jealous bitch – !"

"Don't use that word, Sarah -!"

"And she'd got it into her head that I'd skanked off with Gemma at the youth club disco last Friday."

"Why didn't you tell this to Mrs Selvey today? Not that it would have changed anything."

"Exactly." Silence. "I'm not going to see that shrink."

"You are!"

"You can't make me!"

"An ultimatum is an ultimatum! You've got absolutely no other way out!"

"Slag!"

"What?" Silence. "Do you mean me!?"

"Course not! I mean Polly!"

"You'd better!"

"Why, does the cap fit?!"

"Whaa –! How dar –"

The syllables broke up into a series of guttural animal shrieks and screams and dull thuds.

"Stay away! I'll hit you back! I mean it! I'll hit you back!"

A door crashed shut and as the whole house seemed to shudder in its aftermath wild, stampeding feet echoed on the stairs. A second door exploded. Donna held her breath rigid with shock waiting, waiting. But nothing else happened. The radio programme had been magically switched off and all that remained in the pit of this black unreal silence was a faint woo-woo-woo like a wounded animal calling out for help it sensed would never come.

Chapter 12

Donna liked sitting next to Mrs Harper in the classroom. Mrs Harper made numbers seem fun. She smelled of shampoo and smiled all the time and never told you off. A burden had been lifted from Donna's shoulders, a veritable mountain of self-doubt and misery. In her yellow satchel Mrs Harper carried puzzles and pictures and cartoons and crayons which nobody else in the class got to play with except Donna. It was a kind of treasure chest. A cornucopia of surprises.

"Shall we see what's in the fun bag today?" Mrs Harper would invariably ask after Miss Frobisher had finished the boring stuff on the blackboard that made no sense and then had given worksheets out.

For some days now the topic had been Fractions. Just the sound of the word struck terror into Donna's heart and had been doing so since she first heard it way back in Year One. Fractions. A harsh unkind combination of syllables that grated on your nerves. A visit to the dentist word. A smell of kitchen ammonia word. A black stain on a crisp white blouse word. A word that made you die inside a little every time you heard it.

But fortunately Mrs Harper was much too wise to keep anything as hideous as Fractions in her fun bag. She dipped in a chubby hand, felt around like a magician searching for an invisible rabbit –all the while rolling her eyes in mounting anticipation- and dramatically pulled out a birthday cake! At least a cardboard birthday cake, mounted on a round wooden base like a jigsaw puzzle. Mrs Harper placed it on the table, ran a finger along the whirly pink iced crust and tested the result on the tip of her tongue.

"It'll just have to do," she sighed with mock disappointment. "Oh, well, I'm trying to cut down on the calories!"

"What's calories mean?" giggled Donna.

"Calories, Donna, are the rich nourishing part of the food we eat that gives us energy but also makes us become fat if we eat too much of it," Mrs Harper explained and shimmied lower down on the wooden chair that creaked under her onerous weight and seemed at least three or four sizes too small for her bottom. "Now then, let's pretend it's your birthday party. Okay? You give half the cake to your sister because she's very skinny, the complete opposite of me, and needs fattening up. See?" And with a practised swoop of the hand she removed it, leaving a semi-circular crater which Donna surveyed suspiciously as if it contained a secret trap door. "How much of the cake is left for you?"

Donna considered for a few seconds. "Half?" she guessed.

"Excellent, Donna!" exclaimed Mrs Harper instantly replacing the missing slab. "Two halves make a whole. See?"

"Yes."

"You try it now." Donna lifted the slab of cake, proudly. "They're both exactly the same, aren't they? Two halves make one whole."

"Two halves make one whole?" repeated Donna.

"Excellent. Now then, Donna –"

"But I wouldn't give my sister half my birthday cake in real life. She doesn't like cake very much."

"That's very true, Donna. Have you ever had a birthday party?" Donna nodded. "I bet there were more than two guests, weren't there?"

"I couldn't blow out the candles! They were trick ones! They kept coming back to life!"

"Did they?!" Mrs Harper reconstructed the cake back to its original decorative glory and with a deft sleight of hand released a couple of hidden clips on the outer walls.

"Let's assume you had three guests, Donna. That's three invited guests. Plus you. Okay?" Mrs Harper ticked them off on her fingers. "How many people altogether at the party?"

"Well, er, five?"

"Not exactly. Look again. Three guests plus you makes how many?"

"Four."

"Excellent."

"But five in real life."

"Why?"

"Because you couldn't have a party in the first place if you didn't have a mummy to organise it and lay the table and –"

"Dorghhh!" groaned Mrs Harper in a cartoon voice and banged a fist against her head in self-reproach as if attempting to dislodge an atrophied brain in there. "Silly me! Course you couldn't! Five people at the party. You're right. I'm wrong. Shows you how often I get to go to a party. Dorghhh!"

Donna laughed, covering her hands with her mouth, trying not to disturb the other pupils all bent arduously over their exercise books, excluded from this spontaneous comedy performance. What an amazing mimic Mrs Harper was! She had the voice of Bart Simpson's long suffering daddy to a tee.

"Let's pretend, Donna, that your mummy does not want any birthday cake. Okay? She isn't hungry," said Mrs Harper rediscovering her teacher personality. "So we have one cake. Here. And only four people to eat it. Alright? We divide it equally between them and I give you the first piece." She lifted it up and presented it to Donna. "Watch the crumbs now! That piece is a quarter. Yes? A quarter?"

"Yes."

"A quarter. Think very carefully. How much of the cake is left on the plate? Take your time." Donna hesitated. It was a big piece, much bigger than the first piece, much more complicated. She stared at the shape and it stopped being a cake. It became the head of a baby bawling in frustration, eyes tight shut. Why did babies cry so much? This question loomed up at her now much more urgently than any other question she had been asked and her mind took refuge in it.

"So what do you think, Donna?"

"I don't know."

Donna felt her heart begin to flutter with panic. She had been positioned on a spot and the ground all around it seemed to be crumbling away fast. Did she try to leap to safety or balance where she was?

"Shall I explain it again?"

"Yes, please."

Mrs Harper put the missing slice of cake back and patiently started again, very slowly, bit by bit filling in the cavities that had been excavated on Donna's confidence, flattening and rolling the topography, inch by inch, taming and coaxing her pupil's wayward imagination back into the cage of the problem from which it had strayed.

"So how much of the cake is left on the plate, Donna? Why don't you pick up the quarter pieces and count them? Go on. They won't bite! "

Donna obeyed, her hands fumbling forward and discovering that the big chunk would indeed break into smaller ones. "One, two, three," she counted cautiously. "There are three quarters. Aren't there?"

"Yes, there are! Well done! That's excellent, Donna!"

When the end of the lesson was announced by Miss Frobisher a collective sigh of relief echoed around the room, followed by ripples of excited chatter and snapping pencil box lids.

"Is there anything you want to ask me, Donna?" said Mrs Harper as the assembly broke up. Donna screwed up her eyes thoughtfully, not sure how to put it. "Anything at all?"

"What is an ultee-maytum, Miss?"

"Ultee-maytum?"

"Yes."

Donna watched her teachers exchange looks of inquiry.

"Ultimatum?" said Miss Frobisher. "Do you mean 'ultimatum'?"

"Yes."

"It means, um, a final warning or a last chance," smiled Mrs Harper.

"And if you don't take it there's going to be big trouble!" added Miss Frobisher with a grin. "Does that make sense to you, Donna?"

"Oh, yes!"

"I think we're going to have a candidate for Mastermind on our hands pretty soon," observed Miss Frobisher to her colleague as she followed the last of the children out of the room, "at this rate of progress. I'll leave you two to it."

"Do you want to ask me anything about numbers?" asked Mrs Harper. "Numbers we've done today. Or on earlier days?"

"Well, I want to know the time of things?!"

"Ah! You want to learn how to tell the time from a clock?"

"Yes. But I mean the time of things like rivers."

"Rivers? How do you mean exactly?"

"Well, you know how rivers get high and then go low again? It never seems to be the same time every day. I want to know when it is."

"I see, Donna. You mean river tides," said Mrs Harper applying a tissue to her nose. "Excuse me, I'm about to sneeze."

"Tides. That's it."

"Achooo! Sorry. I'm allergic to chalk dust. Achooo!"

"Geshundeit!" smiled Donna

"Pardon!"

"Geshundeit. That's what you say when somebody sneezes. Tony told me that. He's my new friend. He works in a butterfly factory. Is he right?"

"Yes. He is, indeed. Your vocabulary is becoming second to none." Mrs Harper tucked the tissue back up her sleeve. "Now about tides. They publish a weekly table of the Thames tides in the local paper, you know, and we've got a copy in the staff room. Why don't I make a photocopy for you? Would you like that? You can take it home."

Donna beamed with pleasure.

"Alright then. Come and see me after you've had your lunch.

Okay? And I'll explain to you how it works. Run along now. You must be hungry."

And Donna went skipping off as light as a feather in the direction of the canteen.

In the afternoon Miss Frobisher handed out copies of a poem called "I remember" and read it twice out loud before explaining the more difficult words and asking them questions about what the author meant. Donna quite liked the poem. She could see the intended images clearly, an old fashioned, high- ceilinged Victorian classroom, a teacher with a long black dress, a cane and a severe face. Most of all she could see the children seated in pairs according to ability, ranks of double oak desks lining the classroom, the clean and the talented congregated in the window aisle, the dirty and dim-witted in the opposite corridor aisle. The author who sat with a girl called Irene next to the corner window seemed to feel guilty and proud at the same time about his positioning. At least so his memory informed him. He was an adult with children of his own now.

"Now then, children, you're going to do a piece of free writing in your English books," Miss Frobisher announced as she collected up the duplicated passage. "The first words will be 'I remember.' You fill in the rest. Alright? Give your memory permission to roam around wherever it wants to go."

Donna copied the key words from the board into her book and chewed the end of her pen wondering what to put next.

"You might wish to begin by writing down the very first things you remember," extemporised Miss Frobisher. "Maybe a face or a holiday or a smell or just a feeling. Try to go back to the beginning. It's always a good place to start."

Donna found herself trying to remember a time when Sarah had not been mean to her. That must have been close to the beginning. When was it? A tissue of skin in her mind seemed to split under the effort of recollecting and as the seam inched apart all manner of images crowded into sight. Two boys, for instance, teasing her in the playground. "Look, there's Donna kebab!" shouted one. "Kebab! Kebab! Who wants a lovely kebab!?" guffawed the other and suddenly Sarah appeared like an avenging angel and chased them off with a tirade of bloodcurdling threats. She was fearless even then. Donna felt the security of Sarah's arm around her and fierce pride as they walked to the school gate to meet their au-pair. Now what was her name? A chubby Spanish woman who told her stories at bedtime? It was so difficult to remember names. There had been a new one almost every year. The primary and infants school in Clapham had been located together on the same land. Donna's needling fingers of memory slowly unearthed the detail, strayed in and out of rooms, picked at scraps of conversation and incidents. Curious snapshots of bewilderment and terror vied with ones of serenity and joy.

"Now how are you getting along, Donna?" It was Miss Frobisher bending down close to her head. "Finding it difficult to get started?"

"I was just thinking about Mrs Gaynor," apologised Donna. "She was a teacher at my old school."

"And did you like her?"

Donna nodded. "She used to tell me to remember things when I got upset. Happy things."

"That's very wise," said Miss Frobisher and assisted Donna to write out *I remember my kind teacher Mrs Gaynor*' as her opening sentence. "Now you carry on your own, okay?"

But Donna left alone simply sucked her pen some more and re-entered the sarcophagi of the past. The resurrected images were much more fascinating than any inscription she could tag onto them. Unless memory deceived her Mrs Gaynor had been one of those rare people who never got cross. A smile seemed to play forever on her lips. She liked the bible a lot. Now as the touch, the voice and the features of the teacher all recomposed in her mind Donna felt desperately sad that such a wonderful person should be swallowed up and lost to sight forever in the drift of time. "God doesn't want us to be unhappy, Donna," Mrs Gaynor had encouraged more than once. "That's why he sent Jesus to live on Earth."

Mrs Gaynor had taught Sarah, too, five years earlier, and used to ask after her. "That woman's a religious nutcase," Sarah had sneered once when Donna passed on the message. "Talk about weird. Ought to be locked in a nunnery and the key chucked away! Don't let her brainwash you. Jesus is about as real as Father Xmas, Div!"

But Donna knew that her sister had not always felt like this. Sarah had changed somewhere along the line. How did she know? Donna bit deep into the butt of her pen and tried to remember that too. The answer slowly began to materialise in the form of a cupboard which had two compartments and one door and was situated in a corner of their living room at Clapham. Mummy had allocated the girls this special space for their keepsakes and special treasures. Sarah's was the top compartment and Donna's the one underneath but from the outset Sarah had strictly forbidden her sister to look inside the upper vault let alone touch its tangled contents. Even then Donna had considered it a silly rule although she never summoned up the courage to tell her sister so. The fact that the two compartments shared the same door made it inevitable that you would always see something of the other's possessions whenever you went to dig out an item from your own clutter. And that was how Donna knew about Sarah and Jesus. She kept a picture of Him in there, wedged between some trinkets and toys, and once it had fallen out on the floor.

"I want to read you what Robert has written so far," announced Miss Frobisher. Donna looked round. Robert was one of those children who if he had been alive at the time of the poem would have been seated right at the top of the window aisle. " 'I remember being a baby in a pram. As big as a bus it was. I remember the full moon scaring me when I was trapped in a high chair. I think I must have a good memory. It's like a sponge soaking up water. All the time. Never ending. So what is memory? I think it is me.' " Miss Frobisher handed Robert his exercise book. "Well done. That's excellent. Carry on now, children."

Donna found herself wondering about Robert's sponge. It did not make sense to her. Memory is more like a cupboard than a sponge, she thought to herself, a very deep cupboard extending almost forever into the living room wall. You shove all the details of your life in there, the large and the tiny, the precious and commonplace, the secrets and shames – and slowly everything becomes scrunched up together and sinks out of sight so that eventually it becomes very difficult to find any particular article you might suddenly realise you need. Special treasures are unearthed more by accident than design. You may rummage forlornly after one memory only to rediscover another that you had almost completely forgotten ever existed.

Donna put her pen down with a flash of inspiration. She had arrived somewhere, a strange, open place with contours and colours. The place was called *Answer*. It demanded to be known and brought into being. Her fingers picked up a pencil and within seconds were busy – skilfully etching out a drawing of her first childhood cupboard.

Chapter 13

On Saturday morning Donna was earnestly studying the River Thames Tidal Chart in her bedroom when mummy entered. Mrs Harper had cut it out of the local paper, highlighted the important columns in red and inserted the cutting inside a transparent cellophane envelope to prevent wear and tear. But the neat columns of digits were very confusing and although Mrs Harper had explained how they worked Donna had forgotten already.

"Come along, Donna. We're waiting for you downstairs."

"Can't I stay here?"

"Not today. It's chilly. Put your green jumper on."

"Where are we going?" whined Donna.

"We're taking Sarah to see a doctor."

"Oh? Do I have to see him, too?"

"No but –"

"Well, then, why can't I stay here? I'll be alright on my own."

"Because I say so. Let me help you with that jumper."

"No. It's too big. Will we be back by, er, eighteen thirteen?"

"Eighteen thirteen? Quarter past six? I should very much hope so! Why?"

"No reason."

"What have you got there? Let me see."

"It's nothing."

Mummy took a cursory glance at the chart. "Is this the homework you were telling me about?"

"Sort of."

"Remind me to help you later. You need to understand the 24-hour clock. Come along now. We're late as it is."

The car was parked outside the white house and Sarah had long since ensconced herself in the back seat looking to Donna for all the world just like a spoilt princess waiting to be chauffeured to the next in a long line of tedious royal engagements. "What kept you?" she sneered imperiously.

Donna disciplined her tongue not to rise to the bait and stared at the hollow sockets of the windows hoping to catch a glimpse of Tony or even his friend, Mr Brown.

"Do people who work in factories go to work on Saturdays?" she asked her mummy.

"Sometimes. Why?"

"I just wondered."

They drove for half and hour but it seemed longer to Donna because the traffic was moving so slowly much of the time and she did not know where they were going. The gigantic green road signs that loomed everywhere only augmented her sense of discomfort. Their bold print, their arrows, their bewildering combinations of numbers and letters all served to indicate the overpowering presence of an alien grown-up culture into whose secrets she must one day become inducted, – a culture relentlessly busy, on the move, bewilderingly complex and committed to swallowing her up. And the feeling was made worse by the fact that she had no vocabulary like this to describe it. All these revving machines, all these opaque faceless windscreens, all this motion without apparent destination just made her feel tiny and empty and terrified. She did not want this frenetic world anymore than she wanted a dose of flu or soaking wet feet but there seemed to be no choice. This would be her inevitable inheritance. This hubbub, this scramble, this stress and impatience and danger – Beep! Beep!

"Silly fool! Why didn't you indicate?!" mummy suddenly shouted. "Cutting me up like that! Can't you see it was my right of way?! Up yours too!" Beep! Beep!

Donna closed her eyes tight, trying not to shiver, and hanging on desperately to the comforting dream of her infancy. When she opened them again, encouraged by a sharp nudge of the elbow, everything had magically changed. In place of the two-lane arterial madness hung a tapestry of elegant Edwardian houses, silver barked leafy trees and empty avenue. Mummy had pulled into the kerb and was making last second alterations to her make-up in the car mirror. Sarah opened the door and climbed out onto the pavement but as Donna slid across the vacated seat and made to follow mummy said, "No point in you coming in, Donna. I won't be a minute or two. Stay in here and listen to the radio." And she turned up the volume.

Donna watched them cross the road. A grey saloon cruised leisurely by then a dark blue estate. Nothing else. It was so peaceful now that they might have just landed on another planet. Filigrees of fine young leaves danced in the breeze as far as she could see. Mummy opened a gate and passed into a small garden. There were white steps up to an oval porch and it was only when the two stiff, slightly nervous figures stood on the elevated plinth waiting for the door to be opened that Donna realised she had been here before. When was it? She scrolled through her memory, stopping at intermittent episodes in her life, pulling in the focus of the file then moving on. How long and infinitely detailed her life seemed? It divided quite simply at first into landmarks but then the landmarks sub-divided and the closer she honed in on each subdivision, the more it began to break up into even smaller component parts with their own gravity and colours and emotions, millions of cells in a honeycombed beehive to which she had once belonged and was still connected, all competing to suck her back into their secret heart. But where was it, the cell she wanted to enter? A quarter of her lifetime ago? Half her lifetime?

Suddenly the car door clacked loudly open. "Sorry I was so long," mummy was apologising.

"Were you?" muttered Donna inaudibly, the familiar voice resurrecting her at lightning speed through ventricles of time back to the surface of her life.

"Right! I'm taking you shopping! Okay!" beamed mummy and the engine roared into life.

"But what about Sarah?" exclaimed Donna.

"We'll come back for her later. You need a new pair of shoes. And maybe some trainers."

Donna craned her neck anxiously, watching the house where Sarah had been left, shrinking to nothing in the residential distance and in her imagination she heard again those horrific nocturnal shrieks of defiance.

"Is the doctor going to give Sarah the ultee-may-tum, mummy?" she asked nervously.

Mummy lowered the volume of the radio and asked Donna to repeat the question, which she did more hesitantly, because she realised it amounted to a confession of having been eves dropping on a conversation not intended to reach her ears. But mummy did not seem to mind. "Doctor Williamson is helping Sarah to understand her aggressive behaviour," she replied, "and learn how to control her bad temper and anti-social attitudes."

"Why was she naughty at school? Why, mummy?"

"I don't know exactly, Donna. There are reasons for Donna's naughtiness and there are, well, other reasons, too –deeper reasons."

"But she's always being naughty, mummy. And mean. Isn't she? She makes me cry sometimes and then she just laughs."

Donna waited for an explanation but it did not arrive. The car turned left at a busy junction, edged forward in a queue about fifty yards and then abruptly spurted right into a narrow side street and stopped next to a parking metre space that was just being vacated by its elderly occupant.

"We'll walk from here," said mummy switching off the engine. "It isn't far." Donna watched her click open her shiny black handbag and extract a pound coin from a leather purse.

"How can a doctor stop her from being naughty, mummy? How?"

"He can't stop her. He can help her. He can make her much more aware of how her personality works, how it affects other people. He did it once before – when she was at primary school. Remember?"

"No."

"She'll be going to see him every Wednesday after school," added mummy. "And I expect you to be patient, Donna. Things may well get worse with your sister before they start to get better."

As they walked across the pedestrian bridge and into the High Street Donna tried again to remember a Sarah who had once been mild tempered and not the constant source of telephone calls and letters of complaint from her schools. There must have been one because her mummy said so.

They entered a shop, stood around gawping awkwardly for a few minutes and then mummy was approached by a gushing silvery haired lady who disappeared soon after into a stockroom and returned laden with half a dozen or more white boxes containing the very latest models of leather school approved shoes. The lady sat Donna down on an upholstered chair and proceeded to minister to her feet with loving care.

"Would miss like to put her weight on this one? Would miss prefer a wider fitting? Is miss aware that our company supplied this identical style to the Duchess of York's children?"

"Mummy? Are you sure we can afford them?" whispered Donna when the saleswoman had momentarily withdrawn to attend to another customer. Mummy stroked her daughter's head reassuringly, and yet pampered and pleased as she abundantly was, Donna continued to feel guilty. "Mummy? What will Sarah say? Won't she want a pair for herself?"

"I'll buy Sarah some another time," mummy shrugged indifferently. "Try walking on those."

In the end two pairs were selected, a small plastic card handed back and forth, and they were escorted across acres of spongy carpet to the door as if they were members of the royal family itself.

"Can we buy some sweeties, mummy?" asked Donna.

"No, I don't think so. They'll spoil your appetite."

"Not for me, mummy. For Sarah. I can spend my own pocket money. Please!"

They found a newsagent on the next corner and Donna purchased a large box of Maltesers which she knew were her sister's favourite type of chocolates. When they had got back in the car mummy turned to Donna to ensure that her seat belt was properly secured and said, "That's a very nice gesture, Donna. We both have to try and be kind to Sarah. She can be infuriating, I know. But we have to make allowances. She has suffered a lot. Her childhood has been very difficult."

Donna listened attentively and watched her mother's taut features, head bowed slightly and eyes oddly preoccupied with a rip in the passenger seat casing. The words came leaking slowly out of her mouth like water out of a rusty tap and then suddenly dried up. Donna felt like a curious spectator. It was as if mummy was speaking to herself.

"Why?"

"Why what?"

"Why has she suffered a lot?" Donna watched the varnished nail of a little finger enter the indentation of the upholstery tear and circle about nervously like a burrowing worm. "Why, mummy?"

"Because – because – well, because Sarah was there when her daddy had the accident. She saw it happen, didn't she?"

My daddy, too, thought Donna possessively to herself but as she opened her mouth to fill the silence different words fell out. "Where was I, mummy? When it happened?"

"You were in your pram, fast asleep. In the flat with me, weren't you? You'd kept me awake half the night. You never did like sleeping in the darkness. Not for more than a couple of hours at a stretch."

The worm had burrowed right up to the second knuckle and showed no signs of exhaustion.

"Can you tell me the story again, mummy?"

"I don't want to tell you, Donna. You've heard it before."

"Not for a long time. Tell me the story, mummy. How it happened?"

"It isn't a story. It's real. And I don't want to talk about it again. We have to put things like this behind us. We have to forget and move on. It was a long, long time ago. Nobody can live in the past. But Sarah was very close to her daddy. She was only six years old. That's why we have to make allowances for her behaviour. Do you understand, Donna?"

The worm disengaged itself from the hole with a sudden vehemence that made Donna blink and closed down any further possibility of inquiry. She nodded compliantly and her mummy revolved her head simultaneously exploding the car into life. But she did not understand. The unanswered question spun around in the candy floss machine of her head, spewing out strands of a patchwork nightmare all the more disquieting to Donna for remaining so shapeless and threadbare. She had once, quite recently, – where was it? – been shopping with Katrina when she heard a sickening squeal of tyres and breaks and turned her head to see an old man in the middle of the road facing a car that had stopped so close to him it's bumper seemed to be caressing his baggy trousers. He was shouting and waving a walking stick angrily towards the windscreen as if intent to smash the thing. What if the car had failed to stop? What if the man had fallen down, covered in blood and died like you saw in films and cartoons? Would she have been able to forget all about it the next day, the next month, and move on? Move on to where? Or would she have become bad tempered and naughty at school and have everybody making allowances for her?

They pulled up outside the doctor's house and mummy got out to collect Sarah. Donna watched the door open and close. It had polished brass fittings and two stained glass windows that seemed to be watching her with wry amusement. Then the door opened again and Sarah appeared followed by mummy. She slouched down the steps, her head no less erect than when she had entered, wearing the self same haughty world weary expression, the expression of a dutiful cinema goer for whom the performance did not quite live up to the advance publicity.

"These are for you," said Donna, handing her the box of chocolates as she climbed into the back seat. Donna watched as her sister took the box out of the white paper packet.

"Thanks," Sarah muttered inwardly and deposited it neglectfully in her lap. "Can we have the radio on?"

So they drove on and on immersed in the throb and beat of artificial disco jollity. For somebody who had just received the ultimatum and the help of a private doctor Sarah did not seem any different at all to Donna. Maybe it takes a while to work, she thought, like junior aspirin on a headache? Her candy floss machine spun faster and faster now, one question begetting another. There were feelings, too, dozens of ambiguous and contradictory feelings accompanied by little electrical shocks in the chest region but it was not clear whether these were the source of the energy that worked the machine or the waste product of its efforts.

"Stop looking at me!" snapped Sarah

"I wasn't!"

"Don't!"

"I was looking at the river." The Thames had suddenly appeared there, a convenient lie on the other side of her sister's window, a brown rippling murk spattered by the onset of harsh rain. An incomprehensible rap motive thumped through the speakers.

Maybe you have to take more than one dose, thought Donna, like honey linctus for a sore throat? If Tony came out at quarter past six to watch the high water she would be able to ask him. He did not have to make allowances, to forget things and move on like mummy. He would be able to answer her questions. Tony was becoming her friend after all.

After lunch Donna spent a large part of the afternoon drawing pictures and colouring them in. She had decided to give the best one to Tony as a present. Sometimes they went wrong. It ought to have been easier to draw directly from an object than from memory but this was not always the case. The chimneys on the white house which she could see perfectly from her bedroom window were much too tiny, for example, and the side door was big enough to have admitted a dinosaur never mind a man the size of Tony. On the other hand the texture and colouring of the pine hedges which she could not see from her window seemed very true to life once she had finished jabbing and notching the paper with her needle sharp pencils, a lovely big set that boasted five shades of green. But that willow with its grasping claws and imperious tentacles really tested her patience. She tore up the first two attempts. Then she tried a portrait of Tony but after a promising beginning the head became mysteriously dislocated from the shoulders as if it lived in a more advanced dimension of anatomy and she returned to that swaggering, flirtatious giantess of a tree, determined that if she could not master the whole of its monstrous elegance at least she would tease one of the bunches of tresses into submission.

"I've arranged to go out tonight," said mummy quietly ghosting into the room. "Is that alright?"

"Can I come too?" asked Donna her glance flickering with unbroken concentration between the distant branches and the nib of her pencil.

"Not this time. Can I see? That's really lovely!"

"Where's Sarah?"

"In her room. Working, I hope. She's two sets of geography homework behind. You've got quite a talent for drawing, Donna. You really have. Who's this?"

"Mummy? What time is it?"

"Just coming up to half past five. Who's this?" repeated mummy picking up the sketch of Tony.

"Nobody."

"Well, nobody ought to feel flattered. It's good," joked mummy. "I've laid out a cold supper on the table. Just help yourself. Okay?"

"Mummy? Are you going to see Gerry?"

"No, I'm going to see Keith. He's a new friend. By the way Donna, I forgot to tell you – I bumped into Sian Tyson's mummy the other day. She works in Churchill's, the estate agents –"

"Why doesn't Keith come to our house, mummy?" interjected Donna.

"He will one day. I'm sure. It's just not the right time yet."

"Doesn't he like children?"

"Oh, yes. He's got two of his own. It's not that. He works very hard. Sometimes seven days a week. And so in the evening he prefers just to relax and listen to music."

"Oh."

"Well, anyway, we got to talking and Sian's mummy told me all about Mr Brown who rented the white house. She met him once. He's a very nice man apparently, works in the city. But the bad news is he hasn't got any family. He's divorced and his children are all grown up and live in Scotland somewhere. So that's why we haven't got a reply from him, I suppose."

"Mummy?"

"Yes, dear."

"Don't you love Gerry any more?"

"Erm, well... in a way, yes I suppose I do – but not as much as I love you and Sarah, of course." Mummy placed the pictures back down on the window ledge. "I've got a couple of phone calls to make now. Alright, then."

When her mummy had left Donna looked at her willow picture critically, angling it towards the insipid streaks of sunshine. It was not perfect by a long way but it was not dustbin fodder either. The hanging clutch of fronds had turned out bigger than she had expected and there would be insufficient room for the rest of the tree trunk. Which should it be now? This one? The house? The Hedges? Certainly she could not risk the portrait of Tony himself – it made him look deformed like a monster and he would be badly offended. So after due deliberation, balancing the dictates of art and instinct, she selected the hedges and in the blank space underneath wrote *dear toni when can I see the egs agan? I hop you lik the piture love from donna.*

The kitchen wall clock read nine minutes after six as she clicked open the back door and momentarily hesitated. Sarah had taken a plate of food to her bedroom and mummy could be heard in the living room evidently still speaking on the telephone very quietly and soothingly. There appeared to be more pauses than words and little self-mocking spats of laughter as if mummy was teasing someone and being affectionately teased back in return.

Outside it had stopped raining long since but small puddles or water remained in the ginnel. The wooden fence felt slimy to the touch of her hand and steam emanated in billows from the slats. In the garden the grass was long underfoot. She walked across it gingerly, a sea of sponges clasping and squelching her feet up to the ankles; then through the keyhole, emitting a little gasp of amazement as her gaze fell on the river. It was lapping the bottom of the wall and if it had not been for the fact that the gate was located on a raised platform of flagstones, the water would have been pouring at a rate of knots into the garden. She found a bit of ledge that had nearly dried out and balanced on it side-saddle, excited and privileged to be a witness to this adventure, studying the vastly transformed waterway like an explorer who has stumbled into unmapped territory and is torn between the desire just to enjoy the solitary experience for itself or to rush back home and share the good news. But Tony might be here in a minute. There was no need to retreat. And Donna tried to anticipate his reaction, the slow smile of wonder that would spread across his face.

So she waited and anticipated and gradually the lake began to subside, the concrete mooring reasserting centimetre by centimetre its dark personality. And still Tony did not arrive to share her secret. Very soon the secret would cease to exist. She walked back up the garden slowly clutching her crumpled present, past the garage and onto the patio, hesitant, wondering if she dared to break new ground. Right in front of her were the double breasted French windows, eight oblong panes of glass, overhung by strands of a wispy passion fruit plant greedy for territory. They looked as if they had not been opened for ages. She approached closer, up an esplanade of tiered steps. The living room beyond was obscured from view by a thick, sinister curtain. She moved along the esplanade to the glass door. It, too, had been draped off. She made to put her hand on the ornamental chrome lever but thought better of it. Why should Tony want to have his curtains drawn when it was still daylight? Was he asleep on the sofa? Had he dropped off and missed the high tide? He would be very cross with himself if he had.

She pressed her face to one pane of glass then another, shuffling back and forth between the French windows and the door, uncertain whether to knock, wondering if he would be angry at the sudden disturbance, all the time on tenterhooks of anticipation expecting her indecision to be dispelled in an abrupt unveiling of the drapes from within. Five more silent minutes passed before she finally accepted her fate. Tony was definitely out, – probably at work, even though it was the weekend – and she felt a pang of sympathy. How awful it must be to have jobs like the ones Keith and

Tony had where you were expected to go in every day of the week, she reflected. How tired and fed up you must get!

Nothing had changed in the house as she tiptoed in. Mummy was still on the phone faraway, although her tone had changed. Donna scrunched up her picture and dropped it in the bin.

"Well, you insist he takes the pills!" she distinctly heard mummy advising. "You tell him you won't wash his underpants if he refuses to take them!.......That's right! You tell him a bit of constipation is a small price to pay!"

It must be gran'ma, Donna thought. Mummy always spoke to gran'ma in that kind of bossy joking voice as if she was issuing veterinary advice on how to manage a wilfully disruptive pet dog. Donna went upstairs directly, changed her socks, and returned with the soiled evidence which she buried carefully at the bottom of the laundry bin. Then she entered the living room.

"Look at it like this, at least that allotment keeps him out of harm's way," mummy was saying. "He might start sniffing illegal substances otherwise.....Yes! Ha, ha, ha! Just tell him from me maybe he needs to spend a bit less time mulching his carrots and a bit more mulching a few family relationships.....And to you. 'Bye!"

"Gran'ma sends you her love," smiled mummy as she hung up.

"What about gran'dad?"

"He was digging up the garden. They're looking forward to seeing you at Whitsun. Remember, we're going two weeks today."

"Sarah as well?"

"Of course! Heaven forbid I'd leave her at home for a week."

"Mummy? Is she going to see that shrink man again?"

"Doctor," mummy corrected. "This Wednesday after school. And every Wednesday after that. Why? Did she say something?"

"No."

"Sarah is not as hard as she pretends to be. A lot of it is an act,"

"Mummy? What are we doing tomorrow?"

"I don't know. Any suggestions?"

"Can we go to Thorpe Park?"

Mummy screwed up her face. "Not a good idea, dear. It's very very crowded at weekends – and expensive. We'll go somewhere, though. A little jaunt in the countryside if it isn't wet. Now then, excuse me." She picked up the phone again. "I need to double check with Katrina her availability tonight. The silly girl's trying to hold me to ransom."

"Did you do anything nice at the weekend, Donna?" asked Mrs Harper on Monday morning as the Maths lesson finished and books were being put away.

Donna had been feeling unusually weary for the last ten minutes of the lesson and hoping it had not shown. "Not really. We went for a walk somewhere," she answered languidly. "And it was too late when we got back to do anything else," she added, thinking of Tony whose garden she had been unable to re-visit.

"Well, any questions? Not just about Maths? Anything at all?" coaxed Mrs Harper.

Donna stifled a yawn. "What does it mean to hold someone to ransom?" she pondered aloud as much to show gratitude for her teacher's generosity as any burning desire to know.

Mrs Harper gave a sound explanation but within five minutes Donna had completely forgotten it, so badly was her concentration shot to pieces, and later after lunch when they passed in the corridor the special needs teacher observed, "That walk in the countryside seems to have really taken it out of you!"

Donna nodded back politely but in her heart she knew the walk was not the real reason why she felt tired. Hopefully it would wear off in the comfort period between the end of school and suppertime, she considered, and then she would try to catch up with her elusive new neighbour. In the event she crept into his garden twice after school only to be disappointed. The living room curtains remained ominously drawn and the whole house yet again resided in a gloomy silence as if its tenants had suddenly abandoned the place forever.

Chapter 14

On Wednesday morning Frank woke up to the sound of radio pips then a voice introducing the seven o'clock news and instantly his mind flared up with the energy of anticipation. Even as he rolled out from beneath the duvet his body seemed to surge with the adrenalin of a long wait to get started almost over. Today McLeod would be phoning with the date of the operation. The hijack could even be on for tomorrow with any luck. For a minute or more he prowled up and down the landing feeling like a caged tiger, wrestling to keep his excitement under control. Then he showered and went downstairs to the kitchen where he breakfasted copiously on toast, bacon and tea – never taking his eyes off the mobile which stubbornly remained silent.

Afterwards he drew back the curtains in the living room and peered between the garage and buddleia tree down the funnel of the garden where the briefest snatch of animal movement caught his attention. The sun was edging its way promisingly through a light cloud cover. The willow tree to his right looked majestic. The conifers, the lawn, the rose bushes were a delight to the eye but very soon now this suburban idyll would be left far behind and drop like a stone to the bottom of his memory bank. He switched on the box for the sake of distraction. Even at that time of day the widescreen television was pumping out film footage of beaming politicians all riding the crest of some indefatigable euphoria. So many women, too, posturing like mannequins around their paternal leader. He possessed the charisma of the head of a great dynasty but they, it appeared to Frank, came across more like his badges of achievement than his blood family. Now individual ministers were enthusiastically answering questions and espousing brilliant new policies – milking a moment of public adulation that had already expanded into its twelfth day and showed no signs of abating.

He picked up The Adam's Empire tome and read a few pages. He made another pot of tea. Two hours had crawled by. It was going to be another long, tedious day. His fingers rifled idly about amongst the butterfly collection and selected a purple-yellow specimen which he pinned carefully in the lapel of his shirt. These are my medals, he thought suddenly, my badges of achievement. And every bit as hard earned as our noble PM's.

A bit later still Frank took the photographs down from the board and began daydreaming about Sue and Cesca living in Australia. He did not doubt his ability to locate them once he set foot on the continent but felt less positive about how they would react when he eventually turned up unannounced on their door step, especially in Francesca's case. God alone knew to what extent his absence might have eroded her heart's natural flow of affection. As far as Sue was concerned, McLeod had dented Frank's conviction a bit but not dismantled it. She had been and, no doubt, still was a very attractive woman. She would not have been without ready admirers. And, yes, she had her own set of needs. But even if she had hitched up with someone to help satisfy them, he considered, it would be purely as a pragmatic arrangement. Her heart still belonged to him deep down and with the right degree of coaxing and patience he could win her back again.

"Bollocks!" cursed Frank suddenly aware how far his mind had slid down the bottomless tube of nostalgia and he shoved the photographs away. If he did not find another distraction quickly it might slide a bit too far and never be able to get back. He made more toast in the kitchen. It tasted like cardboard. What to do with the day? The question seemed to hang over his head like an executioner's noose. With all his high tech paraphernalia and a garden it ought not to be a problem. He knew that. But it was all the same. He had learnt techniques for coping from Leppy and from Rosie. But these only seemed to work when he had no other choices, when he was physically banged up. This incarceration was different, self-inflicted as it was and supervised by armed screws. Since his arrival, in strict obedience to McLeod's directives, he had strayed off the premises just four times and then no further than the all-purpose shop on the main road. It was getting him down. He entered the living room again, munching, pacing the floor and peered through the French windows. He had taken to keeping them curtained during school hours and weekends in case that little girl or any other nosy kids came snooping around. The sunshine streamed in, taunting his enforced indolence, splashed against the wall and the still animated screen of the television where a thin faced politician, all horn rimmed glasses and unctuous charm, sat reassuring a table of pundits about his integrity.

"Yes, that's right," he simpered. "Tough on crime and tough on the causes of crime. And here's how we've already begun to deliver..."

"I'll go mad if I stay in this place today," Frank muttered to himself. "I'll do something crazy!"

*

Outside the classroom window Donna watched Year Five marching off across the playground and vaguely envied them, their liberty. She felt tired again and was finding it difficult to concentrate on what Miss Frobisher was saying. Sarah had woken her up making those funny blubbering noises three nights in a row now and she had found it difficult to drop back off to sleep.

"Things may well get worse before they get better," she recalled the words of her mummy. But better for who? And how long would it take? She stifled a yawn and focussed her eyes back towards the map of the world Miss Frobisher had tacked up on the white board.

"They almost certainly sailed in rafts from these islands here," indicated the teacher with the help of a ruler. "And perhaps even from the mainland of South East Asia. It's a long way – thousands of miles. The migration couldn't have happened quickly. What does migration mean? Anybody?"

Some nights Sarah did not come into her room. Why not, considered Donna? It would be nice to be told. It would be nice to be asked. To be prepared for a disturbance. Perhaps I should complain to mummy about it, she thought and instantly saw a mental picture of her sister exploding with rage at the betrayal?

"Very good, Clarissa," said Miss Frobisher. "Now if we concentrate on the continent of Australasia itself – turn to your books please – what do you notice about all the main centres of population, the big towns? Yes, Peter?"

"They're all on the coast, Miss," answered Peter.

"Well done!" purred the teacher. "Now why do you think that is?" She looked around. "In such a huge country? Thirty times bigger than the UK? Anybody?" Then Harry shot his hand up. "Yes, Harry?"

"Because the people were so tired after paddling their rafts all the way from India," smirked the boy, "they couldn't be bothered to go any further, Miss." And everybody laughed.

*

As Frank stepped through the front door he suddenly remembered the mobile phone. It would be very bad form to go AWOL without that, he smiled to himself as he retrieved it from the living room and placed it inside his jacket pocket. There would be all hell to

123

explain if McLeod decided to ring and he was not around to answer. It was just after 10am and the compulsion to break out of the cage had burst like a ripe carbuncle. There was no denying the cure.

Nobody was about on the street apart from a post woman on a bike delivering mail. Frank rounded the corner quickly and strode on down Mansfield Road. That, too, was deserted except for an elderly man cleaning his car. The man looked up from his polishing but Frank kept his gaze steady and decided on balance it was better not to acknowledge him. By the time he had crossed over the hump back bridge, reached the main Richmond Road and cut behind the college grounds via a narrow lane that led to The Thames, Frank was convinced that this perpetual daytime squatting in the house was far more likely to alert the curiosity of his neighbours than his actually leaving it occasionally. And what did that curiosity amount to anyway? This was suburban London. Affluent. Gentrified. Complacently self-centred. Nobody would give a newcomer time of day until he played loud music after hours or parked outside their front gate.

The vast expanse of river opened up in front of him, the footbridge and the freedom of open common land and towpaths. Frank quickened his step. The sunshine, the whole day lay before him, his liberty. Perhaps he would take a boat down to Hampton Court and wander round the palace gardens? The world seemed suddenly to be his oyster. To be on the move, to be on the water – at that moment nothing in life seemed more desirable to Frank. He crossed over the bridge as if walking on thin air. A regiment of schoolkids were standing around the lock listening to some pompous windbag lecturing them from a plinth. "We're also responsible for the maintenance of the river and its tributaries," Frank heard the man say. "In fact we've got a bank rebuilding project about to start just over there." – a sputter of words like gulls' wings suddenly flapping and instantly swallowed up by the breeze. He felt invigorated, as if he could walk forever. His anonymity fitted like a glove and nobody gave him a second look as he marched on behind their backs towards the road bridge and pleasure boat quays beyond.

"Hampton Court! This one's just about to leave!" shouted the ticket manager and Frank boarded the open-decked craft without further hesitation.

He sat behind a group of babbling Japanese tourists whose evident delight in the scenery as they cruised past Eel Pie Island only intensified his own. The skipper came on the tannoy directing public attention to the television studios on the Teddington bank when suddenly the mobile sounded. "Yes?" said Frank waiting half a minute before clutching it to his ear as the tannoy cut out.

"The party's been arranged for this Friday," said McLeod. "Can you be outside the Hounslow East tube station at 9pm?"

"I can," confirmed Frank and the tannoy crackled back into life. "Looking forward to it."

"And don't forget to bring your kit bag. It'll be needed. I'll bring the fancy dress. Okay?" added McLeod. "What's that noise? Is someone with you?"

"I'm listening to the radio," grinned Frank and switched off the apparatus abruptly. At last, he thought to himself and his fingers stroked the butterfly charm as if in gratitude.

*

After school Donna found Katrina consulting a road map book in the car. She joined her reticent sister in the back and eventually they drove off in silence. "Aren't we going home?" she asked as the vehicle turned right at the roundabout. Nobody seemed to hear. Then she remembered about Dr. Williamson and said, "I wouldn't mind being at home on my own." Nobody answered. "I wouldn't be scared."

She opened a packet of strawberry bubblegum and put a piece in her mouth, wondering whether it was safe to offer one to Sarah who sat in a rigid posture, cold and withdrawn. "Want one?" she risked at length.

Sarah took it without speaking and peered out of the window. "Mummy's got a new boyfriend," said Donna encouraged. "He's called Keith."

"I know," grunted Sarah remotely.

"Where does he live, Sarah?"

The question was shrugged away as an irrelevance.

"Does he go into her shop sometimes?"

"Search me."

Sarah opened a magazine as if to prohibit further conversation. In the silence Donna found her mind flitting from one image to another. The curtained off windows of Tony's house were easily the most frequent stopping place. "Katrina? What time do people in factories finish work?" she asked leaning forward.

"Five or six o'clock maybe?" answered Katrina. "Sometimes they have to work through the night."

They drove on a while before Donna spoke again.

"This car's very bumpy, isn't it? I don't mind a short journey but long ones make me feel sick." Sarah took no apparent notice. "I hope mummy stops a few times. When we drive to gran'dad's, I mean. It's so tiring. Last year I threw up. Remember?"

The car pulled up at traffic lights. "He's a copper," mumbled Sarah into her window pane.

"Who?" yawned Donna following the direction of her sister's gaze, mystified.

"Keith. She told me," said Sarah and seemed to laugh inwardly at some private joke. "I'll give it two weeks tops. Then she'll be back with the other one. That's if she's ever left him."

"Sarah?"

"What?"

"Are you going to be sleeping in my bedroom again tonight?" No reply. "No offence. Only you make noises and they wake me up."

"Shut up! Don't speak to me!" snapped Sarah stridently. "I'll do what I please!"

"But –"

"Don't speak to me! Don't!" Her voice had been raised a couple of octaves. "And don't look at me either!"

Katrina finally turned her head. "Calm down, please, girls. I'm losing my way," she said and crunched into the wrong gear.

In the waiting room at Dr Williamson's house Donna tried to read a comic but after a few minutes her eyelids felt heavy as if they wanted to close and she gave up. Katrina was busy writing. Donna watched her, sighing, pulling faces and squinting. "What are you writing?" she asked at length.

"Oh, it's an application for a job," Katrina replied. "It's got to be in tomorrow. How the hell do you spell 'necessary'?"

"A job? In the daytime? Like mummy's?" pondered Donna.

"Hm. Hm," muttered Katrina. "Didn't she tell you?"

*

As soon as he arrived back home Frank began to prepare himself. He spent several hours that evening studying the operational plans, living the moves in his mind and anticipating every critical moment – a process that continued with only a six hour break for sleep right into the next day. The maps. The itinerary. The guns. The precise timings. Everything he was required to do had to be second nature. Indecision and ambiguity could not be part of the equation, nor could fear of failure. They were actors in a play and they had just one attempt to get the performance right. Just before eleven he made a cup of tea and took it outside into the back garden to clear his brain. A woman was working a couple of gardens down on the opposite embankment. A dog barked. This place was a stroke of genius on McLeod's part. They were all so on top of each other and yet all so distant. It had to be the dead of night, though, he considered. You could never risk being seen to load a cargo like that during waking hours.

He went back into the house and lay down on the bed with his eyes closed, listening to his breathing. Tomorrow he would do a final dress rehearsal in his mind. At that point he would psyche himself up to the hilt, focus on nothing else, revert to machine mode. Today was different. He could afford to walk slowly like a jockey round a national hunt circuit checking the elevation of the fences, the feel and the undulations of the ground under foot. He could ask himself the 'what if' questions just to purge them finally from his system. So now he allowed them to come dancing one after another into his head like little mischief making demons. What if?... What if?... What if?... He watched them and answered them and watched them some more cavorting insatiably with the licence he had given them. Most of the questions were totally outside his territory, or course. They belonged to McLeod. Nobody else could answer them. And he had chosen to have faith in McLeod, he reminded himself. McLeod had done it before – not this big, of course – but he knew the ropes. McLeod understood how unequivocally the stakes split – the rest of their lives behind bars or the rest of their lives on easy street with nothing in between. A red eyed demon pranced close to Frank's left ear now and whispered audaciously, "What if you're spotted by the P.L.A. on the river and they make radio contact? What if they don't like your explanation? Now there's a thing, Frank!"

Frank ran through the explanation in his head, ran through the rationale behind it, ran through it from the river police's point of view as well as his own and finally silenced the demon.

"But what if the sponsor anchors his ship in the wrong place in the estuary?" demanded another. "What if you can't find him?"

"And what if Hunter loses his bottle?" shouted a third. "You know he's a land lubber, Frank, and arrogant with it? What if he can't find his way up the Crane from the Thames? What if he misses the tide? And what if -?"

"Get away! A blind dog in a pedalo couldn't miss the entrance to the Crane!" snarled Frank with a yawn and the demons fell back rebuked into disarray.

He must have been asleep for an hour and when he came to his tormentors were nowhere to be seen. He took a long steaming shower and emerged feeling almost totally cleansed. But somewhere on the hem of his consciousness, a patch of oily grime had failed to come out. What had caused it? He lit a cigarette and the mobile rang.

"Everything this end is A okay," said McLeod. "You?"

"A okay. Just one check required." replied Frank. "The boat man? Everything sorted his end?"

There was a short pause and McLeod said, "The boat man's in place. Everything hunky dory. Nine o'clock tomorrow. Hounslow East. Be on time."

"Okay," said Frank and switched off.

Chapter 15

"You seem tired again, Donna," said Mrs Harper. "Is everything alright at home? Or is it just the Friday feeling?"

"Katrina might be leaving soon," nodded Donna and tried to stifle a yawn. They had gone to the library together and been staring at shapes on a computer screen. "To work in a proper job somewhere."

"What will your mother do then?" asked the teacher.

Donna rubbed her eyes and shrugged by way of a reply. "I've brought you in another tidal chart," said Mrs Harper. "Shall we go over it?"

"I've brought you in a drawing," said Donna shyly and footled through her folder. "Do you like it?"

The teacher gazed at it and Donna felt a shiver go down her spine as Mrs Harper's face widened into a smile of appreciation. "It's a willow tree, isn't it?" she said. "You've got real talent, Donna. You've brought it to life. Thank you very much. Do you mind if I pin it up on one of the corridor noticeboards?"

For a while they sat talking about all sorts of things, mostly to do with school – the Australia project, the Whitsun half-term and the reason it was a holiday. Mrs Harper had this way of making you feel relaxed and encouraged you to ask questions. It was easier to talk in the library with no one else about, smirking or trying to put you off. Donna found herself totally at ease just as she had once been with Mrs Gaynor a long time ago. They were similar people. They both went on about God as if he was a kindly magician who rented a room in their home and did hundreds of amazing things called miracles. She felt safe.

"How's your friend? The one who works in the butterfly factory?" asked Mrs Harper with a twinkle in her eye.

"I haven't seen him once this week," Donna answered. "He's never been out in the garden when I've gone looking. And the curtains are always closed."

"That's a bit strange. Maybe he's away from home?"

"Maybe," considered Donna. "He's got a little river at the bottom of the garden and he likes to come out and see it when the tide is up high. I'll look again today."

"I see. So that's why you're interested in the tides?"

Donna nodded. "What's the reason for the tide, Mrs Gaynor?" she asked. "What makes it happen?"

"Donna?!"

"Yes?"

"Have you forgotten my name? You called me Mrs Gaynor! Whose she?"

"Did I? Sorry," burbled Donna apologetically. "Mrs Gaynor was my teacher at the other school."

Donna watched as Mrs Harper threw her head back and chuckled with an amusement that was instantly infectious. The teacher's explanation of the tide was like a tangled ball of string – hard to follow. It led from one place to another and eventually back to the start. But as Donna listened she could not help thinking nostalgically about Mrs Gaynor who had virtually ceased to exist for her now as a complex personality, who had fallen to the back of the memory cupboard and would soon become totally obliterated by the most recent deluge of experiences. And one day, she thought to herself, it would be the same with Mrs Harper. The good lady would sink without trace and there was nothing she could do to prevent it. Nothing. Her eyes felt wet with sadness.

"Is something the matter?" asked Mrs Harper in a warm sympathetic manner. Donna shook her head. "It's quite alright to say, Donna."

Donna wiped a cuff across her eyes and controlled a sniffle. "I'm sorry," she said. "I can't properly explain."

*

By half past one Frank was ready –having treble checked everything – and yet at the same time he was not. Something inside felt incomplete, out of kilter. Was it just adrenalin? Fear of failure? He searched his house and head yet again for clues but could not satisfactorily explain the origin of the discomfort. He knew that he was not the nervous type or ever had been. He switched on the television and relaxed on the sofa for a while but unable to settle he got up, donned a pair of gloves and began prowling from room to room with a kitchen wipe, rubbing at furniture and work surfaces and walls like a neurotic housewife. Even the panes in the French windows were not immune from his fastidiousness. He stripped his bed and dumped the sheets in the washing machine together with a pile of towels. Everything he did was an attempt to eradicate himself. Eradication, it had been agreed, was McLeod's job – and well after the main event – but Frank could not stop himself. I have not been here, his ablutions said. I have never existed. But he suspected that if the forensic men ever came sniffing they would eventually find him in spades. He could burn the house down and still the police might detect his traces. Nobody could entirely cease to exist. All he could do realistically was delay the process of detection, hope that the trail stayed cold til long after the lease had expired. With luck and good management he might be in Australia within a fortnight, maybe less. And what then? He tried to think it all through again. Was that the source of his discomfort – Sue and Francesca? It would be one thing just to find them, quite another to get them to belong to him again. And yet he could not afford to doubt that they still loved him, just as he could not afford to doubt the competence of McLeod or doubt his own resourcefulness in dealing with whatever delays or disappointments might impend on his voyage of discovery. It was too late now. At the back of his head, in his heart, Frank had implanted a hope, a dream, like a seed of redemption and been watering it daily for years, watching the shoots grow slowly, feeling the roots burrow down into his deepest being. They had become his faith and theology, combined, and he needed those shoots to flower every bit as much as he needed food and water simply to survive. No. Sue and Cesca were not the question – the malaise that afflicted him. What the hell was it then? He lay down on the bed to reflect but within minutes his mind slipped its anchor and the question drifted out into a vast expanse of sleep.

*

After school Donna waited patiently for her opportunity. Once Sarah had become engrossed in the first of the evening soaps and Katrina started yapping on the phone she packed a small shoulder bag with pictures and other items and just after 5:30 she made her move, ghosting quietly out through the back door totally unnoticed to make her vigil. But for the umpteenth day in a row, so it felt, Tony was not about. The river was low. That could be the reason. Or maybe he had gone away somewhere as Mrs Harper had suggested? It was a lovely warm evening. A man in a cloth cap appeared on the opposite embankment a couple of moorings up river. He glanced at Donna furtively before tipping a barrow load of grass and plant cuttings into the stream. She did not hang around for long. She knew from her latest chart she had missed the afternoon tide by several hours and the next one would be well after nightfall. A wood pigeon cooed overhead, circling the willow tree, and she trekked up the lawn, her eyes fixed like a hawk's on the windows looming in front of her. Amazing! The curtains were pulled back! Why had she not noticed before? Tony must be at home after all! She ran straight to the patio door and tapped on the glass pane, calling out "Tony? Are you there? It's me. Donna! Hullo?"

*

Frank broke suddenly out of his sleep with the vague impression that someone was in the bedroom talking to him. He checked the radio. It was not functioning. Then he lifted his wrist watch in front of his eyes and was astonished to discover that more than four hours had passed.

"I've done a picture for you?" he heard the voice again. "Shall I try and slip it under the door, if you're not coming out today?" And the truth accosted him like a slap in the face. What a fool he was! He had neglected to draw the curtains and the kid had interpreted it as an invitation to an open house!

He leapt to his feet and peered gingerly down through the casement window. There she was, right beneath him, kneeling on the steps by the patio door. Suddenly she craned her neck upwards and he managed in the nick of time to step back and avoid being spotted. A long silence set in during which he fidgeted around unsure what to do next, trying to remember if he had left the door unlocked. Surely she would not dare to come in even if he had? When he eventually peeked out again it was just in time to glimpse a pair of legs disappearing back through the fence and he breathed a sigh of relief.

For a while he watched the butterflies waltzing around in the plumes of the buddleia and the question with which he had fallen asleep gradually rose up again from the deep like a lifebuoy but this time it had the answer barnacled to the side. McLeod had forbidden him to wear an insect charm in public as a precaution against recognition and he had dressed for today without one, obediently, unquestioningly, like one of the new prime minister's mannequins. It would not do. Call it superstition but he felt naked without one now. And McLeod's prohibition was ridiculous given they would all be disguised behind combat uniforms and balaclavas. He extricated the butterfly collection from his holdall downstairs and poked about until he found one he liked – a member of the Pieridae family. It was not the colouring that attracted him on this occasion. It was what Leppy had told him about its habit of survival. This little creature was extremely tasty. The birds loved to eat it. And so it had learnt to mimic exactly the movements of the poisonous Heliconicus butterfly which the birds avidly avoided and its trickery worked a treat. The birds were totally fooled.

As Frank pinned the brooch onto the lapel of his tee shirt and then pulled a sweater over the top of that he seemed to hear Leppy laughing as if he was actually there with him now in the room. "It's a lesson for life, Frank," he was saying. "It's rarely the truth that counts – just the quality of the camouflage."

Frank drew the curtains across the French windows, then went to do the same at the patio door, trying the handle first. It resisted his pressure. Good. He had not neglected to lock up after all. But on the floor protruding through the bottom blade of the door he noticed a piece of paper. It contained a picture of a bridge with a butterfly hovering above it.

The words *to toni with love from donna will you be my frend plese* had been scrawled underneath.

*

At home Donna sought out the dolls to console her for Tony's continued unavailability. She showed them the brand new tidal chart Mrs Harper had given her and it was Sylvestra who showed especial interest and asked the best questions. "The tides are about twelve and a half hours apart," Donna explained in a voice that mimicked the rhythm and intonation of Mrs Harper's. "It all depends on the moon and where it is in the sky." Sylvestra angled her head, impressed. "You see the moon is like a giant magnet. It pulls the water one way then another," continued Donna authoritatively.

"How can it do that?" puzzled Sylvestra.

"I'm not really sure," frowned Donna. "This is something you need to be a scientist to understand. One day you'll be able to read their books and know it all."

"What exactly is the moon, anyway?" persisted Sylvestra.

"Well, the moon is like the sun," began Donna incautiously and began to founder against the borders of her teacher's wisdom. "It floats around in space." She gazed up for inspiration at the orb of her bedroom lampshade. "Some people call it God's night light."

"Aren't there any strings holding it up?" asked Sylvestra with a glance towards the green Troll who had suddenly pricked up his ears. Donna shook her head. "Why doesn't it fall down then?" persisted Sylvestra.

"I don't know," answered Donna. "But for ages people were amazed like you and thought it was a miracle. And then those clever men called scientists came along and explained it all with lots of numbers and everybody said, 'Oh yes! I see it now! That's why it doesn't fall down! So simple really!' And it stopped being a miracle and nobody needed to feel amazed anymore."

The dolls all listened spellbound and Donna turned to the

green Troll for affirmation. He just grinned back maliciously. "Not everybody believes in God, though? Do they?" asked Sylvestra at length.

"Donna! Dinner is on the table!" intervened Katrina's voice from downstairs. "Donna!?"

Donna shook her head as she recalled the subject of her last Geography lesson. "The aborigines in Australia don't," she said. "They believe everything in the world came out of a dream – a long, long time ago."

Sylvestra tipped off her box seat in apparent confusion.

"Donna!? Can you hear me?!"

"But I can't tell you about that right now as dinner's ready," Donna concluded and went off to eat.

Later as Katrina cleared the dishes Donna returned to the scrutiny of her tidal chart. "What have you got there, Div?" demanded Sarah aggressively.

Donna ignored her and turned to Katrina. "0052. What time is that, Katrina?" she asked.

"Let me see," said Katrina. "Oh, that's about ten to one in the morning, I think."

Sarah snatched the piece of paper out of Donna's hands and peered at it suspiciously. "If you're thinking of strolling down the road to see it or something," she growled, "don't forget to take your garlic – the vampire will be on the prowl. Not to mention the werewolf! And even if you don't, be warned. The thing can dematerialise and find a way into your bedroom!"

"The what?" challenged Donna with a shiver.

"The werewolf. It's half man half hairy monster. And it howls at the moon before eating its prey," glared Sarah menacingly. "Its bloodshot eyes can peer into your darkest secrets!"

"I'm not scared, Sarah. I'm not!" retorted Donna. "You're talking through your bum hole. Isn't she Katrina?!" But the taunt had rubbed a raw nerve of imagination.

Katrina turned her head from the pantry door, unheeding. "Would anyone like tinned peaches and yoghurt?" she asked

Later in bed Donna snuggled up with Caroline and Dawn on either side of her but they provided marginal relief from the mystery of nightfall and the terrors implanted within it by Sarah. Katrina had insisted the light stayed off and, to make matters worse, the torch batteries had failed. Common sense may have informed Donna one version of the truth but her thumping heart in the darkness contradicted it. She lay for ages, victimised by every scrape and jolt that echoed through the house. Finally as she balanced on the very edge of sleep, conscious only of the weird nocturnal creatures that waited to haunt her dreams, the bedroom door seemed to open and footsteps padded into the room.

Involuntary words formed in Donna's throat. "Sarah? Is that you?" she whispered.

"It's me. Mummy," came the muted reply and Donna felt an infinitely gentle hand stroke her forehead. "Don't open your eyes. I didn't want to disturb you."

"Where have you been?"

"For a meal with a friend."

"Who was it?"

"Nobody you know. You feel very hot. It's so mild outside. I think summer's arrived."

"Where's Sarah?"

"She's in her room, of course, fast asleep. I just checked. Sleep tight, darling."

"Mummy?"

"Yes?"

"Is there any such thing as a werewolf?"

"Of course not!"

"Or a vampire?"

"No!" Mummy giggled. "Has she been teasing you again? Take no notice."

"Mummy? Will you take me to the zoo tomorrow please?"

"I can't tomorrow, dear. I've got to work. Sunday. How about Sunday?"

"Okay. Thank you, mummy."

"Unless Katrina wants to take you? I'll ring her now. That would suit me better."

"Okay, mummy. Mummy?"

"Last question now. I'm really tired. And I've got to be up at seven."

"What's a slag?"

All she could hear for a few moments was mummy breathing close to her face. "It's somebody who couldn't care less what other people think of them," she whispered at last. "But it's not a polite word. I don't want to hear you using it – alright? Goodnight now."

"Goodnight, mummy. Love you."

"You too, Donna. Sleep tight."

The door gently closed. The menagerie of mythical beasts dissolved into the night. And within seconds Donna had fallen through a trapdoor into a magical landscape of sweet and contented dreams.

*

It was hot and cramped in the back of the van. Frank sat in the rear with McLeod, crunching the knuckles of his right hand, wondering why Fearon did not open a window. Even though he had discarded his combat uniform and balaclava he still felt overdressed. He peered out of the back window and saw Challinor's decoy transit in which the clothing had been dumped move across the lanes and overtake them. By his calculations it would turn left at the next set of traffic lights and head north towards Greenford and the A40M.

McLeod squinted at his watch. "Can't you go faster?" he ordered. "We can't be doing more than twenty."

"I've got my foot flat down," answered Fearon. "We're overladen. The sump's scraped the road twice."

Frank caught sight of Challinor turning left up ahead at the lights. He could not contain his anger any longer. The lights changed and Fearon brought the vehicle juddering to a halt. Through the red glow of the windscreen and etched like a phantom in the darkness Frank spotted a white police car waiting to pass in the opposite direction.

"You told me no violence, McLeod," he said at last. "McLeod?!"

"I heard you," answered McLeod, the upper half of his body obscured from Frank by a pile of boxes. "There wasn't any choice, was there? Who'd have thought a runt like that fancied himself as a hero?"

"He shat himself ! " retorted Frank. "He wasn't a hero. He was too scared to remember the combination." The high pitched strain of the engine picking up again cut to the quick of his side temples. They were wet with perspiration.

"We're already seven and a half minutes down," said McLeod urgently into the back of Fearon's neck. "Is this thing slowing down or what? We're drawing attention to ourselves."

"We're going up a slight hill, boss," answered the driver. "Once we hit the crown it'll be all plain sailing."

*

The sound that lurched Donna back had its origin nowhere and everywhere at the same time. It was part howl, part scream, prolonged, a rhapsody of terror and agony. Donna opened her eyes in sheer disbelief, the lovely dream she had been enjoying utterly destroyed. The terrifying noise reverberated physically through her as if some monstrous deity had bent down over the earth and ripped the cloak of night slowly in two.

"Sarah? Was that you?" she gasped in confusion. "Sarah!?" She had no idea if Sarah was in the lower bunk and held her breath, listening intently, feeling for her sister's presence in the eerie unresolved silence. "Did you scream out? Sarah?!" Then she remembered her mummy's words and swung the top half of her body downwards, staring into the abyss of the bottom bed, her eyes filtering desperately through the colliding particles of darkness for the outline of security. Then all at once it pierced her again, this dreadful guttural yelp of despair but much closer now, and as distinct as breaking glass, a life unmistakably in the final act of renunciation.

*

"What was that noise? Over there?" demanded Frank. Nobody responded. "Didn't you hear anythin', McLeod? Are you deaf?"

The transit was groaning up and over the hump back bridge in Mansfield Road. McLeod shone a torch at his wrist and replied. "We're just twelve minutes behind schedule. No reason to start gettin' jumpy, Frank. Probably a cat fight. You take a torch and back Fearon down the drive. Okay? Got the keys to the garage door ready?"

"Yeah. But – !"

"Open it up but don't put the inside lights on. They're too fierce. We'll unload under cover of torchlight. No speaking once we get out unless it's absolutely necessary. Just me. Understood?

*

Donna scrambled down the ladder now, plunging her feet into the empty mattress, tottering still dizzy with sleep to the window and forcing her head between the curtains. All she could see was her own pallid face staring back at her. She pressed her nose close up to the glass and the great familiar monuments of her backyard neighbourhood shaped themselves slowly out of the nothingness. Where had the noise come from?

She opened the door of her bedroom. The boards creaked beneath her feet. A loose carpet tack bruised her big toe as she crept along the landing in the half light scrutinising the shadows. When she reached the door of Sarah's room she put her head sideways against the keyhole, listening, then her mouth to the aperture and whispered into it. "Sarah? It's me. Donna. Did you hear anything?"

Nobody answered. Donna lifted a hand to the knob and now realised that something remained clutched tight inside her fingers. She brought the object close to her face and with surprise recognised the outline of Caroline's hard elongated body. At the same moment Sarah's door, which had been only half latched, caved in and Donna tumbled into the room on all fours. The bedside lamp had been left on and the undisclosed lump beneath the duvet shifted slightly and coughed. Snakes of wild auburn hair spread out on the pillow where Sarah's head ought to have been. Donna sat back on her heels, hardly daring to breathe, a sense of enormous transgression clutching her heart, waiting for the werewolf to howl again. But she waited in vain. The husky rise and fall of her sister's body regenerating its energy and the occasional wheeze of an unblocking sinus gland was all she heard. By the time her eyes picked out the luminous red digits on her sister's radio clock, which showed 0006, the howl of the mortally wounded beast had already receded to a far flung outpost in Donna's wilting memory. She stumbled to her feet, faint with fatigue, unsure what had prompted this visit, mumbling to herself something about the tide. Then as she re-entered her own room, snapping the door closed with her backside, she seemed to hear the whine of a tamer animal beneath her window. The whine changed tone. The animal snorted, seeming to approach closer and closer. A shaft of light suddenly streaked the window. Tick –tick –tick –tick –tick –tick. The light went and came again and this time remained like a fiery translucent stain on the curtains.

Donna wanted to know its cause but the lids of her eyes felt so heavy. They had a will of their own. She opened the curtains and craned her neck towards the sound of the stationary beast. Tick –tick –tick –tick –tick. Now she could make out the roof of a white vehicle. It was located just off the road, apparently in the front garden of the white house, three quarters hidden behind the dark fencing. Her lids closed out the scene and Donna prodded them open again with her fingers. She seemed to hear a series of little clicks, then a sharp scrape. The ticking quickened pace, syllables of a mechanical sound eliding into a drone and the white roof came edging slowly down the driveway right beneath her window towards the garage where it stopped with an abrupt muffled squeal and plunged into the deep purple silence of the night. Unable to hold on one second longer Donna groped her way back to the bunk beds and, within seconds of locating a mattress, her body surrendered to the irresistible pressure of sleep.

*

They worked in a chain from inside to out. Fearon. McLeod. Frank. First the porter's trolley then the boxes. Backwards and forwards. Grunting. Scraping. Heaving. Frank lifted a shadowy hand and halted the mechanism for a few moments in order to remove his top sweater. His armpits and groin felt clammy with effort. The minutes passed.

"You start wheeling them down to the river," whispered McLeod. "We'll finish off the rest."

Frank loaded four boxes of bullion on the trolley. Any more and he feared the wheels would not turn on the surface of the lawn. He set off down the flag-stoned pathway, a second torch wedged under his armpit, and had just reached the lawn when another ear-splitting volley of howls rent the darkness. Half yelp, half whine, it seemed to emanate from the very heart of the garden and proceed in spasms of modulated agony before dwindling finally into extinction. Then some writhing, indistinct shapes flickered through the quarter light of his beam at the speed of thought.

"What the hell was that!" gasped McLeod approaching under the giant buddleia where Frank remained as if frozen to the spot contemplating the residue of his fear. For a while they listened and waited like condemned men for their executioner until finally convinced of their security.

"Probably a cat fight," grunted Frank with involuntary sarcasm and he pushed forward again towards the river. "No time to start getting jumpy, McLeod." His eyes surveyed the bank of terraced housing, alert to the probability of bedroom lights being switched on. But none were apparent. It was definitely spooky. Nobody but themselves had apparently been disturbed by the cacophony.

"Loud enough to have woken the living dead," whispered McLeod as if reading his partner's mind and he lumbered back to the garage.

On his third journey down to the river Frank misjudged the angle of the mooring gate and smacked his trolley into it. A box dislodged and he sniped his clothing on the splintered wood as he knelt down to retrieve it. The water was rising quietly now. He shone the torch into the chasm in the direction of the bridge. Twenty minutes at most and the river would be navigable, he calculated. They must have made up the lost time. Round that black bend no more than three hundred yards away Hunter would be tied up and waiting for the full flood to carry him in from the Thames.

But now as he wheeled the trolley back up the garden, Frank's senses, peeled and tuned to the smallest rustle of leaves, seemed to detect the distinct whisper of a new panic in the air and it grew closer with every stride. He strained his ears in disbelief as whispered angry words cohered into meaning. They belonged to McLeod who, barely able to contain his anxiety, was asphyxiating into the mouthpiece of his mobile phone, strangulating his larynx in an ever failing effort to keep it under rules control when all it physically desired to do was scream blue murder.

"What is it?!" demanded Frank urgently.

"The outlet's sealed off. Hunter can't get the boat in," jabbered McLeod. "There's a notice –"

"What do you mean? Sealed off? It ain't possible –"

"They're startin' work on the Crane banking on Monday. It's been sealed off to river traffic."

"It can't have bin," seethed Frank incredulously. "There's got to be a way through. The water's risin'!"

"Hunter says they've sunk iron railings right across the river forty yards in from The Thames – where it passes under the first road bridge. They weren't there yesterday. He can't shift them." The mobile spluttered again. "Just a minute."

Frank stood there his body tingling with disbelief as the enormity of the news flooded against the defensive walls of his consciousness. There had to be a mistake. Hunter was supposed to have been on the Brentford section of the river for three days double checking every detail of the escape project.

"He wants us to take the stuff round to The London Apprentice," began McLeod. "Meet the boat by the Syon Wharf."

"But there's houses there. Right opposite. And street lighting. And people live in that pub," spluttered Frank. "We'd be spotted. It aint possible. I'll kill that bastard! How could he let this happen! Give me the phone!"

But McLeod held Frank at arm's length. "We've gotta keep calm," he said. "We've gotta think clear. Where else could we meet the boat without danger of being spotted?"

"Nowhere!"

"It's the middle of the night, Frank. There must be. How about the promenade opposite the lock?" suggested McLeod.

"They're on permanent duty in that place," spat Frank. "The river police moor up there for tea and toast! And in any case how long d'yer think it'd take?! Reloadin' and comin' and goin' in that thing? More than an hour at least. By the time we'd finished we'd have woken up the whole neighbourhood. If we ain't already done it!" He kicked the garage wall twice. "For fuck's sake! I knew this was too clever by half!"

"Okay, Frank. This is what we do," said McLeod with sudden decisiveness. "Now listen hard. Fearon? You, too. I'm only going to say this once."

Chapter 16

Donna reclined on the golden sand sipping exotic juices from a tall glass and admiring the bronzed surf riders who scudded across the ocean. Though nobody had told her, she knew instinctively this was Australia by the cloudless quality of the intense blue sky and the brightness of the sunlight. It was peaceful, too, and only the distant roar of waves breaking could be heard until a familiar voice assaulted her from behind. "Your mummy says I must take you to the zoo," it insisted peevishly. "First we have to go shopping and it is ten thirty already. Donna? Will you get up now? I'm cooking the breakfast downstairs."

Donna peered over her shoulder to discover who was speaking and saw Tony dressed in red trunks relaxing on a deck chair, his body muscular and unblemished, his hair salt wet and unkempt, smiling as he chatted to a man in a grey suit who she recognised as Mr Brown. But it had not been him who spoke.

"It will be on the kitchen table in five minutes, okay? Donna answer me, shall I pull the duvet off you?" Suddenly Donna felt a cold wind engulf her stomach and back. The image of Tony and the crescent of perfect white beach that she lay on began to fracture and as the pieces fell away like splinters of glass on the surface of a broken mirror the base figure of Katrina's back and legs, bustling out of the bedroom, became harshly revealed underneath.

It had been one of those epics stretching for back into the night, full of twists and turns of plot, dramatic changes of location, a dream which in those first confused seconds of waking leaves a brutal empty sense of incompletion. Donna swung her legs towards the edge of the bed and was amazed to feel them hit the floor. She had been lying on the bottom bunk! But how could that be? She never did that. As she tottered into the bathroom and swilled the sleep out of her eyes she tried to remember. Remnants of the quickly fading dreamscape still scattered and danced like bits of confetti in her mind's eye. It was impossible to hold onto them.

"Did you come into my room last night?" demanded Sarah as they sat at breakfast together.

"No!" remarked Donna automatically but an almost extinguished ember in the ashes of her memory momentarily glowed back to life. Had there been a dream episode in which she had been hunted by a werewolf? And had she gone desperately looking for Sarah to protect her?

"Don't you ever come into my room unless I give you permission!" growled Sarah.

"But you come into mine all the time. "

"That's different !"

"No, it isn't – you get in my bed!"

"It's my bed! Mum bought those bunks for me years ago not you!" shouted Sarah. "I can use them any time I want!"

"It is difficult to think when you two girls are arguing," intervened Katrina.

"I didn't know you bothered," scowled Sarah sarcastically.

"What?" snapped Katrina.

"You heard."

Donna dropped her knife and fork and stood up.

"Where are you going?" asked Katrina.

"I'm not hungry," said Donna and ran upstairs to seek more civil company until it was time to go shopping.

Katrina seemed in an unusually bad mood, barely bothering to talk as they shuffled from one supermarket shelf to another. "Can I have some sweeties from the Pick N' Mix, please?" Donna asked wondering why she had been required to tag along. "I've got some money, I can pay."

"Your mum has been taking advantage of me," Katrina muttered by way of a reply. "Do this. Go there. Not for much longer though. I'm not a slave."

Back home as Sarah helped Katrina to put away the shopping, Donna consulted her window ledge sentinels for news of Tony. None of them had spotted him. "No matter, I'm going to the zoo with Katrina," she answered and gave them a mint each to encourage further watchfulness.

"Haven't you heard? It's all over the news," Sarah was nattering away to their minder as Donna re-entered the kitchen. "It's one of the biggest robberies of all time. In this country, anyway."

"Are you coming with us to the zoo?" Donna asked hopefully.

Sarah pulled a face. "I've got better things to do," she answered darkly.

A bus and two tubes it took to get there. They had lunch near the monkey house. Katrina had never been before. Her attitude had reanimated and Donna seemed glad that no more surly remarks were coming out of her mouth. But after three hours of visiting all the many compounds and cages Donna felt herself growing increasingly disillusioned with the experience. Katrina picked up on the change of mood as they stood outside the gazelle sanctuary.

"Are you bored, Donna?"

"I was just thinking how sad they all look," she replied. "They've hardly got any space to run around in. They're all on top of each other. See that one, he's really fed up. It must drive them mad after a while."

Katrina smiled down from a lofty height. "It is you who is fed up, Donna. Animals cannot feel like us. They are lucky to have regular meals and no threat to their lives, I think."

"But it's so small that space!"

"It is also private, how long do you think they survive in the wild? If all these animals had feelings they would only feel happy to receive such kind treatment."

Donna nodded in agreement but did not feel convinced. On the tube home Katrina briefly extricated her face from a magazine and said, "I've got an interview for a job at a post office. Your mummy will take you to school on Monday." Then she complacently resumed her perusal of the print.

When they were sitting waiting for the bus outside Richmond Station, Donna was surprised to hear Katrina remark, "You are very lucky to live in this country, you know. Look how patiently everybody makes a queue. People respect each other."

"Don't people queue up in your country then?"

"Oh, some of us do, of course. But many people have no manners at all. We have to teach them how to behave." Donna watched in alarm as her minder's face screwed up into a hard angry grimace. "They tell lies and betray their neighbours. They steal the land. They have no recognisable feelings at all."

In the pause Donna said, "Do you mean like animals?"

Katrina stood up, not seeming to hear. "Here comes our bus now. Come along," she said.

It was not until early Sunday evening that a real opportunity arrived for Donna to escape with impunity into the back ginnel, carrying a decoy crust of bread and pretending to look for Chelsea. Mummy had gone out to rendezvous with Keith – just for a couple of hours she had promised – and Katrina summoned once more to take charge, despite Sarah's protestations that it was not necessary. The muscles of Katrina's face had relaxed over night, Donna noticed, and said so privately to her sister.

"Mum must have promised her a pay rise," opined Sarah as she set up the V.C.R to watch a taped film. "Either that or she's got an interview for a proper job."

"Yes, she has," Donna concurred. "Tomorrow morning."

The evening smelt of mildew and damp soil as she passed through the fence. It had been raining but not heavily and tiny pearls hung around on the leaves of the bushes which lined the garden patio. The door and French windows had been curtained off again and she studied the pleats as if they might contain the secret code which would reveal Tony's whereabouts. She sauntered down the path and across the lawn humming a tune as if to advertise her presence and entice him outside to meet her should he be within earshot. Some unseen animal presence darted for cover as she passed through the conifers. It might be worth hanging around for a while, she thought to herself as she began to tear the bread into pieces and approached the latch gate which had been carelessly left open again. Immediately she noticed that one of the wooden ridge struts had been snapped off, – quite brutally, too, judging by the jaggedness of the splinter – and the adjacent strut appeared to be dented. The gate responded to the pressure of her hand by swinging in a jerky lop-sided arc as if one of the hinges had been partially dislodged.

The river had shrunk to a pebbly caricature of itself, all tin cans and bits of effluence stewing in a nauseous trickle of piddle, and the gaping jaws of the embankment exhaled the stench of decay. How quickly things change down here! she marvelled. The great reedy plants that thrived along the embankment seemed to have doubled in number, intertwining thin spindly branches and foliage that mushroomed upwards and outwards, an impenetrable thicket forcing its way out of every niche and cavity of the ground – a veritable army of bamboo on the march in leafy camouflage. This private colony at the bottom of the garden seemed to shrink before their relentless advance even as she watched. And yet here at the apex of the mooring a kind of slaughter of the innocents had very recently taken place. It did not escape her gaze. The war of occupation had been temporally delayed if not halted. The sappy reeds had been violently gashed and trampled. They hung limp and bedraggled like the limbs of corpses still oozing the juice of escaping life.

"Ugly! Ugly!" gasped Donna and turned away on her heels, up one ledge of the mooring, then the next. Something tinkled as if shunted sideways by her shoe, something that caught the sunlight making her bend down to retrieve it. She smiled in recognition. It was clearly one of Tony's butterfly replicas and she turned back up the garden excitedly having acquired perhaps the perfect excuse she needed to announce her presence. But as she reached the garage a sense of sudden propriety made her stop and reconsider. Perhaps he would resent being disturbed? Better maybe to try and shove the brooch under the patio door and risk him treading on it? Or should she keep it safe at home? As she weighed up her options, leaning against the little ancillary side door to the garage, a hard metallic object wedged into the nape of her neck and she let out a gasp of surprise. It was an iron padlock and she remembered now once watching Georgia's daddy open it to search out the garden chairs, which he kept with the mower in the rear of the building. All at once resolved in her strategy, she tip toed across the patio and tapped three times gently on the window. But the curtains failed to stir. Neither did the declaration of Tony's name achieve a revelation. No point in risking his anger, she considered, an alternative idea hatching in her mind. And without further delay she hurried back home to put it into operation.

"What are you looking for, Div?" challenged Sarah without turning her head from the television screen. You could get nothing past her. She had the instinct of a hawk. Donna decided on honesty.

"An envelope. Where are they?" Donna opened another drawer in the sideboard, foraged through a clutch of paper doilies and table napkins, assorted batteries and last year's Xmas cards.

"Why?"

"I need it." Donna waited for the next intrusion, wondering whether to retreat while her secret was still safe. But she got lucky.

"The bottom left, in a brown folder."

Donna dropped onto her knees and found it immediately. She looked over her shoulder as she left the living room but Sarah and Katrina remained impervious, like twin images of the Buddha, gazing into the infinity of the cathode ray tube. The soap action was hotting up. "Sarah! How do you spell 'tomorrow'?" she asked. Sarah ignored her.

"T O M OR R O W," spelled out Katrina proud to display her knowledge of the language.

Donna kept reciting all the way back up to her bedroom where she extricated the letter she had been writing and scratched the final words of her message in red crayon. It was good in that bleak hole of the evening between supper and the indeterminate return of mummy to have something tangible to keep her occupied other than her television muffled anxiety. She chose a nice picture from her drawing pad and placed it neatly folded into the envelope, then the blue tinged butterfly, carefully bending the pin flat against the body and finally the plain undecorated letter she had just written. She wrote TONI in large letters on the envelope but with her tongue already moist against the seal a seed of doubt implanted itself in her mind. Did it make sense? Would he properly understand it?

Donna extracted the letter and read it through out loud one more time to reassure herself.

dear toni I fond the butterfly next to the river I have bin misin you I wil be ther agin at 4oclock tomorrow I hop you likd the oter pitur I left from your frend donna.

She left the front door ajar, as she sneaked outside under cover of tense orchestrated film music. It was still broad daylight and the pink orange glow of an almost defunct son haloed the rooftops to the west of Mansfield Road. She ran straight to the White House, opened the gate and approached the front door as bold as brass, clutching the sealed envelope. When it had disappeared through the letter flap with a dull plop, she dallied on the path in case the reward for her vigilance might be instantly forthcoming but nobody stirred within. Not a sound, not a light betrayed the presence of the tenants and only the dispassionate façade of the lace curtained front windows seemed to witness her long, lingering retreat from the premises.

Chapter 17

When Frank woke up on Monday morning just after daybreak he rubbed his eyes, unable momentarily to remember where he was or how he had got there. Neither the bedroom, nor its contents, nor the building which contained him had any historical context in his consciousness. And yet the sensation did not correspond to amnesia. He knew who he was – at least, who he was supposed to be. Rather he felt as if some divine joker had extricated his personality during the hours of slumber and placed it inside an alien body.

Laboriously now he extricated sticky limbs from a tangle of sheets and lumbered naked across the room towards a stairwell. In the hallway that loomed before him as he groped his tentative way downstairs weird configurations and colour spots appeared to float about and pop in front of his eyes. One of them refused to dissipate – a white oblong shape indented on the tapestry of the floor, close to the front door. He knelt down, stretching a hand suspiciously towards its sharp pristine edges, afraid they might have the power to cut into his flesh. Was this an envelope? Two segments of the recognition process slid into place. Maybe he ought to open it? As his fingers picked ineptly along the paper, a blue butterfly suddenly darted out through the gash and alighted on the carpet where to Frank's amazement it remained motionless, inviting closer inspection and totally transfixing his curiosity.

When eventually he stood up the action seemed to have been occasioned by a desire to explore the rest of this bizarre environment because suddenly he caught sight of himself, as if from a distance, drawing back the living room curtains and collapsing onto a settee in front of huge French windows. In a thoughtless stupor he gazed at the magnificent incandescent sun hanging just above the adjacent roof tops. Then a secluded paradise of shrubs and trees came into focus with shards of dazzling light, bouncing and contorting into one kaleidoscopic image after another as they splattered the glass. Slowly the amnesia was beginning to wear off. A faint tinge of familiarity attached to the outline of his seeing. The world as it had come to be formed in all its awful complexity was reasserting itself. Two voices now started to converse with each other in his head and he recognised them as a memory from that reluctantly returning world. One of them was his own. The conversation had taken place many years ago in prison with Rosie, his regular visitor.

"It's quite normal, Frank. It's a survival mechanism," she was saying again. "Your brain has put your sense of who you are on a kind of autopilot. It's trying to protect you from the increasingly harsh realisation of your predicament."

"Do you mean I've gone mad? Do you mean I'm stir crazy? Is that it?"

"No but –"

"You do, don't you? It's just a fancy way of sayin' it!"

She had hesitated as if flustered then gathered her confidence and replied, "No. You've just temporarily run away from yourself. You've gone to ground like a wounded animal. Psychologically speaking, I mean. You're suffering from a kind of panic attack. Tell me, do you feel any thing else?"

"Yeah. I feel you're lying to me. I feel the screws must be secretly feedin' me some sort of happy drug to keep me tame. Ain't that it, Rosie?" He watched her shake her head and grinned to himself as he considered how poorly she thrived in her own bullshit. Dressed all in lime green, thin and stem like, she suddenly resembled a withered plant. "Thing is, Rosie, I don't care. It's all so pointless. Everythin's a bleedin' joke."

"You're distraught, Frank. That's what's causing these mood swings, these alterations in perception. It's stress. Just stay calm and it'll wear off. Honestly."

"It will!? When!?"

She took a deep breath and furrowed her brow. "Impossible to say exactly. Minutes, hours, even days if –"

"Days?!"

"This kind of dissociation can sometimes act like a fever, gradually reaching a crisis over a period of days then slowly wearing off. But it's rare. Usually we're talking a few minutes – a snapshot of time. And you can encourage the return to normal by taking a cold bath or shower."

"It's you who needs the showers not me! I am a sane man!" he heard himself retort but the words had sounded hollow even back then.

As the residue of this conversation faded in his memory Frank noticed now that the sun had cleared the roof tops and seemed to be scorching the topmost fronds of the willow tree. The windows blazoned extraordinary patterns of orange energy and he suddenly understood how three days of solitude and nervous waiting had reduced him to this state again. There were things he knew he had to attend to, things that urgently threatened his security, and yet the transfiguration of nature continued to immobilise his will power and reduce them to utter absurdities. He closed his eyes and waited for the final release to come as soon it surely must.

After a while he began to sense another presence, close up, scrutinising him with a hard remorseless stare. He opened his eyes and blinked. An animal stood right outside the French windows, fiery and glowing, its fur and massive tail an organic part of the solar corolla beyond and for one chilling moment he apprehended it as a mystic embodiment of retribution waiting to devour him. He closed his eyes again and in the streaky darkness his terror convulsed into another meaning. Maybe Rosie in her clinical diagnosis had economised with the truth to keep his morale up? Maybe he was really deranged by nature – the incurable psychopathic criminal described in right wing broadsheets of the time? And when he reopened them the apparition had vanished into thin air, as if to confirm his suspicion.

*

"You'd have to be mad to think you could get away with a robbery like that," Donna overheard one Year Six teacher confide to another as she shuffled past them into the assembly hall. "Absolutely off your rocker. I mean you can't launder gold bars like you can bank notes."

"The police reckon they know who's behind it, anyway. According to the radio today."

"Really? Have they made an arrest?"

"Not yet. But it's imminent. So they say."

After Mr Knighton had made his announcements Bronwyn came forward and said, "Good morning everybody! And what a beautiful sunny morning it is too that God has given us today. Isn't it?"

Donna loved the sound of Bronwyn's speaking voice. It had a strange lilting rhythm to it that sent shivers down her spine. She was not a classroom teacher as such. She gave advice, organised netball practices and helped out in assembly sometimes. And nobody could tell a story better than Bronwyn. Her every sentence gripped the listener, packed full of colour and drama. The story that she proceeded to tell them now was about a powerful man called Samson and a wicked lady called Delilah who drugged him with potions so that Samson's enemies could cut off his hair while he slept and thereby deprive him of his physical strength and take him prisoner.

It was a chilling tale. You could see every agonising detail of Samson's transition from handsome nobility to abject humiliation. In Donna's mind's eye he looked exactly like Tony – his black hair, his thick biceps, his broad intimidating shoulders – and she found herself loathing the woman that had so deviously bewitched him with every fibre of her body.

At the end Bronwyn concluded, "Whatever gifts we have are given by God and it is for Him alone to decide how long we can keep them."

But Donna did not understand this and as Bronwyn invited the school to close their eyes and follow her into prayer she remained puzzled and quite angry that God had so dreadfully deprived Samson while allowing his evil seductress to retain all her gifts of beauty and royal patronage.

"And finally, children, you will all have heard of the armed robbery that took place at an airport warehouse on Friday night, the containers of gold bullion that were stolen and the two injured security guards one of whom remains in a dangerously critical condition in hospital, the innocent victim of greed and brutality. Dear Father, such a shocking deed casts a long shadow over our community here. We pray earnestly for the recovery of these innocent men from their injuries; we pray for the healing of their families and friends whose mental suffering at this time is too enormous to comprehend. And we pray, too, for the speedy apprehension of the armed robbers who have perpetrated this evil act. Amen."

On the way back to her classroom Donna noticed a couple of year six girls gazing admiringly at the notice board. "That's good," one of them exclaimed. "Who is this Donna Atkinson, anyway? Should I know her?" Donna read the printed caption. *Willow Tree by Donna Atkinson*, it said as if she was famous.

After Maths when Mrs Harper had packed away her yellow satchel Donna said, "Why didn't God punish Delilah?"

"I'm sure he did. In his own time."

"But it wasn't fair. Samson was a good man. He didn't steal anything. He didn't hurt innocent people like those robbers did. Did he?"

"No. But he became a bit too big for his boots."

"My sister doesn't believe in God," mused Donna. "She says only fools believe in God."

Mrs Harper's smile never altered. "And what about your mummy? Does she believe in God, Donna?"

Donna thought for a while. "I think she used to once," she replied. "When she was young. My gran'dad does." There was a story about gran'dad and how he came to believe in God during the war but Donna was sure Mrs Harper would not be interested in hearing it. "Thanks very much for putting my picture on the wall," she said instead.

"Thank you for letting me. Donna," answered Mrs Harper." And I'm really looking forward to seeing your next one."

*

It's a lie that you eventually get used to cold showers, Frank thought to himself as he shivered through his third in as many hours. He towelled himself off and got dressed his body tingling with new found purpose. What they do is torture you back into the real world. They scatter the demons for a while. Stop the slide downhill. Rosie was right about that.

He took the mobile out of his inside jacket pocket and dialled McLeod's number just in case it might by some chance have been left open. But the line remained stubbornly dead. Then he located the regional P.L.A. number in the book and his call was answered on the third ring. "It's about the work on the Crane embankment. Where it enters the Thames," he said. "Can you tell me when you expect the waterway to be reopened?"

"Just a minute, sir. I'll check." One minute passed into two. Then three. " Hullo, sir ?"

"Yes?"

"We won't really have an idea until we receive the surveyor's full report, I'm afraid."

"When do you expect that will be?"

"By the end of the week. At the latest. If you leave me your number I'll ring you back as soon as it arrives, sir. It's Mr – ?"

"Never mind," snapped Frank and hung up.

Now he picked up Donna's note again and scrutinised it with a clear head. What do I do about this? he thought to himself. Seal up the rip in the fencing? Pretend I never received it? He opened the patio door and gazed uncertainly at the row of terraced houses, shuffling through his options, assessing the danger she might represent. She was just a half-witted kid the same age as his own daughter the last time he had seen her in the flesh. Was that why he had allowed her to stay? He bent down and examined the broken fence panelling, and realised that in his own way he had been as casual about the intrusion of the girl as Hunter had been about the monitoring of the rivers. Frank tried to piece together the couple of conversations he had with her, the words he had used to deflect and humour her. They had hardly seemed significant then. They had not mattered. Why should they have done? But now? What if he was stuck there for another week – which seemed more than likely?

What if she had shown the butterfly to someone and that someone had sniffed a rat and spoken to the police? There was only one way to find out. Four o' clock, the note said.

He went to the side door of the garage, slid the key into the rusty padlock and opened the wooden door, groping for the light switch in the dark. The neon tubes blinked twice and spluttered into life. Frank looked around. It was the first time he had been inside the garage since the small hours of Saturday morning. There they all were – the transit van, the piles of boxes, the trolley leaning against the bonnet. He lifted the lid from one of the boxes and took out a bar which he revolved slowly between his fingers. It exuded an intrinsically pure quality. The light bounced of the hard surfaces, dazzling his eyes and enflaming his imagination. So near and yet so far, he found himself thinking. So rich and yet so poor! He pondered how many of them he could usefully stuff inside his holdall and suddenly an illicit idea took root in his mind which threw up boundless shoots of temptation. Why not just simply pick up a share of the loot and walk away, jettison out of the whole stupid mess!

But after a few minutes closer inspection the idea began to wither. Where could he go with the holdall and how would he turn his assets into hard cash? He had no passport and remained utterly restricted in his movements without one, utterly helpless to further his real ambitions. He hurled the bar in disgust against the wall and made his way out of the garage, his brain seething with arguments and counter-arguments, his fingers fumbling with a padlock that stuck and resisted the pressure of his hand to consolidate it. As he made his way down to the river and installed his body in the nape of the low wall, contemplating the pit of the escape route shrunk to a bilious pebbly trickle, Frank found himself entertaining for the second time that day a serious doubt about the nature of his sanity. He suddenly seemed to be up in space looking down on himself like a spectator from the vantage point of an ethereal cinema balcony. An absurdly contrived melodrama of a film was in progress with an impenetrable cops and robbers story-line. The tiny characters below scurried and fretted and planned, heads down, with unblemished conviction in their own autonomy of purpose, apparently unaware of the invisible director who manipulated them scene by scene towards his preordained tragi-comic conclusion. Time passed slowly now. The story seemed to have got stuck in one long, tedious scene where nothing much was happening. Except that the actor who called himself Tony took a cigarette out of his pocket, lit up and smoked it. When it was finished, he smoked another. Apart from the odd water fowl, nobody came and nothing altered.

Frank perused this static performance from an imperious distance, neither bored, nor distressed. I am a merely a player in somebody else's dream, he found himself thinking as his fingers groped for yet another cigarette and watched a smile of contentment unexpectedly spread across Tony's bearded face .

*

Donna uttered a little gasp of surprise as she passed through the conifers. She had not expected him to be there, let alone reclining on the wall in baggy shorts and a T shirt. "I didn't see you come out," she announced cheerfully as she crunched across the gravel. He neither replied nor turned his head. She watched him take a long draw on his cigarette and release the smoke in two blue jets through his nostrils.

"You've bin keepin' watch on me, ave yer ?" he answered at length .

She nodded quilelessly. "From my bedroom window," she explained. "I've got a good view. My sister's jealous. Haven't you been to work today? I only got back from school a few minutes ago."

"You spend a lot of time gazin' out of your winder', do yer?"

"Quite a lot. And when I've got to be somewhere else Dawn does it for me."

Tony turned his head sharply. "Dawn?" he snapped. "Your sister?"

"No! Sarah's my sister. Dawn is my doll. Don't you remember? You said she could come here with me but I didn't bring her today because she's gone for an interview. It's for a job in a post office, I think."

"Which is your house again? The second one down from the corner?"

"Yes. No. It's the third one, I think." And she counted on her fingers. "24, 26, 28. Yes."

"Where did you find the butterfly?" Tony interrupted.

"Right here. Next to the gate."

"When?"

"Yesterday."

Tony stood up on the river side of the wall, shook his shoulders loose as if the muscles had tightened up at the top of his back and began pacing first one way then another, his expression dark and preoccupied. "Did you find any thing else?" he asked.

"No."

He suddenly bent down, grasped one of the tallest bamboo plants and with a quick movement of the arms yanked it roots and all straight out of the ground. A fat ball of earth clung to the base of the stem pitted with tiny pink tentacles. An earth grub fell out onto the concrete and was instantly dashed to a pulp beneath the sole of his shoe.

"If you've lost something else I can help you look for it," suggested Donna helpfully. She came across to the gate, gazing at him expectantly waiting for a response, her left hand resting on the section where the strut had been damaged. She felt the dart of his grey-green eyes land on her arm like a voracious bird of prey. Then he started pacing up and down the mooring once more, bulbous staff in hand, muttering drunkenly to himself as if she had ceased to exist

"Have you been drinking in the pub?" asked Donna as Tony turned on his heels for the tenth time. He hurled his spear into the river by way of reply and muttered less indistinctly now. "Pardon?" inquired Donna.

"I said what are we goin' to do about you?"

"Oh,nothing. I just like being here," said Donna innocently. "I don't particularly want to do any thing. It's a pity the water is so low."

"Yes, it is," Tony grunted. A sneer crossed his face and he resettled himself on the wall, knees bent up towards his chest as if he had suddenly decided to embark on a routine of aerobic exercises.

He is bored, Donna thought to herself. Maybe he's fed up going to work every day? "We can just talk if you like," she suggested.

Tony put his hands behind his head and closed his eyes. "Talk about what?" he said.

"Mummy's taking us to see gran'ma and gran'dad on Saturday," she offered. "They live up north in County Durham." No reply. "Have you ever been to County Durham? It's very pretty. We go there every Whitsun. Sometimes we go at Christmas. I prefer Whitsun. You can go to the beach. In the winter all you can do is stay in or go to the Metro Centre." She waited for a reply. His body had gone very still now, his eyelids unmoved by the leafy light that danced across them. Was he dropping off to sleep? The gravel crunched as she took a couple of steps closer to see. Suddenly in a movement so quick that Donna did not register it until after the deed had been accomplished Tony lashed out his left arm and grabbed her wrist.

"Did you show your sister the butterfly?" he demanded urgently.

"No. I didn't show anybody except Dawn and Sylvestra and, maybe Caroline too. I'm not sure about her. "

"They're all dolls? Right?"

"Yes."

"You never showed it to nobody else? Nobody real?" Her wrist felt as if it had been locked in a manacle. It had begun to hurt. She put her hand against his and silently contorted her features into a wincing expression. "Oh, sorry kid." He let go immediately. "I'm very proud of my butterfly collection, see. They're invaluable. I don't want the word to get about that I own them. Might encourage burglars or somethin'. Promise me you won't say a dickie bird to no one?"

"I promise," smiled Donna rubbing the blood flow back into her wrist.

"Just your secret and mine. Yeah?"

She nodded anxious to please him, privileged to be taken into his confidence. This was what real friendship was all about. She knew that from the things Sarah said about her friend's secrets, or rather from the things she refused to say about them. Being able to keep a secret was the purest currency of friendship.

"Does your sister know about me?"

"I think so. Everybody knows the white house isn't empty any more."

"I mean, did you tell her you've been in here and talked to me?"

"No! She didn't believe me!" giggled Donna.

"But you did tell her?" Yeah?"

Donna tried to remember. She did not want to tell this new friend to whom she was now bound in honour of secrecy a lie. "I just told her I had a new friend," she said, "but Sarah wouldn't believe me. She started teasing me."

"So you never said nothing else?"

"No," considered Donna. "Why should I? She never tells me anything. Not even about my daddy. She can be very mean."

"What about your mum? And your minder? Did you say anything to them about coming 'ere to see me?" Donna shook her head vigorously. She was certain of this. "But why didn't you?" persisted Tony. "You're just a kid. You couldn't just leave the house without it being noticed. How old are you, anyway?"

"Eight," she replied and shook her head again. "I just didn't." And she tried to think of the reason why. Somewhere beneath the rubble of pain and loneliness lay an answer.

"Why didn't you?"

"Because...... because they're both too busy to bother about me." There remained another broken off bit, too, deeper down, but she did not have the machinery of language to excavate it. "There's a lot of things they don't notice."

She had Tony's full attention now. Almost too much of it in fact.

He was peering so relentlessly into her eyes that she felt they were trying to consume her. Suddenly it was over. He threw his head back and emitted a deep throated scoffing noise that she could just about identify as laughter.

"That's the way it was with me when I was a kid," he said, more to himself than Donna.

"I was me own little man from the beginning!" He closed his eyes again, the muscles of his face relaxing now into a wintery smile and he lay his head back against the neighbouring wall. The tension which Donna had not properly understood until that moment drained instantly out of the atmosphere as if some invisible hand had pulled the plug on the sink containing it.

"Are you going to sleep now?" she asked.

"No, kid, I'm just remembering things." She watched him at close quarters. He seemed to enjoy remembering things, judging by the little twitching movements around his mouth and cheeks. "Are you still there kid?"

"Yes"

"What's your name again? Dawn? Is it?"

"No! Donna!"

"Donna – of course!" And suddenly he began to sing. "I had a girl, Donna was her name, since she's been gone, I've never bin the same!" His face screwed up now into a parody of lover's agony, the end words of each banal phrase long drawn out and deliberately discordant like the howl of a wolf. "Oh, I love my girl, Do -onn – onn – onna, where can you be – ee?!"

"Is that a real song?" giggled Donna gleefully. "Or did you make it up specially for me?"

"Well, I'd like to say I'd made it up specially for you – but I'd be a liar. Just popped into me 'ead from the past. I aint 'eard that song in, oh, twenty odd years. At least."

"I like it," said Donna. "Can you sing some more?"

"I can, Donna but I aint gonna. I'll 'ave all the dogs in the neighbourhood barkin' for me blood. Come here, Donna. Come here, closer!" He opened his eyes and squinted at her. "I aint gonna bite."

She moved right up next to him now, close enough to bring the black hairy patterns of his beard sharply into focus, the tufts of hair in his ear and nostrils, the dank smell of his clothes, taking care to keep her hands behind her back, one clasped inside the other.

"So you wanna be my mate, do yer – my friend?" She nodded twice. "Good. I like that idea. I do. But if we're gonna be real mates and not just, well, over the garden wall mates, foller me drift, there's got to be rules, see?"

"Rules? Like in School?"

"Yeah, sort of. But different. For a start I don't want you blabberin' about me to nobody."

"Blabberin? What's that, Tony?"

"Talkin'! Gossipin'! I hate gossip. And I won't blabber to anyone about you. I'm a very private person see? I don't want nobody to know my business. If I think they do- well, let's say, I can get very, very angry. Understood?"

Donna nodded her head, her face composed to a model of sincerity. She liked this turn of the conversation a lot. It made perfect sense. But it made her feel just a bit nervous at the same time.

"Are there any other rules?" She asked seriously.

Tony considered for a few seconds before replying. "Does anyone else know about that loose fencin?" She shook her head. "Good, well keep it that way. I ain't runnin' a recreation centre 'ere for every stray what's in the neighbour'ood. Just *you,* see? Cos you're a mate." It was an endorsement couched in terms so warmly generous that it sent a massive tingle of pleasure down Donna's spine, overflowing into the tissues of her neck and cheeks. "And if somebody's on your case – sorry, I mean if somebody's hangin' around watchin' you, either in your 'ouse or backyard and you were intendin' to come 'ere – then don't! Stay away, okay? Til the coast is clear. There's always another day. Everything comes to she who waits. Eh?" He winked.

"Okay," said Donna who had something else on her mind, something that had squatted there silently for a couple of weeks at least and was now tugging at her larynx for attention. "What if I come and you're not here? Shall I knock on the back windows like –"

She broke off because Tony was already shaking his head in dark agitation. "Never do that," he said "It'll badly disturb me, see? I'll assume it's a burglar snoopin' around. Tryin to break in to steal me butterflies and other valuables." He opened his packet of cigarettes, took the last one out and flicked the empty packet sideways into the stream.

"I can easily go back to my house," enthused Donna, seeing a simple resolution to the problem, "out on to Mansfield Road and walk round to your front door like I did yesterday."

Tony pulled the partly lit cigarette so petulantly out of his mouth that it snapped and hung in an inverted v between his nicotine strained fingers. "No front door either," he interjected emphatically. "That is if you want to be my mate of course, – if you don't –" He shrugged his free arm. "I'm no good on the 'ospitality front. Nothin' personal. Rules is rules. You still wanna be my mate, you do things the way I say, yeah?" She nodded and considered his manner, its quick unexpected shifts of mood, its jagged niceness. "You see, Donna, I'm not ever gonna be goin' round and knockin on your front door, am I?" he added with a smile. "It's only fair. Do as yer done by."

"But you can if you want!"

"Nah! Wouldn't dream of it. Yer mum don't want a git like me treadin' me hobnail boots all round her shiny spic-an-span manor! Not in a million years!" He tapped her jovially on the shoulder. "Eh, mate? Would she? A great cockney lump who can't properly speak the queen's English?! Eh, mate!"

"Can I come for tea sometimes, though?" asked Donna choking on her laughter.

"Wot? Out here in the open?"

"No! Silly!" It was like a fit. The giggles had a life of their own surging up from her stomach at the slightest hint of catching something funny in the air. "There's no kitchen out here. No 'lectricity. You couldn't boil water for a start."

"I could build a camp fire and put a pan of water on top. Like a boy scout." Tony made a silly boy scout salute and a cherubic face to accompany it. "Dib dib dib. Dob dob dob. Leaf tea or leaf tea, miss? We've got sycamore leaves and willow leaves. Oh yes and dock leaves."

"You're too big to be a boy scout," Donna howled. "You're too hairy!"

"I beg madam's pardon! Hairy? Moi? I've just had my legs waxed at Scallywags – woz it?"

"No, I don't just mean tea like a cup of tea," continued Donna fighting off the fit as best she could. "I mean cakes and sandwiches and biscuits. And I want to have them inside your house! In the living room! In front of the telly!"

She watched Tony's mouth fall open his eyes roll about and a blank imbecilic expression descend on his face. "The telly? And what exactly is a telly?" he asked.

"You know! You know!" wheezed Donna "It's –"

"No, don't tell me! I think I can get it. Just a second." He stood up and protruded the lower muscles of his abdomen so they shaped into an enormous semi-circular dome. "Is it anything like a belly?"

"No! No!" retorted Donna almost cracking up with mirth "There's one in –"

"No. I think I've got it.!" He drew in his stomach and protruded his rump at an impossibly vulgar angle. "Is it anything like a smelly?"

Donna's helpless little body shuddered and spasmed under this outrageous assault. Great hoots piped up her throat. It was worse than being tickled. "There's one in your living room" she managed at last. "In a big wooden box. Near the fireplace, you can't miss it"

"You don't mean the coal scuttle do you? Or the poker?"

"No! I mean the telly! The thing with the glass in front. It glows when you switch it on!"

"Oh that? I wondered what it was for! I 'ang me trousers over it. An' sometimes my jacket." He indicated how. "Like a coat'anger, see?"

"You're very silly," hooted Donna. "Anyway, can I please come to tea sometime?" she asked in between chortles, one slow adamant syllable after another.

"Yeah, sometime you can," said Tony suddenly relinquishing the performance as abruptly as he had assumed it. "When the place is straight."

"And when will that be? Friday?"

He sat back on the wall and rubbed his cheek with the knuckled back of a hand, aloof, waiting for the hilarity of his audience to extinguish itself in the silence. "Nah. Not that soon."

"When I come back from Durham?"

"Yeah. Okay, maybe."

It was her turn to pace around – now on one side of the conifers and then the other- frightening the sparrows, pretending to be looking for Chelsea but secretly spying on the object of her idolatry who had lapsed suddenly back into that impenetrable solitary world of his own. A jack-in-the-box with a time lock on the lid. Primed and ready to go off any second. Eventually, when nothing else happened, when her ribs had stopped hurting, she approached him and said casually. "What shall we do now, Tony?"

"I need another smoke," he muttered, "and I've run out." Then he added absent mindedly. "Do you ever go down to those shops at the bottom of your street?"

"I'm not allowed," replied Donna. "Not usually."

"Neither am I. Not any more," he mumbled to himself and picked up the broken stub, struck a match and puffed it into dwarfish life. "This'll just 'ave to do."

Donna studied him trying to suck some enjoyment out of the pathetic broken stub and felt a jab of pity. "You're a grown up," she said. "Why aren't you allowed?"

"Did I say that?" She nodded firmly. "Yeah, well wot I meant was I've torn a muscle in me leg and it wont get better unless I rest it completely."

"Where in your leg?"

Tony pointed to the hamstring area at the back of the thigh on his left leg.

"But you were walking okay just now, weren't you?"

"Well, I wasn't actually. I was in pain all the time. I shouldn't 'ave bin doin' it, that's the whole point. Keep right off yer feet, said the doc. Only walk when you absolutely have to. Otherwise the tear'll never mend." He took one last greedy finger pinching draw on the stub and hurled it into the reeds.

"Oh, I see," said Donna. It made perfect sense – the pained expression on his face as he had walked up and down, the grunts and mutterings. She had twisted her ankle once coming down some steps and her patience had been severely tested by the instruction to keep it rested at all times.

"I could go and buy a packet of cigarettes for you," she offered. "I have been down to the shops before. I'm not scared."

"That's kind of you, Donna" answered Tony shaking his head. "They won't give 'em to yer unfortunately. You 'ave to be sixteen to buy fags."

She watched him retrieve the other half of the cigarette from the ground and try to repack its tattered entrails before finally giving up in frustration. What magical properties these smoking sticks must have to reduce a grown man to such a state of irritation when his last one was broken! "I've got an idea!" she announced, suddenly darting away through the keyhole like a cat whose just spotted a field mouse. "I'll be straight back! Don't go away!"

Within seconds she had re-entered her house, sped past Katrina's back hunched over the telephone, up the rickety stairs and into her mummy's room. It was a lovely room. She had painted it herself in pastel blues and pinks, bought a caftan rug for the floor and Laura Ashley curtains for the window. There were bottles of perfume, little alabaster and wood carved boxes in which she kept her brooches and ear-rings and other treasures. It smelt of dry rose petals and lavender. Now where would she keep them? thought Donna to herself. She looked under the wide four poster bed on an impulse and found nothing but a pair of blue slippers. The pine bedside table had three drawers. One after another she opened them, craning her neck all the time towards the door. The last thing she needed now was for Sarah to blunder in on her. Where was Sarah anyway? She ought to have checked first. She had just assumed that Sarah would be in the living room watching the telly. None of the drawers contained a packet of cigarettes and to make matters worse, the last one decided it did not want to close. Donna struggled, projecting the fulcrum of her body weight now one way, now another. It could not be left open. That would be sacrilege, and in such a neat, well ordered room as obvious a sign of burglary as a broken window. Then suddenly the drawer gave up its stolid resistance and collapsed inwards with a sharp thud. Nearby somebody coughed twice and a door opened with a creak across the landing.

Donna in a fit of panic instinctively threw herself on the floor along the side of the bed which was hidden from the door. The pad of feet approached close up now then stopped. She held her breath, knowing her sister stood there, eight feet away, on the threshold of the room, peering in. Ten long seconds passed before the feet began to move again but this time in the opposite direction, along the landing – pad, pad, pad – away down the stairs and dissolving into the furry silence of the house. Very quietly she resumed the search.

The cigarettes were stacked at the bottom of Mummy's wardrobe, camouflaged by the hem of a deep indigo blue evening dress. Eight cellophane unwrapped packets, all smooth and silky to the touch. Donna had pre-supposed she would find perhaps an open packet and take a couple of cigarettes which would never be missed but here was a veritable trove of unwrapped treasure and she hesitated to break clumsily into it. So after a few moments consultation with her conscience she picked up a whole packet, placed it carefully inside the rim of her knickers and tip-toed furtively out of the room after carefully eliminating all evidence of her intrusion.

Katrina, telephone receiver in hand, still bound on the wheel of her private tragedy, barely registered the minx-eyed little figure flitting past her. Tony too, had not shifted his position. He slouched against the junction of the wall, self-contained, almost statuesque, presiding over the river like a daylight incubus. "I'm sorry I took so long," panted Donna producing her prize from its hiding place without any coyness. "Are these alright?"

"What?! A whole packet?! Whose are they?!"

"My Mummy's."

"Didn't no-one see you take 'em?"

"No. I found loads of them in her bedroom."

"But she'll miss it"

"No she won't. She only smokes about five a week."

"Five packets? Take it back, she's bound to notice."

"No, silly! Five cigarettes! She's told me."

"I 'ope yer right, Cesca," chuckled Tony ripping into the packet with practised fingers. "There's clearly more to you than meets the eye. You could just be the saviour of my sanity. Help me stay on the straight and narrow."

Donna watched the tension seep out of his face as he filled his lungs with smoke, holding it to the count of three before exhaling into the sunshine and she shared his pleasure all the more happily because she had been the creator of it. "Donna," she corrected.

"What?"

"My name. You called me something else!"

Tony pointed two fingers at his head and exploded a consonant in the back of his throat as he pulled the imaginary trigger. A bird fluttered out of the conifers. "Have the eggs hatched out?" she asked.

"I reckon. Your cat keeps chasin' the parents."

"Please will you lift me up to see the chicks?"

"Another time, okay? I'm just nicely relaxed now"

"Okay," agreed Donna reluctantly. "I like that name. Chesca? Was it? Is it short for anything?" She noticed Tony's eyes suddenly cloud over with a kind of sadness. At least he did not reply and she wondered if he wanted her to go away and leave him in peace. She decided on one last ploy. "The grass is getting long," she remarked. "You know there's a cutting thing in the garage, don't you? I can help you do it, if you like."

"You've bin in there, 'ave yer?" guffawed Tony and he discarded a long filament of ash. "Silly question! You're just about the busiest little girl I ever met – apart from one! Go on now. Yer gonna be missed."

"I'll come back tomorrow. After school," announced Donna, emboldened by his demeanour. "Oh, unless you'll be late home from work?" And she thought about his injury. "Are you going? With your legs?"

"No, I'm staying home with my legs. They've bin given time off for good behaviour," Tony replied and she looked on in amazement as his body rocked with laughter as he if he had just cracked the funniest joke in the whole wide world.

*

Dinner had not long been eaten when the living room door unexpectedly opened like an intrusion on the three of them, huddled around a television soap opera. "It's mummy!" spluttered Donna.

"Hasn't anyone got any homework to do?" asked mummy catching her youngest daughter in her arms. "Sarah? Can I check your day book schedule please?"

"You're back early!?" said Donna.

"I took a couple of hours off and went up to Kings Cross to buy the railway tickets."

"To Durham? We're going by train?!" Mummy nodded. "Wowee! Sarah? We're going by train! I won't get sick, will I? I won't get cramp in my legs! Oh, thanks mummy! Love you mummy!"

Sarah condescended to half turn her head now, spotting a possible opportunity in her mother's good humour. "Can I take Friday afternoon off school to get ready?" she asked.

"Certainly not," snapped mummy and turned to Katrina who

had stood up immediately and begun collecting a few personal things together. "How did the interview go?"

Katrina grimaced extravagantly. "Not very well. I was so nervous – I kept stumbling over my words. They did not receive your reference yet either."

"They didn't? That's strange. I definitely sent it last week. When are they going to let you know?"

"By the weekend they said. They're going to interview another three applicants."

"Mum. Did you buy a newspaper today?" cut in Sarah.

"Yes. But I'd prefer you to get on with your homework than read that."

"Actually, I can't do my homework without it. We've got a sociology project on the influence of the media."

"Oh. It's in my bag. Here."

Sarah took the bag and pulled out a scrunched up copy of the Daily Mail with a self-righteous sneer on her face. "Tha-ank you," she said ironically.

"Sarah? Who will look after us, if Katrina goes to work in the post office?" asked Donna later in the still darkness of her bedroom. It had just been invaded by the apparition of her sister. "Sarah?"

"What?"

"I said –"

"She won't go to work in the post office, Div. She's just pressuring mum for a pay rise. She's too thick to be offered the job and too foreign."

"Oh? Is she?"

"Yeah. She's only got a temporary visa. She's an alien."

"Oh? Will she be going back to her own country soon?"

"Yeah. To stand trial for her war crimes, I hope, like the rest of her family. Now leave me alone. I want to go to sleep."

Chapter 18

The last Friday before Whitsun Donna found her morning English lesson unusually interesting. Was it, she wondered, because she had so much to look forward to at the moment? There was a special phrase for this feeling and she had learnt it quite recently. What was it? She began to thumb through the pages of her vocabulary exercise book. Miss Frobisher had been talking about one of her favourite films, all about a man who was condemned to live through the same day again and again, a prisoner in time. She was making it sound really funny. Suddenly she stopped talking in her narrative voice and said dryly, "Are you listening, Donna?"

"Yes, miss,"

"What were my last words then?"

"Don't know, miss." A couple of boys tittered and Donna felt the heat rushing to the surface of her face.

"Well close your exercise book, please, and try to listen a bit harder. Now then, where was I?"

A thicket of arms shot up. "Yes, Clarissa?"

"You were saying about how Phil stole the groundhog and drove off with it in a car, miss, and the Police were chasing him."

After she had finished telling the story Miss Frobisher invited somebody to volunteer to talk about a film they had seen recently and enjoyed. Donna noticed that the same eager hands shot up and the same sullen eyes widened in panic. "Can't we have somebody who hasn't contributed for a long time?" implored Miss Frobisher menacingly over the heads of her zealous acolytes and the wide eyes began collectively scrutinising their table tops praying for an invisible shield to descend and protect them from further tyranny. But Donna knew she would not be chosen against her will. It had not happened for ages. A sort of unspoken agreement had been formulated between them. She did not understand why exactly. It might have something to do with Mrs Harper. So as the badgering and disaffection continued Donna slyly reopened her vocabulary book to look for the phrase. Where was it now? It was a very pretty phrase. She liked it a lot, and today, if she could only remember, would be a perfect day to use it.

Bit by bit the contributions began to dribble out. First Beccy described a shrill giggly version of the Little Princess, then Colin added a few words about Aladdin, and finally Ivan tackled E.T.

"Yes, very good Ivan," announced Miss Frobisher. "The children regarded E.T. as a friend. They saw the good qualities in him, the warmth and intelligence. But the grown ups were scared of him. They just saw an ugly wrinkled alien." Ivan grinned from ear to ear with sheer relief. "Can anyone explain what an alien is?" asked Miss Frobisher, writing the word on the board in bold capital letters.

Donna looked up from her exercise book, alerted. She knew this. She had only recently heard it at home. "Anybody?" repeated Miss Frobisher hopefully. Donna raised her hand uncertainly to the half-mast position and was about to withdraw it again when the teacher noticed. "Yes, Donna?" she smiled encouragingly.

"Is it somebody who-?" She stopped. Her mouth suddenly dry with the heat of thirty pairs of probing eyes.

"Carry on, Donna. Don't worry about being wrong. You're the only one brave enough to try."

"Is it somebody who comes from another country? Where a war is?"

"Yes! It can very well be," explained Miss Frobiser. "That's excellent. Well done! E.T. actually came from another planet – but it amounts to the same thing."

Vastly emboldened by this praise Donna added, "My child minder is an alien," and felt her heart crumple into tiny mortified pieces as a serpent of laughter wriggled round the room.

"I beg your pardon, Harry," chided Miss Frobisher to the smirking head of the beast. "Have you something intelligent to say for once?"

It was a tactical mistake. Harry refused to be intimidated into the remorse his teacher had anticipated. "I said, 'her daddy was an aborigine and her minder is an alien', Miss," retorted the boy to Donna,s further anguish. "What's wrong with that?"

After that Miss Frobisher quickly settled everybody into doing what she called "free expression composition," meaning that you could write down in your English exercise book anything you wanted to. A poem. A conversation. A story. There was absolutely no limit. "Just go with the flow of your imagination," she explained. "Ask yourself the question 'what am I really burning to say?' and put it down on the paper." For the majority of the children this acted like a starting pistol on a sprinter. They were heads down and out of their blocks almost instantly. "If you don't feel there's anything you're burning to say," added the teacher a few minutes later for the habitual pencil suckers, "I suggest you describe a film you've seen recently, or, maybe a friendship that is important to you. Okay?"

To Donna this was a red rag being waved at a bull. She charged at the blank open page with her nib so ferociously that it broke and had to be impatiently restored. "I hav a secrat friend he makes me laff a lot. He live in the wite hose, this week I hav seen him for times in a row" she wrote. "His nam is caled t...."

It was not until she had written the T in Tony and was beginning the O that she remembered her promise. She stopped writing and clasped her hand to her mouth like someone in a state of awful real-isation. Miss Frobisher noticed immediately.

"What's the matter, Donna?" she asked walking over to Donna's table. "You've got a face like someone whose just burnt the Sunday roast. Can I see?"

Donna covered the exercise book with her arms and leant for-ward across the table. "It's all wrong, miss. I'll start again."

"Oh, I'm sure it isn't. Your writing is lovely these days. Let me see?" Donna did not move. Her face was on fire. Her body quaked. She felt like a fox cornered by hounds. "Come on now. You have to be prepared to learn from your mistakes –"

In a movement so agile that it could have had no premeditated origin in thought, Donna ripped the offending page straight out of the book, crumpled it into a ball and pelted out of the class-room. By the time the startled teacher had caught up with Donna in the toilets she had scarcely flushed it down the bowl and was sitting above the scene of her offence, ashen faced, awaiting her punishment. Her eyes filled at the first sight of Miss Frobisher bearing down on her and the tears followed in great rivers down her cheeks.

"It's alright, Donna. It was entirely my fault," consoled Miss Frobisher bending down to her pupil. "I'm really very sorry." And nothing more was said about the matter, neither that day nor any subsequently.

*

Frank could not remember the last time he had seen a downpour like it. He stood at the bedroom window fish-eyed with wonder watching the bombardment, bolts of electricity fracturing the black mid-afternoon sky. Something had settled in his lower chest like mild indigestion although he had not eaten for several hours. What was it? The image of Francesca formed in his mind, then the image of Donna. For a second the images fused together as if they were the same person and Frank knew simultaneously the cause of the discomfort. This foul weather would prohibit Donna from coming today, and the instant he realised it Frank's solitude hardened into a composite lump of pain. So when the mobile suddenly rang he fastened onto it like a leech in need of life blood.

"I'm sorry I haven't been able to ring before now –"

"It's bin a week! I've bin tryin' to reach you on the phone!"

"I warned you not to. I have to keep the thing switched off," replied McLeod nonchalantly.

"Have to? Have to? I don't get it! Why is it all one way!?"

"You know why. Security. And it's more imperative than ever now. "

"But –"

"Drop it. I said drop it. I haven't got time to argue. All the omens are good. Don't spoil them."

Frank felt suddenly speechless, whether with rage or relief it was impossible to distinguish. Only now that it had been delivered a temporary escape hatch did he realise how grossly inflated his brain had become with tension. "What have you bin doing wi' yourself ?" asked McLeod into the void. "Tell me. You still there?"

The answer forced itself out of Frank's throat like a series of quips. "Oh, a spot of gardening, mate. A few hours baby sittin'. I've found meself a girlfriend –"

"Lay off the sarcasm. Have you seen anyone, son?"

"Like who?"

"Uniform, of course. Has anyone bin snooping around the neighbourhood?"

"Impossible to judge. I aint bin out once."

"Good. Keep it like that. Nobody been to the door then?"

Frank hesitated, wondering whether to confide about the girl. But why should he? That situation had previously been discussed and the kid represented no real risk. She could be managed on the terms already agreed between them. Besides he could never explain to a man like McLeod what the kid's visits had meant to him. How they broke up the tedium. Kept him from losing his trolley altogether. And how easy they were to contain. "Not a soul," he said. "Tell me about the cabin cruiser. When's Hunt –" He corrected himself. "When's our friend gonna be bringin it in?"

"He isn't. I'm handling the job myself now. The bad news is the river's going to stay closed for at least another three weeks –"

"What?!"

"Could be longer. Depends on the weather."

"Find another way out then! Forget the river. I'm puttin' 'alf a dozen bars in me bag tomorrow and walkin' unless –"

"There's no other way, son. You've got to keep your bottle. The uniforms are chasing up blind alleys. In three weeks time the trail will be stone cold. Our friend's cock-up is working to our advantage. Think about it."

Frank thought about it and said, "Bring me some cash then. I'm short. And my passport, too."

"You'll get cash in the post but –"

"Why can't you bring it in person?"

"I can't risk it at the minute. Sorry."

There could only be one reason for McLeod's caution. "They've got a tab on you!" exclaimed Frank in realisation. "They're watchin' you, aint they? That's it. I'm walking. Right now –"

"Look son, if you walk, you probably wont last a week," insisted McLeod with cool equanimity. "They'll pick you up. It isn't just me they've got a tab on. Half the ex cons in the country are under suspicion. Stay in the house. If you run short of grub use that Paki shop but only after hours."

"So what if they do pick me up? They can't pin anything. They can't make one and one add up to thirty-two, can they?"

"They can ask you why you haven't been reporting to your probation," McLeod reminded him pointedly. "Sleep on it. You're bound to feel better in the morning. Believe me, all the main omens are good." And the line went dead.

Frank put the mobile back inside his pocket and resumed his scrutiny of the deluge, the prematurely darkening sky, the willow flailing and beaten into imminent submission.

*

There was no question of a secret meeting this evening, Donna reflected. Tony would never venture out in a thunderstorm. "It's just not right," she expounded to her dolls. "Why can't the rain fall at night when everybody's asleep?"

Sylvestra could not fathom the reason, neither could Dawn from her perch on the window ledge. If God was really in control, pondered Donna aloud, why didn't he organise the weather to fit in better with the habits of his people? Why couldn't every day be cloudless and sunny? How much more cheerful everyone would be! It was such a simple thing to arrange. Dawn agreed and Donna decided to consult Mrs Harper about the matter after the holidays. She was bound to have an opinion. Perhaps even an influence with the deity?

Soon she settled down to some drawing, beginning with the willow tree, it's magnificent green tresses sodden to the conical roots but totally unbowed by the onslaught of nature, the grey morbid backdrop of cloud only serving to intensify its phosphorescent glow and defiance. Skipping effortlessly from one sheet to another, describing first from nature, then from memory, touching lightly, amending constantly, uncomplicated and thoughtless, pursuing her sense of delight and instinct for form. When Katrina summoned her to supper two hours had passed in an instant. Her stomach appeared to have forgotten how to feel empty connected as it had been to an invisible fuel pipe of creativity.

"What is the matter? Aren't you hungry today?" complained Katrina peevishly. "Have you been secretly eating sweets again?"

After supper she helped Donna pack her holiday bag upstairs and explained that mummy would not be home before ten. Sarah had already packed hers. Donna caught up with her sister, installed in front of the television screen watching the news, replete with note pad and pencil, scribbling furiously.

"Sarah, can we watch -?"

"Shut up! I missed that!"

A man with a flat northern accent and combed sideways black hair was answering questions.

"All we're going to do, Martin, is ask the regional water companies to meet agreed annual targets for reducing piped water loss. If it means a few fat cats cutting down on their bonuses, what's wrong with that?" and his chubby face dissolved into a Mr. Blobby kind of smile.

The newscaster, unimpressed, turned over a fresh sheet of paper and launched into another topic. "Sarah –?" asked Donna.

"Shhhh!"

"In the wake of the news that Britain is now the world's seventh most flourishing economy, sharply improving its competitiveness in the last year and now outranking the rest of the E.U. countries....."

None of it made the remotest sense to Donna. It might just as well have been Katrina talking on the phone to her family back home. She noticed how all the people being interviewed seemed to positively shine with smug contentment and well-being. The programme presenter alone had not caught the charismatic disease but if the parade went on much longer surely he must succumb too?

"... Meanwhile, the Prime Minister, Mr. Blair, appears to be using the worldwide interest in Labour's landslide election victory to advance Britain's agenda overseas as long as his government's honeymoon lasts. Downing Street officials are preparing for President Clinton's visit," he ploughed on and the screen began exhibiting more images of confident, beaming, handshaking men and women. The only one Donna recognised was the Prime Minister himself.

"Honeymoon? Honeymoon?" Donna salivated the word on her tongue. She thought she knew what it meant, but the newscaster's usage did not make sense.

"Mr. Clinton is said to feel a trifle envious of the massive powers the British Constitution confers on the Prime Minister with a 179-seat Commons majority and will be keen to discuss the mechanics of New Labour's triumph which owes some debts..... "

"Sarah?"

"Not now."

"....a day of mutual congratulation and razzamatazz mixed with hard nosed politics. The President was the first foreign leader to congratulate Mr. Blair, describing him as an exciting and able man..."

Donna knew how important her sister's homework project must be. It was all part of mummy's ultimatum thing. She wandered out and came back, patiently nursing her curiosity, and was about to wander out again to where Katrina stood jabbering dementedly on the kitchen telephone when the newscaster said, "Father of three, Raymond Lensbury, who was brutally attacked by masked robbers during the gold bullion raid near Heathrow last week, died in hospital this morning." Pictures of buildings, and desolate faces, and a white transit van followed in quick succession and then a man in a dark blue uniform began to answer the newscaster's questions. Donna eyed her sister, head bowed over the pad, the pace of her writing hand never slackening.

"We now have reason to believe a second van was used. An identical transit," said the policeman. "And we are requesting people who live in the Thames Valley area, particularly Maidenhead, Slough and Oxford to be particularly vigilant."

"Do your men have any positive leads yet, Chief Superintendent?" asked the newscaster. There was a short pause and Sarah stopped writing to look up at the screen.

"I am not at liberty to say but you can take it from me these murderers will be caught," contested the Chief Superintendent through thin tight lips. "It is only a matter of time."

"That means you aint got a clue, pal!" scoffed Sarah and resumed her writing.

The news did not seem to want to end. But end it eventually did. When Donna wandered in for the fourth time the screen displayed a map of the British Isles, pitted with drawings of clouds and lightning flashes.

"Look at that lot on the way, Div!" moaned Sarah. "Won't be much of a holiday, will it?"

"Sarah? What's a honeymoon mean?"

"It's a holiday people have after they've just got married."

"Did the Prime Min-man have a honeymoon?"

"I suppose so"

"Did mummy and daddy?"

"How should I know? I wasn't around at the time."

"Sarah? What did da – ?"

"No more now! I'm busy!" exclaimed Sarah, her lips trembling suddenly. "I've got to write my notes up!" She switched the television to another channel and dispatched the remote onto the sofa. "You sit and watch this garbage. I'm going to my room. And I don't want to be disturbed again! Understand?"

That night Donna fell asleep while speculating about her mummy and daddy on their honeymoon holiday together and these thoughts quickly became transfigured into the texture of a dream. The familiar beach with the white sand and the surf and the mass of palm trees. The beach loungers with mummy in a pretty bikini, hair tied back, her tanned pretty face blissfully happy and the man she loved beside her, clasping her hands as if he never wanted to let them go. In the romantic story which ensued, sometimes her daddy's face belonged to the Prime Minister, sometimes to her best friend Tony, and sometimes to nobody at all. It was the first dream narrative of the night and was quickly swallowed up by the prolific weave and weft of sequels that flowered from its roots.

Chapter 19

The train journey to Durham passed off uneventfully for Donna, if a trifle too slowly. The family found themselves sharing a table with a dapper young man dressed in blue corduroy who described himself as a musician and kept dropping the names of the famous singers he knew. Donna felt he was trying to impress her sister who, made up to the nines and sporting a tight fitting open necked top, could easily have been mistaken for a 20 year old.

She spotted gran'dad well before the train had crunched to a halt on the Viaduct high platform of Durham Station. He looked like a bald eagle perched on top of a metal luggage trolley, knuckled fists like talons clasped to the handle as if he was afraid somebody might try to steal it from him.

"This is a surprise!" smiled mummy as they approached him. "We were going to take a taxi, dad"

"I 'ad to pop in the Toon Hall about soomthin', lass," he smiled back. "It weren't a problem."

Gran'dad wore a jerkin with leather patches on the shoulders and peered at his grandchildren through thick lenses, unsure how to greet them. "Kiss your gran'dad," ordered mummy to resolve the awkwardness, and he bent a weather beaten pate down to Donna. She shyly offered up her cheek to white whiskery topped lips. His face felt bristly and she shivered a little under the embrace.

"Who's this? One of those cat walk supermodels?" said gran'dad pretending not to recognise Sarah. "What you been feedin' her, lass? Spinach and bean sprouts?"

Sarah hugged him without hesitation. She looked flattered and relaxed to be in his company and stood exactly the same height. It was amazing to all of them to realise how much she had grown in a year.

The drive due west of the city to the village of Waterhouses took about 25 minutes. Donna found herself wondering out loud how a place as small as Durham could be called a city at all, the way the houses surrendered so quickly to the great rolling hills of the countryside. The road twisted and turned along with the conversation, mummy skilfully providing gran'dad with questions enabling him to display his pride in the local community and repair the damage that she knew a year's absence would do in the memory of at least the younger of his grand daughters.

As usual the two sisters were invited to share the same peachy frilly bedroom and Donna was amazed that Sarah failed to raise her usual graceless objections. Sarah seemed in a very happy mood. Indeed, Donna had noticed, it seemed as if some heavy burden had been lifted off her sister's shoulders the moment she had alighted from the train and that phrase Donna had been unable to recall during the final English lesson magically came back to her now precipitated by this wondrous transformation in Sarah's behaviour. Sarah was looking at life "through rose coloured spectacles." The brooding, short-tempered, spiteful side of her personality had apparently taken a holiday, too, and left Sarah in peace!

"Which bed do you prefer to sleep in, darling?" Sarah asked affectionately, the first night. And "Do you need an extra blanket? In case it gets cold in the night? Do you? I'll get it, dear, no problem."

Everything was "Donna dear" and "darling" and not once did Donna feel the sting of those poison-tipped nicknames. The whole stock had been abandoned somewhere down the track of Durham.

It was great fun just rediscovering the nooks and crannies of the three bed roomed house, fingering all the brash clay figurines and ancient trinkets and framed photographs. Gran'dad never failed to remind them how he had built the place himself in his younger days between the villages of Esh Winning and Waterhouses where his father had worked in the coal pit, how the colliery had been shut down the year England won the world cup with two Geordies in the team, how badly the local community had suffered. Nor did he tire of showing them once again all his special places. The gaping holes. The rusting pieces of machinery. The derelict co-op warehouse. The still trim terraces of colliery cottages. The red brick chapel where he and gran'ma worshipped religiously every Good Friday – and Christmas Day, too, hangover permitting! Wherever they went Sarah prompted gran'dad with the same polite questions she asked every year, and everyone they met on the streets smiled and had the time of day to chat to them.

They had married in 1957 when he was 32 and gran'ma barely 20. Neither came from a religious family but gran'dad had become converted during the war, the final year of which he had spent on active service. The story still amazed Donna. Gran'dad had killed a German soldier with a bayonet knife in the stomach. A few days afterwards he claimed to have met a celestial being who forgave him and blessed his life in the name of Jesus Christ. Mummy explained this away to Donna as an hallucination brought on by guilt feelings, but to this day, gran'dad insisted the experience really happened and would merely smile knowingly to himself if anybody tried to tease him about it.

As for gran'ma, the sisters agreed, she was putting on a lot of weight. She walked with a bit of a hobble due to something she called varicose veins. She sported the same bright lacquered hairstyle as ever, though, and never missed a Friday visit to the posh city shop to keep it properly groomed.

"They once used gran'ma's head to light up the Women's Institute during a power cut, you know" joked mummy not for the first time to her daughters.

Donna thought that her mummy did not take either of her parents very seriously the way she teased them and mentioned it to Sarah who strongly disagreed. One evening Sarah was invited to go with them both for the first time ever to a W.I. meeting and reported back later with hilarious descriptions of a draughty corrugated hut, pock marked with buckets in case of rainfall, a totally inept demonstration of origami making, silly party games and a so-called gourmet French cuisine served on tacky paper plates with plastic cutlery. Donna had laughed so much at her sister's colourful description that mummy had burst into the bedroom to tell them off for fighting when they ought to be sleeping.

There were special outings almost every day and the weather stayed improbably fine while, according to the meteorologists satellite maps, the lows continued to centre on the southern counties. They romped on a duney beach in Northumberland, rode enormous chestnut brown horses at a nearby stables, went to a concert performed by the Esh Winning brass band in which an increasingly purple – faced gran'-dad played the trombone, and made their annual pilgrimage to the Metro Centre in Gateshead where mummy liked to stock up on her wardrobe with clothing and knick-knacks that cost half the price she paid in London. Donna was given spending money which she used to buy a male companion doll to add to her collection.

"Have you given him a name yet, lassie?" asked gran'dad later when she paraded her treasure. They were watching the news at the time.

"He's called Tony."

"Jus' like the man o' the moment, eh?" grinned gran'dad.

Donna did not understand until he pointed to the screen which was transmitting pictures of the prime minister with the president and their respective wives.

"Oh? He's Tony, too, isn't he?"

"Ay, lass! There's only one Tony Blair! He lives jus' doon the rood in Sedgefield."

"I thought he lived in London?"

"Ay he does an' all, Donna. But his real home is oop 'ere with us – his constituency. Come 'ere and I'll tell yer somethin'." She sat on gran'dad's knee now to watch the rest of the news while he rattled on with tales about street parties and other spontaneous demonstrations of joy that took place on election night and the days that followed it. "There's not bin a feelin' like it since the war ended, lass. Eighteen years of blight an' greed finished! Eighteen years of listenin' to them fat sleazy polecats peddlin their lies to the people –"

"Hark at him trying to indoctrinate his grandaughter," remarked gran'ma laying out the supper things. "It were a Labour government who closed down yonder colliery, Fred. Don't forget to tell 'er that."

"And it were the making' o' me, weren't it?" chirped back gran'-dad who had retrained in the aftermath as a landscape gardener.

"If you want my opinion, –" said gran'ma.

"I don't actually," grinned gran'dad mischievously.

"If you want my opinion that lad's hypnotised the whole bloody country into believin' they're going to get somethin' for nothin'" continued gran'ma undaunted. "All he's done is stolen the other lot's clothes an' relabelled them, lass. Mark me there'll be disappointment ahead. I give it a year at most before people start waking up to the truth."

"People aren't hypnotised –"

"Oh, no? Day dreaming with their eyes open? What else can you call it Fred?"

"Are you having an argument?" asked Donna with growing anxiety.

"Course not lass!" smiled grandad tickling her suddenly in the ribs. "This is a discussion. At one time it used to be as regular with us as movin' our bowels –"

"Disgustin', Fred! What will the child think of you?"

Sarah, who had not been listening at first, began to laugh quietly to herself. Donna's eyes flickered from one person to another, utterly confused now and directionless.

"You do politics at school, Sarah, don't you?" asked gran'dad.

"Sort of"

"What do you think of the feller?"

"He's alright, I suppose," considered Sarah. "Everybody seems to like him, even Mrs Crosby voted for him and she always supported the Conservatives before."

"That's because she knows a Conservative when she sees one," chimed in gran'ma, "even if he calls himself by another name."

"No, that's because she needs to believe in somethin'" said gran'-dad, "and she'd find it impossible to believe in the other lot. There was nothin' there, lass." He seemed to be addressing himself directly to Sarah now. "There 'adn't bin for years. It was like looking into a black hole. The Tories allowed a massive void to grow in the political consciousness of the country and they never realised it. That's why they lost so heavily. If it hadn't bin Blair it would have bin somebody else with a penneth of nouse."

Mummy, who had arrived carrying a pot of tea in time to catch the rest of this, observed dryly, "Most of Blair's manifesto policies are unworkable. They can't be resourced. I heard you saying so yourself to Bernie, dad! Last year."

Gran'dad sighed deeply. "Unworkable or not, lass. It doesn't matter. The fact is most people believe in those policies. They're like signs pointing back to the real world. Folk can safely get on with their lives again, confident like. Eh? We feel we know where we're going now – which we didn't before – and this bloke Blair has provided us with a map and a route planner."

"And here endeth the lesson!" mocked gran'ma with a shrug of final indifference. "Supper is served. Come along now, lasses."

Home baked bread and cakes were never in short supply. One day when mummy and Sarah were weeding the borders, Donna found gran'ma and gran'dad in the kitchen, preparing sandwiches for afternoon tea. "You've got lots of photos of us," she remarked. "I was wondering, er –?"

"Wondering what, lass?"

"I was wondering why you haven't got one of my daddy?" She waited but neither of them seemed to hear. "Mummy hasn't got one either."

"Pain. That's why!" snapped Gran'ma suddenly. "He led her a right song and dance, and she never found out the worst til after –"

"Elsie! Don't!" interrupted gran'dad. "What's got into you?"

Donna stared abashed at gran'ma's back bent over the work surface. "Well, it's true, Fred."

"I don't care," said gran'dad and turned to Donna with a smile. "Can you take this plate of butties outside on the patio table, lass, and tell your mum to pack up 'cos the grub's ready? Ta, love."

Donna obligingly took the plate and hurried out through the living room but a voice raised in anger behind her made her hesitate in the hallway. She listened and crept quietly back towards the kitchen.

"He was a philanderer, Fred. A lying two-faced philanderer," she heard. "And the girl's entitled to know what her mother had to put up with!"

"But you're not entitled to tell her, Elsie. That's up to Margaret. Let sleeping dogs lie, I say."

That night in bed Donna struggled to remember the word. "Sarah? What's a Filler?"

"What, darling?"

"Fill something, Fill-under?"

Sarah giggled. "Search me. Fill-under? Where did you hear it?"

Donna hesitated, wondering whether to bring daddy into it. But Sarah was in such an angelic mood and she decided not to risk contaminating it, so she said only, "I think it's someone who sings and dances, is it?" Sarah's giggles expanded into prolonged gales of laughter and within seconds Donna felt her body helplessly joining in.

The day before their departure was a Saturday and Donna could not help contemplate it with pangs of regret that felt like indigestion. She knew they must have shown on her face because after breakfast, mummy took her aside and warned, "Don't play up when we leave, Donna. I don't want a big weepy scene again."

"Alright then," muttered Donna and bit her lip. Her heart wanted to stay in County Durham, close to all those lovely people and countryside and most of all her grandparents but she did not dare to say it in case the tears began. Mummy did not like tears. And if mummy became angry she might always refuse to bring them back again.

"You're not a baby, Donna. Stop moping," she scolded. "You're old enough to recognise when you feel sorry for yourself and control it. Now off you go with gran'dad. He's waiting with Sarah in the car to take you to the old vicarage."

The vicarage no longer belonged to the church but had been recently purchased by a couple of retired teachers along with the adjacent gardens and meadow. To Donna it seemed like a stately home and park. As gran'dad took them on a leisurely ramble round the estate he explained his own involvement in the landscaping project. By turns they threw pebbles into the ornamental pond, sniffed aromatic herbs, chased baby rabbits through the long grass and played badminton on the lawn. The air so sweet and intoxicating. The views so expansive and soothing. It was as if for a couple of hours they had alighted in Heaven. At lunchtime they were summoned into a high ceilinged kitchen, all pine and polished copper, and were served bowls of vegetable soup with wedges of country fresh bread and goats cheese. The bantering affable conversation encircled them like a gentle hug.

"So what did you like best about our garden?" asked the bearded man who was called Ed.

"I liked that tree, the one with all the butterflies in it," confessed Donna eagerly.

"Oh yes. That's called a Buddleia. Butterflies love it. It's the purplish blossom that seems to attract them."

"I've got a friend who makes butterflies," said Donna thoughtlessly and Sarah emitted a good natured snort of laughter. "Not real ones," she added defensively. "They don't fly. You can wear them." And suddenly she bit her tongue with shame as she remembered the promise that she had been on the verge of breaking.

"We've been reading about that big robbery that happened near where you live," consoled Ed's wife tactfully. "Forty million pounds worth they got away with!"

"Forty-two," corrected Sarah smugly.

"Anyway, the police have made some sort of breakthrough in their investigation. According to the lunchtime news one of the robbers has been arrested. Would you like to see the music room?"

The sisters could not contain their enthusiasm. Ed ushered them through and left them to explore at will. The room contained several string and wind instruments but Sarah made a beeline for the polished grand piano by the window and instantly began the entertainment with a repertoire which included two fingered versions of 'Green Onions' and 'The Grand Old Duke of York'. Donna reclined full length on the chaise longue and politely applauded during natural breaks in the recital. When they returned to the kitchen, Donna was instantly struck by the animated atmosphere. The three adults had a newspaper wide open on the table and were trading long complicated sentences punctuated frequently by howls of derision and laughter.

"Come on, darling, let's go and play badminton again," suggested Sarah leading the way out into the garden. "Isn't Durham an amazing place? Even the rich people here vote Labour!"

*

The inter-city train back to London was less than half full when it pulled into Durham station and they had a section of carriage virtually to themselves. Sarah was very quiet and kept to herself. She had been all morning, too, remaining aloof from the ritual panic of packing and farewells until it was absolutely necessary to join in. Something had begun to change in her. While Mummy and Donna played cards at a table comfortably designed to seat four, Sarah remained unsociable across the passageway, her face in a book. The train made stops in Darlington, Northallerton and York and was accelerating towards Doncaster before the subject that had really been consuming Donna's thoughts discovered a voice.

"When are we coming again, mummy?"

"Next Whitsun, dear, I expect, as usual."

"But a year takes ages." No reply. "Why can't we come sooner?" Donna looked across the gangway to see if she could elicit support from her sister but the look was not returned.

"It's expensive, for one thing, and it's tiring. Not just for me, I mean, on a journey like this, but for your grandparents too, having three of us on their hands."

"But gran'ma said she loves having us around? It makes her feel young again?"

"Shall we play blackjack again Donna? Or do you prefer rummy?"

"Rummy." The cards were dealt and the first moves made in silence. "Why don't we all go and live in Durham mummy?"

"Two of hearts discarded? Are you sure? You've just seen me pick up the three."

"Yes. I don't want it."

"Very well then, – your turn."

"Why, mummy? We could buy a house. We wouldn't have to stay at gran'ma's."

Donna picked up the jack of clubs and matched it against the ten and eight of the same suit. "Is it because of Keith?" she asked incautiously. Mummy did not reply. "Is it?"

"Not really. You're holding eight cards"

"Oh, sorry." Donna discarded a black four.

"Why then?" she persisted, feeling the tight-knot of mummy's secrecy beginning to loosen a little against the weight of curiosity

"I lived there for the first eighteen years of my life, Donna. Nothing much goes on. It's boring for young people. I couldn't wait to leave. I wanted to go to a really big city and train as an actress. I've got rummy by the way." She displayed her hand, a red flush and three fours.

"But you're not an actress now, are you?" said Donna, suddenly aware that the double image of Sarah's reflected face in the opposite window had stopped reading and was now seriously absorbed in a study of the landscape.

"No, but I like London."

"Why, mummy?"

"You are full of questions, aren't you? Well – I like the shops and the cinemas and I suppose I like not being known. In Waterhouses everybody knows everybody else's business. It's like living in a goldfish bowl."

Later as the train raced through the Midlands, mummy gave the children money to spend on drinks and snacks in the buffet. They stood unspeaking, rocking in a queue for five minutes, then Sarah ordered coca colas, crisps and Maltesers which they took to a vacant table and began avidly to consume.

"What was mummy saying to you before?" asked Sarah coldly.

Donna did not understand. "About what?"

"About Durham? Weren't you asking her if we could go and live there?"

"She said – she said it was like living in a goldfish bowl!" replied Donna, laughing at the silliness of the image, and instead of joining in, her sister's close up oval face darkened menacingly. "What does that mean, Sarah? Is it bad?"

Sarah tossed her head back defiantly, a thin bitter smile playing on her lips. "What do you think, Div?" she replied. "It means we are going to be stuck in the smoke for the rest of our lives. Give me some of your crisps. I'm hungry." And she snatched the packet out of Donna's hands.

It had taken half a day, and 150 miles of railway track, but the transition was now complete.

At Kings Cross they quickly procured a luggage trolley and set off across the station concourse towards the underground escalator. "Isn't this where the fire happened?" whined Donna, anxiously clutching at her mummy's jacket hem. On the final leg of the journey from Northampton Sarah had found entertainment by painting her sister's imagination with infernal scenes of smoking tunnels and burning bodies. "Is it safe to go down there?" She refused at first to step onto the moving staircase and Sarah was inveigled into making a special return journey unaccompanied to disprove her own malicious theory of disaster.

"See, not so much as a charred mark," she sneered as her head veered suddenly over the ascending escalator parapet.

The Heathrow Piccadilly tube rattled its way across London and at Hounslow East they alighted stiffly into the late afternoon sunshine and found a taxi whose driver could only manage a few words of pigeon English. Donna soon began to recognise the landmarks of her neighbourhood, consuming every mundane detail with the relief of an Arctic explorer returning from a transcontinental treck. The Newsagent's, the off-licence, the butcher's shop – all standing glassy eyed and straight to attention, like a personal guard of honour as the taxi turned into Mansfield Road. Then the hump backed bridge over the river, suppurating in the haze like a swollen boil any second about to burst.

"Look, there's Sidney!" gasped Donna, as the driver angled his cab obediently into a prescribed space, "and Chelsea too! Just look at him, Sarah!"

The tortoiseshell moggy reclined on the bonnet of Sidney's red ford in a nonchalant stupor of satisfaction while Sidney polished the carriage work that enthroned him. It was impossible not to exchange pleasantries given the situation of the vehicle right next to their home.

"Your girls look as if they've caught the sun," said Sidney as Donna stroked the cat. "Where have you bin? Tenerife?" Mummy told him and he stroked his grey head in exaggerated disbelief. "This is the first time we've seen it. Rain, rain and more rain. What a week! And Chelsea went missin' for three days to top it all."

"Where did he go?" asked Donna alerted.

"No idea. I was beginnin' to think he must have bin run over. Then yesterday ev'nin' I'm watchin' the telly and hear the cat flap shudder. His fur was all tattered as if he'd bin dragged by the tail along a barbed wire fence. And hungry! He gobbled two tins of cat food straight off!"

"Oh, poor Chelsea!" cooed Donna gently caressing the languid animal. "Did you get lost then, you poor dear pussy?"

"And the only other thing you've missed is the police."

"How do you mean?" asked mummy.

"They've bin round, knockin' at all the doors. Two of them. It's about that bullion robbery at Heathrow."

"Oh yes, I heard about an arrest. But do they think the gang might live around here!? Surely not?"

Sidney shrugged. "Search me what they think. They were pretty tight lipped. They were askin' who lived here, what we were doin' on the night of the robbery, whether we saw or heard anythin' unusual. That sort of thing."

"And did you?"

"Course I never, and neither did no-one else. I need me shut-eye. 'What do you take me for', I says to them, 'a bloody barn owl?' I think they're just clutchin' at straws. The villains'll be long gone by now, not 'angin' round south Middlesex waitin' for Plod to knock on the door. Seen today's Mirror?"

"No, what's in it?"

"A four page special on the robbery. Very carefully planned it was. I'll lend it you if you like," said Sidney turning towards his front door.

"Oh, please don't go to any trouble, Sidney."

"No trouble, Margaret. Just a tick."

Mummy unlocked her own front door impatiently and instructed Sarah to take in the luggage. "Come on, Div, give me a bloody hand," she ordered, instantly transferring her mother's impatience in the direction of her cat – doting sister.

"Can I take Chelsea home to play with, please, Sidney?" implored Donna as their jaunty little neighbour reappeared carrying the newspaper.

"No problem. Just be careful how you handle him," warned Sidney. "He's still a bit tender in the underbelly region." Donna picked up the animal very carefully and gently. He twitched his head a couple of times and flexed his claws ready to strike the instant the pain was inflicted. But Donna expertly rolled him onto his back, avoiding the scarred area, and cradled him into her arms like a baby.

"Come along, Chelsea don't be frightened," she exhorted carrying him towards the front door. "All your family are dying to see you upstairs."

"Alright, is it?" Sidney asked mummy.

"Thanks," she nodded with a sudden rush of gratitude as she realised that Donna had acquired the perfect parachute she needed to bring her safely back down to the ground.

Chapter 20

I wish I had brought him a present back from Durham, Donna thought to herself as she crawled through the fence after school on Monday. The curtains were shut and so she walked around the garage towards the garden. It was bad manners to turn up empty handed to see your friend after you had been on holiday. But this reservation instantly evaporated as Donna's eyes plunged into the greenery of the lawn and the splendid seclusion of her special space. The smell of grass filled her nostrils. It had been recently mown and bristled under foot. The borders looked neater too and on closer inspection she realised the worst patches of weeds had been dug up. Several little shrubs were now clearly identifiable, floating like islands in a sea of finely raked soil, and rose bushes close to full pink and red bloom. These were all positive signs even though Tony himself was not around. He must certainly have recovered from his injury and gone back to work. A green plastic sun lounger had been set up in a corner of the lawn. It extended towards the willow tree and she quickly surrendered to the urge to try it out. She lay there like a lady of leisure listening to the deep throated calling of unseen wood pigeons waiting for her Sir Galahad to arrive home on his white charger and serenade her with funny stories and songs. After a while, however, her conscience intervened and she knew that she ought to return home before someone missed her. Later, she decided. I'll try and creep back later. How exciting all this subterfuge was! Stealthily she sneaked back through the fence and into her home without further ado, totally unnoticed.

Sarah sat curled up in front of the early evening television news. "Sarah? Will you be sleeping in my room tonight?" Donna asked.

"Ssssh!"

Donna dropped onto the beanbag. "The man held in custody since Friday and thought to be a suspect in the Heathrow gold bullion robbery was unconditionally released today" she heard.

"Sarah?"

"Belt up, Div! I'm listening!"

There was a programme on another channel she wanted to watch. Why did Sarah always have to monopolise the box?

"And are we to understand that Henry Challinor has now been eliminated from police enquiries, Chief Superintendent?" the newsreader was suddenly demanding.

"I think that's a reasonable assumption to make," replied another man stiffly.

"Then why did you need to hold him so long? The public perception is that you are as far away now from apprehending the gang than you have ever been. How do you respond to the criticism?"

"By reiterating that I have every confidence in my colleagues. They're working round the clock. Leaving no stone unturned. Several lines of enquiry have been established as a result of the interviews with Mr. Challinor and these are being vigorously pursued even as we speak."

*

"The police have said that several vital new lines of inquiry have been instigated as a result of the interviews with Mr Challinor and further arrests are imminent. Now for the sport...."

Frank's eyes jerked open, his right hand spasmed towards the radio switch – killing the voice instantly – but the message continued to pulse through his nervous system like an electric current.

Since the news about Challinor's arrest had first broken, Frank had been tortured by indecision, unsure whether to run or stay put until instructions arrived from McLeod. But for ten days now the Scotsman's sole communication had been by post, a package stuffed with banknotes. As the pressure intensified, sleep had become virtually impossible. Whenever sheer physical fatigue forced his eyes to close, a kind of delirium set in and Frank would see the film of his live flowing before him in disjointed episodes. Brilliantly clear images bombarding the retina of his imagination in random and often repetitive order. Out of control, faster and faster crowding his brain as if they intended the whole of Frank's experience to become present in a single animated moment of time. As if they intended to suffocate him in their overwhelming intensity. The past, the present and the future all enjoined together in a terrible fever of retribution.

Suddenly he felt his body jerk into an upright position as if it had independently made a decision to act and Frank began gulping for fresh air, gripped by the compulsion to escape. Every fibre of his flesh demanded it. Go! Move! Before it is too late! He felt his legs thrashing about, landing on solid ground, stumbling down the stairs. He felt his hands picking up his jacket and stuffing the pockets with whatever objects lay within the proximity of his panic – stricken departure, insensible now to everything but the front door crashing closed behind him and the urgency of pure movement.

*

Donna pressed button 4 on the remote and the television instantly flared with canned laughter. Sarah tucked her legs under her buttocks and discarded her notepad. Donna knew Sarah had wanted to watch the sitcom, too, because "Friends" was one of her favourite shows. She just wanted to be awkward first. "Thanks," acknowledged Donna momentarily turning her head away from the screen. Through the window a familiar profile came into view, no more than a few yards away, marching along the pavement. She emitted an involuntary gasp of surprise and scrambled to her feet.

"Who is it?" asked Sarah vaguely alerted.

"No-one" insisted Donna and walked out of the room, intent on catching up with him. But as she opened the front door Katrina emerged from the kitchen.

"I'm just putting the supper on the table, Donna," she said. "Can you come now with Sarah?"

"Er, yes, okay," stammered Donna. She closed the door and waited til Katrina had gone back into the kitchen before making her move. Quick as a flash she was out onto the pavement, peering down the road towards the hump backed bridge. "Tony!" she shouted. "Tony! Wait for me!" and began to skip after him. But he was walking really fast and did not seem to hear. As she hesitated wondering how expedient it was to give chase, the decision was made for her by a brusque voice behind.

"What do you think you're doing, Div! Didn't you hear? Supper's ready! Who's that anyway?"

Donna turned on her heals indifferently and shrugged off the question as best she could. Tony's unresponsive receding figure was too far away to matter now.

"I thought it was Sidney," she muttered and led the sprint back into the house.

*

Frank had no destination in mind as he walked. He had nothing in his mind. Neither seeing nor hearing, the act of walking comprised the totality of his being. At some stage a distant roar like an aeroplane in flight appeared on the edge of the exterior world that encompassed him and it stuck like a semaphore, signalling to his numb brain across the void and gradually growing louder and louder until the roar was all around, behind him and in front of him. Like blood surging through the veins of his temples and magnified a thousand times. Suddenly he was sensible again.

He stopped and blinked in each detail of the scene confronting him with the astonishment of a blind man who has miraculously regained his sight. The turquoise belt of river. The exploding waterfalls and weirs. The barrage walkway splitting a hundred metre length of water before it doglegged via a rectangular arch and bit into the opposite embankment. Lifebuoys lodged at regular intervals along the weir winked at him like bloodshot eyeballs. A man walking a white mongrel along the towpath towards him from the opposite direction. A grey predatory heron, sharp and still as a steel sculpture. The word 'DANGER' in bold capitals at the zenith of the arch.

"This is where the tide ends," he realised. "This is where they apply the brakes. Teddington Lock!" He had been there once with Sue but the place had hardly changed. His body suddenly felt gutted with the effort of walking what must have been a good four miles.

A wooden fence hung like a low washing line closely guarding the river. He ducked under it and flopped down on the slope of the bank, inhaling the spume, which stuffed his nostrils with salt-sweet memories of that day long gone by. Sue had been three month's pregnant with Francesca and they were living in a one bed roomed council flat in Tower Hamlets. As he closed his eyes a fever of nostalgia flooded into his heart, joyful at first but accompanied by an increasingly violent undertow of despair. Once again he saw them taking the slow train from Waterloo, walking down Teddington High Street, past the mock gothic church with its flying buttresses, crossing the river bridge and strolling like the pair of carefree lovers that they were back upstream along the Surrey towpath. Once again they boarded the little ferryboat at Ham wharf and landed at Marble Hill Park where they discovered a quaint little café, converted from stables, and bought high tea. What a perfect day it had been! But every detail, every word and glance remembered felt like a knife being shoved between Frank's ribs as he understood with renewed clarity how badly he had betrayed the trust of his beloved family and blighted his life. The stark truth reared up before him – the devious way he had kept his criminal activities a secret from Sue, all those after hours scams which had grown bolder in conception as time passed and his underworld contacts increased. He had chosen to assume that she knew – after all, he had rationalised, how else could they have afforded to buy a five bedroom home in Lewisham on a mere lighterman's wage? But Sue had guessed nothing. Frank's arrest and trial for armed robbery had been a hammer blow. And now as he relived again her shock and humiliation, Frank's dream of reconciliation became depleted of all credibility. He was a self-deceiving fool, a total waster. He had nothing to live for. It was time to let go. And this conclusion reached, Frank felt his body offer no further resistance. It slid limply into the water, submerged, and quickly became caught by the powerful current.

*

Donna picked up her blue rubber dolphin and slipped into the warm sudsy bath that Katrina had prepared while the children ate supper. "Katrina, do you think mummy really loves Keith?" she asked.

"I don't know. She spends a lot of time with him. This is the second evening in a row."

"Sarah says he's divor- divorc-?"

"Divorced. Yes, and he has got two children just about your ages, I think."

"Katrina?"

"What?"

"What are war crimes?"

Donna noticed her minder's eyelashes begin to flutter.

"Why do you ask me?" demanded Katrina

"Sarah says they happened in your country. War crimes. Does it mean killing people? Or stealing their money? Or what?"

Katrina pursed her lips and marched to the window where she pulled the blind so abruptly closed, Donna thought it had ripped. "They collaborated with the Nazis. They killed many of our people," she said. "That's okay. Yes? Long time ago. Everybody is supposed to forget and to forgive. My people stood side by side with the allies. Through thick and thin. These judges in The Hague forget that too...." And the sentence trailed off in her own language.

Donna understood nothing of the reply apart from the solitary idea of killing. "Did you kill someone?" she asked perplexed.

"Me!? Course not me! Soap yourself all over now and put all these silly thoughts out of your mind. I'm going to speak to Sarah about this."

"But why do people in your country kill each other? I don't understand?"

"'Course you don't. You are a child," snapped Katrina. "Let me tell you these are not people, they are animals. Worse than animals. They are infected. What do you do with an animal who has a disease and wanders all over your land spreading it? Eh? Tell me!" Donna shook her head totally bewildered by the outburst. "You put it down, of course. You kill it. For your own safety. Got your shampoo there? Don't forget to use it." And she scurried out of the bathroom.

Donna closed her eyes and slid down deeper into the water, guiding her dolphin through imaginary waves. Within seconds she saw herself swimming with a whole school of them through a beautiful coral sea.

*

The river seemed bottomless to Frank, the water amazingly clear. Small silver fish and eels seemed to dance all around him. Showers of bubbles and auras of colour delighted his eyes. If this was the journey into oblivion, his only regret was that he had delayed it so long. Then, out of the depths, two large shapes began to materialise, human swimmers moving towards him with effortless grace and serenity. He recognised them as Sue and Francesca. They were speaking to him telepathically and he could hear their exhortations perfectly. But how could this be? Were they dead, too?

"Go back, daddy! We forgive you!" called Francesca.

"Swim back to shore! We're waiting for you in Australia! Everything's going to work out," urged Sue. "We need you!"

"I don't deserve forgiveness. I deserve to be dead," Frank answered. "I've gone mad with remorse. Isn't it too late, anyway?"

"No!" Sue had approached so close now that Frank could see every pore on her face. "And you're not mad. You're upset. It'll pass like a fever. Be patient. Remember, we need you. Go back now. I love you, Franco!"

Obediently Frank twisted his body through a semicircle and opened the blades of his arms for the first time, pumping and powering his limbs through the growing turbulence, inch by inch, now floundering, now defying the physical suction of the weir, until his face finally broke the surface and gasping in huge lungfuls of air he galvanised the remnants of strength he had left to paddle his way to the bank and drag himself out.

"Is everythin' okay, mate?" This was a male voice, urgent and repetitive. Frank craned his neck upwards and opened his eyes on a world drastically altered. A man with a small white dog on a leash a few yards back on the towpath.

"Meanin' me? Course it is!" Frank grinned back manically. "I aint mad! They've forgiven me!"

"That post you're leanin' on isn't safe," warned the stranger, "and the embankment's eroding. A kid fell in from just about there a couple of month's back and cracked his skull on the sluice gates. They found his body a few days later. Floated up to Chiswick Eyot."

"Couldn't you see? I'm a strong swimmer" said Frank and closed his eyes in an attempt to eclipse this rash of pedestrian anxiety which had allied itself now to a shrill ringing sound.

"That may be," was the reply he heard, spoken slowly as if to a simpleton. "All the same it'd be a pity to slip in and get your clothes wet, wouldn't it? It's not exactly drying weather this evenin'. Well, aren't you going to answer it?"

"What?"

"That phone? In your pocket, isn't it?"

Frank watched the man tug his dog's leash and walk away shaking his head in disbelief. His hand found the mobile in the inside pocket of his jacket. How had it got there? How long had it been active? And why were his clothes dry? He pressed the 'okay' switch and waited, bewildered, for a voice to be discharged.

"Where have you been?" it demanded irately.

"Nowhere," he answered remotely and suddenly his mind was back in the river but this time struggling to comprehend how such a vivid experience could not have been real.

"Well then?" demanded McLeod.

"Well what?" Frank muttered.

"I said, have you heard the news about H.C.?...Hello?"

"H.C? What's that?"

"What's got into you? Did you receive the money?"

"The money? Yes. Is that you, McLeod?"

"Of course it is!"

"What about Challinor? Has he told them everythin'?"

"'Course not. He's bin solid as a rock. They've had to let him go."

"Go where?"

"Are you pissed?! Where are you?"

"On the river bank."

"Good. Make sure you stay there. Don't allow their broadcasts to spook you. It's all flannel. They're digging in the dark, and don't break cover. That's what they want. One of us to get spooked. They havn't' got nothing – except a file of old lags. I'll ring again when it's safe, and go easy on the booze!"

The phone went dead. "They're diggin' in the dark," Frank kept jabbering to himself as he ambled back down the towpath the way he had come. "They haven't got nothin' except a file of old lags." The words were the anchor, keeping his feet firmly planted on the ground, while, somewhere miles above, his imagination strained and tugged for its freedom like a sail in a storm.

*

How long she had been asleep, Donna had no idea. It felt like a long time. Right away she knew the noise that had woken her up was not part of a dream. "Don't look at me! Just don't look at me! Please!" her sister begged pathetically again and again as if her life depended on it.

Donna groped for her torch, leaned far across the edge of the top bunk and shone the beam downwards where it found Sarah's contorted face. The eyelids remained tight shut and she was evidently fast asleep but possessed by some awful nightmare. Donna turned away and killed the light, unsure what to do. She could not bear to watch or listen. Whatever demons of the dark had penetrated Sarah's dormant consciousness they appeared to be slowly torturing the life out of her.

Chapter 21

The flood tide peaked at 5.44 on Tuesday evening. Donna knew this because she had asked Mrs Harper, and the kindly teacher had looked it up in the staff room newspaper. If work permitted, Tony would surely be out to watch it. She sat next to Sarah in the rear of the car concocting a strategy.

"Sarah? What homework have you got tonight?" asked Katrina. Sarah pretended not to hear. The question was repeated with ice on top.

"History and Maths," sneered Sarah.

"Donna?"

"We've got a test on Friday, all about Australia," Donna replied in a wheedling tone. "I'm supposed to be revising for that. Do I have to?"

"Yes, your mummy asked me to ask you. She'll be home before 7 tonight."

"Whenever," said Sarah with utter indifference.

"What've you got there?" asked Donna pointing to a video cassette in her sister's hands.

"Some stupid history crap I'm supposed to watch." Donna thought she noticed Katrina's eyes flicker with hostility in the rear view mirror. "You'd better not have any ideas about the telly, Div. I'm going to play this Wars of the Roses tape as soon as I get in. Get it out of the way."

Donna could not believe her luck. "Oh alright then," she pretended to complain, "but don't be long."

"I'll be as long as I like," gloated Sarah maliciously.

Donna knew he was down there as soon as she reached the end of the garage, even though she could not see him. Somebody else was there, too, behind the conifers. She could distinctly hear talking and laughing. Her feet hesitated, then halted halfway across the lawn. Suddenly she had lost confidence in the privilege of her access. Mr Brown must have come back home, she realised. Who else could Tony be chatting to? And he *was* chatting – she could make out most of his words now – and going at it fifteen to the dozen, too! It would be really rude to interrupt, wouldn't it? And she posed this question to her latest doll acquisition who was being specially honoured to receive his first tour of the estate. Let's just listen for a while, his smile seemed to infer, and together they edged closer.

"Nah, nah. I don't wanna disturb you in any way at all. I just want you to know I'm totally at your service....What? Ha, ha, ha! Nice one! Manservant! Yeah. Think of me as your unpaid manservant. I don't want nothin' back in return.......Nah, there's no catch. I don't even need to live with you. I mean, it'd be nice, eventually, of course, but you mustn't feel any pressure...."

Mr Brown must have a sore throat or something, Donna thought to herself. I can't hear anything he's saying. Her doll companion looked perplexed too, and silently encouraged her to move right up close to the keyhole where the solitary figure of Tony appeared, strutting about as if he was rehearsing a speech.

"I'm truly sorry – truly, madly, deeply sorry for all the hurt I've given you and Francesca," he said with deep feeling and then hesitated as if correcting himself. "Is that over the top? Madly, deeply? Yeah. S'pose it is....Er? Okay, then." He cleared his throat and began again like an actor attempting new lines. "If in the course of time you can find it in your heart to love me again I'd be the most grateful man whoever drew breath..... God! I'm sorry, I'm so bad with words!....What? Ha, ha, ho! Yeah, you're right there, Cesca. It's so beautiful 'ere in Australia, innit? So much space and sunshine..... Course you did the right thing!....What?......I dunno yet. Money aint such a problem. Maybe I'll breed kangaroos and koalas on a farm....ha, ha..."

He stropped in mid laugh and turned abruptly peering back through the keyhole. Donna gave a little gasp of dismay. She was too slow to avoid detection, too fascinated. "I'm sorry," she whimpered. Her voice tailed off in discomfort. "Shall I go away?"

But Tony did not answer and she saw him properly now, face on. His eyes were strangely enlarged and seemed to be about to bulge out of his face. His mouth hung wide open biting on thin air. He looked a real sight with his unwashed hair and scraggly beard, his baggy shorts and earth-stained tee shirt.

"Is Mr. Brown there?" she asked uncertainly. "I don't want to disturb you."

"Mr Brown? Why should he be 'ere?" answered Tony in a more sinister voice and approached closer, his gaze suddenly consuming hers with animosity. "Did you say Mr. Brown?"

192

Donna could clearly see now there was nobody else behind the conifers, that is unless they had jumped into the river. "You were talking to yourself, you were," Donna blurted out nervously.

"Was I? Fancy that! Am I talkin' to myself now?"

Donna giggled with relief. Tony was in a good mood after all. "Course not, silly! You're talking to me!" she exclaimed. She felt Tony's index finger prod her twice in the ribs and giggled even louder. "You've done it before, you have!"

"I'll 'ave to be more careful. What was I saying?"

"Things. Names. You should know. You were saying them!"

"They say talkin' to yerself is the first sign of madness. Do you know what the second sign is?"

"No," giggled Donna, rising to the game.

"Allowin' strange little kids like you to wander into your garden and listen."

She watched Tony walk past her towards the sun lounger and then settle down on to it without a second look back. "Where did this come from?" she asked following after him. "This bed thing?"

"I made it, of course," he replied with his eyes closed.

"Did you!" Donna exclaimed in admiration and then on instant reflection realised that the construction of garden furniture must be a simple task to a man who could create butterflies with his fingers.

"I made it come out of the garage," he added and she watched a hairy smile form on his lips. "I've missed you," he said as an afterthought.

"I've missed you, too. You've been doing a lot of gardening while I was away, haven't you?"

"Yeah. Keeps my mind occupied."

"It's all neat and pretty now." His smile did not alter. He seemed to be thinking about something especially nice. Maybe about life in Australia? "Is that why you're in such a good mood?"

"The fever's almost blown over now. I think I've turned the corner. Come out of the tunnel"

"Oh?" said Donna wondering which tunnel he meant. The only ones she knew were underground tunnels. "Did your train get stuck in a tunnel on the way back from the butterfly factory?" she opined.

"I saw some people I really love yesterday and it's made all the difference," Tony mused. "But fer them I'd have signed off. No question. One of them's a little girl, not much different from you." He opened his eyes and shielded them from the glare of the sun. "She was so real, Donna. As real as you are standin' there. Er, you are real, aren't yer? Let me feel again. Yeah!"

This time Donna felt his fingers tickling her ribs and flinched backwards with a volley of giggles. But his words continued to puzzle her. "Does she live in Australia?" she asked and Tony nodded. "But you can't have seen her yesterday. It takes a long time to get to Australia – at least a day, and I saw you walking past my house!"

"Let's just say she visited me then. In my head," grinned Tony mysteriously. "In my dreams, if you like. Like a premonition. And she's given me hope. I aint gonna quit. See?"

"Oh?" replied Donna who did not see at all. A long silence ensued before she added, "I dream about you sometimes."

"Do you? I'm flattered."

"What's she like?"

"Who?"

"Fran-chesca?"

"She's got her mother's eyes and skin colouring and she's very sweet – like you. I'm going to see her properly soon." He stopped talking abruptly and blinked twice in the sunlight. "How did you know her name?"

"You said it," smiled Donna. "Don't you remember? Sometimes you say 'Chesca' – is she, er –?"

"What? I need to be more careful," he muttered.

"Your daughter?"

"You promise not to tell anyone these things, don't you? I mean I told you before – I don't like no-one knowin' my business. I can trust you, can't I?" Donna felt herself hesitate. She wanted to say yes, but she knew it was not entirely the truth. Tony lent forward in his seat now, his face becoming stern. "You have done already, ain't you?" he demanded. "Tell me!"

"No! Honest. Only sometimes –" She hestated.

"What? Go on!"

"Sometimes I nearly forget. It starts to come out and........"

"And what?"

Donna shook her head. She did not want to make him angry. "I don't let it."

"Sure?" he demanded and she nodded her head. "I need to think about this," he muttered and lapsed into silence as he slouched back down again and closed his eyelids.

"I'm going to look at the river," Donna said after a bit, but Tony may as well have fallen asleep for all his reaction. The ebb had been underway for twenty minutes or more and the wet tide mark on the concrete embankment showed a band several inches in height. Very slowly and in as much scientific detail as she could muster, Donna explained the tidal cycle to her companion. Then she pointed out landmarks along the riverside, the place in the conifers where the hedge-sparrows nested, cat-pooh corner, a timid pair of mallards and even the obscured hump-backed bridge that straddled

Mansfield Road and might become visible for the doll if she held him at arms length out across the dark brown water. "Can you spot it, Tony? It's all made of bricks and shaped like an arch...No? Shall I stretch further then? ....How's that?" Her feet were now at the very edge of the mooring, teetering.

"That's dangerous!"

A massive hand clasped her arm. Had she been about to slip? It was impossible to tell the order of events. Certainly one foot had buckled. "Why did you do that?" she gasped in surprise.

The real Tony guffawed. "That's what I'm wondering myself," he said. "Lettin' you drown would 'ave solved one of me problems, at least!" He let her go and turned away to sit on the wall, muttering something to himself that sounded like, "A dotty little kid who talks to her dolls! Who in the world's gonna take notice of anythin' she says anyway!"

Donna walked up to him deliberately affronted and challenged, "Were you talking about me!?" His hand descended on her head and she felt a lovely warm inner glow as he ruffled her hair.

"Whose your pal?" he smiled. "Your fergettin' your etiquette, aint yer, Donna. Nobody's introduced us yet."

"Tony", she announced with a giggle as she held him aloft like an Olympic torch in both hands. "This is Tony. He's from Sed.... Sedge...? Er, he's from the Metro Centre."

"Pleased to meet you, Tony," said Tony with a stiff little bow. "Welcome to my manor. What's he, er, do? I mean fer a livin'?"

"He's the prime minister" said Donna proudly.

"I thought as much."

"I was wondering if...." Donna hesitated.

"If what?"

"If you were named after him or something? I mean because he's famous. There's a boy in my class called Michael who was named after Michael Jackson. Honest. And I was named after my dad. He was called Don. So I became Donna. Gettit?" She waited for an answer but all she received in return was the controlled curious scrutiny of his grey green eyes.

"I saw another grey heron this morning," he remarked at length. "Standin' just here."

"What's a heron, Tony?"

"It's a wadin' bird," he explained. "Got legs like knittin' needles. I think it's tryin' to build a nest in that tree." He nodded towards the willow. "Talk about popular though. There must be a two year waitin' list to get in there."

"Can't it make a nest on the ground? I mean if all the trees are full?" asked Donna guilelessly.

"'Course not. It'll be gobbled up for breakfast." Donna felt her gauge rise at the horrible thought. "Look! There goes another applicant!" exclaimed Tony. A beautifully proportioned bird with a proud head and blue and white colouring to its wings spurted across the river from the roof of the timber gardening hut, swerved, arched and came to a dead halt on a low branch where it settled as discreetly as a sapphire ear-ring. "So, tell me about your holidays then?" he asked settling himself on the wall and lighting a cigarette. She needed no second invitation. It poured out of her system, an incontinence of anecdotes washing over Tony who listened with the equanimity of a tired child at bedtime, occasionally damming the progress of the flood with a terse question or correction.

"Buddleia! Not Buddha, kid. That's a God. Budd-lee-ha. There's one at the other end of the garden. Aint you noticed?"

"No."

"And you an artist!"

When the ebb had settled to a pebbly trickle and her throat had dried up, Donna lapsed into silence. She waited for something more from Tony, but it did not come. Somewhere along the line his eyes had closed. His head become angled spastically against his right shoulder. Surely he could not have fallen asleep, draped as he was along that narrow concrete ledge? She walked along the mooring and foraged about with a stick among the bamboo reeds, now an impenetable phalanx of sky- scratching warriors and still multiplying. She felt peaceful herself and yet oddly incomplete. There was something else she wanted from Tony in addition to his attention. Gradually, cautiously she inched her way back towards his prone body, all the time trying to summon her courage to say what she felt. But the words that now formed in her head were simply unsayable. She wanted Tony to touch her again.

"I'm not mad. I've got to be patient," he suddenly began to mutter. "Everythin's goin' to work out. I'm gonna make it. I have to. They need me."

"Are you talking to me?" The question hung over him unanswered. "Did you say something to me?" Donna persisted.

His eyes remained closed. "Carry on kid, I like listening to you," he mumbled eventually.

"You seem very tired, and I'm tired too," she yawned. "Sarah woke me up twice last night. The second time I couldn't get back to sleep." Tony seemed to mouth a response, which was consumed in the courtship rhapsody of the wood pigeons. She lowered her head to his face.

"I never did any of it for myself, Sue," she seemed to hear. "I did it for us. It was stupid, I know that. If only I could put back the clock. If yer don't want the money give it away. It's no use to me. It's you I want." And the rest of it trailed away into gibberish.

"I think I'll take Tony back home now," Donna said. There was clearly no point in staying despite the protestations to the opposite. "Shall I come again tomorrow?" More mumbled nonsense followed. "I said shall I -?"

"Yeah! Why not? I'm not goin' anywhere. Not yet, Cesca. For a few days, anyway. I'll be 'ere."

"Donna!" she corrected with a giggle, but he made no reply.

"Bye!" she chirped, skipping off up the lawn, content with her discontent. Whatever unspeakable manifestations of affection her body craved could easily wait another 24 hours. She had almost passed the garage before she recalled his mention of a buddleia bush. Her skip faltered. Where could it be? she considered, gazing all around. A low lying plant with vaguely obscene tuberous branches and prickly leaves attracted her attention. Was that the buddleia? Surely not, unless they bred a stunted, non-flowering species in the south? Thin spindly tentacles of a vine clung to the walls of the garage. Opposite stood the gnarled ancient tree which guarded access to the patio. Her eyes followed the twisting trunk vertically upwards now for the first time. It divided and sub-divided into serpents' bodies, all thinly serrated and rutted with age. Beyond them were the lilac – tipped spears she finally recognised as buddleia branches. And amazingly there were dozens of butterflies, orange ones and white ones all caught up in a dance of adulation around the tips. As she craned her neck to the sky, totally entranced, one of them spiralled drunkenly downwards and settled on her shoulder in the exact place Tony wore his broaches. It seemed to look at her but as she moved her left hand slowly to cup it, the butterfly took off and capriciously hovered around her head before waltzing way up to the highest branches and rejoining the others.

"Where've you been?" snarled Sarah who was peeling ice into a tumbler of coca cola as Donna entered the kitchen.

"Only in the garden."

"No, you weren't. I've just come in from there."

"And then in the ginnel," extemporised Donna with affronted invention. "I was looking for Chelsea."

"No, you weren't. I would've heard you!"

"Yes I was!" replied Donna insolently imitating her sister's tone of voice. "I went into Sidney's garden the back way. See!" and she flounced sarcastically out towards the stairwell amazed at the extent of her own cunning.

Chapter 22

"Guess what? We're having a sports day!" announced Donna as she climbed into her car after school on Wednesday wafting a bulletin, which Sarah snatched instantly out of her hand. "Will you come and watch me, Sarah? There'll be prizes and – what else, Sarah? Read it out!"

"A parents race and – Ha! Ha! Ha!" tittered Sarah maliciously. "A raffle! The first prize is an Olympic running vest autographed by Linford Christie. Ha! Ha! Ha! What's the second? One of his old jock straps. Ha! Ha!"

"This isn't the way home, Katrina!" exclaimed Donna as the car veered right into the main dual carriageway and sped across the river.

"It is Sarah's day to see Dr. Williamson. Have you forgotten?"

"But – but I want to go home! There's something I have to do!" complained Donna. She had begun three new drawings during her break times and wanted to share them with Tony.

"Yeah, why not Katrina?" chimed in Sarah. "Do a U turn right there. It's no skin off your nose if I miss one measly appointment".

"It's not my nose I'm worried about. It is my job. I cannot afford to lose it."

"Really? I thought you were all set to work at the post-office."

"They turned me down, finally."

"'Course they did," Sarah muttered under her breath. "Silly of me to ask."

"What?!"

"Nothing."

The consultation lasted a tedious forty-five minutes during which Donna occupied herself improving her drawings, particularly the portrait of Tony. "Whose that? Frankenstein's monster?" sneered Sarah as she rejoined them in the waiting annex. Donna ignored the affront. "Don't you want to know what I talked to the shrink about, Div?" Sarah taunted as they drove home.

"No."

"Just as well. I wasn't going to tell you."

"I know what you were talking about, anyway."

Sarah bristled. "You're full of shit."

"You were talking about daddy," said Donna and instantly felt the humiliating sting of recrimination smack against her cheek.

It was just before six when Donna finally contrived an opportunity to keep her rendezvous with Tony. "Where are you going with that bag?" challenged Katrina distractedly as she rummaged in the pantry.

"In the back garden. To do some drawing."

"Your supper with be ready in ten minutes. Okay?"

"Okay."

But Tony was not there. The river had died and the blue cabin cruiser beached in the mud displayed a pregnant underbelly to the scalpel of the sun. She sat on the wall for a while wondering if he had got stuck in that railway tunnel again. A dog appeared on the opposite embankment, barking indignantly at her presence as it scrambled impotently to the edge of its canine world.

"Donna! Where are you? Supper is on the table!" she heard in the distance and ran back up the garden, stopping only to wedge a couple of her drawings on the sun lounger beneath a stone for Tony to find – the frugal evidence of her being there.

On Thursday in the Art lesson, as Donna tried unsuccessfully to stifle her third yawn in as many minutes, Miss Frobisher pounced. "I didn't sleep very well," she apologised sheepishly. It was particularly galling to be told off because Miss Frobisher had just given praise to the butterfly drawing Donna had brought in and shown to the class.

"Have you been watching too much TV?" asked the teacher. "I've warned you before, it makes the brain overactive."

Donna shook her head, embarrassed. "My sister keeps making moaning noises and talking in her sleep," she confessed in a low voice.

At lunchtime Miss Frobisher kept Donna behind and privately asked her all about Sarah's sleeping habits. "Have you told Sarah she wakes you up?" was the final question. Donna shook her head. "She gets cross with me and I'm scared," she explained. "But she didn't moan once while we were in Durham."

"Thank you for being so honest," said Miss Frobisher and produced a bar of chocolate from her drawer, which she gave to her pupil. "It may be that Sarah's just having a lot of bad dreams. She's that age. Run along now."

When Donna arrived home and went upstairs to change out of

her uniform, she was particularly delighted to spot the patio door of Tony's house wide open. She had resisted the temptation of the chocolate bar all day in order to share it with him. But as she burst out of the kitchen door dressed in red shorts and white tee shirt, something totally unexpected pulled her up in her tracks as abruptly as if the earth had quaked and a chasm had opened at her feet. Sarah had placed a beach towel on the ground and sat on it in a skimpy blue skirt and bra, pampering her skin with sun lotion.

"Have you seen Chelsea?" Donna improvised quickly, wondering how to navigate the obstacle.

"No. Can you rub a bit of this on my back?" Donna obeyed, spreading the white sludge with her fingertips, massaging it in as instructed. "Thanks, Div. Is that for me?"

Before Donna could answer, her sister had picked up the bar of chocolate from where she had placed it on the ground and began unwrapping it. "Oh, Sarah, it's mine," objected Donna and stamped her feet petulantly. "I hate you! I hate you!"

"Thanks a bunch," retorted Sarah with an ironic smirk on her face. "You weren't going to scoff it all yourself were you?" She snapped off a couple of squares and tossed the rest of the bar casually over her sister's head into the pile of debris. Donna retrieved it, scraping her knee on the edge of a broken brick as she did so.

"Ow!" moaned Donna, studying the abrasion. "Ow!"

"What have you done, Div?"

"Nothing."

"Need some help?"

"No." Donna walked towards the gate that led into the ginnel with an exaggerated limp intended to make her sister feel guilty. But Sarah just opened a magazine and lay down on her stomach to read it in a calculated display of indifference. "Chelsea! Here Chelsea!" cooed Donna cunningly as she edged bit by bit down the ginnel, gradually rounding the corner, accumulating confidence with every step. "Here Chelsea!" Within two or three minutes she had reached the place where the fence had broken loose and calculating that she had now stalled long enough to prevent any danger of detection, bent down to lever the gap open.

"What are you doing?" demanded Sarah menacingly. She was standing ten yards away at the junction of the ginnel, her hands on her hips like a model posing for a photograph. Donna toppled over backwards in surprise. "I said what are you doing?"

"I told you, Sarah. I'm looking for Chelsea."

"You won't find him down here" scoffed Sarah. "He's just jumped over the fence from number twenty-six."

"Has he?" gulped Donna, scrambling to her feet with guilty relief. "Oh, thanks for telling me."

"You're most welcome," nodded Sarah holding her ground all guile and composure. Donna walked back past Sarah feeling the scrutiny of suspicious eyes in her back. "Aren't you coming, Sarah?" she said looking over her shoulder nervously.

"Of course I'm coming, Div. What on earth could I find to detain me down a grubby back passage like this?"

As 4F jostled back into their classroom following Friday assembly, Donna heard a voice nearby say, "Hi, Donna! Feeling nervous about the Australia revision test today?"

She turned round and saw Abigail smiling grimly at her. They had not exchanged pleasantries for weeks. "I completely forgot," answered Donna in confusion.

"Don't worry, I'll help you," whispered Abigail confidentially. "Wait for me at break, and Donna? Will you be my partner in the three legged race?"

"Settle down quickly now!" urged Miss Frobisher before Donna could sufficiently overcome her astonishment to reply.

When break arrived Donna found herself led to a shadowy niche in the elbow of the playground where Abigail proceeded to leaf through an illustrated book all about Australia which her mummy had borrowed from the library. "Coogan's Creek. See? Lake Eyre," indicated Abigail.

"Lake? But where's the water?"

"There isn't any. It's flat. See here. It say's Donald Campbell set a world speed record there in 1964."

The scraps of information fell thick and fast from Abigail's lips and when the bell rang to signal the end of the bombardment, Donna seemed to perspire with learning.

"What about the three legged race?" asked Abigail as they walked back inside. "Will you partner me or not?"

"Don't you want to do it with Laura?"

"She's not allowed because of her asthma. Will you?"

Later, on the way home in the car Donna flushed bright with contentment as she told her captive audience how she had been able to write answers to all twenty questions in the Geography test and how well she had practised three-legged running with Abigail, never falling down once.

"Please come to the Sports Day and watch us!" she begged Katrina who grunted evasively and informed her that mummy would be staying at a friend's house tonight after work.

Back in her bedroom, Donna found that her newest doll was an altogether more attentive listener to her news. "Miss Frobisher's invited a famous Australian explorer in next week, Prime Minister," she explained. "He's going to talk about the abo-rig-ines."

"Excellent!" grinned the Prime Minister. "Please call me Tony."

But even the enthusiasm of the national leader became scant consolation to Donna for having her access to the real Tony blocked. Sarah had taken possession of the back garden again and when she did it on Saturday too, Donna began to wonder if her sister had discovered the secret and was deliberately persecuting her.

"Why don't you go round to see your friends today?" asked Donna affecting nonchalance.

"I'm grounded – remember?" sneered Sarah, spraying lotion on her cleavage.

"Katrina will be ages at the shops. If she misses you later, I'll say you've got a headache and gone to bed."

"You just want me out of the way or something?"

"No. It's cos you're my sister. You could let me play in your bedroom sometime, though. Only if you wanted."

"Yeah, well I don't want. If you told Katrina I was ill, she'd be upstairs like a shot to check. That's what paid spies do, Div. Especially the ethnically pure ones."

Sarah was still lying in the sun when Donna saw a black cab pull up outside and rushed to greet her mummy.

"I've had some good luck," mummy gushed as she handed over a pair of pretty bags. "Give this to Sarah. The other one's for you."

"Guilt money," announced Sarah darkly as she emptied the Body Shop paraphernalia into her lap. "We're being softened up. This means one of two things, Div. Either she's decided to marry Keith or something much much worse!"

"What?!" squealed Donna in a panic.

"She's got pregnant. How do you fancy an ugly deformed little imp of a step-brother howling away in its cot all night?"

Donna hurtled back into the living room wailing hysterically for an explanation. "There's no baby, Donna," consoled mummy gently amused. "Are you telling me I look fat? That I'm a Miss Piggy Porker?"

"No," moaned Donna burrowing deep into the maternal bosom. She closed her eyes and suddenly saw herself in a lovely sheltered garden mingling as an equal with all kinds of tame animals.

So peaceful there. So uncomplicated. If only she could stay in that place forever!

Chapter 23

Frank stood at the bedroom window in the half-light just before dawn on Sunday. He was watching the final moves of a territorial performance, two foxes circling each other in deadly enmity on the lawn – the king and the challenger to the royal estates. Since he had first spotted them a few mornings ago the howls emitted when one animal eventually dared to strike the other no longer curdled his blood. They were huge beasts, unearthly in their beauty and their bearing. They held their heads erect and their brushes radiated defiance through every orange-red fibre. In this magical hiatus of time nothing about their being appeared sly or skulking. One animal ruled the land while the other had determined to usurp it. And it was not just Frank's garden being disputed. It was clearly the entire patchwork principality this side of the Crane. The dance of rivalry moved up and down the embankment only ending at daybreak, when intrusive humanity began to stir from its slumber and the pretender wandered off to lick his wounds. But he never gave up. It was not in his nature to do so. Frank recognised that with a twinge of satisfaction.

Frank returned to bed and managed to doze back off. Although his patterns of sleep remained disturbed, at least the quality had improved. Several news reports had criticised the police for their false optimism and failure to produce. His dreaming had become less intense and he no longer woke up feeling as if his mind teetered on the brink of full-scale insanity. Whenever raw emotions flared up in his heart, he now had confidence again that he could control them, as Leppy had once taught him, by channelling them into practical activity.

It was sometime after seven-thirty before he stirred again, soaked in a cold bath and towelled himself in front of the same window. Already the sun seemed high. The foxes appeared to have long gone. Instead, close to the conifers Frank, spotted a grotesque creature with a long snout like an anteater's casually sniffing the lawn.

Then after a couple of seconds it metamorphosed into the prosaic familiarity of yesterday's labour – a wheelbarrow heaped up and over spilling with herbaceous cuttings. Yet Frank maintained an intuition that something real was prowling close-by, and no sooner had he sensed it than the victorious beast appeared like a courtier to his thoughts, padding through the keyhole, imperious and sovereign of all he surveyed, destroyer of all who defied him. In the fox's dripping mouth something was gripped like a prize, – something grey and still squirming, perhaps a squirrel in the last throes of life.

Frank blinked twice, but the image remained. This was not an illusion and he felt strangely elated. But why? His gaze pulled back and moved like a camera, first to his left, panning along the small square parcels of garden that divided him from his anonymous neighbours along Mansfield Road, then straight ahead where trim fenced off plots of private land ran like so many individualised bowling alleys down to the river bank. He nodded to himself with sudden insight. Yes. This was the real illusion – suburban civilisation. These landscaped remnants of privacy had been created by people to conceal from themselves the awful uncertainty of life. To the creatures – the natural occupiers – there existed just one huge wilderness, a battleground for survival. While householders uprooted weeds or moaned about a hike in their mortgage rate, Terror and Appetite went inconspicuously about their sordid business.

He was half way thorough a plate of scrambled eggs on toast when the mobile rang. "I've been worried about you, son," McLeod began.

"That's why it's taken you six days to phone again?"

"Don't take umbrage. You know how careful I've got to be. They can monitor these things. You've not been on the booze -? Last time you sounded groggy sort of. Spaced out?"

"I've had some viral thing," Frank prevaricated. "A touch of fever. But it's passed now."

"Sure?"

"Yeah. When are we moving out?" Frank put a forkful of egg in his mouth and waited.

"Soon. Look, I've had a tip off about increased police surveillance in the western boroughs."

Frank felt a stab of anxiety. The evening before he had noticed a police vehicle stop in Clifton Road. A man had alighted and entered a house. The car had quickly moved on and so had Frank's malaise – until now. "What sort of surveillance?" he demanded.

"Och, routine stuff, apparently, – no more than a public relations exercise, but you'll need to be extra careful. Don't answer the door to nobody. "

"I never do. I aint stupid."

"They haven't bin your way yet then?"

"No. Well, maybe. I aint sure."

"Don't go out now, even at night."

"What?! I'm eating my last three eggs. The pantry ain't exactly stuffed with grub."

"Try to manage. What are you going to do with yourself today, son, to occupy your mind? Eh? Thought about making some more pieces for your butterfly collection?"

Frank felt the urge to laugh. Suddenly McLeod had adopted the patronising tone of an agony uncle. "Are you avoidin' the question? When's the river gonna reopen?"

"Sorry. I haven't got a date just yet. I'll ring the minute I have. Don't lose faith. We're gonna do this, son."

Frank ground his teeth in frustration and mentally cursed Hunter. "Can you give a message to our friend the boat master?"

"What?"

"Tell him I'm seriously thinking of removin' his head from his shoulders once this is all over."

"Funny you say that, son," chuckled the Scotsman. "It's already bin taken care of. Cheerio."

"Is that supposed to be a joke – !?" barked Frank but the line had already broken up.

*

Donna felt ill at ease. The cooked meal that mummy called 'brunch' had stuck in her throat.

"Have you finished?" asked mummy gazing up from the Sunday newspaper.

"Yes. I can't eat any more."

Mummy stretched out her hand to take the plate, but Sarah intervened. "Leave it mum. I'll do the washing up," she simpered as sweetly as you like.

"Oh, thanks" said mummy. "That's very kind."

"Would you like another cup of tea?" offered Sarah as she busied herself clearing the table.

"I wouldn't say no."

Donna watched the fresh cup poured out and delivered. Her sister's behaviour was totally nauseating. The whole thing was. This stupid new deal! She got up from the table, flounced into the living room and switched on the television. Pictures of police cars and a river appeared suddenly on the screen, two men in wetsuits and goggles diving beneath the surface. Donna flinched as a voice explained, "The decapitated body is thought to have been in the river at least three days. An identification has been made, apparently, –"

"Donna? I'm taking Sarah over to Jeannie's They've arranged to go skating. Then I thought I'd go for a walk in the Isabella. Do you want to come with me?" Mummy was standing in the doorway completely unaware of how offensive her presence was.

"I'll stay here – I'll be alright," muttered Donna self-pityingly.

"Are you sure? I won't be very long."

"Yes, mummy," insisted Donna, suddenly recognising that a major window of opportunity was opening up in front of her. "I need to tidy my bedroom, and then I might play at market stalls with my dolls in the garden." She watched mummy hesitate, her gaze move towards the screen. "I won't go in the street or answer the door. Promise! Mummy, why do people kill...?" She hesitated, unsure how safe it was to ask. "Why did you tell Sarah once that –?"

"How dreadful is that!" exclaimed mummy. "Make sure you put sun block on your face and arms if you go in the garden. What were you saying, dear?"

"Oh, nothing," said Donna she went upstairs to pack a bag full of goodies for the stall.

Her luck was in. Minutes after Sarah and Mummy's departure, Donna spotted the man she intended to be her main customer amble outside and begin mowing the lawn.

"Watcha, mate! Awright – ?" he greeted her approach. The rest of his words were swallowed up in the din of the motor. "I said –!" It was no good – even Tony's vocal cords could not fight off the opposition. He swivelled the mower in its tracks, simultaneously snapping off the power. Donna watched the line of trimmed grass tail off to the left. It was like putting the curl on a gigantic letter J.

"You brought your overnight bag then?" he asked, brushing a bare forearm over his brow.

Donna grinned shyly and said, "I thought you might like to visit my market stall – if I can set it up on the sun bed?" Tony bent down and disengaged the grass collector from the machine. His arm disappeared into the obscene rear duct and pumped out shard after shard of thick clogged vegetation, which it proceeded to stuff into the bulging container. "I've been trying to come but my sister's been lying in the back garden sunbathing," she explained. Tony said nothing. "I was scared she might follow me. I did right, didn't I?" Tony lifted up the grass collector with a grunt. She followed him through the conifers where he removed the plastic lid of the mulching kiln and unpacked his parcel bit by bit into the putrid pudding below. Donna had to summon up all her courage to watch. Tony stirred the pot with a stick, releasing a nauseous odour into the air, and as the newly textured surface took shape all manner of sticky, terrified bugs, disturbed in the habit of gluttony, went scampering in terror of their parasitic lives.

"So? Where's your family today?" asked Tony settling himself on the wall his back to the river. Before Donna could answer, a rustling noise close by, followed instantly by a cacophony of bird squawks, provoked the questioner to add, "It must be that cat of yours. It thinks it owns the place. Too busy by far. It's gonna come to a sticky end one of these days." Donna bit her lips nervously. "Oh, thanks for leavin' those drawings the other day," he continued. "I appreciate it. I do." Donna smiled shyly and shrugged her shoulders. "I stuck your drawings on the wall in my bedroom."

"Did you?"

"Yeah. You're a real talent you are. Honest. Who was the man, by the way?"

Donna looked him full in the face, massively pleased yet incredulous. Was he was kidding her?

"That was you," she replied quietly and peered back down at her feet. "I didn't think it was any good , either. Sorry."

"Me? Nah, Donna! Don't put yourself down! It was brilliant. I just never properly looked at meself lately. The mirror's a foreign object. You made that man, I mean me, look sort of handsome." Donna angled her head at him, smiling, and moved it away again the instant his eyes latched onto hers. "What were you sayin' about your sister? Katrina, is it?"

"Sarah!" exclaimed Donna in mock school-mistress exasperation.

"Oh, sorry. Sarah, then," Tony fluttered his eyelids apologetically.

Sarah was the one subject Donna was bursting to talk about more than any other. "Mummy's given ten pounds to Sarah so that she can go out with her friends to the ice skating rink," she began. "I don't mind the money cos mummy's given me some new clothes and other things which I've brought to show you, but she's supposed to be grounded. Do you know what grounded means?" Tony nodded. "It means her behaviour is very bad, she's naughty all the time and can't go out anywhere until she stops. Well, she hasn't stopped. As far as I'm concerned. She's mean and nasty. She smacks me in the face for doing nothing – pardon me for breathing! Smack! And it really really stings for ages afterwards and I'm too scared to tell on her to mummy in case she does it again when mummy's at work! And she's always in my bedroom making noises at night and sometimes it's so bad I can't sleep, and then I get told off at school or something because I can't concentrate!"

"So Sarah's gone out, has she?" asked Tony.

Donna's eyes began to well up with the pain of the injustice as she answered. "Yes and all because mummy came home in a good mood, because her boss has given her a bonus and – do you know what a bonus is?" Tony nodded his head. "And a pay rise, too, all at the same time. So she wants to be happy and kind to everyone and she tells Sarah that because she's had much better reports from her teachers she's decided to give her a clean – clean something –"

"A clean slate?"

"Yes, a clean slate which means she isn't grounded anymore and there's no ult-ee-may-tum now and she can carry on saying what she likes to me and slapping me in the face and nothing has really changed at all! Hoo, hoo, hoo!" A grey drizzly mist descended in front of Donna's eyes rendering the shape of her feet and the texture of the ground all but invisible. Then she felt a hand on her shoulder, her frail sobbing torso being pulled firmly but gently against his. Faraway on the other side of the fog, a wood pigeon cooed as if mocking the extravagance of her grief. "I'm s-s-sorry," she blubbered and simultaneously felt her body lifted and turned and cradled in his lap.

"And 'ere's me thinkin' I've got problems," said Tony stroking her temples with the tips of his fingers. "She sounds a proper fruit and nut case your sister. Why did she slap your face then?"

"For nothing at all!"

"Don't you want to talk about it?"

"Yes. I don't mind. She goes to the doctor to talk about daddy and she thinks it's a secret but I knew all along, and I told her."

"Yeah, well people get angry when they find out you know their secrets. Don't they? When you touch a raw nerve?"

"I suppose."

"Donna?"

"What"

"Didn't you tell me once your dad was dead?" She grunted affirmatively, sniffed and shifted her head to a snugger position on the massive pillow of Tony's chest. "Maybe that's what's at the back of it then?"

"At the back of what?"

"Your sister's behaviour." No reply. "Do you mind me speaking about him?"

"Course not!"

"Did he get very ill?"

Donna felt puzzled. After a few seconds, she said, "I don't think so. He got run over by a lorry when I was a baby."

"Do you, – er -?"

"What?"

"Do you go and visit his grave?"

"You mean the hole in the ground thing, where -?"

"Yes, – do you?"

Donna peered down the funnel of her memory looking for a signpost marked "daddy's grave" but, if it had ever existed, she certainly could not spot it now. Yet her daddy must have a grave. Everybody who died was automatically laid in the ground, weren't they? In a box so that their body could rot and return to nature while their soul flew off to Heaven? "Do you believe in Heaven, Tony?" she asked searching out his grey eyes.

"Sort of," came back the hesitant answer. "Yeah. I suppose now I think of it I do. Not that there'll ever be enough room in there for me, of course!"

"Mummy doesn't believe in Heaven. Or God. She told me once. And neither does Sarah. Not any more."

"You can never say nothin's impossible. Not in this world or the next. Most things are a mystery"

"Bronwyn believes in Heaven. So does Mrs Harper. Bronwyn says there's more than enough room for everybody."

"Yeah. And I'll bet your dad lives on the most beautiful patch of it, too."

"Bronwyn made us pray for the soul of that man to go straight up to Heaven."

"Which man?"

"You know. The guard man who got killed at the airport by those robbers. He had two girls just like me and Sarah." She felt his body flinch in surprise and stiffen against her. "Didn't you know about them?"

Tony shook his head and let go of her waist. "I've got to stand up. My arse has gone numb," he announced gruffly.

Donna giggled as she slipped onto the gravel. It was such a funny word in the mouth of a grown up. She watched him limber to his feet and seem to wiggle invisible creases out of his body. "Tony? Can I come to tea soon? You promised." He muttered something incomprehensible and turned away, fixing his gaze down river. "Shall I finish cutting the grass for you?" No reaction. "I don't mind. I can do it." More silence. Had she said something to upset him? Or was he just engrossed by the antics of the stray ducks, she wondered? "I'm going to set my market stall out in the garden now. You can come and visit when you're ready. There's no hurry."

She lugged the bag back through the keyhole towards the sun lounger. There was indeed no hurry today. Mummy would be gone for ages. She felt weightless with freedom. That great tangled serpent of pain and humiliation which had been feeding off her stomach only a few minutes earlier seemed to have been magically expelled from her body. And as she arranged her booty like a fussy shop window designer into whose reality her imagination had involuntarily wandered, her voice broke into song.

"I had a girl – Donna was her name. Since she's been gone – I've never been the same!"

*

It is not the antics of the ducks which have distracted Frank's attention. It is his memory of the robbery and the heroics of a stubborn security guard, refusing to surrender the numerical code that gives access to the bullion room.

"I tell you I can't remember! I can't! Give me more time!" Frank hears the man pleading.

"You've had enough time. You're takin' the piss," says McLeod and even as the trigger of his gun is cocked, Frank is certain it will not be pulled. That is their firm agreement.

"If you just stop pointing that thing, I'll remember it! Please! This is not a trick – !"

A single shot and the guard flinches, tries to run in panic even before it is fired. His collapse to the floor is so theatrical, Frank momentarily wants to laugh.

"I'm dead. You've killed me!" wails the guard and rolls his eyes towards his colleagues who remain rigid like granite extras staring nowhere and everywhere simultaneously.

"You're not dead," says McLeod. "You've got a flesh wound, but you will be in three seconds if you don't tell me how to open this room. One – !"

And to Frank's amazement, the combination is instantly delivered, – the programmed robotic voice of a man with a hole in his chest calling out the winning numbers in a highjack lottery.

Suddenly during the third consecutive repeat of this scene in his imagination, Frank hears an unscripted voice intrude. "The stall's ready, Tony. Do you want to come now?" it says.

"What?" he asks it back.

"The stall. You'll be my first customer."

A frame of the memory film has been frozen as if stuck in the projector gate of time. Slowly the image turns brown and then bursts into flames and as the flames die away another image appears, a bundle of animation and chatter. It is that little girl who looks like Francesca. "I mean if you prefer to look at the river, I don't mind. I'm not in a hurry today," she is smiling. And the smell in his nostrils of sulphur and fear is overtaken by another, mud and pine needles.

"One is called Fiona and the other Kay," the little girl says.

"What?"

"The guard man's children. The one who got shot. Tony? Can I ask you something? Why do people kill each other?"

Frank feels his legs weaken at the knee joints. Has she been there too? In the audience? Has she followed him into his mind? "Search me," he hears himself mumble. "Why do you ask?"

"I heard mummy saying once that she felt like killing Sarah."

A wave of relief floods through his chest, followed by another containing flotsam of pity and hilarity and a desire to protect. "But she didn't do it? Right?" he asks.

"No, course not. But she wanted to. She said it, didn't she?" The face stares plaintively at him, a mask of infantile uncertainty.

"It's normal for people to say things like that when they get angry," he gropes for an explanation. "It don't mean they're killers. All they're thinking at the time is how much better they'd feel if the person they was angry with no longer 'appened to be around. It's a fantasy. They never do it."

He watches her features. They are transparent and pure. They are entirely open to whatever words and catastrophes come their way. The lips slightly parted and pouting. The skin unblemished. Some long hidden part of him has become suddenly exposed to the light and he wants to scream with shame and self-recrimination.

"Your eyes were grey before," she says, approaching him. "Now they've gone sort of greeny blue." His tongue tries to form a reply and fails. "But some people do, don't they?" she continues. "Why do they, Tony? Why do they kill other people?"

Suddenly Frank sees himself, full frame, thirteen years earlier, projected on the lens of his remorse. He is running on cobblestones, which hurt his feet, hinder his escape. It is night. A siren screams close-by. A headlight beam sweeps across his body. He ducks low into a doorway, sweating. The stench of the dog shit polluting his nose. Litter everywhere. Gripping the pistol so that it becomes the steel centre of the foetus into which his terrified body curls itself up. Shouts. Doors banging. Feet pounding. Waiting. Waiting. Finally, silence. He sees himself stand up and begin to walk like a ballerina on the cushioned balls of his feet, noiselessly. He reaches the outlet, the corner and flattens himself against the wall. No more than twenty yards to his right stand a pair of uniformed constables, peering into a shop window with ludicrous nonchalance, appraising a display of ladies' underwear. They have not seen him. He takes a balletic step backwards into the ally, treads on a discarded can and watches it out of the corner of one eye, roll tortuously along the pavement, before dropping over the precipice of the kerb with a crash that echoes loud enough to wake the dead. Now he is running again. The pounding feet, the shouts and whistles closing in on him. He slips, gets up and twists around to confront his pursuers.

"Get back! Get back! I'll use it!" he shouts. One of them freezes in his tracks, but the other keeps coming, his pace slowed to a walk and he is speaking, coaxing, his right arm stretched out. He is not intimidated. "Stop walking! Right now!" pleads Frank.

Frank sees the fear in his own eyes. He hears a voice in his head demanding, "why don't you shoot?" Still he hesitates. The response demanded of him is wrong. He has to find another way, a compromise. The policeman will not be cowed. "Throw it on the ground," the courageous young officer insists. But the gun explodes in Frank's hand and the constable spasms in agony, clutching his thigh like a sprinter whose hamstring has snapped. Now Frank is running again. Two officers emerge from a white car, which pulls up ahead of him. They are not armed. He stops. The red flashing light on the roof of their car seems to pulse in the same frantic tempo as his heart. He knows there are nine rounds left in the magazine. Nine is his lucky number. He points the gun at the targets. Neither of them move or speak. Beyond them two more cars pull up. A decision is made but how or why he has no idea. He sees himself throw the gun on the ground and sink to his haunches, head in hands.

"Why do people kill each other?" the little girl is repeating.

"I don't reckon there's just one reason. There's quite a few," answers Frank who has relived the scenario of his arrest in the time it takes the girl to walk two paces closer. "But in the end it probably boils down to one thing. Fear."

"Fear? Is that the same thing as being afraid?"

"Yeah. One feller will kill another cos he's afraid if he don't the other will kill 'im. Or at least make his life not worth livin'."

The little girl continues speaking. He sees her mouth moving but the words he hears do not belong to her. They are the words of the judge at the Old Bailey passing sentence.

"Orsi, you are a ruthless and practiced criminal. You do not hesitate to carry a gun or to use it. You are a danger to society and the sentence I impose must properly reflect the gravity of your crime. Moreover you have chosen to remain obstinately silent about the identities of your partners in the foiled raid, and I find this misplaced sense of loyalty compounds the offence. There has been some suggestion that you fired deliberately low into the pursuing officer's legs to immobilise him and that you made no attempt to kill. Weighing up all the available evidence, I am hardly minded to regard this as mitigation although in sentencing you now, my ardent hope is that some small ember of decency did indeed hold you back from the act of murder and will not be extinguished as you face up to fifteen years penal servitude. Take him down."

"Would you, Tony?" the little girl persists, her voice now filling the void.

"Would I what?"

"Would you ever kill someone?"

The question feels like a bucket of cold water smacking him in the face and he suddenly knows the answer now unequivocally in a way he did not know it, all those years ago. He knows he will never let anyone threaten his liberty again – whatever the price. "Cor, you ain't 'alf comin' out with the difficult ones today, Donna," he tries to joke. "Bin watchin' too many of those quiz games on the telly?"

"It's alright. I know you wouldn't," she giggles turning on her heels. "I'm going back to my stall. The customers are waiting."

As she skips away through the keyhole, Frank finds himself regretting all those conversations that prison deprived him of with his own child. Then he begins to anguish about the conversations that he will need to have with the grown up Francesca to reassure her about his love once he has found her again.

"Tony! Are you coming?"

It is the voice of Donna breaking into his self-absorption again and he realises with sudden clarity that he ought to deter her random incursions, not so much because they threaten his safety but because she sets his mind flowing in dangerous emotional directions. He cannot afford to allow his will power to be undermined by sentiment. But how does he manage to exclude her now without hurting her feelings? Without jeopardising the understanding they have? How does he say goodbye?

*

What a lovely smell, freshly mown grass! If summer has a perfume this is it, considered Donna as she knelt on the lawn shifting her treasures around the plastic slats like chess pieces. Her thoughts flitted across the surface of Tony's words, alighting on a sentence, probing its meaning and quickly moving on to the next. She wondered at the first port of call why Tony thought there would not be enough room in Heaven for him. After all, he was not a giant or a mountain range! What did he mean? Surely anywhere worthy of the name Heaven must have more than enough room for everybody? But she delighted at the picture conjured up by her daddy, living on the most beautiful patch of Heaven. What would he find to do there all day? She pondered. Grow vegetables? Play card games with ether other residents? In real life daddy had been an actor. Maybe a drama group might exist on his patch and daddy might be given some interesting roles to play by God? And one day, a long time in the future, if she was very, very good and there was still enough room left for her to get in, she would be able to see him perform them. You could never say nothing is impossible, after all. Tony was right. "Most things are a mystery." Living. Dying. People. Just to mention three! Even those people closest to you were a mystery much of the time. Mummy. Sarah. Gran'dad. Gran'ma. Katrina. You never knew them completely even though you loved them. They were always capable of doing something that surprised you, something that hurt you when you touched one of their raw nerves. Take gran'dad, for example. He was a gentle, kindly man who would not hurt a fly, and yet he had once killed that German soldier with a long knife thrust right in the tummy. Just the thought made her feel sick. How had Gran'dad been able to plunge like that? To feel another man's life come trickling out onto his fingers? But now after talking to Tony she thought she understood, just a little bit.

"I had a girl, Donna was her name. Since she's been gone, I've never bin the same!"

The butterfly of Donna's thoughts darted off into the blue quilt of the sky as she heard Tony break suddenly into his ludicrous song. "Cos I love my girl, Donn-onn-a, where have you been?! Where have you been?! Oh, Donn-onn-a! O, Donn-onn-a!"

She watched him, her sides aching with laughter, as he came loping across the lawn, the very parody of a lovesick crooner, pleading for the return of his sweetheart, and dropped to his knees in front of her. As he finished the song, he started baying on all fours like a hound in a bizarre finale of distress. It was simply hilarious.

"So? What we got 'ere then?" he asked eventually. It came out in a series of little yaps, and as she showed him each item in turn he sniffed and nuzzled with canine curiosity.

"You're a fruit and nut case, you are!"

"Take's one to recognise one. What's this? A tube of glue? Sniff, Sniff"

"No, silly! That's bubble gum in there. You can squeeze out just a little or as much as you want. Want some?" She picked up the plastic tube and unscrewed the top.

"Yuk! No thanks. What's this?" Tony edged his nose sideways a few inches.

"Those are joss sticks, sir," answered Donna, slipping into the obsequious role of shop assistant. "You light them at the top and they smell all sort of flowery. Are you looking for anything in particular, sir, or just, er, brooding?"

"Browsing, don't you mean?"

"Oh, yes, sorry. Browsing!"

"Fancy having your grammar corrected by a mutt!" he joked and Donna almost doubled up with laughter. "Actually, miss, I'm looking for a goodbye present for a friend."

"Right, well then? What sort of friend? A doggie friend?"

"Oh no, miss. This friend has two legs and a big, big heart. She's very special. Any ideas?"

"Let me see, sir." Donna meticulously studied the alternatives. "I have a very pretty bracelet. See? It's all in different colours, or? You could buy her this tin. It's got a lovely picture. People having a picnic by a lake."

Tony nuzzled up to it curiously. "Anything inside?" he asked.

"Well, I haven't opened it yet, but – let me see?" She picked up the tin and rattled it uncertainly. "It may be empty? Anyway she can put pencils and stuff in. Is it for Fran-chesca?"

He shook his head and picked up a tube of mints. "Okay, the tin it is, and I'll buy these for myself. I love mints. How much, miss?"

"Oh, shall we say thirty pence altogether, sir?" Tony pulled a ten pound note out of his back pocket and gave it to her. "Oh? Now I don't think I've go the change for that?"

"Keep the change. Please."

"Are you sure, sir?"

"Certainly, miss. Still cheap at the price, and no need to wrap it. Thank you." Tony took the tin out of her hands and stood up. "I'm not being funny or anything, Donna," he added in his normal voice, "but hadn't you better be goin'? Your gonna be missed soon."

"May-be," agreed Donna reluctantly and started to pack away the contents of her shop. "It's early closing day, Sunday, isn't it?"

"And I've got to finish cutting the grass."

They walked back up the garden together to where Tony had left the lawn mower.

"Shall I push it for you?" Donna asked, trying to stall her departure.

"No thanks. I'll manage. Here. Don't forget this." He held out the biscuit tin to her.

"Oh? What about your special friend then?"

"It's for you, Donna" smiled Tony. Donna looked at him uncertainly. "It's yours!"

"Yes it is but – oh, alright then." She grabbed it innocently out of his hand and put it in the bag, took a couple of paces toward the garage, then remembered the banknote. "Here," she grinned, holding it out to him. "My turn to forget!"

"No. That's yours too"

"Mine?"

"I gave it to you. You're the special friend! Get along now"

"But -?" This was confusing her.

"Yeah?"

"What shall I do with it?"

Tony suddenly looked serious. "Good point, "he muttered. "Haven't you got a piggy bank you can put it in? I mean if Sarah or someone spots it they'll want it for themselves, and there could be a lot of awkward questions to answer. Have you got one?"

"No."

Tony walked towards her. "Well, maybe in that case –"

"But Sylvestra's got one."

"The doll? Yeah?"

Donna nodded her head with the excitement of a suddenly burgeoning idea. "It's not a piggy though, it's a clown, and all she's ever put in there is a ten penny piece and two black buttons. She'll be rich beyond her dreams!"

"Good. You do that then, and promise not to tell anyone I gave it to you. It's our secret."

"I promise, but are you sure? I mean, you've never even met Sylvestra, have you?"

"Nah – but I feel as if I have." He turned back to his mower, chuckling to himself.

"Tha-nks, Tony! See you soon! I'll try and come tomorrow after supper, when Sarah's finished sunbathing."

"'Fraid I'm working afternoon an' evenin's the next coupla weeks," said Tony. "And all the weekend too. I ain't gonna be around. This'll have to be goodbye fer a bit."

Donna felt a pang of disappointment. "Oh?" she gulped. "Working in the butterfly factory?"

"Yep." He kept his back to her while he fiddled about with the mechanism, his face averted. "No point in looking for me, is there?"

"No. I s'pose not. Bye then?"

"Bye, Donna. It's bin nice. Take good care."

Something about the words and the way they were spoken made her feel a bit sad. But she knew that she had no reason to fret. Tony had been excellent company and would be again. If not this week or the next then... whenever... as Sarah would say! As she approached the garage she noticed the buddleia seething above her head with white and orange butterflies. It seemed a positive omen. For a few seconds she marvelled at the intricacy of their celebration of approaching midsummer before skipping away in the direction of home.

Chapter 24

On Monday evening, Donna was singing to herself in a warm soapy bath when mummy came in wearing a frown. "Mummy! You're back early!" she exclaimed.

"Miss Frobisher's sent me a letter," said mummy. "You can guess what it's about, can't you?" Donna nodded. "I just wish you'd told me yourself, Donna. I feel ashamed to find out about it like this."

"Sorry, mummy."

"Anyway, I've already spoken to Sarah. She knows the score. But please come and tell me first if you've got problems with her in future."

"Yes, mummy."

"And don't forget to shampoo your hair."

"Did Miss Frobisher say anything else?"

"She said you're doing much better in Arithmetic now, and that your vocabulary is improving. What else? Oh yes, she said you've drawn some very nice pictures recently and that you're getting quite a reputation for it."

Donna felt gratified. This is what she hoped the letter had been about. "Mummy? Why does Sarah want to sleep in my room all the time?" she asked.

When mummy did not know the answer to something, or could not properly explain, her eyelashes would flutter like butterfly wings. This is what they did now. "I think it's just one of those insecurity things," she replied. "Anyway, she's been given strict orders that it won't happen again."

"Can you come and watch me on sports day, mummy?"

"Donna, I've told you twice already. I can't afford to take an afternoon off work."

"But you did when Sarah was naughty."

"That was different. You know very well"

"Can I play in the Metro Centre with my dolls tonight? Just for a bit. I'll go straight to bed when you tell me. Please, mummy!"

"What? You mean the utility room? Alright," sighed mummy, leaving. "There's something I want to watch on the Television now. Goodnight."

Later, when the doorbell rang, Donna had the distinct impression mummy must have forgotten about her. The Prime Minister was making an official visit to the Metro Centre and crowds of invisible admirers had been queuing up to shake his hand, hanging over the balustrade for a better view of their hero, riding the escalators, waving. "It's what we call a walkabout," Tony confided to Sylvestra as she offered him a small pot of coffee. "Whose that ringing your doorbell?"

Voices sounded in the passageway. Heavy shoes approaching. "Not for us thank you," somebody said.

A chair leg scraped then another. They were sitting round the kitchen table, it seemed, two of them with mummy. Donna stretched her torso. All she could see from her sitting position was a pleat of dark blue material.

"Just let me put on my specs. Right then?"

A rustle of papers. "Take your time, Mrs Atkinson."

"Hmmm? I'm sorry. I don't think I recognise any of them. I'm usually pretty good with faces."

"Look at this one again, madam. It's an old prison photo. He doesn't have a shaven head any more....No?"

"No. Sorry. Mean face, sensitive eyes. I'd remember him. Is he a prime suspect?"

"He's broken his parole. We need to find him. Do you know the family who live in the detached white house just round the corner, by any chance?"

Donna pricked up her ears.

"Yes. That is, I used to," replied mummy. "They've gone to the States for a couple of years. It's been let out now. Why?"

"It's the only one in Clifton Road we haven't been able to get access to. There appears to be a light on inside."

"Maybe he's having a bath or something?"

More likely he's still not back from the butterfly factory, thought Donna to herself.

"He? Do you know the tenants then?"

"Not personally. It's occupied by a Mr. Brown – through Churchill's, the estate agent in St. Margaret's Road."

"So you've not seen him?"

"No. I don't think so. I dropped him a note once asking if he had any children my daughter could play with but he didn't reply. I think he spends quite a lot of time in Scotland on business, according to someone I know who works in Churchill's."

"We'll go back round there now. Sorry to bother you so late, madam."

"It's no bother. I'll show you out. Do you want to show my kids the photos? Oh, the eight year old's already in bed."

"Maybe the other one then?"

Donna breathed a sigh of relief. What sort of people just marched into your house and started asking questions, she wondered? They were very nosy – even if they were polite with it. Maybe they were trying to sell something?

"What's his name, your suspect?"

"Orsi. Franco Orsi. Usually known as Frank. He won't be using his real name on the street of course, if he's involved in the bullion robbery. Well, shall we see her quickly then?"

The chairs scraped again. Shoes clumped on the tiled floor. Donna held her breath. The conversation had taken an unexpected turn. Suddenly she realised who the visitors were.

"Officer you really think – ?"

The question was lost in the shutting of the kitchen door. They had gone to pester Sarah in the living room. Donna waited and a short silence ensued, momentarily filled by the falsetto hilarity of a television audience. The coast was clear, and she suddenly felt tired. So clutching her companions to her chest, she crept stealthily upstairs to her room and as she got into bed, she found herself wondering if Tony would be quite so anxious to please those late-night visitors as Mummy had been.

*

Frank was still sitting in television darkness, rock still, as if mesmerised by the all seeing eye of an oracle, when the doorbell sounded in two prolonged bursts for the second time that evening. Instantly he killed the screen and grabbed the gun before opening the door and crawling, cockroach fashion, down the gloomy passageway towards the stairwell. The long seconds passed. The bell repeated in three short, impatient volleys. If it was the police again why had they refused to take 'no one home' for an answer? As he reached the upper landing and inched his way towards the vantage point of the master bedroom, another blast of electronic terror severed the building. He screwed the silencer onto the barrel and listened with the focus of a hunted rabbit for its predator. What if they vaulted the iron gate and came snooping round the back of the house? Had he remembered to secure that stupid rusty padlock on the garage door? The sudden doubt pierced his skull like a poisonous arrow. He gritted his teeth with determination. Nobody was going to take him – at least not alive. That was the one certainty pumping adrenalin round his body.

Suddenly a torchlight streaked the lace curtains and hovered its orange halo like an alien spacecraft against a corner of the ceiling. One of them down below was speaking. Feet crunched across the gravel patio. The halo played slowly along the bedroom wall and Frank deflated his body like a punctured balloon onto the floor beneath the windowsill. Sweating. Rigid. Light years away in a remote galaxy of his terror a metal flap seemed to rattle. Then the halo was extinguished. Another muted voice and scrunching feet, followed by silence like white noise infecting his ear-drums. What were they doing, the bastards? Climbing the gate? Forcing the door? Then a motor car engine roared into life and tyres squealed. Frank lifted his head just above the window sill and saw a white police car disappearing round the corner. They had gone.

*

Donna had almost dropped off to sleep when she felt the bunk stanchions vibrate slightly. "Sarah?" she whispered. "You're not supposed to be in here." No reply. "I'll tell mummy."

"Just tonight. Go on!"

"If I let you stay, then you've got to answer my questions. Okay?" No reply. "Sarah? Where is daddy's grave?"

"He hasn't got a grave. He was cremated. Now go to sleep, I'm not answering any more."

"Cream-mated? What does that mean? Sarah?!

"It means his body was burnt. Shut up now."

"Burnt?!" shuddered Donna, her mind igniting with horrific images. "How was it burnt? Tell me, Sarah!"

"I'm not listening! Go to sleep, you bitch! Leave me alone!"

Suddenly the door burst open and the ghastly silhouette of mummy appeared in the gap. "Sarah! Get back to your bedroom this instant!" she stormed. "You woke me up"

"I won't forget this, bitch!" backfired the trespasser as she scuttled out.

Tortured on the rack of her unanswered question, Donna had been sleep-deprived for ages when howls of agony suddenly began to orchestrate her thoughts. Surely Sarah was lying? Surely nobody burnt human beings any more? But the bonfire effigy of Daddy, flames dancing, skin dissolving into an orange inferno continued to haunt her imagination. Finally she stumbled out of bed to the toilet. Maybe she could flush the nightmare away altogether with the pain in her bladder? Far away the howling continued to echo.

Hands covering her ears, she collapsed to the floor where her body finally surrendered to exhaustion.

*

"Donna?! For God's sake?! Are you all right?!"

Donna opened her eyes and brought her mother's face miraculously into focus. The hazel jewels, the microscopic pustules of oily skin, the blood beneath the cellophane lips, tiny tufts of hair, the furrows and fissures of encroaching middle age – so beautiful and frightening at the same time.

"It's seven o'clock. How long have you been lying here?!"

"I don't know," she muttered hoarsely. "I went to the toilet and – and –" Her limbs felt stiff. Her neck ached. "I must have fallen asleep."

"On the landing!" said mummy, lifting her up. "You scared me to death for a minute. You can snuggle in your bed for twenty minutes. But it's straight up when I call you."

As she slid out of her mother's arms on to the mattress a single word plopped suddenly like a long submerged buoy back to the surface of her consciousness. "Cream-mated," she uttered in automatic recognition.

Mummy turned abruptly on the way out. "What did you say?" she asked with unexpected severity.

"Nothing," Donna replied. It was not worth the risk. She knew someone it would be safer to ask.

*

The water thundered into Frank's upturned face. He invited it to hit his chest then turned round and took the full force of the icy cascade on his shoulders and spine, thousands of sharp little darts vibrating the flesh, pummelling him out of the hangover of broken sleep and unresolved anxiety dreams. His left hand groped for the thermostat and wheeled the marker much deeper into the blue territory. A massive chill suffused his back. Shoulders jerked. Lips shuddered like a horse in panic, but Frank bit hard and hung on, until gradually the torture reached its zenith of pain and the magical transformation into pleasure began to kick in. When he turned off the water the mobile asserted itself in the silence, ringing distantly downstairs.

"Progress at last –" the Scotsman began.

"We gotta sort this phone thing out!" cut in Frank, a towel round his shoulders, dripping a puddle onto the kitchen tiles. "Look. I tried everythin' to reach you last night – directory enquiries, even that caff The Silver Spoon. Aint you got a home?!"

"I'm ex-directory –"

"The old Bill came round!"

"And? You didn't let them in?"

"Course not! But they came twice. And the second time they left a calling card – a bloody polite little note! They only want the tenant, Mr. Brown, to contact them at Brentford nick a.s.a.p.!"

"Consider it done. I'll ring them now."

It took the wind right out of Frank's sails. "You're a cool one!" he gasped. "How did they get the name?"

"Estate agent, I suppose. Look, it's routine door stepping. If they were acting on solid information received your door would've caved in and you wouldn't be sitting there now."

Frank reflected on the truth behind this before retorting, "But what if they want to see you?! In person?!"

"Then I'll go. They're local plods. They aren't detectives."

McLeod's composure utterly confounded Frank. He took a deep breath and said, "Look, mate, I keep seein' police cars in the street. There's one bin outside number seven three evenin's in a row now. A man gets out and goes in there –!"

"So? He's probably a copper finishing his shift. Even coppers have to live somewhere, son, you know. The good news is –"

"This one is different! He's in civvies and he keeps starin' over 'ere! I'm certain he's watchin' me!"

"Och! Getta grip on yourself! You're just imagining things! Here's the good news. I spoke to the PLA again yesterday. The waterway reopens on Wednesday the eighteenth – barring any unseen delays. I suggest we leave on the night tide – Friday. Check your tide tables. Should be just after 1am. Anyway, I'll confirm on Monday next – okay? I'll only ring before that if I hit a snag with the Brentford police. Keep a grip on yourself, son. Don't panic. We're almost there. Okay? And stay off the street completely."

"Look, I need a reliable phone number – fer me own peace of mind."

"Sorry. It's too risky this end –"

"But you made me believe I could get you on the mobile! You conned me! What if there's another emergency!? I'm up shit creek stuck here incommunicado!"

"It's for me to decide what an emergency is. It's for you to exercise self-control. That's why I hired you. Don't make me regret it."

A string of oaths flowed from Frank's mouth in reply. None of them were returned. "Are you still there!?" he bawled frantically but McLeod had long gone.

Chapter 25

"Are we going to practice our three-legged race after lunch?" Donna asked Abigail as they crowded into the canteen to collect their boxes.

"I don't think so," pouted Abigail. "You see I've promised to play hopscotch with Laura."

"Can I play with you then?"

"Not really. Only two people at a time can play."

Donna felt the invisible weight of humiliation squashing her into the floor. She knew that she had somehow to try to stand tall and swat away the offence. Suddenly she thought of Tony. Why did she need Abigail anyway when he had adopted her as his special friend?

"But you can watch us if you like," added Abigail with a thin smile of pleasure.

"No thanks. I think we've probably practised enough already," retorted Donna turning away towards the canteen assistant as if butter wouldn't melt in her mouth. After she had finished eating, Donna watched a bank of sombre rain clouds accumulating above the playground and squeeze the last shreds of sky into emaciated columns of blue. It looked really beautiful. I wonder if I could draw that, she thought. All around her clusters of children screamed and cavorted, totally unaware of the imminent downpour. Then unexpectedly a laser beam of sunshine knifed through the cloud cover and Donna felt a drop of moisture hit her cheek. The dramatic effect of the light took her breath away and she dashed straight to the classroom to search out her drawing materials.

"What are you drawing?" asked Abigail when the class began to reassemble early, bedraggled by the electric storm. Perfectly contained in the nib of her pencils, seated up against the window, the view from which was now dominated by an amazing rainbow, Donna felt not the slightest need to answer. "Look at Donna's picture, Laura." enthused Abigail. "It's really pretty!"

Donna knew her classmates were pressing around to see the picture but did not allow her concentration to falter for a second, even when the anxious voice of Miss Frobisher began to establish order. As the knot of admirers loosened under the duress of authority, Donna heard a latecomer demand, "What's going on? Who is it? Tell me!"

"It's Donna drawing one of her pictures," answered Abigail with maternal pride. "She's going to be my partner in the three legged race. Aren't you, Donna? And she doesn't want to be disturbed by you. So go and sit in your place and maybe you'll get to see it later. Come along."

The weather continued dull and showery right through Tuesday and well into Wednesday. On the journey home from Dr. Williamson's on the Wednesday afternoon, Donna decided, if the rain held off and a safe opportunity arose, she would take a stroll in Tony's garden. She had new drawings she wanted to leave him, including the rainbow one, and also a packet of those mints he liked. She would locate them in a waterproof bag like treasure to be discovered in his own time. This was the kind of nice surprise "special friends" ought to arrange for each other, especially ones deprived of each other's company for a couple of weeks, she considered as she forced her body through the gap in the fence. It appeared to have shrunk, as if some new panels had been nailed in, but they did not detain her conscience or her progress very long. Once inside she gazed at the silent curtained-off French windows then wandered into the heart of the squelchy lawn, inhaling the musk scent of the roses, now nearly all in full bloom.

Everywhere the garden's secret occupants, encouraged by the moisture, had left the traces of their presence – slug and aphid trails, serrated pantries of leaves, all manner of animal burrows, and tiny indentations that shone out like silvery fossils in the borders and gravel patches. In one corner she stumbled upon an ugly rash of greenfly disfiguring a rose bush, in another a tiny crustacean scaling the dizzy heights of a red hot poker in search of a flower feast. Momentarily it occurred to her that although Tony had made the garden appear all neat and pretty, beneath the surface nothing was really different. Once the evidence was properly examined, a constantly changing micro-world astonished her eyes. Every nook and cranny, every minute petal and stem existed as either food or camouflage for the numerous species of creature which lived out their lives there. Except for a very short while, nobody could really stop the garden from changing. Nobody could tame it. The garden belonged to itself. Completely.

This thought was baptised in a squall of rain which sent her running for the cover of the buddleia tree. She stood a while watching the wooden side door of the garage wobbling in the wind. Was the clasp thing loose? Her fingers examined it inquisitively, – turning, twisting – and as the padlock suddenly came away the door flew open with a bang, revealing a black, forbidden hole. "Oh my God!" she gasped in surprise. Her face felt wet. The shower had grown much heavier, pressing through the overarching fronds and she made an instant decision. A stink of petrol and fusty newspapers attacked her nostrils. It was like entering a cinema. Nothing was visible except the tiny rectangular screen of a rear window. Groping, shuffling slowly forward, Donna felt her toes stub against something hard. Tentatively, she bent to her haunches. A frisson of surprise as her bottom touched the concrete floor. Then locating the bruised part of her foot she began to rub it. The offending object quickly followed to hand. It had the invisible contours of a small brick. She could just begin to see it now indistinctly as her fingers played along the surface slowly. Whatever else it might be, she realised, this object was not a piece of masonry. She made to pick it up and was surprised by the weight. Heavy and cool and smooth like metal, the edges true and neat. Whatever could it be? Donna considered that it had a similarity to the paperweight Miss Frobisher kept on her desk but this was altogether more impressive and simple in its jaundiced beauty. Why on earth would it have been left on the grubby floor like that to gather dust?

No matter the reason, she thought. It certainly did not deserve to remain there. She stood up and looked around her. The black fog had thinned out and the apparitions of the outbuilding were ghosting themselves into existence – a bicycle, a work bench with iron things on top, a filing cabinet, lawn mower, paint cans, spades and a host of other gardening implements. On the concrete floor dozens of identical boxes stood piled up, the kind of boxes you found in shoe shops, and dominating the centre of the garage like a slumbering beast a transit van. Had Georgia's daddy exchanged it for their family saloon then, she wondered, before they went to America? More likely it belonged to Tony or Mr. Brown, she continued to speculate. Perhaps it was something to do with Mr Brown's business? Yes. That must be it. He sold shoes. Suddenly the door swung shut and night closed in dramatically.

"Is that you, Mr. Brown!?" she called out in a spasm of guilt and fear. "It's Tony's friend – Donna! I don't mean any harm!"

But only the wind and the steady patter of rain on the corrugated roof answered her plea. She stood stock still, listening. The weight of the bar she was still holding seemed to immobilise her will power, to anchor her to the darkness. Some entity more tangible than the elements was definitely out there. She could hear movements now, breathing. A bestial scrape, a snarl. Her tongue seemed to freeze to the roof of her mouth. Then as she stared and inched forward in a mounting state of agitation, the door flapped open again and Donna blinked, her face picked out by the ribbon of daylight like a rabbit's in the beam of motor car headlights. She watched the door hanging on the hinges, swaying, creaking, teasing – but nobody came through the aperture. The scraping had ceased and Donna felt the adrenaline of release flow suddenly through her body. She bustled out of the door, flexing her head one way, down the garden, then the other. Nobody was to be seen. Lawn. Conifers. Patio. Curtains. Nobody.

It must have been the weather after all, she thought with a sigh of relief, or maybe Chelsea scurrying for shelter. That would teach her to be nosy! She re-entered the garage, stopping only long enough to place the paperweight on one of the piles of shoe boxes and to pick up her shopping bag from where it had been left on the floor. She looped the bag handle over a knoll of the buddleia trunk where it would remain protected from the weather by the thick fronds, hopefully to be spotted by Tony the next time he came down the garden path and quietly closed the garage door, returning the rusty padlock to its proper position, despite being unable to exert sufficient pressure to secure the thing, and darted off towards her secret escape hatch.

"I saw you in the garden," said Sarah. They were watching Eastenders in the living room while Katrina tidied the kitchen.

"Which garden?"

"You know very well which garden, Div. I saw you from your bedroom window. How did you get in?"

Donna's cheeks flushed. She could feel the vacuum sealed lid of her secret being prised open. "You shouldn't have been in my room!" she retaliated. "I'll tell on you to mummy!"

"I was looking for the protractor you borrowed from me. How did you get in? Sprout fairy wings and fly?"

"I climbed the fence," Donna lied.

"What?! That rickety old fence? In the rain?!" Donna said nothing. "How many times have you done that before?"

"Twice."

Silence ensued. A long television minute passed. The crisis seemed to have dissolved. Then. "Donna? If you let me start sleeping in your room again, I'll give you my favourite red Troll for keeps and a bottle of mauve nail varnish. Donna?" Donna said nothing. "Mummy won't find out. I'll set my alarm and go back to my room early. Donna?"

A curious sensation of power and pleasure began to seep across Donna's chest, displacing the apprehension. A little circuit of memory drunkenly connected in her brain. "I don't think so," she simpered momentarily becoming Abigail.

"Why not?! I'll give you my eyelash curler too!"

"I don't want them, I want something else."

` "What? It'd better be something I've got."

Donna took a deep breath. "I want you to tell me everything about daddy. Answer all my questions and –"

"You bitch! You viper!" screamed Sarah as she leapt from the sofa, her face and body taut with outrage. Donna closed her eyes in terror expecting a slap or worse. It did not come. "I hope you rot in hell!" she heard instead as the door slammed shut on her sister's exit.

Chapter 26

"Before I introduce our special guest, I want to give back the test papers you did last week," announced Miss Frobisher to an expectant silence on Thursday afternoon. "No-one got lower than half marks and two people actually got nineteen out of twenty. I think it's safe to surmise you're going to have an informed and appreciative audience today, Mr. Burridge," she added as she distributed the papers. The elderly man, his head a thatch of white, unkempt hair, returned the teacher's smile.

"Miss? Who got the nineteens?" asked Harry with gum chewing audacity.

Donna blushed and squirmed with embarrassment even before Miss Frobisher mentioned her name. And once the debriefing of the answers began, the smiles and implied congratulations, she became utterly self-conscious. The staring eyes of her peers seemed to generate a force field of energy that impeded her concentration. Time almost stopped still. She listened uncomprehending as if to a record being played at the wrong speed. Suddenly her ears seemed to pop and normal sensory service was resumed as dramatically as it had been disrupted.

"... which was the only question Donna got wrong," the teacher was saying. "The capital of Australia is Canberra, isn't it, Donna? Not Cranberry! Maybe you were thinking about the sort of juice you'd packed in your lunchbox?!"

Warm comfortable laughter broke out, totally devoid of malice, and Donna felt encouraged to nod her assent to Miss Frobisher's supposition with a comedic wince of pain, that parodied one of Harry's mannerisms. Something had changed in the culture of the classroom, she realised. Not today. Not yesterday. But gradually like a sea tide rising, like the moon waxing in the sky, her position in the complex geography of personalities had moved from the wastelands close to the centre of things.

The affable guest was introduced properly now – Mr. Howard

Burridge, anthropologist and writer – and he explained how Australia had become his second home. He had trekked across the continent in the footsteps of Burke and Wills and been active in a campaign that had won financial compensation for the Aborigines from the British government which had secretly used the outback to test atomic weapons. "But you'll be relieved to hear that I'm not going to talk about politics," he grinned.

"About what?" whispered Rupert in Donna's direction.

"Polly-ticks," she whispered back, flaring her nostrils in a zany gesture of complicity with his ignorance.

While Miss Frobisher set up an easel, Mr Burridge unpacked a satchel of paintings in which the various artists had attempted to illustrate the stories and myths of The Dreamtime. He reminded everyone how the original settlers had begun travelling to Australia in boats over fifty thousand years ago, using the stepping-stone land masses between continents, a journey which would have taken several generations for prehistoric men.

"And women!" chirped in Miss Frobisher to general amusement.

"Yes, indeed" smiled Mr Burridge. "These odysseys would have foundered at the first port of call without womanly participation."

"He means sex!" beamed Harry for the hard of understanding.

"Yes I do. But until they became colonised by the modern world," said Mr Burridge, cleverly reining in the hilarity, "the Aboriginal peoples never realised that was how babies were made! They believed in the existence of tiny orphan spirit children who were constantly on the look out for a mother. When one had been found the spirit child would secretly enter her body and wait to be born."

Miss Frobisher mounted a picture of magical, over-lapping desert landscapes upon which sylph-like creatures dodged and darted their chameleon shapes. Donna gazed in wonder and admiration. One story quickly followed another. Each illustration once removed was circulated round the tables. In some cases Donna found the story compelled her attention, in others the picture, and sometimes the fusion of both together felt so powerful it made the hairs on the back of her neck stand on end. The image of a gum tree exploding into a holocaust of crimson flames, for example, and consuming crowds of naked bushmen who fled in terror while Mr Burridge narrated the myth of Nature taking revenge on a tribe who had desecrated the environment. And again a picture teeming with exotically coloured butterflies intended to illustrate the essence of the aboriginal belief about the origin of the four seasons.

"According to the Dreamtime stories the Earth is flat," announced the anthropologist displaying a starkly surreal landscape. "If you wander to the horizon, you fall off the edge into nothingness. Imagine the anxiety, therefore, – the heightened sense of awareness experienced by the hunter-gatherer on his every journey! Look carefully. This is not how he would have experienced the outback."

But Donna had already got there ahead of his explanation. She knew all these pictures were invitations to climb inside the skull of a primitive person and gaze out through his eyes.

"Nowadays our perception, our quality of seeing comes through the distorting lens of familiarity placed over our eyes by men of science. Our perception of the world has been blunted. Except perhaps in drug induced or other life threatening circumstances," Mr Burridge continued.

Puzzled frowns, whispered questions and several yawns followed in the wake of this statement. "Yes, Abigail? Maybe you could share your observation with the rest of the class?" intervened Miss Frobisher.

"Well I was saying they weren't very intelligent, were they?" began Abigail. "If they had been they wouldn't have felt scared all the time. Isn't that what Mr Burridge means?"

Donna felt her head shaking spontaneously. "Donna? Do you wish to add something?" coaxed the teacher.

"No – well yes, – that is, – well," stammered Donna trying not to wilt in the blinding spotlight of the invitation. "I mean, I don't think the aborigines were stupid to be scared. I think they – er? – noticed things, lots of things we don't notice any more. Very nice things as well as very dangerous things."

The words seemed to hang in the air in front of her inspecting their own naked banality. What had she said? Why had she bothered? She waited for the ceiling of mockery to fall in on her head – one second, two seconds – but nothing happened. Her eyes refocused on the personnel of the classroom. It was amazing! Everybody was looking at her with serious expressions as if waiting for her to drop further pearls of wisdom into their ignorance and Mr. Burridge more than anybody else. His eyes had narrowed. He was stroking the wispy ends of his beard and actually nodding in agreement!

"Why, in your opinion, don't we notice things in the same way as the Aborigines?" he encouraged her in a kind voice.

"Because – because we don't live close enough to them any more," she replied. "We're too –" And her tongue faltered on the word she wanted, a long word beginning with the letter P. She could see its meaning in her mind. A meaning that applied to mummy and Katrina and almost every grown-up she knew – although it did not really apply to Tony, at least not in the same way. Pre-something?

"Yes?" prompted Mr. Burridge

"Busy. We're too busy," said Donna. It was not the right word, but it was the closest she could get and she looked up at the visitor apologetically.

"Thank you. That's a very helpful contribution, Donna," he said. He now explained that the Aborigines with about five basic tools had been able to survive and flourish for thousands of years in a hostile, frequently waterless environment and that this was not just evidence of normal intelligence but also of a practical resourcefulness and complex knowledge of the land that civilised peoples, even today, could not match. The most amazing thing to Donna though, was that at the end of the explanation it was she who received the respectful smiles of appreciation and not the speaker. Or so it felt.

"We'll take a few minutes break now," announced Miss Frobisher. "Relax and stretch your legs if you wish, but please don't leave the room. Alright?"

Donna was examining one of the pictures at close quarters when she heard a voice above her say, "He goes on a bit, doesn't he? Too many big words. Our table's really bored. Aren't you?"

She looked up at Laura, all prim and smiling, like a lady in waiting. Donna hesitated uncertainly. Laura had never once spoken to her before. "No, I'm not," she replied.

Laura's milk white teeth instantly disappeared behind thin sown-up lips. "Of course not. You're a boffin now," she sneered. "You only got nineteen because Abi showed you her book. She told me. It's cheating! And I'm going to tell on you! Nobody likes a cheat!"

Donna felt her heart sink with guilt. Her new status, less than an hour into its existence, had been exploded. Suddenly several tables away, she glimpsed another little girl's face, fretted with worry and dark as thunderclouds. It belonged to Abigail. "You tell anyone you like," Donna heard herself reply. "I don't care. Nobody likes a jealous cow. Not even Abigail. She told me." Laura's eyes widened and filled with tears. Donna held her breath, mortified and amazed by the poisonous demon of retaliation that had possessed her.

"I'm sorry if some of the things I've been saying have passed over your heads," Mr Burridge suddenly started up. "I get a bit carried away. You see, I am used to talking to extremely old pupils in Universities – some of them as ancient as your mums and dads."

This produced a titter of relief which Howard Burridge followed up with a promise to show just three more pictures and then leave them to their own devices. Those children who were standing returned to their seats and Donna glanced towards the window tables where Laura sat glum and chastened while Abigail had noticeably brightened. She did not know how exactly she had desecrated the sovereign territory of that relationship. All she knew was that she had been given no choice – Laura had been the aggressor – and if a similar situation arose she would be able to act as ruthlessly again. It felt a bit like something Mr Burridge had been saying about the Adam and Eve story. A spell had been broken in her life. A kind of innocence ended.

As the lesson continued, Donna noticed how much slower Mr Burridge was speaking, how much less elaborate his sentences had become. He told them two more illustrated stories about how the Aborigines conceived the creation of the world but it was the third one that really captivated her imagination. It was all about what happened to the natives when they died. "This is one of my favourites," said the anthropologist erecting what appeared at first glance to be a simple painting of water by moonlight. It could have been a sea or even a river, not dissimilar to the Crane in full flood, Donna considered. There were lots of shimmering reflections and blue-grey colour textures. A wooden dingy drifted close to the bank or shoreline. Apart from a thin mast, which sprouted in to the air, the open hull lay bare and empty. "Look carefully. What do you see reflected in the water?" prompted Mr. Burridge.

Donna now detected the inverted image of a tribesman. Was he drowning? She twisted her neck through a semi-circle. No, she realised. He was statuesque, holding a paddle identical in every respect to the thing she had originally assumed to be a mast. He had to be the boatman. But why was he not in the craft? After all, his paddle was! Erect and unsupported!

"The spirit man is called Wulawait," explained Mr Burridge. "His job is to receive the soul of the next dead native and ferry it in the bark canoe to an island called Purelko. When the newcomer arrives he is greeted by the inhabitants who hurl their spears into his spirit body to revive it. Eventually he is transformed into a healthy young person and takes up his new life on the Island. Purelko, you see, is the aboriginal heaven – full of secure camping places where everyone lives in perfect contentment."

Donna instantly thought of her daddy's spirit body. If only there had been someone to prevent it from being burnt! And her head was still brimming with this story later after school, as she made her way towards Katrina's rendezvous place. "Are we still going to be partners in the three-legged race?" shouted Abigail running after her.

"You startled me!" exclaimed Donna and walked on past the Winchester Arms, across the first small road junction, wondering why Abigail continued to dog her steps. "Aren't you going the wrong way home?" she snapped at last.

"I didn't mean to tell Laura about the book. Honest, Donna!"

pleaded Abigail pitifully. "She made me. I don't think I like her any more."

They stopped and stood in silence, studying the map of each other's faces like lost explorers searching for a possible route home to base camp. Then Donna spun decisively on her heels and with a cheery "See you tomorrow!" walked away briskly round the corner.

Chapter 27

Sarah's latest silence had spread now like an Arctic winter across two whole days. Nobody else knew about its existence, apart from Donna. This was a major part of its meaning. You are a disease, it demonstrated. You do not belong to the territory I inhabit. You have less relevance to me than a footprint in the snow. When her sister was present, Sarah wore these slogans in every inflexion of her body but, like one of those massive electronic advertising boards which straddle major trunk roads, she could alter the message at an unseen flick of a time switch the instant anybody else entered the room to one that beamed good humour. This strategy of exclusion would have utterly mortified Donna in the past. Now she seemed to detect the outline of its foundations and felt resilient if not entirely immune.

On Friday afternoon as Katrina drove them home, Donna could feel the chill in the backseat, creeping down her neck and along her arms, even though it must have been 75 degrees outside. It did not otherwise undermine her mood. She was quite buoyant in all sorts of ways. In her bag she had a Certificate of Achievement, the first one she had ever been awarded, and the applause when she had gone up on stage to receive it from the headmaster, Mr. Knighton, was still resounding in her ears. She knew in her own way too, that the freeze was a temporary affectation, not a long-term seasonal change. Sarah was put out. She wanted something that had been refused her. It was a tactic. Once Sarah realised it could not work, the tactic would lapse. They would begin to communicate again, at least in a language more conciliatory than the "Move!" "Shut up!" one that prevailed now, and the deal that Donna had decided to hold out for, come hell or high water, could follow hopefully in its wake.

While Sarah took a shower, Donna decided to sneak into Tony's. He would not be there, of course. But she had an idea for a drawing and it had been on her mind ever since yesterday afternoon. Katrina occupied the kitchen as usual.

"Can we have supper early? I didn't each much lunch," Donna asked politely.

"Okay. What shall I make? Pasta?" But the phone rang before the question could be answered, and Katrina leapt on the receiver, snaffling it jealously to her ear as Donna escaped outside unnoticed.

No sign of human life greeted her intrusion. The house remained muffled up and silent but the plastic bag had gone from the buddleia. Tony had been there! Instantly Chelsea, who had been stalking the garage roof in search of sparrows, leapt down and fell into step beside her till they reached the sun lounger which he mounted and occupied like a sphinx, awaiting adoration. Donna was not slow in supplying it. She knelt on the lawn and caressed long sonorous notes of pleasure out of the beast. The wounds it had suffered seemed to have completely healed up.

"What's this? It's full of dirt!" observed Donna as her interest panned out to the plastic slats of the lounger. "You should wipe your feet before you jump onto this, Chelsea, you mucky thing?!" They were pock-marked with flat dry blobs of mud, unmistakably animal paw in origin.

Chelsea sniffed disdainfully and leapt onto the lawn. After a while Donna ambled after the cat down towards the gravel patches and was delighted to see the river high, lapping the upper reaches of the mooring. Someone had rowed a dinghy in with the tide and tied it up opposite. Apart from the iron oar struts, the craft bore an uncanny resemblance to the one in the Wulawait painting. She sat on the wall idly attempting sketches of the hull and the watery reflections it cast, until hunger got the better of her and she vowed to come back and try again tomorrow.

"Is supper ready yet, Katrina?" she asked as she entered the kitchen. But Katrina did not hear. Her eyes, two vast limpid pools of misery, Katrina remained as if organically connected by the right ear to the telephone, simpering and biting her knuckles raw. In normal circumstances Donna would have asked her sister what this awful new peak of anguish might portent in their minder's life, but she knew she would receive short shrift. Especially when Polly, of all people, arrived a few minutes later and was bundled immediately upstairs by Sarah like a jealous possession.

So all is forgiven, thought Donna as she listened to the rap beat and giggles leaking through the living room ceiling and wished there was some way she could accompany them to the Friday Youth Club. For a few self-pitying moments she felt about as relevant to the functioning of the house as an influenza virus but then she recalled that mummy had promised she would leave work promptly tonight and come straight home. That was a huge bonus, and her rapidly depleting mood of weekend anticipation enjoyed an abrupt recharge.

*

Frank was lurking a couple of yards back from the window in the master bedroom and periodically checking his watch. From this vantage point he had an excellent view almost to the bottom of Clifton Road. The vehicle was two minutes overdue. Now three minutes. Now four. He took a mint out of the packet and sucked it hard, suddenly aware that he needed to visit the toilet. Five minutes overdue. He knew that his apprehension was not irrational. For five straight days in a row now the white police car had pulled up outside number seven, dead on twenty past the same hour each evening. Whatever that bastard McLeod reckoned, this was not the product of an over-active imagination.

Six minutes overdue. A yellow van rounded the corner from Mansfield Road and was forced to stop, veering tight to the line of parked cars to permit a red Ford to exit from the opposite direction. Frank could wait no longer for the toilet. He walked towards the bedroom door and was still reaching for the handle when a horn sounded sharply. Outside a cyclist had evidently swung carelessly across the road, almost colliding with the police vehicle as it turned blind round the corner. Here we go again, said Frank to himself and spied on the car as it moved on forty yards and pulled up, depositing a passenger before leaving. Frank knows what will happen next and sure enough it does – a déjà vu experience. The passenger opens a small gate that leads to the terraced house and as he takes the key out of his trouser pocket to unlock the door, he looks over his right shoulder diagonally across the street and stares unmistakably at Frank's place – always the same hard, suspicious stare – then he disappears inside and the door closes.

By eight o'clock, ninety minutes later, the tourniquet of anxiety in Frank's head has ratcheted up a notch too far. He has to unload the burden on someone. He has to try – despite all McLeod's prohibitions – to make contact. Having previously discovered the number in the London directory he telephones The Silver Spoon. It is an Asian voice that answers. Polite but brusque. Frank can hear from the background noise the place is busy.

"I'm trying to contact a Mr. Brown," he says. "He's one of your regular customers. A Scotsman with –"

"Didn't you ring before? Wanting a phone number?" interjects the Asian.

"Yes. A few days ago."

"Well, I asked the boss. He has no idea. Sorry."

"Is there anyone else working in there who might know him? Please. It's very urgent." Frank garbles out a description of McLeod.

"Hold on a minute."

Frank realises as he waits that beads of sweat have formed on his forehead. The kitchen smells of burnt toast and stale fat. He is food as well as sleep deprived. He sticks another spearmint in his mouth and rolls it around with his tongue, trying to suck comfort out of the hard shell. Since last weekend when he ran out of sugar and jam his taste buds have been in revolt. These sweets materialising suddenly in the garden have brought relief to the craving.

"Hello?"

"Yes. I'm here."

"Someone here thinks he's seen your friend in The Rising Sun –?!" The Asian intones a street name and district. Frank hangs up ungraciously and contacts directory enquiries immediately.

A flat robotic voice eventually delivers the digits. Frank taps them out and listens to the ringing tone. A woman answers. "I'm sorry to trouble you," he begins. "I'm trying to trace an uncle of mine. Apparently he drinks in your pub. I aint seen him for twenty odd years."

"What's his name?" Frank hesitates, suddenly unsure whether McLeod would be using an alias or not. "Don't you know his name?" the woman laughs. She sounds a bit tipsy. "How much does he owe you?"

"Plenty. He's a Scotsman. About sixty. Wears a trilby. Wart on his nose and –"

"You mean Alex McLeod. Yeah – he's in here most nights, I think."

Frank can hardly believe his luck. "Is he there now?" he demands.

She speaks to somebody else. "No. Apparently he's not been in all week. I'll be happy to take a message, though."

Frank is gripped by another anxiety now. What if McLeod came unstuck at Brentford nick? What if they are holding him like they did Challinor? What if.....what if.....?

"Hullo?....Are you still there?"

"Can you tell him his nephew Anthony is desperate to speak to him. There's bin a death in the family," he nonetheless says. "Do you know his phone number by any chance?"

The woman guffaws then corrects herself. "Sorry," she simpers. "I do apologise. What's your phone number, Anthony?"

"Oh, er, he knows it."

"You mean its bin the same for over twenty years?!" The woman laughs like a hyena – uncontrolled raw incredulity.

"Yeah, that's right."

"And there's been a death in the family?" It sounds like a party now. Somebody close by has joined in the mirth. Frank wants to strangle her.

"Correct", says Frank bitterly. "And just tell 'im if he wants to avoid another one, to ring me back a.s.a.p."

Chapter 28

"What time did you come in last night?" muttered Donna hoarsely as she padded into the kitchen, still dopey-eyed with sleep, drawn by the smell of fresh coffee.

"Good morning, sleepyhead! Not much before eleven. Last minute change of plan. I'm sorry," apologised mummy with a hug. "Didn't Katrina tell you I'd rung?"

"Don't think so. I must have gone to bed already. I thought –"

"Here drink this orange juice. The good news is I don't have to go in today. It's a Saturday of leisure. How about we have brunch at the supermarket? And then go to the outdoor pool?"

Donna felt the residue of last night's disappointment dissolve immediately. "Will Sarah come with us, mummy?" she asked.

"Shouldn't think so, dear. She's been sleeping over at Polly's. God knows what time they'll surface."

"Can I have a sleepover sometime?"

"Maybe on your birthday. Why? Do you have a little girl in mind?"

Donna yawned. "Does it have to be a little girl, mummy?" The clock said half past nine but her body felt it needed another two hours sleep.

"Well, a little girl would be easier to manage," said mummy fluttering her eyelids. "I mean in terms of, er, sleeping arrangements and –"

"But I don't mind having a man in my bottom bunk."

"A man?"

"Yes, I don't mind."

Donna watched her mummy's mouth gape open, her eyes widen. "Don't you mean a boy?" she queried.

"Oh yes! Sorry. What did I say?" gasped Donna quickly.

"You said a man, dear. Didn't you?"

"Mummy! I almost forgot! I got a certificate of achievement!" exclaimed Donna with the inspiration of sheer panic and she bolted in search of the camouflage.

*

Frank studied the meagre contents of the fridge. His body felt groggy. It had barely slept a wink. He chewed a crust of stale bread and waited for the kettle to boil. The butter had long gone but tea remained in abundance. Was it hunger making him light-headed, he thought as he peered through a chink in the living room curtain, or was it this constant gnawing vacuum of waiting and isolation? Rays of sunshine pierced his eyeballs. At least the weather augured well.

He carried a mug of black tea outside and slumped down on the garden lounger, trying to clear the fog from his mind. Four times last night he had rung The Rising Sun and each time they had nothing to....nothing to....his brain seemed to freeze, momentarily unable to complete the most basic circuit of thought. Within minutes his eyes closed and scraps of experience from every quarter of his life came randomly crowding into his consciousness. Neither asleep nor awake, his mind gradually relocated to a narcotic place midway between the two states and became becalmed there, anchored by the image of his daughter. He found himself thinking about the family members Francesca had never known, about the details of their history which he had kept from her because she was too young to understand and they were too difficult to confront, even in the privacy of his own head. An immigrant father who, after years growing sour in the catering trade, found lucrative work on a project in Saudi Arabia – or so he had said – and was never seen again. An English mother, betrayed and broken-hearted, who had never recovered from the loss and died, a cancer victim, three years later. A brother who had gone off the rails in his own way, aloof and ascetic, last heard of in a far flung Norweigan monastery. But most of all, Frank was thinking about how as a growing boy he had buried his emotions rather than confront them and about how they had distorted his life.

A monologue of remorse seemed to shape itself out in his mind, addressed directly to his daughter. "This is difficult for me to say, Cesca," it began. "I know I've behaved like a fool. I know I don't deserve no respect from you or mummy. It's bin like torture for me just trying to imagine how much I must have hurt you. But the thing is this – you 'ave to let go of the hurt. Not for my sake, I mean. For your own, cos if you don't the bitterness might just eat you up like it did me after Dad left. You might even blame yourself. Take it from one who's found out the hard way, these things can poison your life. I love you, Cesca. I don't want that. The heart's a strange place, bloody strange. D'yer foller me?"

He waited as if for an acknowledgement but Francesca seemed no longer to be there. She had slipped away and something else had taken her place in his mind – an unseen presence, a prowler, a series of indistinct noises. Sniffing. Panting. Why did he not show? Suddenly Frank felt his eyelids open with a jerk and he was back in the garden, gawping in amazement. A fox stood right in front of him, almost close enough to touch, a piece of meat that had recently been a vole hanging from its jaws. The animal had no fear or malicious interest, and to Frank at that moment of awakening it seemed neither wholly real nor wholly a figment of his imagination. It simply inspected him with curious detachment as if recognising a kindred spirit, a comrade in the art of terror, and Frank understood just how shallow were the machinations of his conscience. The fox turned now and with a few lightening fast bounds disappeared behind the conifers.

Frank rubbed his eyes and made to stir. The mug of tea lay cold and half-finished beside him. There were things to do, The Rising Sun to ring again. The adrenaline of urgency began to flow harder through his veins with every step he took back towards the house. The mobile lay as ominously as a grenade on the bed waiting to be detonated. He pressed the redial button. A moment passed and then a bleary, irritable voice began to speak in answer to his question.

"But if he comes in at lunchtime you will tell him, won't you?" persisted Frank.

"Don't worry, I'll tell him and his wife," snapped the woman. "In fact, I'll probably never let him forget it. Now piss off and stop pestering us!"

*

"Push the trolley into that corner and grab a table," ordered mummy. "I'll come and find you with the meals." The supermarket cafeteria was busy and it took Donna a while to find a couple of empty chairs. "Can we sit here please?" she asked a fat man with his head in a tabloid newspaper. He grunted reluctantly.

"Thank you," she said and gazed across to mummy queuing at the counter, all powder blue femininity. This man would be an intrusion on their intimacy. But within a minute he dumped the paper on the table and left as if reading Donna's mind. The front page contained a large picture. She revolved it slowly and focussed on another ugly man, his head and face unshaven, his expression mean and desperate as if he had been starved of food for weeks, his eyes so full of defiance and hatred they made her heart quiver – although there was something familiar about him too.

"Orsi has not been seen since his...." she read slowly in the small print underneath until she ran into a cluster of polysyllabic obstacles. Her eyes went back to the top of the page. Three large words hung like a halo over the convict's head. WHERE IS HE?

She dropped her gaze and foraged back into the paragraphs searching for oases of clarity, words she understood. "The police need to elim-elim-elim … are being warned not to app-app …him in any circ-circ …" Scanning for known landmarks. "Gun … prison … London … wife … hobby …"

"Uggh, not him again!" exclaimed mummy plonking a full tray suddenly on the table. "That's yours, Donna. Help yourself now." And without further ado she whisked up the newspaper and returned it to the wall rack.

"Katrina's going to be leaving us," announced mummy as they tucked into their meals. "Her brother's been arrested. He'll have to appear at the War Crimes Tribunal, and she needs to be home to support her family. Take one of my sausages. Here. I don't need two. Next Friday she's off."

"So soon? I'll miss her, mummy," whimpered Donna. "What will we do?"

"Do you –? Is it possible –?" answered mummy hesitantly. "I mean, we could try and manage without a home help? She how it goes for a while? What do you think?"

Donna felt confused. The thought of her being alone with Sarah for long periods at the mercy of her sister's moods and tantrums without recourse to a referee scared her. She said nothing and put a chunk of sausage in her mouth.

"Anyway," added mummy after a long silence, "I haven't definitely decided yet."

Chapter 29

The best part of the Saturday afternoon had leaked away when Frank woke up with the distinct impression that someone had just rung his front doorbell. He strained his ears and heard nothing, then faraway like the fading remnant of a dream, he seemed to catch the electronic jingle of an ice-cream van playing Che Sera Sera, a popular Italian tune from years ago. A directory toppled off the bed as he moved his stiff legs and it came back to him now how he had been randomly phoning around numbers listed under the names of Fearon, Challinor and McLeod in the desperate hope of a lucky hit when sleep must have overtaken him. Still groggy with fatigue, he made his way to the roadside bedroom and opened a peephole in the lace curtains.

Things had taken a drastic new turn. The police spy from number seven stood beneath the window on the driveway facing the wrought iron gate and scribbling into a notebook with the earnest demeanour of an estate agent conducting a property survey. Almost at once an ice-cream van turned the corner, pulled into the kerb and began hailing the public with its jingle. Utterly mesmerised by the unreality of the scene as it presented, Frank suddenly felt compelled by the notion that a police raid must be in progress and that the ice-cream van must conceal an armed support team who were about to leap out at a given signal and storm the house – an idea which, on the grounds of its sheer Hollywood absurdity alone, he was instantly proceeding to dismiss when, to Frank's further amazement, the spy abruptly withdrew from the driveway and marched up to the van with the obvious intention of speaking to its owner.

*

Donna was still smiling at the ludicrous thought, now firmly implanted in her imagination, of Sidney being ceremonially married to a cat, as she trailed mummy back into the house.

"Just look at the mess in here!" complained mummy, as she

243

unpacked their wet swimming things in the kitchen. "You'd think a bomb had hit it!" A sticky trail of pots, plates, glasses and empty tins snaked round the work surfaces while the culprits responsible had evidentially absconded to a higher plane from where the repetitive thud of hip-hop music betrayed their illicit presence. "Go and see what your sister's doing and tell her to come and clear up the mess immediately or she's grounded again. I'm going to put my feet up in front of the telly. I think I've earned the privilege after six hours entertaining you at the pool!"

As they had alighted from their car they had bumped into Sidney, polishing his own vehicle, and accepted an impromptu invitation to share a pot of tea. Donna, who had never ventured over the doorstep before, was intrigued by the untidiness of the rooms and the odour of the cat, which lingered everywhere. Mummy had once confided that Sidney had acquired Chelsea to fill the space his wife used to occupy. They were really a couple. It had sounded like a silly joke at the time, but now that she had seen the house from the inside, with its litter trays, balls of wool, half full tins of Whiskas and assorted playthings strewn around, Donna understood exactly what mummy had meant.

She ran up the stairs obediently and thumped twice on Sarah's door, confident in the authority mummy had given her.

"Who is it?"

"Me! Mummy's in a bad mood!" A splinter of giggles broke out. Donna opened the door. "What are you doing?" she challenged one, then the other. Polly looked taken aback and covered her turquoise rimmed eyes as if caught in the act of something vulgar.

"Who wants to know?" snarled the mask of Sarah's moisturised face as she plucked her eyebrows with surgical intensity.

"Mummy. I just told you."

"We're getting ready to go out to the charity disco at school tonight."

"You've got to clean up the kitchen, or you'll be grounded."

"God! Shut the door behind you."

"Now. She means now, Sarah."

"Okay! I heard! Scram!" Donna retreated. "Div!" A petulant command followed after her. "Come here!"

"What?" asked Donna reopening the door.

"Can you lend me some money? I've spent my allowance."

"I haven't got any money. Sorry."

"You will be. Don't come back. Ever!"

"I don't intend to!" Donna went unruffled into her room to see if Sylvestra, who had been placed on window ledge patrol, had any news for her. The school bulletin lay there, too, in the sunlight, which had just a hint of orange afterglow about it. Outside the tresses of the willow shimmered in a halo of well-being. Surely nobody could resist an evening like this. Not even a recluse. "Is he back from work?" asked Donna grabbing the doll with one hand and the bulletin with the other. "He is, isn't he?" And an audacious idea occurred to her.

*

A huge ice-cream had changed hands and Frank had felt his mouth salivate with envy as he had watched the spy slowly devour it, leaning nonchalantly against the garden wall. What was the man playing at? Then suddenly he discarded the remnant of cone and made his move, walking directly up the garden path. Was this the signal for attack?! Frank's gaze darted back to the van but no reinforcements emerged and the elderly driver was merely serving a couple of kids with lollipops. As the spy approached the front door, he became momentarily passed out of sight; then he reappeared apparently in full retreat, striding away without a second glance back, across the street and finally disappearing into his own house.

For several minutes Frank stood motionless listening to the gurgling of his deprived stomach, his mind inert and baffled. Eventually the van also departed and the strangely empty street seemed to mock him now, to accuse him of having imagined the whole episode. Then in the distance he heard the distinctive melody of Che Sera and the spell was broken. The dreamscape dissolved and the adrenaline flowed back through his body. He rushed downstairs and discovered a folded scrap of paper lying on the mat by the door, covered with neat loopy handwriting. The spy must have just delivered it!

"Sorry to trouble you," it began. "My name is Jack Cummings. I rang your door bell but there was no reply. I recently brought the house at 7 Clifton Road. It is the one with the green garage and narrow drive. Anyway, I've been admiring the beautiful wrought iron gate on your own driveway and wondered where I could buy one like it?......"

What followed did not matter. Neither the fact that Jack Cummings said he worked shifts nor that his place of employment was a police station. Frank felt his shoulders fall several inches out of his neck and he began to laugh with relief, a deep bellied, self-mocking laugh which continued as he flung open the patio door and cavorted out into the back garden. He headed directly for the embankment, resolved to enjoy the remaining hours of sunshine.

Within minutes of stretching out along the low brick wall barrage, his back propped against the gate stanchion, the mood burnt itself out and left only a residue of fatigue behind. A gentle breeze dusted his face and gradually his eyelids gave up the struggle. He did not notice the red booklet which slipped out of his pocket. Now he seemed to be floating weightless in a black-purple balm that smelled of honeysuckle and barbecuing meat. His mouth salivated with hunger. Then faraway, in an unseen corner of the past, a frail soprano began to sing.

"When I was just a little girl, I asked my daddy what would I be. Would I be happy? Would I be rich? Here's what he said to me –"

Off Frank went scurrying down long winding burrows of memory to locate the source, his voice falling in with the chorus, and suddenly he arrived in a living room full of children and decorations. A banner read; HAPPY BIRTHDAY – EIGHT YEARS OLD TODAY and Francesca stood in her pink floral party dress singing the song to perfection, just as he had taught her.

*

Donna read back what she had written in the top margin of the bulletin. *Plees, plees come and wach me on sports day! Luv from Donna xxx I am in the 3 leg race.* The map, the times and all the relevant details were on the front page, so Tony could not miss them. Maybe, just maybe, he would find the time? She folded it up, tucked it into her knickers and hurried downstairs.

"I'm going out the back to look for Chelsea," she told mummy. "When are we having supper?"

Mummy shrugged indifferently. "Half-sevenish?" she suggested. "I'm going to order a Chinese takeaway." And she took a languid sip of wine.

Donna could hear Tony singing before she reached the keyhole and tiptoed through so as not to alarm him. She need not have bothered. Arms folded, eyes closed, he seemed lost in a world of his own singing, "Che sera sera. Whatever will be, will be. The future's not ours to see. What will be will be."

One verse followed another and always the same chorus in between. He had a nice singing voice, she considered as she edged round directly in front of him hoping to be noticed. Should she announce her presence? Eventually he lapsed into silence.

"Tony? It's me," she whispered. "Am I disturbing you?" But he did not seem to hear. She waited, and waited. His lips were twitching. She moved closer and listened to his breathing, unsure whether he had now dropped off to sleep. A small red booklet lay just beneath him on the concrete mooring in a patch of dry mud, and there were also paw marks like those left by Chelsea on the sun lounger the other day.

"Hullo – it's me," she announced more boldly now. "I hope I'm not disturbing you?"

Suddenly, without opening his eyes, he appeared to hear. "Course you aint disturbin' me, Cesca," he mumbled back. "I'm your daddy."

"My name is Donna!" giggled Donna with amused relief. "Not Cesca! You silly man!"

*

Frank opened his eyes with a start and one reality dissolved instantly into another, smothering him in confusion. A metamorphosis had taken place. Francesca had evaporated back into the past and the little girl from Mansfield Road hovered in her place. He gazed at Donna's guileless sky blue eyes, the light brown shoulder length hair, the dimpled smiling cheeks – unable to find his tongue. Then a sleek black creature swooped down from the sky, alighting on a gatepost and curling up its wings into an angular miserly attitude. It instantly cleared his head and he heard his lipsmumble, "Look at that cormorant, kid. Ugly bird, aint it? Must be waitin' for the tide. Like me. I thought I'd got rid of you, anyway. Didn't I tell yer I'd be workin' all weekend?"

She seemed to grimace with embarrassment and Frank instantly regretted how mean spirited his words sounded. The truth was he needed a dose of her company. "Well, never mind. Your 'ere now, ain't yer? And I'm glad," he made amends. "Er....I don't suppose you've got any sweets or anythin' on yer?" She shook her head. "No matter. It was kind of you to leave those things the other day. The pictures got a bit wet."

"Did you like them?"

"Course." Her eyes lit up. "They were 'triffic. I wish I 'ad something' as good to give back in return. I reckon you'll be a famous painter one day." This delighted her and so he laid the praise on thick, dimly aware as he did so how Donna's mere presence revitalised his thwarted paternal affections. To be the recipient of the trust and high regard which Donna could not help but betray in every inflexion of her face was indeed an honour.

"Are you feeling hungry then?" she asked when he lapsed into silence.

"A bit. Have you already eaten?"

"Not properly. I had a cake at Sidney's. Mummy's going to order a Chinese takaway tonight."

It took a couple of seconds to light up. Like a neon sign. Lying dormant in a dark unused billboard of his mind. "What? Takeaway? How do you mean?" he gawped. "Oh, my God! Don't tell me, kid! You ring up and they deliver it!"

"Didn't you know? You can get pizza delivered too, and other things."

247

"I bloody well forgot," he guffawed. "I never 'ad need of it where – never mind! You're an angel you are, Donna. I love you!"

"Tony? You could give me a butterfly," she said suddenly. "I mean only if you had one to spare."

"Oh, yeah?" He watched her face beam with expectation and hated what he had to say next. Giving her a butterfly would be a risk too far. "The thing is they're all spoken for, the ones I've got at 'ome. They're going to be sold."

She looked upset and it mortified him. "Will you have some more by next week?" she asked hopefully.

"Oh very likely. By next weekend. I could give you one then." The words just slipped out like an apology and Donna pounced immediately.

"Well I could come for tea on Saturday and you could give me a butterfly then?"

"Er.....but what if your mum's got other plans for you?" Frank flannelled. "Or what if – ?"

"I don't think she will," said Donna. "But if she does, no problem – we'll do it another day."

Frank shrugged off the problem with a smile. By next Saturday afternoon he would be long gone – if McLeod's plan held good.

"Have you always made butterflies? I mean for work?" the little girl was asking in the background of his thoughts which had strayed back to the banquet of Chinese food, available at the end of a phone line.

"No. I done other things," he answered. "It was a geezer called Leppy got me involved. Funny the way it happened though."

"Did he work in the butterfly factory before you then?"

"Yeah. You could say that," chuckled Frank. "I only knew him by reputation at first. Educated in natural sciences, he was."

"Go on then," demanded Donna. "Tell me the story."

"There aint much to it. I was banged up in solit..." Frank instantly corrected himself. "I mean, I was in this toilet on me own once, and I found a beautiful butterfly down the pan. Right where I'd bin doin' me business so to speak. Am I disgustin' you?"

Donna shook her head. "Was it dead?" she asked.

"No, Far from it. It loved the place, flew around for days. Not always in the pan of course. But that was its favourite part of the room. How it got in God only knows. I used to watch it all the time. It kept me goin'. Seemed like a bloody miracle at the time. I mean the way something as delicate as that could survive life in a shit house, er, sorry in a toilet!"

"And did you show it to Leppy?" asked Donna giggling at this profanity.

"Yeah, eventually. I put it in a cup, and he looked it up in one of 'is books. This is the really amazin' part of the story. It turned out to be a rare Scandinavian type which nobody'd seen for years anywhere!"

He watched with a smile as Donna's eyes rolled in innocent wonder. Then suddenly she said, "Is this a joke story? It is, isn't it?"

"Cross me heart. Swear on me mother's grave!"

"But what made it stay in a toilet?"

"Food, Donna. It was eatin'," Donna pulled a face. "That's right it was gorgin' itself off me waste products."

"Ugggh!"

"Leppy told me. Full of nitrogen, see." Frank levered himself up and walked towards the keyhole as he explained why butterflies needed nitrogen to procreate. "Anyway, that was my first butterfly experience," he concluded, "and it kind of motivated me to study them."

"Where are you going?" exclaimed Donna in alarm.

"To order a takeaway. Maybe two or three," he grinned.

Donna looked disappointed. "Are you coming back? I wanted to ask you something very important!" she pleaded.

Frank felt touched. "You sure you aint gonna be missed at home?" he said.

"Not til half past seven. Please!"

"Okay then," he reassured her. "I'll be straight back."

*

Donna sniffed the air. In one of the gardens a barbecue party must have been taking place. She could hear animated chatter and smell the meat cooking. The wrinkly old man who owned the dog four moorings down appeared pushing a wheelbarrow and the beast let off several yelps of reproach at her presence. The man kicked it once in the ribs then skilfully disgorged a pile of refuse into the cavity below. Now she noticed the red booklet and bent down to retrieve it from the mooring shelf. There appeared to be paw marks everywhere, baked hard in the mud film which must have been deposited by the last high tide. On the cover of the booklet two embossed words stood out – TIDE TABLES – and she sat on the wall to study her find.

Inside the cover she read the names Sue/Cesca, scribbled by a neat hand, and then an address in Sydney, Australia which presumably belonged to them. The actual layout of the tables surprised her. They were differently structured, far more intense than the small one which Mrs Harper cut out from the paper. Each page divided into four vertical columns and packed with lateral rows of five, six – she counted them carefully – seven digit numbers. Yes. She checked again. Seven. Between the fourth and fifth digit was a gap. And this was a consistent gap right down each column, as too, was the full stop printed between the fifth and sixth digits. Right then, she thought to herself, what is it trying to say? A few weeks ago her brain would have fled in terror from this arithmetical contagion and never looked back. But now the bacteria of numbers seemed to have lost their virulence. She had developed antibodies of self-confidence which came rushing to her assistance as she turned the pages one after another.

Quite quickly she realised that this was a tidal calendar, dealing with all the months in the year as well as individual days and each parcel of numbers had been anchored to an abbreviated date, situated in the margin. The layout was both clever and beautiful, she considered as she perused the data and began systematically to distinguish between the timings of high and low tides. The same pen which had scribbled the address on the inside cover had been busy in the months of May and June, too, where a plethora of circles, asterisks, and doodles caught her eye. The final and boldest circle by far appeared on June 21 around the digits 0103 6.57 and a tiny butterfly doodled in the margin next to it as if for good luck.

"What you got there?" came the voice of Tony suddenly behind her.

"Your Tide Tables book. You left it on the ground, silly man!" she grinned. "Listen. Is this right?" And staring hard at the page she announced, "On Saturday, June the twenty-first the high tide will be at um? three minutes past one in the morning and will reach a height of six point five seven, um now, is it feet or metres?" She held the booklet out to him for clarification.

"Metres," he said grabbing it out of her hands brusquely.

She watched it disappear into a trouser pocket. "That's next Saturday, I think," she added to dispel her awkwardness to which he said nothing. "I don't know why you marked it. It'll be too dark to see."

"Look, Donna, it's on the move now," he remarked at last.

"So it is!" agreed Donna with relief. Almost imperceptibly the fulcrum of nature had shifted. She noticed that the pile of old man's garbage had become half submerged and informed Tony about the incident. "Isn't that naughty of him?" she asked.

"Yeah, I've seen whole bins chucked in. That's what attracts the foxes, I reckon."

"Foxes? Here?" gawped Donna unsure if it was another tease.

"Course here. Aint you ever 'eard them at night? Terrible racket they make when they start fightin' over the pickings an' all."

"You're teasing me, you are!"

"Look down there. You can see their paw marks," he said with a gesture towards the ground.

"Chelsea made those! They're on your sun bed, too!"

"Nah, kid," he grinned. "Cat's don't have paws that big. In any case, the animal that left those prints has been in muddy water and cats hate water."

So they do, thought Donna and she gulped, "Do they live here in the gardens then?"

"On the railway embankments, I reckon," he tried to reassure her. "The one who bosses this patch is fearless, mind you. He don't tolerate intruders – unless they're bigger than 'im. Pure killin' machine he is. No conscience, no guilty secrets hold him back. All this land belongs to 'im."

Donna felt even more terrified. "I – I – I thought it belonged to Georgia's mummy and daddy?" she stammered and was relieved when Tony affectionately tousled her hair and coaxed the conversation in a different direction. She told him all about the school sports day and Abigail.

"Is Abigail your best friend then?" he asked.

"Course not!" she objected. "You are.....You are, aren't you?"

"Yeah," he chuckled. "Just testin'. And you passed."

"Anyway, could you maybe come and watch me? Mummy can't take the time off work." She discreetly produced the bulletin. "This explains where it is and everything."

"Work'll be a problem for me, too. Sorry, Donna."

"Couldn't you make more butterflies than usual the day before and take some time off?" she pleaded.

"It aint as simple as that," retorted Tony stuffing the bulletin into his pocket, "but I'll consider it. Okay? Now tell me what else you've bin up too."

She told him about her success in the Geography test, then about the policeman who had come to her house at night. "I think he was looking for those robbers," she said. "And he wanted to see Mr Brown, too. Did he come?"

Tony leant forward and stared at her hard. "What day was that?" he demanded and became impatient when she could not recall.

"M – Monday, I think?" she guessed and this seemed to settle his agitation. "My daddy's body was burnt."

"What?"

"The same night the policeman came. I mean....er....Sarah told me the same night. It was cream – cream something?"

"Cremated," muttered Tony and peered deep into the gathering river as if suddenly preoccupied with his own thoughts.

Donna realised now that her eyes had become wet and she

turned away, not wanting him to hear the intermittent piston of sorrow which had begun to convulse at the trigger of this unresolved memory.

"Donna? What are you crying for?" she heard. "Is it about your sister?"

"No. It's about my daddy being cremated. It's so horrible," she sniffed and Tony instantly tried to console her with an explanation of the process. She squeezed gratefully at the hand he offered to her but now sobbed louder than before. "But how can you go to Heaven if your body's been turned into ashes? I mean even if Heaven exists?" she complained. "It's impossible, isn't it?"

"No it aint. Look, it needs a vicar to explain it proper," he replied. "Maybe.....er.....this body is like a shell. When it dies I just carry on somewhere else with....er....a new one – only it's made out of spirit and air and....er....can move about much more easily....Am I making sense?"

Donna nodded. His description reminded her of the Wulawait story.

"Now then, brainy box, who was it said energy can't be created – just changed from one form into another?" he asked suddenly in a silly quizmaster's voice.

"Dunno," gulped Donna.

"Dunno? Dunno?! And you the one with the certificate of achievement! The only certificate I ever got was fer swimmin' across the baths doggy paddle."

Donna could not help but smile at the mime which accompanied this remark and she dried her eyes with a little apology. "Did he speak to you?" asked Tony in a suddenly altered tone of voice.

"Who?" she replied puzzled.

"The policeman?"

"Oh. Not me. Just mummy and Sarah. I was playing in the Metro Centre. He didn't see me."

"But you heard him – yeah? Can you remember much of it?"

She tried to recall. "Mummy told him your friend spent a lot of time in Scotland. And....um....oh yes, there was a man who had broken something. I think he had been in prison. "Then it came to her all at once – two pieces of a jigsaw sliding neatly together to form one integrated island of sense. "The policeman showed mummy his photograph. I think it must have been the same one that was in the newspaper today. Did you see it?"

She watched Tony give a faint negative movement of his head. "Did you?" he asked back.

"Course I did."

"And?"

"And what?"

"And did he remind you of anyone?"

Donna considered carefully. "Well, he did look a bit like a football player."

"Any particular football player?" asked Tony with an odd glint in his eyes.

"That French one with no hair. The ugly one. Don't know his name," offered Donna.

Tony ripped a twig from a nearby shrub and revolved it pensively in his mouth. "So you reckon that the police are lookin' fer an ugly, bald French professional footballer with forty million quid's worth of gold bullion in his kit bag, do yer?" he said with a sudden guffaw of laughter. "Shouldn't be too difficult to find! And they're searchin' all the trainin' grounds round here?"

"But not just round here," Donna giggled back. "They're searching everywhere. That's what the policeman said. Suddenly she remembered something else. "And there were two of them!"

"Oh? Two bald footballers? They travel in pairs like London buses, do they?" grinned Tony. "Never one around when you need it, then two arrive at the same time!"

"Stop it! You're always teasing me!" laughed Donna. "Two policemen, I meant!" And she thought about adding gratefully, "You're trying to make me feel better about daddy," but that was too obvious to need saying. "Tony?" she asked instead. "Do you mean like a butterfly?"

"Do I mean what like a butterfly?" he said leaning back relaxed again the stanchion.

"Changing one body for another? You know – it starts as a caterpillar and then –"

"Yeah – sure. That's what I meant."

"But butterflies die at the end of summer, don't they?" persisted Donna. "They don't change into anything else?" And she watched Tony's eyes fix on the unbroken tract of blue sky as he pondered.

"I don't know," he confessed at length. "I hope they do. I hope they have a reason fer bein' what they are that don't just stop with their physical existence. I hope people do an' all. Look at the sun up there. What makes it come up and go down every day? Why don't it just fall on our heads? Fer thousands of years nobody knew why – it was a total mystery. But now we've discovered the reason."

"What is it?" asked Donna shielding her eyes from the orange glare.

"Gimmme a break, kid! I aint an expert!" snorted Tony. "All I know is there's a reason of sorts an' it's got somethin' to do with gravity."

"So why haven't they found a reason for people yet?" challenged Donna.

"Search me," chortled Tony. "But you can bet plenty of egg-heads are busy lookin'! And sooner or later they'll discover one. At least a reason that keeps them happy til a better one comes along."

"Sarah doesn't believe in Heaven or God," considered Donna. "And neither does mummy."

"Do you?"

"I don't know. All my teachers do. And so does gran'dad."

"My mum did," mused Tony. "I used to grill 'er just like your doin' me. Brought up a Catholic, see. And never recovered. Ah, yes, long dead she is. She once 'ad a job in a pastry shop – makin' gingerbread men, yer know – our larder was always chock full with the broken ones."

"Hmmmm! Love – lee!" cooed Donna.

"Not fer breakfast, dinner and tea they aint! Anyway," recalled Tony with amusement, "'The world aint a factory, Frank,' she used to lecture me, 'and we aint created just to be gobbled up by old age and despair. God's put us here to love and have children and to fulfill his hidden purpose!' My dad thought she was barmy. He left her when I was twelve."

"Frank?"

"What?"

"You said Frank. The world aint a factory, Frank!?" Donna watched the smile seem to drain out of Tony's face, his eyes shift around nervously.

"Frank's my brother, see. She used to tell 'im and all," he replied swinging his legs suddenly over the wall where they sat. "Well, time up. My takeaway'll be arrivin' soon –"

"Tony?" Donna interrupted quickly, positioning herself in his way. One further question had been long squatting on her mind like a vulture. "Does it hurt when you die?"

"It depends....I....er....think it often looks much worse to the people watchin' than it actually feels," said Tony hesitantly. She noticed the way he prodded his foot into the gravel as if the answer might lie buried there.

"Did you see your mummy die?" she risked and Tony shook his head silently. "Sorry, Tony," she added.

"It's okay to ask," he reassured her. "She was on pain killers fer days beforehand, the ones that give you lovely sensations. The doctor told us she would 'ave just slipped away in a dream."

"But my daddy died in a road accident," complained Donna trying now to prise open the catacomb chamber of her memory in which the details had been long ago interred. Then she felt Tony's arm snake around her shoulder.

"I'm sure it would 'ave bin all over in a split second. Your dad probably never felt a thing."

A chink in the mausoleum seemed to open and Donna described what she saw inside. "Daddy died three days later in hospital. Mummy told me once."

"Well, you can bet the doctors would 'ave given him the same special drugs me mother had," he said kneeling down and pulling her into his chest. "Your dad would 'ave felt....I don't know....like he was floatin' out to sea in a boat on a beautiful, calm moonlit night."

Donna closed her eyes and the scene composed itself in her imagination. A sky littered with stars. A warm balmy breeze. A tribesman silently paddling daddy across the vast expanse of ocean to his new island home. Time seemed to stand still. Then suddenly she felt her whole body propelled into the air. The spell was broken. "Where are you taking me!?" she squealed with delight.

"Back up the garden," Tony replied without breaking stride. "Your goin' home now and so am I."

*

The work surfaces in the kitchen were spotlessly clean now and an odour of disinfectant filled the room. Donna padded upstairs to her bedroom where she was instantly greeted by the sight of Sarah's back. She knelt on the carpet examining the contents of a doll box, illicitly extracted from beneath the bunks.

"What are you doing?" Donna demanded indignantly. "That's private."

"You told me you didn't have any money," sneered Sarah and revealed the ten pound note. "Where did you nick it from, liar?"

"Mum – mummy gave it me!" stammered Donna. "Now put it back in the box!"

"I'll put the change back when I get home from the disco – if I'm feeling generous."

"But – but why can't you spend your own pocket money!?"

"Because I've already spent it, witless one."

"Right. That's stealing," determined Donna. "I'm telling on you." Sarah instantly sprang across the room and blocked her sister's move towards the door. "Get out of my way!" screamed Donna.

"Make me, bitch!" screamed Sarah back and Donna felt two wild hands flailing her to the floor.

"What's going on!?" shouted mummy scurrying up the stairs.

"She's stolen my money and hit me," blubbered Donna.

"I wasn't stealing it – I was borrowing it!" insisted Sarah self-righteously. "Here, take it, you tight arse! I don't want it now!"

255

Mummy turned in exasperation to Polly who had strayed out of Sarah's room to see what the commotion was about. "Sorry. I didn't see," shrugged Polly loyally.

"Where did you get this, Donna?" asked mummy as she retrieved the banknote from where Sarah had flung it on the floor. Donna bit her tongue.

"She said you gave it her!" pounced Sarah.

"Certainly not. Donna, who gave it you?"

"Nobody. I found it on the pavement," groaned Donna in exaggerated agony.

"A liar and a prima donna!" jeered Sarah flouncing off in triumph. "She probably stole it."

"Get up, Donna. You're not dead," exhorted mummy. "I'll keep this money for now. We can discuss where you got it another time." She walked out on the landing before announcing loud enough for Sarah to hear as well, "And tomorrow we shall be doing something altogether as a respectable family unit for once. So Sarah, don't make any alternative arrangements."

*

Frank could not be bothered with a plate. His fork pitched wildly into one silver carton after another, loading the gourmet cuisine into his ravenous mouth, the new anxieties which had begun to coalesce in his mind since Donna's revelation of a newspaper photograph now totally obliterated by this enormous satiation of appetite. It was the mobile suddenly vibrating into life that gave temporary pause to the process of his gluttony.

"About bloody time!" he exploded. "You were supposed to ring me after you'd bin to Brentford nick! I've bin sweatin' 'ere! Somethin' came up!"

"Monday I told you. I said I'd only ring before that if there was a hitch," replied McLeod with total equanimity. "And there wasn't a hitch – at least, not til you started belling my local. It's a nark's watering hole. So what's the problem?"

Frank felt rebuked. He garbled an explanation which sounded hollow even to his own ears. McLeod did not comment. He simply outlined the schedule of Friday night's business in a cold almost contemptuous voice. Hunter's final contribution, it transpired, had been to rebirth the river cruiser at a managed mooring adjacent to the ferry in Twickenham.

"You sure it'll be properly fuelled up and runnin' good after all this time?" asked Frank.

"Yes. The ferry master's been well paid."

"When's the last time you spoke to 'im?"

"Och, a couple of weeks ago. The man's totally reliable."

"So was Hunter accordin' to you, mate," challenged Frank suddenly annoyed by the Scotsman's laconic attitude. "That boat's gotta long journey ahead of it. If the engine dies on the river we'll be kippered. It needs a proper service."

"I'll ring him again tomorrow...." McLeod's voice seemed to break up suddenly and twenty seconds passed before it came back halfway through a sentence. "......but it's a really shit likeness."

"I missed most or that. What's a shit likeness?" retorted Frank. And as the Scotsman proceeded to explain Frank felt a wet patch of panic spreading across his groin.

"The photo's been put out on the telly, too," said McLeod, "but it isn't as bad as it sounds. All they've got is this old prison mug shot. They havn't even tried to enhance it. And anyway, according to the early evening news, the suspect's been sighted already –"

"What!?"

"In the East Midlands."

"Your 'avin' a laugh! You must be!? East bloody Midlands?"

"The report said that C.I.D. are shifting the focus of their inquiries up there. Check the box yourself. It could be a police bluff, of course, to convey a false sense of security. So no silly risks between now and D day. No stray phone calls. No little outings. Stay tight inside. I'll be backing the boat in around quarter to one. Show the green torchlight. After this sentence, you won't be hearing from me again til 4 pm on the day which is when I collect the cruiser – confirm."

"Confirm," rasped Frank. The mobile hiccoughed twice into silence. He reached out again with his fork to the special fried rice carton but suddenly found his appetite had completely deserted him.

Chapter 30

"Where is this poxy place?" asked Sarah as they finished their breakfasts.

"Newlands Corner. It's near Guildford," snapped mummy through firmly clenched teeth. She was busy at the ironing board.

Donna studied her sister's antagonistic expression. "She's trying to punish us," muttered Sarah confidentially then added more stridently, "I've got two essays to finish for tomorrow."

"You'll have plenty of time for homework when we get back," snapped Mummy and handed them each a neatly pressed pile of clothes to wear and insisted that all rights of style objection were summarily withdrawn.

On the drive nobody smiled or spoke. "Where is Guildford mummy?" asked Donna after a while just to thaw the ice.

"You'll see," chirped mummy knowingly and veered the car into the relentless conveyer belt frenzy of the M25. "It's quite spectacular. A nice walk in the countryside is what we need right now."

They had parked the vehicle and walked back to the Heritage Centre to consult one of the maps pinned to the hoarding out front when Donna heard their mummy exclaim "Oh Keith! What a surprise to see you here!"

A man with a rapidly balding pate and baggy hiking shorts stood next to them, grinning like a monkey. Sarah's face turned instantly to thunder. The introductions were conducted with a minimum of fuss. Keith had a son a bit younger than Donna who wore thick-lens spectacles and walked with a limp and a daughter two years older with freckles and lank over-shampooed hair. The grown-ups quickly decided to set out together and the children were encouraged to forage ahead spotting the correct colour coded boundary markers. The views across the Surrey Downs were breathtaking.

"Have you been here before?" Donna asked the little boy as he peered into the distance.

"Once, I think. No. Twice," he replied uncertainly.

It was his most expansive outburst of the afternoon, in Donna's company anyway, except when they reached the cafe at the end of the circuit and Keith insisted on treating everybody to ice creams and drinks with conspicuous largesse.

"Where's your mummy today?" she asked him while the children congregated at the table.

"She died," replied the boy glumly and retreated back into his cocoon of owlish solemnity.

"I'm going to the toilet," announced Sarah suddenly. "Coming, Donna?"

"Yes," replied Donna, taken aback equally at the correct use of her name and the fact that Sarah seemed to have deliberately waited until the other girl returned from her ablutions before issuing the invitation. There was only one available cubicle and Sarah took it ungraciously.

"What's Rachel like?" asked Donna as she waited outside.

"Boffin," came Donna's retort. "Mum's set all this up and thinks we're too stupid to realise!"

"Sarah?"

"What?"

"Is Keith going to be our new daddy?"

"Not if I've got anything to do with it." And the end of the sentence got flushed away in the operation of the lavatory system.

*

Frank finished what was left of the chicken chow mein and prawn fried rice for his lunch. Four pristine cartons remained unopened. He had slept well for a change and felt resolute and lucid despite everything. A memo pad lay on the coffee table in the living room. It contained a shopping list of concerns which seemed outstanding now that the food problem had been resolved. He picked it up again and read: *Mugshots, Reply Neighbour, Fix fence, Hommertons.*

The first Item he could do nothing about. There were no other recent photographs available to the C.I.D. No help his brother Paulo could give them or any other relative. He supposed C.I.D. could 'age' the mug shot in some way, or otherwise 'doctor' it, but if that was their intention, why had they not done so already? The second and third items he decided needed definitive action. What if Cummings had come back to see why his note had not been answered? What if Donna blundered into the garden with her mother and sister in tow? He had spotted them all drive off together earlier dressed in their best bib and tuckers. It was a good time to sort the problem.

The job did not take long. A makeshift strategy involving the wheelbarrow and a load of spare paving stones but one Frank felt confident would frustrate the most persistent efforts of a child twice her size trying to break through. Subsequently he scribbled a brief reply to Cummings explaining how he had recently rented the property and had no idea where the owners had purchased the fancy gate. He signed it with McCleod's alias and determined to post it through the man's letter flap well after dark. That left just Hommertons to address. Impulsively he dived into the local directory and found a number. Off and on all afternoon and early evening he rang it unsuccessfully, finally asking the operator to intervene.

"Sorry, sir," she cooed. "No fault on the line. Nobody appears available to answer."

So he abandoned the task. He suspected the ferry and the chandlery must be a one man enterprise and the gaffer would have his hands more than full on a Sunday coping with the pedestrian traffic. Even so it was odd, he considered. Why no voice mail service? He crossed the first three items off his memo list, resolving to ring Hommerton's ferry again tomorrow.

*

It was too humid to sleep. Donna lay in bed reflecting on the meaning of the day's unexpected events. A solitary plane droned distantly through her sense of apprehension. The family had ended up at Keith's house, eaten a meal, watched a video and listened to Rachel play her recorder. Suddenly the bedroom door clicked open and Donna rolled over just in time to spot the ghostly outline of her sister duck beneath the upper bunk.

"Sarah?" she said but no reply came. "Sarah? You're not allowed – unless you're going to tell me about Daddy." No reply.

"Sarah, is it you?"

"Yes."

"You can't stay unless –"

"Can I get into your bed, please?" cut in Sarah.

"Why?" hesitated Donna. "Are you going to tell me?"

The bunks creaked as Sarah's head appeared again like an apparition followed by a material body scrambling up the pine ladder, the mattress sagging with the sudden implosion of added weight.

"Are you – !?"

"Sssh. Keep your voice down. You'll wake mummy."

An invisible elbow bounced off Donna's cheek. A knee thudded into her thigh. Was this a physical assault? An act of revenge?

"Sarah -!" she shuddered in alarm.

"Sorry. Move over. You've got all the room. Okay. That's better. God you're sticky!"

Donna felt herself suddenly attached to the sweating incubus of her sister like a Siamese twin. A smell of cold cream and toothpaste pervaded her nostrils.

"So are you. Sarah?"

"What?"

"I want to know about daddy."

"What do you want to know about him?"

"Well," began Donna startled as much by the open invitation to pry as the calm measured tone in which it was delivered, "why hasn't mummy got any photographs of him?"

"She has got some wedding photos but they're hidden away."

"Not in a frame on the sideboard she hasn't. Didn't she love him?"

"Course she loved him."

"Then why?"

"I think she's scared."

"Scared? What about?"

"I don't know, Div. The past, I suppose. She thinks – never mind."

"She thinks what? Go on."

"She thinks he cheated on her with other women."

"Cheated? Do you mean sex and all that?"

"Yeah."

"I heard gran'ma say something like that."

"But he didn't. I would have known. I spent more time with daddy than she did. And even if he did, it was her own fault, I reckon. She was always nagging him to get a proper job, always shouting."

"Did he shout back at her?"

"Never once. Daddy wasn't like that. He never lost his temper. He'd just turn the other cheek, play games with me, or take me to the park." Donna heard her sister's voice falter and choke with emotion, only to collect itself again after a pause. "Anyway, that's why she won't put his photo on the sideboard."

"Sarah?"

"What?"

"Are you scared of the past?" Sarah muttered an inaudible answer. "What?" persisted Donna.

"Not really but sometimes at night I get scared.......I imagine things. It's stupid, I know – but I can't help it."

"You mean things like ghosts?" Silence. "Sarah? Is that why you sleep in my room?"

"Yeah. I'm not so scared when someone else is in the room with me."

Donna felt her sister's breathing on the nape of her neck. They had not been this close for years if, indeed, ever. Certainly Donna found it difficult to remember a time when Sarah had cried or admitted weakness like this. "It's not fair, is it?" she asked.

"What isn't?"

"About daddy's photograph. She's got photographs of gran'ma and gran'dad on the sideboard. And photographs of us when we were little."

"That's different."

"Why is it?"

"Because we're still alive."

"Sarah?"

"Yeah?"

"What if they die. I mean gran'ma and gran'dad? Will she hide their photographs away?"

"That's different. I thought you wanted to know something about daddy? If you don't let's go to sleep -"

"I do!"

Sarah opened her mouth in a great mint flavoured yawn that almost devoured her sister's head. "Were you there when he died?" asked Donna. Sarah grunted and shifted her right arm. "What happened?" persisted Donna.

"You know very well."

"I don't. Not properly."

"Mummy told you."

"But that was a long time ago. I can't really remember it – except?"

"Except what?"

"Nothing."

"Except what, div!?" repeated Sarah suddenly hard and aggressive.

"Except you were there." Silence. "Was I there too, Sarah?" Silence. "Sarah?"

"You were asleep in your pram."

"Was it night time?"

"Course not. You never slept at night when you were a baby. Only during the day."

"Did I?" giggled Donna.

"You were a pain in the arse."

Donna giggled some more. "Go on," she said.

"He'd just won some money on a horse race, I think," reminisced Sarah slowly. "I don't know how much, but he was very happy and we were all going out for a meal in a restaurant later."

"How do you mean 'won it'?"

262

"He did a bet in a shop. You know, like Sidney does."

"Oh yeah. Was he rich then?"

"Course not. He was an actor. He only worked about three weeks a year. That's why..." Sarah stopped in mid sentence.

"Go on," coaxed Donna.

"That's why we got to spend so much time together. Mummy had the proper job."

"Even then?"

Sarah grunted. A composite picture had begun to shape itself out in Donna's mind, scraps of memory and celluloid spliced together with imagination. She put herself in the pram. She could see the giants sliding intermittently in and out of her narrow frame of vision. She could hear their guffaws and whoops and shushes. She was not yet asleep. She was just pretending to be.

"And mummy kept telling us to keep our voices down," Sarah was continuing. "'I'm popping out again to buy some fags,' whispered daddy. 'Won't be long.' I wanted to go with him. He wouldn't let me at first. But I insisted. Kicked up a fuss I suppose. I knew if I went with him he'd have to buy me some sweets. 'For god's sake take her, Don,' ordered mummy, 'before she wakes the baby up.' He'd already left and I had to run after him, through the front door. We lived in a side street, a couple of houses from the main road. Do you remember?"

Donna tried hard to squeeze an authentic image out of her memory bank. They had vacated that flat when she was three to go to the other one upstairs in Clapham.

"Anyway, it was a really busy road," continued Sarah, "Always full of traffic. The south circular it's called. I wasn't allowed anywhere near it on my own. He was in a good mood. 'Alright, go back in now, I'll get you something,' he laughed. But I wouldn't take no for an answer. 'Let me come with you and choose!' I kept whining. By that time we had reached the corner and he had to bend down to talk to me above the noise of the traffic thundering past. 'Just tell me what sweeties you want and I'll buy them,' he said. I couldn't think properly. I told him the name of a couple of things. 'Okay. Straight home!' he grinned and pointed. I turned round and pretended to set off. Then I remembered something else I wanted and turned back. Daddy was already marching off towards the zebra crossing."

"Oh yes," muttered Donna to herself, envisaging it all like a film running in her head. A film she had been shown once before but whose horrible details she had pushed to the remotest corner of memory. The baby was irrelevant. The head belonged to Sarah now. She would see the film reaching its awful climax through Sarah's eyes and was powerless to stop it.

"'Daddy!' I shouted," continued Sarah with increasing emotion. "'Can you get me a packet of Lovehearts, too!? Daddy!' He seemed to half hear and hesitate, looking back towards me, grinning, and sort of waving with a thumb turned up....... and then he walked out onto the crossing, still looking in my direction and there was this, this sudden long screech like an animal in pain.....I think daddy must have looked round to see what it was and as he did....he just seemed to fold up and disappear into the ground. And where he'd been was this enormous recycling truck."

The sobs and groans of wrenching anguish began quietly at first and slowly accumulated to a crescendo. Donna had heard them many times before but never like this. Now she could feel them, against her body. They belonged to her, too. She suctioned herself onto her sister's convulsions, simultaneously seeking and offering comfort until finally Sarah spoke again.

"It was my fault," she whimpered.

"No, it wasn't, Sarah. Daddy wasn't looking properly. He should have been."

"That's what Dr. Williamson says. But I know it was my fault. I hate myself. And I always will."

The sobbing resumed but now had a quiet more resigned rhythm, waves retreating back to the ocean.

"Sarah? Have you got a photo of him?"

"Somewhere."

"Can I see it?"

Sarah's body convulsed in what felt to Donna like an affirmative statement. "Do you hate me?" she moaned.

"Course not," objected Donna.

"Then you should. I killed our daddy and he died in horrible pain!"

Wave upon wave of grief reared up and crashed down in the darkness. All Donna could do was cling on to the black rock of her sister's body and search for words of consolation.

"I love you, Sarah. You're my sister," she whispered and eventually the sobbing diminished to an intermittent whimper. "The doctors would have given him special drugs to stop the pain and make him dream lovely things, they would."

Much later in the very pit of night when Donna was awoken by a hideous noise her first thought was that it must belong to a nightmare – the shrieking, panic-stricken brakes of the recycling truck – then it repeated locally, outside the window, and she realised instantly the true origin.

"Sarah? The foxes?" she whispered. "Can you hear them'?"

But Sarah's breathing did not falter. Donna sensed how completely her sister had let go of the world and sunk too far to be reached by the most loving of voices. She listened to the cacophony completely unafraid. Then after a couple of minutes it ceased as abruptly as it had begun and the vast abyss of sleep swallowed her up, too.

Chapter 31

All day Donna had felt bored and out of sorts. It was a condition mummy sometimes referred to as Mondayitis. Normally the mood dispersed by mid-morning break but not today. She had been unable to concentrate properly on anything – not even her drawing. School just hung in the atmosphere like a toxic cloud menacing the free expression of her life and when the release came at 3.25 she was out of the place like an Olympic athlete trailing everyone in her wake including the importunate Abigail. Sarah sat in the car chatting to Katrina with an unexpected degree of animation.

"The project's run by a bunch of youth workers," she was explaining. "Anyone can go along."

"Well, if your mother gives permission it is alright with me," answered Katrina. "But you'd better ask Donna. She may not want to go"

"Go where?" asked Donna instantly.

As Katrina drove them home Sarah explained all about an after school club in the park where you play sports and swing on ropes until as late as 8 o' clock in the evening if you want. She made it sound like a children's paradise. How come nobody had told her about this before?

"It's not been open long," smiled Sarah. "Would you like to come with me?"

"When?! At the weekend?"

"Now."

"Yippee! Now? Can we really?! What about tea and stuff?"

"Oh, we'll have some first and then get the bus down. Won't we Katrina?" Katrina grunted affirmation.

"Thanks, Sarah! Thanks! Have they got lollipops and ice creams there as well?"

"You bet."

The telephone promises, the Welsh rarebits, the change of clothes took thirty minutes. Sarah's make up another twenty, during which interval Donna paced her bedroom hardly able to contain her excitement at the unprecedented act of generosity. A lovely surprise like this was just what she needed. Through the window she spotted Chelsea. Sidney's cat had found his way onto the garage roof. A terrified thrush spiralled into the sky for safety.

"I can easily run you down to the park," offered Katrina. She seemed a bit put out when Sarah declined, as if the consequences of her resignation had already been assimilated.

"I'll take the spare keys," said Sarah. "We can let ourselves in if mummy isn't back. You don't have to stay, Katrina."

On the journey, which Sarah punctiliously supervised, Donna waited for her sister to talk some more about their daddy but decided not to risk souring things between them by initiating the conversation herself. She sensed that she had to be patient and bite back her curiosity for a while.

The activity club lived up to all the superlatives Sarah had used to describe it. A bit shy at first, Donna had hung around on the periphery of things, unsure of how to bond to the various manic clusters of children who occupied the space. Then she recognised several from her own school and with a little diplomatic shove from Sarah suddenly found herself in, leaping, whooping, climbing, all self-consciousness vapourised. So thoroughly adsorbed did she become, in fact, that some considerable time had elapsed before she noticed what Sarah was doing.

She had left the fenced off arena and was chatting to a group of fellow teenagers in the shade of a beech tree. They had a football. Some of the boys wanted to play with it. Others preferred to talk under the tree. When the ball came her way Sarah controlled it and kicked it back with a deftness that induced wolf whistles and applause. She gestured slightly in acknowledgement like a queen, all cool, self-contained condescension.

The living room clock showed 8.20 when they arrived back home. Mummy returned shortly afterwards. Donna felt tired and sweaty and was persuaded to take a bath and go to bed with only token resistance. Nothing had been agreed between them but she assumed Sarah would come again. An hour at least passed. No Sarah? Where was she? The battle to stay awake was almost lost, the questions put to flight when finally the door opened, the familiar padding of slippered feet heard, a rustle of bedclothes.

"Sarah? You can get into bed with me again, if you want?" Donna managed to mumble.

"No thanks. Sleep tight". Silence.

When Donna woke up the next morning in answer to her mother's call Sarah was gone from the lower bunk. Twice now she had been as good as her word. If she had set her alarm it must have been very quiet. Donna rubbed her eyes and peered at the carefully made up bed. The red Troll lay unblinking on top and next to it a 6 by 4 inch colour portrait photograph of a smiling, chubby-faced man. She knew immediately who he was and placed it carefully in the side envelope of her CAT bag.

Are they for me?" asked Donna in the car later as Katrina inched towards the roundabout junction. Sarah nodded. "I don't have to give them back?"

"No."

She removed the photograph from the bag and stared at it lovingly.

"He looked like you," remarked Sarah after a bit. "Around the forehead and the eyes. The rest of you is pure Ramsey."

"Have you got another?"

"Course. Several."

"I'd like to put it in a frame on the sideboard."

"She won't let you. I told you."

They lapsed into silence again. The sense of unfairness wedged in Donna's throat like a fish bone. After all it was their sideboard as much as mummy's. "Can't you tell Dr. Williamson about it?" she said at length. Sarah raised her eyebrows slightly. "I bet he could make her do it." Sarah did not reply. "Have you told him?"

"No."

"I think you should. It's – it's very important. Tell him tomorrow. Tell him to phone her."

The car swung out almost grazing a startled cyclist's shoulder and spurted round the chicane.

"Drop it, will you, div," ordered Sarah. "Just drop it!"

Mrs Harper worked with Donna as usual during the Maths lesson and as the class dispersed for a break she said, "You've done well. Is there anything you want to ask me?"

"Not about the sums," considered Donna.

"Then what? Tell me. I'm all ears."

"If someone tells you one of their secrets – oh, it's silly!"

"No it isn't Donna. Go on. I'm the only one listening."

"Well, if someone has a very big secret and they tell you it, I was wondering if you should tell them one off your own in return?"

"It depends," said Mrs Harper thoughtfully. "Do you have a secret you would like to tell them?"

Donna nodded. "I do. But I'm not sure. He may not like it if he finds out."

"But he will find out if you tell him?" blinked the teacher querulously. "Won't he?"

"It's not him I'm telling. It's her."

"And it's about him?"

"Yes."

"What is it you want to tell her about him, anyway," grinned Mrs Harper self-mockingly. "Is it really so outrageous? Very few things are, you know. They just seem that way at the time."

"I can't tell you. It's a secret."

The teacher patted her pupil affectionately on the head and stood up. "Then you've got to make your own decision," she said. "As a rough guide you should just consider first whether anybody's feelings are going to be hurt, if you tell the secret. Come on now."

This dilemma was still busy gnawing away at the back of Donna's mind when she arrived outside the sweet shop that afternoon.

"I'm going to the park," announced Sarah by way of a greeting and waited manipulatively for a reaction.

"Can I come too?" begged Donna despite herself.

"Get changed as soon as we get in. I don't want to be kept waiting."

Katrina made a few sandwiches and as the sisters left the house still munching, Sidney crossed the street and accosted them. "Have you seen Chelsea? She's not been in since yesterday."

Sarah shook her head and looked at Donna.

"I saw her on the garage roof," said Donna. "I think it was yesterday."

They promised to keep their eyes skinned and walked on towards the bus stop.

"I'm going to show you something else today," announced Sarah when they disembarked a stop too soon.

"What is it?"

"Just wait and see."

They entered the park by a different gate and strolled past a putting green, tennis courts and café, towards the river. Then just before they reached the embankment Sarah indicated an exit back onto a road. In front of them stood a public toilet, beyond that, a modern children's playground with roundabouts, swings and gleaming slides. Further left a flotilla of little boats could be seen parked in the water.

They walked round the first building into a landscaped patio area with benches. A tall slim youth in school uniform who stood lounging against the wall turned and stared at them in recognition.

"Go and play then," ordered Sarah peremptorily.

"Donna's eyes moved quickly from the boy to her sister and back again. "I don't want to," she said defiantly. "I prefer the other place. Can't we go there?"

But the wrath of ingratitude that Donna half-expected to fall on her head did not materialise.

"Wait here a minute," replied Sarah with a haughty smirk and nonchalantly approached the boy who shifted uneasily from one foot to the other. Donna noticed a little boat chugging towards them from the far bank.

"So where's Jimmy and the others?" demanded Sarah. "Skanking again?"

Donna did not hear the reply or most of the conversation that followed. By comparison to the boy's contributions though, Sarah's were confident and bellicose.

"Soon? What's that mean?......I bet he's pulling himself off in the bushes......Yeah, I'm in big awe. I'm an emotional jelly. Piss off!......To the activity centre with my sister. Tell him to suit himself......Our time's too precious to waste."

Sarah turned on her heels back in the direction of the park simultaneously beckoning to Donna, who trotted off in pursuit, amazed equally by her sister's fearless ebullience and the privileged enclosure she has been offered within it. They cut diagonally across the playing fields. Donna noticed that a series of long parallel white lines had been painted onto the lush grass.

"What's this for?" she asked.

"It's a running track."

Then it hit Donna. "Is this where we're going to have our sports day?" she asked.

"Must be. If it's in the park"

There were no curves like you saw on television when it showed running. Just nine straight lines like an aeroplane runway.

"I'm going to be in the three-legged race and the egg and spoon race."

"Yeah, you told me."

"And my best friend's coming to watch me."

"I didn't know you had one."

"He's called Tony."

"Yeah? Just Tony? No second name?"

"I don't know it."

Donna looked at Sarah. She did not seem very interested or properly appreciate the momentousness of this revelation. They walked in silence past some boys playing cricket.

"Does he go to your school?" she asked unexpectedly.

"Who?"

"This Tony?"

"No. He's not from round here really. He's from somewhere else," answered Donna cautiously, unsure how much more, if anything, to give away.

"Oh yes, I remember now. You bought him at the Metro centre. To be Dawn's boyfriend wasn't it?"

"Don't be silly! That's another Tony. This Tony lives very very near us. But don't tell anyone, will you? He'll stop being my best friend if anyone else knows."

Sarah laughed out loud, but there was no spite in it at all, just something else which Donna could not define but felt like affection.

"He's invited me to his house for tea at the weekend," she continued.

"Is Dawn coming with you?"

"I haven't asked her," smiled Donna. "I suppose she can if she wants. Tony won't mind."

"You're crazy you are!" laughed Sarah. "Remember now, two's company and three's a crowd. Who was that little boy you were chatting to on Phil's Folly yesterday?"

"Daniel I think he was called. Why?"

"Maybe he'll be here again today. He seemed to want to make friends with you, I noticed. Did you like him?"

"Yes, he was alright, I suppose," replied Donna without enthusiasm.

"At least he was real," muttered Sarah under her breath and chuckled inwardly.

"What?" asked Donna, confused.

"Nothing," said Sarah, breaking into a trot. "Come on! Last one there's a wally!"

Well, if you don't believe me, thought Donna to herself in annoyance, I'm not going to tell you my secrets, not ever again.

Chapter 32

"Is that the P.L.A. office at Richmond Lock?" asked Frank.

"Yes, sir. How can I help"

"A couple of things. The first one's about the works on the River Crane."

"The passageway from the Thames will be reopening at mid-day today sir. Are you a local boat owner?"

"Yes, I am."

"Then you should have received a letter?"

"Oh, it's probably been mislaid: The other thing is about Hommerton's ferry. Nobody ever answers the phone down there. I've been trying since Sunday. Do you 'appen to know if there's some sort of problem?"

"Hmmm? Hold on a minute, sir."

Frank waited impatiently, rapping his fingers on the draining board, studying the accumulating cloud formations through the kitchen window.

"Hullo, sir?"

"Yes, I'm still 'ere"

"I'm told the ferry has been running normally. Could be he's just too busy to answer. What was it you wanted him for?"

"He's temporarily moorin' my boat. Supposed to be servicin' it, too," explained Frank. "I need to know if it's ready."

"I see. Well, Stan's a bit of a one man band, sir. Your best bet is to go down there. He's very amenable."

"Thank you. You've bin very 'elpful."

Frank went outside and strolled down to the river. Nobody was about. The first high tide of the day must have been twenty minutes into the ebb, he calculated as he perched on the wall and lit up a cigarette. He had persuaded the Chinese takeaway owner to send him a couple of packets of cigarettes and a newspaper with yesterday's delivery. The weather seemed to be changing for the worse. It would be raining soon. There was nothing in the paper that personally referred him or the robbery. He gazed at a photo of Clinton in conversation with Blair and tried to read the story underneath but something impeded his concentration, something other than plain lack of interest. What was it? Buzzing like a fly between the columns of print? He dropped the paper and instantly saw the distraction spiralling to the surface of his mind.

How come if the geezer's too busy on his ferry to answer the blower, Frank thought, can he find time to service his customers' boats?

*

It was not until Donna rounded the corner and saw Sarah nattering away to three of her girlfriends outside the sweet shop that she remembered the significance of the day.

"But butterflies?" giggled Jeanie. "It's such a naff thing to do. I mean for anyone – never mind a big tough villain!"

"It's better than sewing mailbags!"

"Maybe he's sensitive deep down – like that birdman of Alcatraz bloke Mr Chapman talked about? Look, here's Donna."

"Where's Katrina?" asked Donna. "Aren't we going to Dr. Williamson's?"

A horn peeped twice in reply and Katrina pulled into the kerb, missing a lamp post by inches. "What were you talking to Polly and Jeanie about?" Donna asked as the car sped eastwards.

"Oh, we did some stuff in Sociology today about the penal system."

"What's that, Sarah?"

Sarah winked confidentially as she answered and raised her voice so that Katrina could overhear in front. "We read a magazine article about what people who get long prison sentences do to stop from going crazy."

"What?! Are you talking to me?" snapped Katrina.

"Course not," smiled Sarah mock-sweetly. "I was talking to Donna about that gold bullion robber everyone's looking for. Why?"

Katrina said nothing. Donna saw her stare daggers into the rear view mirror and wondered how her sister could be so wilfully mean like that, especially in Katrina's last week of employment.

Afterwards, on the way home from the consultation, a moderate drizzle began to splatter the windscreen. The Thames as they crossed it looked swollen and angry in perfect contrast to Sarah's unusually carefree face. "I don't think I want to go to the adventure playground today," said Donna tentatively in case her sister had inflexible plans to the contrary.

"Me neither, not in this weather," smiled Sarah.

Encouraged by the manner of reply Donna asked, "What did Dr. Williamson talk to you about today?"

"Oh, this and that," answered Sarah evasively. "He said he was pleased with my progress."

"Did he? That's good isn't it? You don't –" Donna thought twice about finishing the sentence.

"I don't what, Div?"

"Nothing, Sarah."

"Go on," coaxed Sarah. "It's alright to say."

"Well, you don't – I mean you haven't been talking and moaning in your sleep lately."

Sarah seemed to flinch slightly with surprise but the expression on her face barely altered. "Sports Day, tomorrow, Div," she said. "Feeling confident?"

"Not really," grinned back Donna sheepishly.

Katrina was able to park outside Sidney's house where the man himself stood tying a cellophane covered poster to the lamp post. "Oh, good coincidence," exclaimed Katrina. "I want to speak with him."

"Has Chelsea come home yet?" blurted out Donna, alighting first from the vehicle.

Sidney looked sad and Donna knew the answer before he gave it. "I'm offering a twenty pound reward to anyone who can find him," he explained. "You never know. He could have accidentally got locked inside someone's garage or potting shed."

"Margaret wants me to clean the downstairs outside windows," said Katrina. "But I can't reach the high ones. Do you have something like a stepladder I could borrow please, Sidney?"

"Yes. I'll bring it round after I've finished with these posters, okay?" offered Sidney.

"Or tomorrow will do. Thanks, Sidney. Bye."

After supper as she changed out of her school clothes Donna eyed the clouds now gathered to a fearsome violet bruise, threatening unprecedented retribution on the proud tossing tendrils of the willow tree. Dawn, on window patrol, had nothing to report on Tony's movements. She assumed he must still be working the late shift.

"But I have to speak to him, Dawn," confided Donna. "Not just to remind him about the sports – you know how dreamy and forgetful he can be – but to ask him to look in the garage to see if Chelsea's there. What's that you say? He may have left the garage unlocked again?"

Prompted by this brilliant insight Donna waited on the stairwell until Katrina had vacated the kitchen and slipped out the back door into the ever-hardening drizzle, then skipped down the ginnel wondering if she had the courage to bang on his French windows, too. It was quite a shock when, bent low to her secret entry place, she found that the fence would not give way. She pushed and tugged as best she could but to no avail. Through a vertical chink she suddenly recognised the problem. The silly man had left a wheelbarrow there, pushed hard against the timber! A sudden roll of thunder unnerved her. She staggered to her feet just in time to see the first lightning bolt and ran back to her house as fast as her feet would carry her.

"And where have you been, muddy knees?" challenged Sarah as Donna turned up the stairwell.

"Nowhere," said Donna wiping the rain from her eyes. "Just looking for Chelsea. Poor thing. I thought I saw him through the kitchen window."

Donna tasted the awkwardness of the words even as she uttered them. She did not want to be deceitful to her sister any more but what else could she do when Sarah treated the first disclosure of her secrets with such amused disdain. There were Tony's wishes to consider in all this, too. He needed to be consulted.

"And did you find him?" inquired Sarah loftily.

Donna shook her head. "No," she said. "I made a mistake."

Chapter 33

Frank pondered if the hairy eccentric staring back at him from the living room mirror looked just a bit too weird for its own safety. He had found a pair of sunglasses and a white floppy hat – the type cricketers wear – on a shelf in the utility room and was trying them on for size. One thing was certain, he thought. His own family would not have been able to recognise him in a police line-up, let alone Joe public.

Keeping tight along the Middlesex embankment via Ducks Walk he calculated that he could be at Hommerton's Ferry in twenty minutes and he had to go if only for his own peace of mind. He had to see the boat and be reassured that it could perform to all the requirements. The die was cast. The front door opened and closed. He walked quickly outside into an eerily quiet sun-stained street.

*

The two girls were waiting at the junction of the Crown and Richmond Roads for the rest of the snake to catch up. "What have you got there?" asked Miss Frobisher approaching them.

"It's a photo of my daddy," beamed Donna. "I was just showing him to Abigail." She held it up for her teacher proudly. "See?"

"My word! What a handsome man he was, Donna! A lovely smile. Just like yours," said Mrs Frobisher.

Donna felt her chest swell with pleasure and she looked towards Abigail who nodded in spontaneous agreement. "His ashes were taken back to Australia and they're kept in a beautiful place by gran'ma Atkinson," she explained. "My sister told me last night."

They crossed the road and entered the park by the tennis courts. "Is your daddy coming to support you?" asked Donna.

"No. He can't take the time off," smiled Abigail. "Just mummy and James. She's bringing her camcorder. Do you mind appearing in the film?"

A system of narrow ramps strutted down from the towpath to the landing stage. One of them veered left giving access to a floating home. As he shuffled along Frank could see the ferry across river picking up passengers on the Ham wharf. The door had been left open and a sign on the wall said: BOAT SHOP AND CHANDLERY. Inside the air smelled fusty.

"Hullo? Anyone around?" he called.

Somewhere in an adjacent room a dog began to yap. Then the phone rang. Nobody came to answer and eventually it rang off. He went back outside and studied the progress of the ferry until it docked. It looked to Frank like a converted police launch. Two mothers with buggies alighted laboriously followed by an elderly couple and a cyclist. They all brushed past him without a second glance. "Mr Hommerton, is it?" he called out to the skipper.

"Stan," corrected the boatman with an easy smile. "Are you after a ride?"

"Not exactly. My friend's got a cruiser moored – what the hell was that!"

The sharp distinctive crack of a gun being fired punctuated Frank's words in mid sentence and he turned towards the embankment where an invisible cacophony of shouting had broken out as a result of the shot.

"No cause for alarm," grinned Stan. "There's a school doing sports events in the park."

*

"Who won that one?" mumbled Donna for something to say.

"Blues," answered Abigail. "Greens came second, I think. Want a sip of my water?"

Donna declined and gazed forlornly towards the huge encampment of spectators which thronged the café side of the track, ten deep at least. Manic parents jostled each other for better vantage points and aimed their cameras like deadly weapons as competitors came lurching past propelled by a rising crescendo of screams and exhortations. Once again she scanned the faces, sifting carefully through the landscape of animation for her solitary nugget of support. He had not come. Bit by bit now she found herself herded into launch pad position for the egg and spoon race, the implements of self-conscious torture thrust into her clammy hands by a P.T.A marshal and the raised pistol with its acrid, saltpetre after-stench firing her unwillingly into the breech. On her eighth stride – disaster! The plastic egg fell out. She grovelled and fumbled on the ground as the beast roared. Up on her feet again she limped home last, feeling utterly humiliated.

*

"It's no problem. Nobody's waiting," smiled the affable ferryman as he led the way along one of the jetties. "I had her ticking over just yesterday."

He stopped opposite a low roofed blue and white river cruiser. "She's fuelled up and had the once over. Not a blemish as far as I can see – apart from the cabin fridge. It needs resealing. Is that a problem?"

Frank appraised the craft. He was pleasantly surprised. "Not in the least," he smiled back. "She's bigger than I expected. What? Twenty-six feet?"

"Twenty-seven," corrected Stan. "Hundred and twenty-five horse power diesel engine. Single screw."

"Speed?"

"Twenty, maybe twenty-five knots full throttle."

"She sits well in the water. I was wonderin' how she might perform under a lot of weight?"

The ferryman looked amused. "You could travel six fatties comfortable on this," he said.

"Yeah? And their luggage an' all?"

"Nothing's going to sink her easy – if that's what you're driving at, mate. I mean the more load, the more speed you'll lose – but the limit's eight knots down river. You know that?"

"Yeah, course."

Somebody began to shout from beyond the park railings then the gun fired off yet again. "Like bloody bonfire night!" joked the ferryman. "Got to go, I've got a customer."

Frank took a twenty pound note out of his back pocket and offered it. "I told you I've been paid up front," demurred Stan as they walked back.

"I want you to do me a favour," said Frank. "Don't tell Mr. Brown when he comes tomorrer that I've bin down 'ere, okay? You see, this is supposed to be a birthday present. I don't want him to twig that curiosity got the better of me."

"Cor! Wish I had a friend that bought me prezzies like that!" grinned Stan taking the money. "I shan't say a word."

"Is that caff in the park still doin' business, do you 'appen to know?"

"Yeah. They do a nice lunch. Bin there before, have you?"

Suddenly Frank saw himself with Sue sitting at the table on the terrace, ordering sandwiches and scones, glowing with love – all those years ago. "Once," he replied. "I think I might just amble back that way. Cheers now."

A line of trees and iron railings divided the park abruptly from the towpath. As Frank entered by the corner gate he spotted the old coach house café perched exactly as he remembered it at the apex of a gently sloping field. Twenty years ago they had found this stretch of parkland virtually deserted but now as he strolled towards his destination a boisterous crowd of several hundred thronged the lower section. One person stood out, a grey-haired man who seemed to be directing operations through a megaphone.

"All remaining sack race competitors must report to Mr Marsden by the yellow flag now!" he crackled. "The three-legged races will follow immediately afterwards!"

Three-legged? thought Frank and felt a mental jolt which made him reach spontaneously into his trouser pockets where he located Donna's bulletin, crumpled up and neglected, and even before he finished unfolding the thing his legs had automatically changed their direction.

*

"Let's do a practice run over there," suggested Abigail as she finished adjusting the ribbons that bound their legs together.

Donna agreed reluctantly and made a listless attempt to co-operate. "Left first!" prompted Abigail. "After the count of three! Come on now! Towards my mummy's camera! One – two – three!"

They managed two steps before collapsing in a tangled heap.

"Left not right! Left!" complained Abigail petulantly.

"I thought you meant your –"

"Come on now! Again! Concentrate this time!"

The red eye of the camera stared unerringly into Donna's discomfort making her feel like a cabaret turn on one of those embarrassing Saturday evening game shows. They lumbered and staggered some more, a hopeless parody of the unified technique mastered in previous practise sessions. Within minutes their event was announced and the teachers herded them into linear ranks at the head of the track led by the youngest year four competitors.

"May I again request spectators to give way a little bit," Mr Knighton's voice spluttered above the din. "Some parents are encroaching upon the track area!"

It was the briefest of delays. Donna watched the obscene bulges of the crowd quickly being flattened out as if suddenly entwined in an invisible corset. Then a fat woman lost her footing and was helped to her feet by a man in a floppy white hat who had his back to the track.

"We can win this," exhorted Abigail but Donna did not bother to reply. All she wanted to do was escape the imminent embarrassment. One last time her eyes slid disconsolately along the rim of spectators.

"We can win this, Donna," repeated Abigail clutching her partner's wrist. "Just listen to me and not the pistol. And make yourself go loose. You're too stiff."

Suddenly the man in the white hat turned his head to the front revealing a beard and sunglasses that seemed to be focussed in her direction. It was several long seconds before Donna allowed herself even to hope. Then she raised her free right arm to the half-mast position and gave it an uncertain waggle in his direction. The gesture was immediately reciprocated, albeit with a minimum of exertion.

"Who's that?" asked Abigail.

"That's Tony. My best friend." The words issued from Donna's mouth in a kind of lovesick simper. Her heart seemed to have melted with gratitude and her body had gone limp with joy. The pistol fired. The first tier of victims pelted into the tunnel of bedlam, human starfish flailing and wheeling as if scalded by boiling water.

"He looks funny," giggled Abigail. "Has he been to a fancy dress party or something?"

"No, he's been to the Butterfly Factory. That's why he was late."

The crowd expanded all along the track like a great diaphragm as the athletes sped past, the din rising to a peak of squealing ecstasy and chanting of victorious names. Donna's tier was now ushered onto the grid. The starter reloaded his pistol and the diaphragm drew itself back in with a hush of anticipation.

"Good luck," said Abigail. "Listen to me and go when I say."

"Ready!" shouted the starter.

"Go!" ordered Abigail and out shot Donna's left leg in perfect synchronicity with her friend's, the retort of the gun echoing a split second behind them. They ran like the wind, leading from false start to finish, the second duo trailing a good fifteen yards behind. – too quick for the eye, nobody had seen, nothing mattered.

"Don-na! Don-na! Don-na!" the children were chanting on their side of the track.

In the bedlam that followed Bronwyn gave them the winners' token and a group of back slapping green team mates huddled round, quickly followed by Abigail's mummy.

"Brilliant Abi," she explained breathlessly. "I got it all on camera! You too, Donna!"

But a gap in the huddle had opened up and Donna peered down

the track in a state of speechless elation, hoping to spot the one person with whom she really wanted to share her emotion. She was not disappointed. Momentarily the bizarre shrunken figure of Tony, arms aloft, stood clapping and performing a miniature jig of triumph. Then he was gone.

"Was that your daddy?" asked Abigail's mummy.

"No, it's her friend, Tony," replied Abigail with a laugh. "And I think he was just the tonic Donna needed."

*

Frank was glad that Donna had noticed him. Her obvious delight in his presence touched a paternal nerve. In some small way it even served his conscience as token compensation. He walked directly to the café, found a vacant table on the terrace and ordered a prawn salad which he washed down with beer. The place was busy but nobody except the waitress took a second glance at him. He felt entirely safe and relaxed and increasingly engulfed in nostalgic memories of his visit there with Sue.

"Come here, James! This is where we'll sit!" a harassed voice broke into his reverie. "No, not there. You'll disturb the gentleman."

Frank turned his head. A toddler stood impishly grinning up at him.

"Oh, I think you have done already. Sorry." The speaker lifted the boy away and plonked him into a high chair wedged into the adjacent table. "I'm Abigail's mother, Felicity," she announced with a degree of familiarity that made him look over his shoulder to see if anyone else was there. "I'm going back for the relays. James wants an ice cream. They did really well, didn't they?"

He opened his mouth but confusion immobilised his tongue and, worse, she seemed to read it. "Donna's been telling us about you. How thrilled she is you came." Still he could not speak. "Tony? Isn't it?"

"Yeah," he blurted out at last.

James dropped his menu on the floor and gazed into his mothers eyes defiantly. "Were you a friend of his father's?" she asked picking it up. "We heard he died prematurely?"

"Er, yeah. That's right. He did," he heard himself mumble and noticed two shirt-sleeved policemen walking towards the café from the direction of the regency house.

"Amazing imagination children have, don't they?" she suddenly smiled. "Donna told us you work in a butterfly –"

"Sorry to interrupt. Do you 'appen to know where the toilets are?"

"Oh? You go round the back, I think. Through a little cobbled courtyard."

"Right. Thanks." His knee thumped into the table upsetting the sugar bowl as he rose too quickly. "Bit of an emergency. Sorry."

Bloody stupid sentimental fool, he cursed himself as he hurried in the direction the woman had pointed, round the old coach house, past the tennis courts towards the Crown Road gate without once glancing back.

Chapter 34

"I thought we might do something special for supper tonight," suggested Katrina as she drove the sisters to school on Friday. "This is my last day you know."

Donna felt sad. Sarah asked, "Like what?"

"Ah! Just wait and see!" smiled Katrina enigmatically.

As the children waited in the assembly hall for Mr Knighton to begin proceedings Donna noticed Abigail and Laura on the row behind, huddled together in whispered animation. The headmaster thanked everyone for participating in the sports and presented little trophies to team captains. Greens came third overall.

"It wasn't our fault, was it?" Abigail commented directly to Donna when the classes were filing out. Donna grinned and Abigail asked, "Did you see him again? After you went home?"

"See who?"

"Tony?"

"No. I went to the adventure playground with my sister. Have you ever been, Abi? It's great."

"No. Are you going tonight?"

"I'm not sure," mused Donna. "It depends. Why?"

"Perhaps we could go there together sometime?"

"Why don't you go there with Laura?" asked Donna cautiously.

Abigail glanced shiftily around then said, "I told you – she's not my friend any more. I have to talk to her because we sit at the same table."

They stuttered forward in pensive silence. Out of the hall. Across the verandah. Into the main building. Donna was thinking about Tony; how he had mysteriously melted away in the crowd after the race, how she had peered from her bedroom window about eight o' clock hoping he might be in the garden but been disappointed, how she could possibly thank him for coming.

"Was Tony your daddy's best friend?" asked Abigail suddenly, as if reading her companion's mind.

"Course not. I told you before daddy died when I was a baby," answered Donna and could not help but notice how Abigail's eyes narrowed with puzzlement. "Don't you remember, Abi?"

"But – but –" faltered Abigail.

"Yes?" encouraged Donna.

They were approaching the hallowed portals of their classroom now. "But my mummy...er...well, never mind that. I wondered if I can be your best friend now?"

Donna considered her loyalties momentarily. "Alright," she decided. "You can be my best friend, Abi. But only in school time."

*

Frank struggled momentarily to open the patio door. The blade had jammed once more in the frame, apparently the victim of heat expansion. Outside in mid garden the skies looked benign. A patchy cloud cover was clearing quickly from the west. Fifty-four days it had been since he moved in and this was the last one, not just in the posh white house but in England too. He took the mobile out of his pocket and pressed in the eleven digits he had just scribbled on the back of his left hand.

"British Weather Services?" he asked the respondent. "Can you give me a weather view please? The Thames Estuary tonight, particularly the North Kent coast."

It was an even better forecast than he had expected. He looked at his checklist now and began systematically working through it, beginning in the garage. Replacing torch batteries. Oiling the wheels of the trolley. Stacking away the sun lounger, the fork and hoe. When it came to the bullion boxes he tried three on the trolley. No problem at all. It ran fine on the concrete floor and the lawn outside had become virtually as hard. Each box held fifty one kilo bars. It would be heavy work just him on his own but there was no way he could risk shunting them until well after dark. Why an odd bar had been removed and placed on top of the boxes he could not recall.

He picked it up in due course and examined the indentations of the tiny serial numbers, pondering the current price of two pounds of pure gold alloy on the world market after it had been smelted down. An illicit idea flickered into his mind. One bar out of several thousand – the sponsor was hardly going to hold anyone to account over that, was he? Even if he noticed? And the sponsor owed him a bonus for sure – leaving him holed up like this for fifty-four days. Yes. The sponsor owed him big time! Frank held the bar against his cheek. So small and yet so precious! It would virtually disappear within a fold of his travelling bag. He carried it into the house without further hesitation and dumped it on the coffee table to await packing with the rest of his gear. Nothing else remained to be done outside, it seemed. He peered at the checklist again. Number Plates removed from van? Done. Rear uplift door fully secured? Yes. New batteries in both torches? Yes. Ramp facilitating the trolley path where it dropped six inches from the riverside gate to the mooring ledge? Done. Loose fencing next to garage?

He went outside again and examined his wheelbarrow barricade. Solid as a rock it felt. Unmoved. On a whim he mounted the pile of paving stones it held and peered along the ginnel. Cooking smells prevailed but nobody was about. You would have to be a sumo wrestler to shift that obstruction, he considered as he secured the garage again and went back inside. He checked the time – precisely nine minutes after twelve. All the clocks in the house agreed. When he next ventured outside in approximately ten hours it would be for the very last time.

*

After school Donna could not help but notice how cheerful Katrina seemed on the drive home. "No more school runs for me!" she sighed as she applied the handbrake.

They had parked next to Sidney's car and Donna saw the man himself taping a brand new flyer to the lamp post. "Why are you putting another one up?" she asked as they disembarked.

"Oh, the other one got torn off by vandals," answered Sidney mournfully. "Four days it's bin now. Chelsea's never kept away this long. I've got posters on every road on the estate."

She stared at his glum wizened face. Why should he have to be so miserable when she was so happy? It didn't seem fair. If only she could find Chelsea for him.

"I have finished with your stepladders, Sidney," remarked Katrina. "Shall I bring them back now?"

"Don't bother. I'll pick 'em up myself at the weekend," said Sidney. "You haven't got five minutes to do me a favour, I suppose?"

"Of course, what is it?"

"Only I've bought a steam iron and I can't get it to work proper."

Katrina let the children into their house and returned with Sidney to his. "Poor old Chelsea!" muttered Donna as they dropped their bags onto the hall floor. "If he's got trapped in the big garage over there he must be starving by now." And she felt guilty that she had not even tried to find out from Tony.

"He'll turn up. A cat's got nine lives and Chelsea's only used two," quipped Sarah. "Come on. Let's go and get changed."

"Changed? For what?" asked Donna.

"The adventure playground. What do you think!?"

Donna followed her sister upstairs reluctantly. She still felt flattered to receive the invitation but there was something not quite right about the way Sarah issued it. Cocky and off-hand as if taking Donna's complicity for granted.

"I don't think I want to go today," said Donna.

"Why not?" objected Sarah at the top of the landing.

"I don't have to if I don't want to, do I?"

"If you want to stay a sad, lonely, doll playing div for the rest of your life," sneered Sarah with a flounce into her room, "that's alright with me." And she slammed the door shut after her.

As Donna lethargically changed out of her school clothes she was unaware of the tears intermittently trickling down her cheeks. She wanted to go. Of course she did. But she wanted to go on her own terms. And in her own time. Beneath the surface of her sister's generosity Donna had begun to detect the outline of a selfish motive – boys. Within the environs of the Activity Centre Sarah could safely flirt and socialise with the older Tertiary college crowd, and if the banter threatened to get out of hand, if the moves of the game turned sour Sarah had an instant excuse to remove herself from the proceedings and not lose face – her little sister. "Got to go now. Somebody's bullying my little sister over there." That kind of thing. And to be fair to Sarah, Donna reflected, occasionally her interventions had justification. She sat on her bed in a quandary.

*

Frank rummaged through the clutter in the living room looking for the mobile. He had decided on pizza for supper, his appetite having just been whetted by an advert on television. So far had pizza technology advanced since his incarceration they could now insert cheese into the usually inedible rim of the crust! The absurdity of this marketing angle made him smile. In any case he would have one delivered, a large American with extra pepperoni and olives. As he thumbed through the directory for the number of a local agent the mozzarella cheese seemed already to be melting in his mouth.

Where was the damned mobile? He searched the house eliminating rooms. It was almost four o' clock. McLeod would be ringing soon if he had not rung already. Then he remembered that he had taken it with him into the garage that morning. He picked up the keys without a moment's hesitation and forced open the patio door at the third push.

*

"Would you like to come with me and Sarah to the park? Or do you prefer to stay here and help Dawn pack her suitcases?" Donna asked Sylvestra as she placed the doll on the catwalk of the window ledge. "Oh, my God! He's home!" she exclaimed in reply to her own question, and rapped several times on the glass.

But down below Tony was moving too fast to notice her. He had emerged from behind the garage, crossed the patio and disappeared back into the white house with the alacrity of a sneak thief. Donna did not hesitate to seize her opportunity, speeding down the stairs and out through the garden into the ginnel. Not until she put her shoulder low to the fence and felt it resist her did she remember the obstacle.

She leapt up and down in frustration and tried to find a climbing foothold on the fence but none existed. It was only when she had meandered dolefully back to her own garden that the solution occurred to her. The stepladders! There they stood leaning against the wall where Katrina only yesterday had been using them to clean the upper kitchen windows. But could she lift them? It turned out to be no problem at all. They were light and manageable despite being made of metal and they provided exactly the elevation needed to reach the ridge of the fence from where she surveyed the wheelbarrow below, piled high with slabs of paving stone. What had previously served as an immovable barrier, she now realised, could assist her descent. Then as she maneuvered her body over the top her left leg accidentally tilted the bridge of the ladders and sent them tumbling. It did not matter. She was safely in and now slid down onto the loaded barrow using her newly acquired adventure playground confidence.

The blue curtains were closed along the length of the French windows and, as she walked past them towards the patio door, a phone began to ring inside the house. She hesitated. On the third ring it stopped in mid-cycle and she tentatively reached for the handle. Surprisingly, the door gave way. It had not been closed properly. The way gaped enticingly open. Slowly, cautiously, she craned her neck, expecting to glimpse Tony through the gap. Her feet remained on the patio steps, her body leaning further and further forward until suddenly she overbalanced and with an involuntary shimmy found herself inside the living room, holding her breath, simultaneously thrilled and unnerved by the extent of her daring.

The word "sorry" started involuntarily to form on her lips to soften Tony's surprise but never became spoken because she saw immediately that the room was empty. Instantly a smell of sweaty socks and burnt fat and tobacco smoke all mixed up assaulted her nostrils. The place was an utter tip. A clutter of dirty plates and cups, clothes and food cartons had been randomly strewn around the floor and furniture. Mummy would have fainted from the neglect of it all. Neither the surfaces nor the carpet, judging from the film of dust, had been cleaned for ages.

"We'll 'ave forty minutes buoyancy on either side of high water," she suddenly heard the unmistakable timbre of Tony's voice in another part of the house close by. "Yeah, even with the load...Course I bin measurin' it! What else would I be doin' with me time? Startin' an Open University course?"

The chuckle that followed served to reassure Donna that it would be alright to stay. Her friend was in a good mood. She would sit down on one of the settees, if she could find space, and wait politely to surprise him.

"I'll be starting with the boxes at eleven...What?" said Tony as she inched her way around the huge, low level coffee table in the centre of the room. "No, it'd be a bit risky before that. You never know who might be takin' the evenin' air on the other embankment."

She stopped to examine the debris on the table – ashtrays, crockery, papers, and several of her very own drawings, held down by the pretty yellow paperweight she had seen in the garage. Her fingers strayed along its smooth surfaces for a moment then clutched it up for closer inspection and she perched on the nearest settee attentively waiting.

"Yeah, it's possible, I 'spose but very unlikely," she heard. "I've never yet seen a boat moving out there after dark...No."

It was obvious Tony was on the phone, she considered, but what was he talking about? A boat trip on the river and with Mr Brown's boxes? She placed the paperweight on her lap and allowed her eyes to roam round the room again. A dark fabric bag caught her attention and next to it a pile of clothes ready to be stuffed inside. Then right next to her on the settee cushion she noticed two shiny black objects like workman's tools, or maybe pieces of a mechanical toy that had to be slotted together.

"So how far outside Whitstable bay will the yacht be anchored?" she heard Tony's voice echo down the hallway as she stretched out a curious hand. "Course it matters. It probably won't be first light when we get there...I take it you've got a compass bearing?"

The tip of an index finger had touched the L-shaped piece and probed along the serrated surface of its grip before the truth dawned. Then with a little gasp of pleasure she clutched the handle and lifted the gun into the air. How awesome it felt! How solid and powerful and realistic! She pointed the toy weapon towards the verandah door and felt her finger fall lightly on the trigger.

"Yeah, I know. It's on channel four tonight," she heard. Tony's voice had become more distinct than before. "I'm sorry you'll miss it, mate. Do you want me to video it and bring the tape?" he added with a chuckle.

But the chuckle was no longer disembodied. It had suddenly crossed the threshold of invisibility and reverberated through the room. Donna swung round and caught Tony full in the centre of her sights. His mouth stalled in mid-word and hung open for a second before collecting itself.

"Somethin's come up," it muttered. "Ring me back later."

Chapter 35

It is impossible to tell the exact order in which the thoughts occur to him. Perhaps they arrive collectively in a shower of fear and enlightenment – a momentary dousing by hundreds of tiny needles of consciousness only a few of which manage to cling onto Frank's sensibility? The muzzle aiming directly at his chest. The sweet smile intending no malice. The troublesome patio door swaying on its hinges. The index finger caressing the trigger, gradually beginning to exert pressure.

He knows the pistol is loaded. What he does not know is whether the girl has inadvertently fumbled off the safety catch which makes it operative; whether in fact her presence in the room is real or an illusion somehow induced by the build up of tension. He thinks about the fox and the first time he saw it. He blinks twice, but nothing changes. This is deadly serious. The gun remains intact, poised between Donna's hands.

He thinks about the small American comedian he had been watching on television last night. "I'm not afraid of dying," the comic is remarking dryly. "I'd just prefer not to be there when it happens."

He thinks about his last visit to Leppy's prison cell. Leppy is set to embark on a one way trip to hospital to have his tumour removed. Leppy knows he won't be coming back but refuses to be consoled. "I just hope there isn't an afterlife, Frank," he confides sardonically. "The thought of having to rub shoulders with that bitch of a wife for eternity is more than I can bear."

Then the image of his mother on her deathbed arrives in Frank's mind. She has been heavily sedated and unable to recognise him or even utter a coherent word for three long days. But suddenly her eyes flicker open, her lips try to smile and she offers a single sentence which until this precise instant he has always dismissed as a delusional raving caused by the morphine. "Be true to yourself, Franco, and God will always be true to you." Yet now as he hovers on what appears to be the last edge of his life those last maternal words resonate with layer upon layer of significance.

"Bang! Bang! You're dead!" Donna shouts gaily.

The words break the spell, terminate the bombardment of memories and Frank becomes fully engaged in the immediacy of the experience. He can feel his heart pounding. "Can you please put it down?" he hears his voice trying not to tremble. "Carefully now."

He watches the little girl's arms twitch, the bead of the muzzle lurch down to the level of his groin, then to his knees. He steps deftly sideways. "Put it back on the coffee table," he coaxes and she obeys. "Gently. That's it"

"Heavy!" gasps the girl flexing her fingers with relief. "Is it a real one?"

"Course not. It's a toy."

"I thought so. Did you buy it for someone?"

He becomes aware of his left arm now, still bent at the elbow holding the inanimate phone, and he lowers it to his hip.

"I didn't mean to come inside," she explains. "I tripped against the door and sort of flopped over the step."

Then he hears her say something else about the cat and the garage but it does not exactly sink in because his eyes have discovered the gold bar lying in her lap. "What are you doing with that?" he interrupts.

"What?"

He can no longer keep the anger out of his voice. "That!"

"Oh, I'm sorry," she apologises and replaces it on the table. "It must be valuable. Is it real gold? Or just painted on?"

He does not answer. His mind has become contaminated by a poisonous weed of truth and almost instantly it has propagated to every furrow of the imagination. There is no way now he can afford to let her walk away.

"The cat's not in the garage, kid," he hears himself mutter. "I've just bin in there." And his hand launches the mobile through the air in a gesture of profound exasperation. It hits the back of the other settee and falls down with a scrunch on the plastic bag that contains his butterflies, partially spilling the contents onto the cushions.

"Wow! Beautiful!" Donna exclaims. "Can I – ?"

"What?!" he barks.

"Do you want me to go home now, Tony?" she asks with a flinch and stands up to leave.

"No. Don't do that," he answers quickly and she seems to smile with relief. "Sorry, Donna. I got out of bed on the wrong side. How long 'ave you bin in 'ere?"

"Not long. I heard you on the phone so I thought I'd just wait. Are you going away somewhere?"

"How did you get in?" he asks in return.

"I borrowed Sidney's stepladder and climbed over," she grins. "Are you sure about Chelsea?"

"Yeah," he murmurs and begins to sort through the options and consequences of extermination. He would have to come clean with McLeod. It would be far too risky to leave her body in the house. They would have to take it with them and dispose of it at sea. "What did you hear me say on the phone?" he asks slyly.

"Something about Whitstable, was it?" she answers gazing towards the settee. "Are you going there? Mummy took me and Sarah once. Can I look at them please?"

"What?"

"The butterflies."

"Help yourself"

He watches her cross the room and kneel down to examine them, her face a picture of wonder and delight. Then he thinks about the stepladders. He will have to remove those. They point in his direction. Once she is reported missing – which will be tonight – how long will it take for a police search to grind into operation? What other evidence might point in his direction?

"Beautiful. Just beautiful!" he hears her purr with admiration. Donna has her back to him. Bowed over the butterfly collection on her knees it suddenly looks to Frank as if she has adopted an aspect of prayer.

*

To Donna's untutored eyes no two butterflies had been made in exactly the same way. They were individuals – not just according to species – but according to the building materials. Tony had used scraps of wire and wood, twine and cardboard, metal and cloth in various ingenious combinations. The wings were daubed and patterned with bold oil-based colours. Some insects had been mounted onto tiny pedestals, others left unhinged to their own puny chances of survival and it was the blue ones which particularly caught her eye.

"Beautiful, Tony!" she sighed again as she held one between her fingers and thumb.

"Donna? Did you tell anyone you were comin' over 'ere?" he asked somewhere behind her.

"Course not. It's a secret," she chirped with the merest half turn of her head. "Always was. Always will be. You promised to give me one. Remember?"

"Course. Yeah. Donna?"

"How long did it take you to make them?"

"Twelve years, one hundred and thirty seven days. Donna? Would you like to see how my nephew's gun works?"

She twisted fully round now, still holding the butterfly. Tony had the gun in his hands but appeared to be fixing the other bit onto the muzzle that made it much longer and clumsy looking.

"Won't he mind?"

"Course not. Come on. Let's go upstairs and try it. There's a target on the wall."

"A target?" she asked scrambling to her feet. "Does it really shoot bullets out then?"

"I'd better just shut the back door first," he said walking towards it. "We don't want any stray cats wandering in behind our backs, do we?"

Suddenly Donna heard her name being called.

"Donna! Are you there! Donna!" It was the distinct timbre of Sarah's voice.

"Who's that?" demanded Tony urgently, his limbs seeming to freeze in mid-movement.

"It sounds like my sister," Donna answered apologetically.

"Donna! Answer me! Are you over there?! Or do I have to come in and look for you?! Donna! You're wanted! We're going out!"

The voice, petulant and uncompromising, seemed to approach closer with every phrase it uttered. Tony rushed to the French windows and using the curtains as camouflage tried to spy the intruder. "I thought nobody knew you were here?" he muttered. "I thought it was our secret?"

Donna's heart suddenly flooded with remorse to see her best friend in such a state of nervous agitation. "Sarah found out," she confessed miserably. "She saw me from the bedroom window. It wasn't my fault."

"You'd better go before she comes blundering through the fence."

"I'm sorry Tony," Donna whined, tears beginning to well in her eyes. "But she doesn't know about you. Honest."

"Donna! Are you there or not!"

"Quickly now. And promise me you won't say anything."

"About what?"

"About me, of course! About being in the house! About Whitstable Bay! About anything at all! Promise me, Donna! Before I change my mind!" His voice had become so desperate. He was pleading with her as if his life depended on the answer.

Donna felt her heart beating wildly in confusion and her hand closed tight on the butterfly as she anguished how to reassure him and herself. "Course I promise," she said. "Can I still come for tea tomorrow?" Tony grunted, his head half-buried in the velvet curtain, his attention fixed on the ginnel fence. "Would four o' clock be alright?" she added hopefully.

"Donna?! What are these stepladders doing here!?" interceded the impatient voice of Sarah.

"Yeah. Tea. Fine," stammered Tony turning towards her. The gun slipped from his fingers. "I'm being kind to you, kid. All I ask is that you be loyal to me in return. Promise it. Go on. Cross your heart and hope to die. Promise it!"

He sounded so earnest, so pitiful that even though she could not properly understand what he meant her head found itself nodding in bewildered agreement. "Cross my heart and hope to die," she repeated and instantly felt his powerful hands dig into her waist and launch her into the air. Her body seemed to pivot in a semi-circle and then her feet landed with a thump right on the threshold of the patio door.

"Now get movin' fast," Tony said, "before she comes over too! Go on!" And her body was propelled outside.

"I'm going off now!" yelled Sarah. "Stop pretending you can't hear me! And if you're not home within two minutes we'll leave without you!"

Donna glanced back at the glass panelled door but it had already been closed and the curtain was drawn across like a veil.

"Sarah! Sarah!" retorted Donna running towards the wheelbarrow. She climbed onto the paving stones and, stretching her body as tall as she could, caught a glimpse of her sister disappearing down the ginnel with the stepladders. "Sarah! Come back! I'm here!"

"Why didn't you answer me, Div?" demanded Sarah meanly. "I've a good mind to take these away and leave you there all night."

"Sorry, Sarah. I was right down by the river looking for Chelsea," whimpered Donna, "and I slipped and hurt my bottom."

"Serves you bloody right," cackled Sarah wickedly. "That's trespassing that is. You could get six months in clink for that. Here. Come on."

As Sarah set up the stepladders Donna suddenly realised she had something crunched up in her hand. She looked at it forlornly. It had once been a beautiful butterfly and might with a few repairs be one again. She wedged it inside her knicker elastic and as Sarah appeared grinning malevolently above her head was able to grasp her sister's wrists and scramble bit by bit up the fence until her flailing legs straddled the ridge.

"Did you see him?" demanded Sarah coldly as they walked back up the ginnel to their house.

"Who?!"

"Chelsea. Who else?"

Donna shook her head. "Where are we supposed to be going to, anyway?" she asked.

"Katrina wants to take us to the park."

"Oh. Sarah?"

"Yeah?"

"What does loy-loyalty mean?"

"It means when you don't skank on a friend," answered Sarah. "Or grass them up like you did to me that time you told mum I went to the pub."

"Thanks. Sorry, Sarah."

"It's alright div. You're forgiven. Almost."

"I don't think I want to go to the park," complained Donna. "I told you before that –"

"You've got to! Katrina wants to buy us high tea! It's her last day. Remember? She's leaving tomorrow."

"Oh. High tea?"

"In that posh coach house place," enthused Sarah. "It's her goodbye treat. Come on. Quickly." And she led the cavalry charge back into the kitchen where Katrina stood in an anaemic trance, her right ear wedded to the telephone receiver.

*

Frank sat slumped in an armchair watching his right hand shaking. Whether it was doing so through fear or relief he could not decide. He knew he was not noble. He had simply reacted by instinct, taken the less awful of two awful options. Only the next few hours would tell whether his judgement had been flawed or not, whether his luck held, whether his life was charmed.

Suddenly the ringing of the mobile snapped him out of his reverie. He quickly recovered it from amongst the debris on the settee.

"What happened there?" demanded McLeod.

"False alarm. Some kid floggin' stuff at the door."

"You alright?"

"Yeah. Why shouldn't I be?"

"It sounded as if..." McLeod's voice hesitated.

"What?"

"Och! Nothing. Look. The boat's fine. I'm going to find somewhere nearby to eat. Okay? I'll start moving her as soon as the flood tide begins to bite. Be ready for me. Time is the essence."

"You don't say. Be lucky."

"I told you, already, luck is for chancers." Frank could hear the grimace in the voice, and something else, too – cold and sinister –

but before he could compose an appropriate retort the line went dead.

He thought about ringing for the Pizza but decided against it now. There was food enough in the fridge and anyway the shock of the kid turning up had taken the edge off his appetite. The spillage of insects needed to be sorted, the bundle of clothes, too. What should he wear anyway? A denim shirt would suffice, he reckoned, and his navy pullover on top. He stripped to the waist and donned the shirt quickly. Then as he reached for the pullover his hand seemed to hesitate and change direction. It went to the insect collection instead and his fingers sifted through the pile searching for the mascot that would complete his apparel. Where was it? The beautiful survivor butterfly that had got him started, the specimen that had refused to become extinct, that took strength and nourishment even from the most sordid and rotten environments? One after another he prodded at the replicas but that unique Scandinavian blue stubbornly eluded him. Frank shrugged. No matter. He would pin another to his shirt. He spread the insect army across the cushions of the settee with the flat of his palm and surveyed them like a field marshal. A small white winged butterfly with fiery orange tips stood out and he tried unsuccessfully to recall its species name. An index finger flipped it onto its back and he appraised the mottled green of the undercarriage which would provide excellent camouflage for any insect at rest in nature. Yes, he decided, this one fitted the bill. He found a pin and carefully pierced the abdomen through its central membrane, the sharp print emerging clearly on the other side and now it was a simple matter for his practised fingers to attach the charm behind the collar where it could reside safely hidden away from McLeod's cynical disapproving eyes.

*

Katrina had appropriated the very best space on the coach house veranda and they were served with platefuls of manicured sandwiches and after that with currant scones and raspberry jam and little silver bowls of clotted cream. Then an elderly man sat down at an adjacent table who Donna thought she recognised but even when he ordered a meal in a Scottish accent she could still not quite place him. Lots of people were strolling around and she felt a bit privileged like royalty being surveyed by casual promenaders. Jeanie walked past with a couple of boys and was regally hailed by Sarah.

"One will catch up with you when one has finished dining," she declared and made an ostentatious show of signalling to the waitress for another pot of tea. The Scotsman looked unimpressed.

"Would you like to come and visit me one day?" asked Katrina out of the blue.

"Could we really do that?" replied Donna. "Isn't it very far away, your country?"

"Not so far in a plane!"

"I thought your family were moving to another part of the country?" asked Sarah with a mouthful of scone.

"Well, yes, they are. That is one of the reasons why I am going home to help them. But it will not stop you visiting us if you wish."

"Which part are you going to?" said Sarah.

"To the South. Near the border with Macedonia and Albania. It's called Kosovo."

Donna watched her sister nod thoughtfully, silently admiring her grasp on the impenetrable mysteries of geography. "But it's still in Yugoslavia, is it?" Sarah asked with a glint in her eyes.

"Serbia we call it now," corrected Katrina. "Yes. It is."

"Serbia? Oh, sorry," simpered Sarah a trifle too apologetically. "I must have forgotten."

Afterwards they walked across to the Activity Centre and while Donna swung on the ropes Sarah played soccer with Jeanie and the gangly boys and Katrina relaxed on the grass reading a book. Donna felt strangely remote and detached from them and not just because they were separated by railings. It was like being an extra in a play whose plot she didn't fully understand, waiting for the prompt and cue of the principal actors to trigger her few walk-on, mostly non-speaking appearances.

And when they arrived back home the feeling had still not left her. Mummy had got in ahead of them and dramatically presented Katrina with a large colourfully wrapped parcel "as a small token of our gratitude," at which point Katrina broke down in tears and began hugging each of them in turn and complaining like a broken-hearted lover she would never forget them or their kindness as long as she lived. It was a performance so unprecedented and out of character that Donna could only stand there and be mauled in silent bewilderment.

After Katrina had finally left mummy said, "You look very tired, Donna. Go and have a shower and get ready for bed."

"But we never go to bed early on a Friday," moaned Donna. "I want to watch the telly."

It was only token resistance. Her body had tottered within sight of a busy week's finishing tape and virtually hit the wall, waiting only for the undisciplined mind to catch up. The ablutions were completed in minutes. She donned a pair of patterned pyjamas and retrieved the butterfly from where she had left it in Dawn's safe keeping on the window ledge. Then stifling a yawn she examined the squashed thorax and straightened out the ruffled wings as best she could. The damage could have been much worse. Tomorrow she would find a tube of glue and effect the insect's resurrection as best she could.

"Donna! There's a cup of cocoa for you here! Do you want me to bring it up?!" called mummy.

Donna sprang towards the door. "I'll come down, mummy! Just a second!"

Footsteps sounded on the stairs. "Are you in bed, dear?"

"No, mummy! I said I'm coming down!"

She wedged the butterfly into Dawn's chest where it instantly assumed the proportions of a prehistoric bird of prey and bustled out of the room in search of her nightcap. Sarah and mummy were already sipping theirs on the settee, contented co-conspirators smiling at an American sitcom.

"Can I watch it too?" asked Donna placing herself on the bean bag close to mummy's feet.

"Yes. Then straight to bed."

"Are you going to work tomorrow?"

"No."

"What are you going to do then?"

"Sssh!" hushed Sarah peevishly.

"Well, Keith's coming round with his children," whispered mummy. "We're all going to drive up to Richmond Park, maybe visit the pen ponds. And later have lunch in the lodge."

"Oh? Is Sarah coming too?"

"Yes. If she wants her allowance this week," smiled mummy pointedly. Sarah pretended not to have heard.

"Will we be back home by four o' clock?" whispered Donna.

"I don't know. Why?"

Donna shrugged petulantly. "I want to that's all. Please mummy! I'll be very polite with those children."

When the sitcom finished mummy urged Donna to go straight up to bed. "Are you coming too, Sarah?" yawned Donna, her eyelids drooping.

"Not yet."

"I think you ought to, dear," mummy coaxed remotely from somewhere in the thickening gloom. "I won't be long myself."

"There's a crime reconstruction programme I want to watch," came Sarah's reply. "It's about the gold bullion robbery and that bloke they're looking for. I'll go after that, okay?" The words echoed remotely in Donna's sleep-deprived brain as she groped her way upstairs. "Okay? Okay?"

Chapter 36

The operation had so far gone like clockwork. Apart from a brief squall and the wind threatening to churn up the water as they began to enter the estuary, nothing else had happened in transit to remotely concern them.

Before steering through the Thames Barrage at Woolwich Frank had made phone contact with the duty officer. Far from smelling a rat the man had cracked a joke and warned him about the number of midsummer revellers cavorting around in dinghies.

Twice they passed police launches but nobody so much as hailed them as they kept tight to starboard and within comfortable limits of the speed restriction. Even the main shipping lanes in the estuary had seemed unexpectedly devoid of traffic.

For his part McLeod provided an efficient if taciturn companion. He had ghosted the cruiser in backwards with minimal noise and exact timing. He had more than shared the exertion of loading, never stopping once for a breather. He had thoughtfully brought sandwiches, cans of soda and cigarettes with him and been prepared to take a back seat as Frank assumed navigational control.

"You lost your tongue?" Frank probed at one point on the voyage. "Something on your mind?"

"No. Cigarette?"

"Light it for me, will yer?"

Then they smoked in silence until McLeod seemed to be ready to impart a further gobbit of information about the ship they were meeting, their destination or whatever else needed telling.

"Is it because I rang you at that pub?" Frank asked casually as he bit into a ham sandwich later.

McLeod's lugubrious manner did not alter. "Is what because you rang me at that pub?" he asked back indolently.

"This mood. You could 'ave come round. You could 'ave given me your phone number. You left me danglin' in thin air!"

"Hunter left you dangling, Frank. Not me. He left the rest of us, too. Think on that. Me. Fearon. Challinor. Especially Challinor! But you were the only one who got spooked."

"Was I?"

"Yeah. For a while there I thought you were going off your rocker."

They listened for a long period to the phut-phut-phut of the engine, the thump of hull on waves. The river had widened considerably now, the darkness thickened. The lights on the embankment twinkled few and far between like low flung stars beyond the galaxy.

"Who decided to nail Hunter?" Frank asked eventually.

"The sponsor. Hunter was a junkie, it turned out."

"I knew it! I told you he was a dud!"

McLeod said nothing and Frank felt justified but he did not crow. He allowed his thoughts to blend into the balmy night air. And so it had stayed beyond Gravesend, round The Lower Hope and past The Marshes until the lights of the Medway Estuary and Sheerness filtered into sight.

"What about my passport?"

"It's on the yacht. Together with your whack."

"In francs?"

"Some. But mainly dollars."

It was McLeod who spotted the cutter first, pulsing green and red beacon lights across the void. As they disembarked Frank discovered the three man crew spoke no English. McLeod did the talking in pidgin French for both of them. The sailors seemed agitated, in a hurry to pulley up the boxes and start the engines.

"What about the cabin cruiser?" Frank asked.

"They're going to tie her up and scupper her in mid-channel," McLeod explained. "Relieve us of a problem."

And Frank suddenly remembered Hunter again, the crack addict, scuppered in the Thames and relieved of his head.

"Come on Frank. Michel is going to show us where to kip."

Michel looked disappointed when Frank declined. "Tell him later, McLeod. I aint tired. I'll stay on deck."

Left alone to watch the first grey patterns of dawn, then a huge orange corolla budding organically out of the water, Frank had found himself unexpectedly needing to express gratitude for his safe delivery. But to whom or what did he address his thanks? Flecks of spume spattered his face like confetti and he fingered the charm beneath his collar doubting that this could ever be the instrument of such amazing providence. He thought of his mother and the simple unquestioning faith that never deserted her, even at the very end. Her God had not been a talisman, small enough to be tucked into a lapel or back pocket in times of uncertainty but otherwise ignored. Her god had existed in a space simultaneously too close and too far from his creation to be described by human reasoning. "We are His purpose, Franco," he recalled her once saying. "We are His work of art – and not the other way round."

Suddenly Frank tore the butterfly off his collar and dropped it into the churning waves – an act of contrition if not quite faith. Then he found a seat on the deck. What he knew for certain as the first minutes of liberty passed into hours was an overwhelming sense of calm and tranquillity. He felt healed. Reborn. Entirely purged of illusions. Everything he saw from the tip of his nose to the edge of the horizon defined itself with perfect clarity and was complete.

"Thank you!" he shouted with religious fervour. "Thank you!" and he gazed around the firmament as if expecting some divine acknowledgement to be returned.

But nothing changed. Nobody answered. High above him in the wheelhouse stood the solitary figure of Michel, stony faced and unmoved, staring straight ahead. And so Frank heard his words picked up like a gulls shriek in the wind and instantly extinguished.

*

When Donna woke up a sensation close to perfect happiness came squeezing into her consciousness together with the rays of morning sunshine. For a few minutes she lay in bed studying the process of its retreat until only a shadowy bliss remained, recalling nothing at all of those scavengers of her dreams who must have planted the emotion in her heart. Then she crept down the rickety pine ladder. Sarah grunted once and turned over, still deeply asleep, her face spectral white. Quietly out onto the landing. Mummy's door stared back, silent and forbidding.

In the kitchen as she helped herself to cereals and juice the weekend seemed to spread out in front of her like an unexplored continent. The only visible landmark which loomed on the horizon was tea at Tony's house, latitude 4 p.m., but how she plotted a course there across the tundra of family directives remained as yet unclear. If only they could do it now with nobody else yet up to complicate the issue! And why not? Breakfast and tea amounted to pretty much the same sort of thing. Perhaps Tony was sitting in the living room right now eating alone? The thought instantly motivated her to action. What did she have to lose? If Tony was not around she could sit by the river and draw him a thank you picture for later.

Upstairs a toilet flushed. Feet padded on the landing. Returning to her bedroom Donna discovered Sarah back in bed but propped on an elbow studying something in her hand.

"You'd better go back to your own room now," she warned, "before mummy gets up and sees you."

"It's okay. She knows," announced Sarah with a yawn. "I told her last night. What's this?"

Donna's eyes widened in surprise at the sight of the butterfly. She began to get dressed. "Is it yours?" persisted Sarah.

"Yes."

"Who gave it to you?"

"I found it."

"Huh? In the same place you found that ten pound note?"

Buckling her sandals. Running a brush through her hair. The questions seemed to have dried up. Sarah's head had fallen back in a swoon of fatigue on the pillow. Donna collected her pencil box and drawing pad together in a shoulder bag and was halfway out when the voice of the inquisition reached after her again. "Have you got any more?" it demanded suspiciously.

"Course not. You can keep it if you want," countered Donna as casually as she could. "It's not important to me." And she closed the door behind her.

Scaling the fence with the aid of the stepladders was easier the second time around but she made a mental note to ask Tony to shift the wheelbarrow. He was so forgetful. Once Sidney took them back what would she do? Very gently she tapped on the patio windows but when the curtains failed to ruffle and disclose Tony's bearded face she took a deep breath and tried the door handle. It, too, declined to budge. No matter. Suddenly a noise to her right alerted her. A voice, was it? She peered up towards her own bedroom, half expecting to meet Sarah's prying eyes but it was a false alarm. Those windows remained steadfastly curtained too.

Nimbly she made her way past the garage, under the buddleia tree and directly onto the lawn. The grass was dewy and needed a cut.

"Bother!" she said, inspecting her damp sandals.

Then she noticed a pattern on the lawn, a tramway of parallel lines up and down the length of the garden, almost overlapping, as if Tony had been roller skating there or pushing a baby's buggy; and, instantly realising they could be used as a kind of protective furrow to keep her feet dry, she tiptoed forward like a ballerina.

The shrunken trickle of water beyond the conifers had a faint odour of scrambled eggs. She emptied the bag, and resourcefully utilising its potential as a dry cushion she sat on the concrete plinth, her back against the wall, her legs bent into a makeshift easel and opened the pad. The sketches which met her gaze had definite potential and her mind wandered off to the aboriginal painting which had inspired them. Yes, these could be developed. Her fingers sorted and selected a pencil. Slowly at first the grey nib moved into action. Faint horizontal lines appeared followed by vertical ones and subtle curves and swirls. One by one the conscious burdens of life fell from her shoulders. Fingers groped. Eyes focussed. The nibs of comrade colours gradually, painstakingly pressed into service. A gentle breeze intermittently wafted the smell of dank river into her nostrils as she worked to reinvent the aboriginal scene within her immediate context, to blend the enigmatic shapes of what she remembered with those which she witnessed now.

Occasionally a thought would rise up like a bubble from the pool of concentration in which she existed to the surface of her mind. This was the next best thing to having tea with Tony, it said, creating him a gift to compliment the one that he had inadvertently given her. She would explain to him the idea of the picture – the empty canoe on the river of life in full flood, the invisible ferryman who waited patiently to transport the soul of the next dead tribesman across the ocean to an island paradise where he would in time become reunited with his relatives and friends. Maybe she would ask Tony to be her model?

And so time passed imperceptibly for Donna, a perfect synthesis of past and present, of action and reflection.

*

The day was really warming up now. Frank took off his woollen top and strolled around the upper deck at his leisure admiring the craft, all spruce aluminium and stainless steel surfaces with an overlay and trim of wood that felt like teak to his touch. His eyes wandered up the main mast and rigging approvingly, taking in the struts and the backstays, the radar scanners, electronic antennas, the booms and winches. A fully automated floating home if ever he had seen one and the property of a very rich person. He found himself wondering if the mysterious owner was aboard. The sails remained unfurled. The diesel engines virtually noiseless. Suddenly a head appeared, emerging from a port side hatch, Frank watched the thickset muscular body attached to it, bare tattooed arms carrying a tin tray. The crewman offered its contents to him with total Gallic indifference.

"Not bad," smiled Frank biting a chunk out of a chocolate pastry. He sipped at a mug of sweet coffee. Still the sailor said nothing. "Nice boat your boss has got here. Cuts through the ocean like a knife through butter."

"Quoi?"

"Your boss. Any chance of meeting him?" The Frenchman stared back blankly. "Le patron?" offered Frank from a derelict corner of his memory.

"McLeod. You," barked the man by way of reply and gestured back down towards the hatch. "En bas. You!"

"Tell McLeod to come up here if he wants to see me," grinned back Frank. "And tell him to bring my wad and my passport."

"Quoi?"

"Passport," repeated Frank. "You understand alright."

The Frenchman's face hardened now into a sneer of pitted teeth and he muttered a phrase which, though incomprehensible, stung like a poisonous dart.

"Lovely day," beamed Frank refusing to have his blissful mood adulterated by the oaf.

"Fends-toi bien la guele tant que tu peux," responded the sailor. "On est en train de te preparer des bottes en beton pour t'aider a nager."

It meant nothing to Frank. "Francais!" he hailed as the sailor walked off. "Bordeaux? How long?" And without glancing back the man held up two podgy fingers.

If they were intended to signify units of time in hours then not more than half of one had elapsed when the nautical silence was next broken by a repeated banging on the starboard bow.

*

The nib of Donna's umber pencil momentarily paused as an aeroplane sauntered out of the sky a long way off. It veered sharply left and dipped, the rotor blades of a helicopter now glinting unmistakably. She studied the whirring linear progress shielding her eyes from the sun. Then it twisted directly above her and circled the houses like a monstrous dragonfly hunting some tasty morsel of prey. A clutch of birds, all flailing wings, could be heard vacating the willow in terror. She stood up and stretched. Her bottom had gone numb. Her legs felt stiff. Behind her in the conifers an unseen creature shuffled and crawled. Donna passed back through the gate to look, suddenly excited by the possibility Chelsea had turned up.

"Chelsea?" she called. "Is it you? Chelsea?" But the gravel path was deserted, so too the paved enclosure opposite. She peered towards the mulch, whose fat, sagging belly protruded obscenely from a tangle of bamboo and bindweed. The vegetation trespassed along the wall, totally obstructing now what only a few weeks ago used to be a view of the river. Something rustled again low down in the verdant entrails. Donna peered hard and inched closer, risking her feet in the tug and tear of the undergrowth. A limb of foliage flicked her in the eye. A bramble clutched her shoelace. Then her face split into a smile as she saw the cat's unmistakeable tortoise-shell haunches and tail, spread eagled and dormant against the mulch.

"Chelsea!" she called. "You bad bad boy! You're here all the time! Why don't you go home?"

She bent down to stroke him but before her hand could ruffle the stiff, petrified fur the answer starkly presented itself. Where the cat's head should have been Donna perceived only a black hole seething with maggots and reared away with such a shriek of horror she completely failed to anticipate the silent intruder into whose body she helplessly careered. He caught her by the arm to prevent her from falling and she saw his thin lips moving but the words became lost in the roar of the helicopter. The dreadful machine had plummeted out of the sky and now hung a few feet above the willow whose startled tresses billowed out in the wind funnel.

"I said 'have you seen him today?'!" shouted the stranger full in her face.

"Seen who?" whimpered Donna reeling from this double shock.

"The man who lives here? Has he been in the garden today?"

*

Frank craned his neck around the door of the sail locker. He was comfortably settled on a bench, inhaling great lungfuls of ozone but these intermittent bursts of hammering had begun to feel like a deliberate reprimand for his indolence. Nobody was in sight and reluctantly he got to his feet and walked across the upper deck seeking out the location of the noise. It led him to a vantage point right above the stagi ladder where he and McLeod had docked. Instantly he recognised the perpetrator of the din. The river cruiser had been winched above the water line and McLeod knelt down in it labouring clumsily with a jemmy and a mallet intent on driving a hole through the hull bottom.

Not a pretty sight, thought Frank as he watched his unfit travelling companion fumbling on his knees and momentarily felt his heart soften with something like affection for the Scotsman.

"Relievin' us of a problem, eh, McLeod?" he shouted ironically.

"Stop grinning like a monkey and give us a hand," snorted McLeod.

Frank came stepping down into the boat and examined his friend's workmanship. "Looks like you're almost there to me," he remarked. "A bit wider, maybe?"

McLeod gave way and Frank with a few deft blows on the jemmy significantly developed the size of the gash. "Did you get my message?" asked Frank still bent over the wound, teasing away its edges like a fastidious surgeon with a scalpel.

"Yes," Frank heard somewhere behind him. "I just want you to know it wasn't my decision, son. I voted to keep you – despite your becoming a liability. Sweet dreams now."

And during the fleeting moment of awareness between this valediction and the explosion in the back of the skull which seemed to signal the curtailment of his life on Earth, Frank to his own surprise experienced neither fear nor rage. Had there been sufficient time to trawl his vocabulary the embryonic emotion might more adequately have been called relief – though that word, too, imperfectly represents the sheer physical power of the sensation, a surge of benevolent energy purging him of every negative impulse and gathering him to its centre.

*

Donna felt too numb to think clearly. She understood only that she had to remain seated on the mooring wall until the stranger who had introduced himself as Gerald told her otherwise. Some people who lived across the river had gathered in their gardens. They peered upwards towards the roaming helicopter and occasionally, she got the impression, at her, too.

Suddenly a man dressed in green clothes like a soldier burst through the keyhole carrying a rifle. She could not hear much of the news he imparted to Gerald, except that he used the word 'sir' and waited to take orders.

"It's alright now, Donna. Come along with me," smiled Gerald and beckoned her forward, through the conifers and back up the garden, his podgy hand a dead weight on her shoulder.

The huge green jaw of the garage gaped wide open and more soldiers were prowling about inside. Two others stood with rifles pointing at the French windows.

"What's happening?" asked Donna as they passed directly up the driveway. Faces were peering out of the bedroom windows to her right. One of them belonged to Sidney.

"Keep walking. There's no time to lose," came the reply and now, beyond the wrought iron gate which hung back flat against the wall of the house, she sensed a huge commotion. The street as they entered it was choked with people, staring, craning necks and with officers in navy uniforms herding them back. Somewhere a megaphone boomed out instructions then behind her a massive crunching thud reverberated like a sledgehammer on wood. Once. Twice. Three times. And a sort of gasp, half cheer and half panic, arose. She tried to see but the funnel through the crowd had folded in behind them. Her guardian issued orders to someone they passed. Then round the corner, past a police car and at last the familiar front door followed by the urgent enfolding constriction of mummy's arms.

"Mummy! Chelsea's dead!" Donna heard herself whimper.

"Thank God you're safe! I'd never have forgiven myself!"

Again the darkness of maternal love folded in. Now she stood in the kitchen. It seemed like a foreign overcrowded land, the apparitions of familiar and unknown faces gazing sympathetically at her. One of them belonged to Keith, another to Sarah but the attempt at a sisterly smile seemed to have frozen in mid act. How vast and moist appeared her eyes!

"Please sit down, Donna."

It was the kindly voice of Keith speaking. She did what she was told automatically. "Can I get you a drink?"

There were other solicitations and introductions but Donna only vaguely heard them. Her eyes wandered from one unreal face to another, round the room and finally downwards towards the table where a mug of tea had magically appeared and a pair of slender feminine hands. In one of them rested the crumpled blue butterfly.

"I'm your friend," said the owner gently. "Please call me Julie. How did you come across this, Donna? Take your time to think. There's no hurry."

Donna felt her whole body flush with confusion. Had she done such a terrible wrong to take it? She glanced all around desperately searching for Sarah's face but it must have departed from the kitchen already.

"Well, I –" she began hesitantly.

"Yes, Donna? It's perfectly alright to explain."

Chapter 37

The train carriage was almost empty. Donna gazed around blinking in every unfamiliar detail, the immaculate white head napkins, the smooth check-patterned table top, the bold row of digits, – one in the middle of each window to frighten off trespassers, – the four reservation tags on the seats and her chaperone, Miss Julie, replete with off-duty hairstyle and carefully made up face sitting opposite.

"Why are we sitting in first class?" she asked trying to stifle a yawn.

"Why not?!" grinned Julie. "Are you hungry at all?"

Donna nodded. Just lately she had been feeling hungry quite a lot, even a short time after a meal. She felt tired, too. She had not slept too well.

"I'll order something from the waiter when he appears," said Julie. "Did you bring anything to keep you occupied on the journey?"

Donna nodded again and placed her shoulder bag on the table by way of evidence. The intercity whooshed in and out of a tunnel. A field spun into view. They already appeared to be reaching the edge of the city.

"It's a pity Sarah couldn't come with you. Will you miss her?"

"It couldn't be helped. She's got to be in Wales for three days with her geography class," explained Donna as much to comfort herself as to answer her travelling companion. "It's called field-something?"

"Field trip?"

"Yes."

Donna inserted her hand in the bag and pulled out the first object it touched, the drawing pad. She opened it and stared indifferently at her still incomplete version of the Wulawait painting, wondering if there was any point now in trying to finish it.

"Oh, I've got something for you," smiled Julie mysteriously dipping into her handbag. She produced a box about four inches square with glass sides and placed it on the table.

"The blue butterfly!" gasped Donna in surprise. It had been repaired and mounted in its own little compartment like a precious museum exhibit. "Don't you need it any more?"

"No. It's yours."

"Thank you so much!" she said and found herself trying to stifle another yawn.

"You look tired, Donna. I'm not surprised with the week you've had to suffer! Why don't you stretch out and close your eyes for a bit?"

"But somebody else might want to sit down – ?"

"Well, they can't. We've paid for all of these seats," smiled Julie. "Go on. Put your feet up. No-one's going to tell you off."

She did not need further encouragement and within minutes lapsed into a deep sleep. When she woke up the train was standing at a station platform. Doors slammed. A whistle blew. She rubbed her eyes, momentarily disorientated. Her slumber had been full of agitation, the most significant voices of the week weaving in and out of her dreams. Mr Knighton. Bronwyn. Mrs Harper. Mummy. Abigail. Sarah. Coaxing, sympathising, praying, suggesting a week's leave of absence. And those other voices too. The police ones. Pleasant on the surface but severe and inflexible just underneath. Asking. Repeating. Never taking no for an answer. Not once. One of them spoke again now.

"Feel better, Donna? Do you want to order something to eat?"

The menu was placed in front of her and a decision made. The waiter came and went. The train soared through the East Midlands conurbation.

"I phoned your gran'dad. He'll be at the station in his car to collect you, after all."

"Are you coming with us?" asked Donna, uncertainly.

"No. I'm coming straight back on the next train. I've got my job to do. I'll be back to collect you in a week's time. Okay?"

"You don't need to."

"It's all part of the service. I'm off to holiday in Italy next month. Have you ever been?"

The change in manner was infinitesimally small, the eyes marginally harder. Here it comes, thought Donna instantly. The game was on again. Only the start had been strategically delayed. "No," she replied.

"You'd love the beaches. And the food's to die for," Julie persisted. "Did Tony ever talk about going there at all?"

"I don't think so."

"He has cousins in Naples, you know. Does that name ring a bell? Naples?" Donna shook her head. "Of course, he also has a wife and daughter in Australia. He must have mentioned it?"

"Really? No. I don't think so."

Julie sneezed suddenly. Once. Twice. And pulled out a tissue from her handbag. "Sorry. I've got a touch of hay fever," she apologised. "Do you mind if I close the top window?"

Donna shook her head with a smile of affirmation.

"We'll be looking for him in Australia, of course. He can run, you know, but he can't hide forever," said Julie as she stood up. "Murder is a capital offence."

"Australia's a very big place, isn't it?" remarked Donna.

Julie sneezed again and snapped the panel shut with an irritable bang.

"Gesundheit!" said Donna sympathetically.

"Whoever taught you to say that?" asked Julie.

Donna frowned pensively for a second then replied, "I can't really remember."

*

The day after she arrived was a Sunday. Gran'ma encouraged her to phone home. "Hullo? Sarah? It's me!" she announced.

"Hi! How's it going? Everything alright?"

"Fine, Sarah, when are you going on the field trip?"

"In a couple of hours. I'm all packed."

"Can I ask you something?"

"What?"

"How did you feel after daddy – ? You know, after he was dead?"

"What?!"

"I said, how – ?"

"I've told you before."

"Tell me again. Please."

"God!" Silence. Then; "I kept thinking he was going to walk in the flat. Every day. I kept expecting to see him."

"Sarah? I keep feeling hungry."

"Aren't they feeding you properly?"

"No. It's not that. I still feel hungry even when I'm full. It's like a pain."

"Hold on, Div. I'll put mum on. Could be you've got worms? Maybe you need to see the doctor? Mum! It's Donna!"

Mummy reassured Donna that the emptiness pains would gradually pass. They were not something to bother the doctor about. And that evening a large cellophane bag containing individually wrapped sweets appeared on her bedside table as if by magic, comforters to suck in the night, though nobody said as much.

There were plenty of treats and distractions in the days that followed. Nothing seemed too much trouble for her grandparents. The only rules were that she had never to wander into the main road alone and always be tucked up in bed with a warm drink by nine in the evening. Donna wondered how much they knew. It seemed like nothing at all. They asked no questions. They subjected her to none of those sly sidelong glances that so many other people in her neighbourhood had taken to doing. She appreciated this discretion. She felt relaxed and unselfconscious. County Durham could have belonged on another planet. Most nights she slept like a log. Gran'dad put it down to the country air.

Thanks to the persistence of the police Donna could remember virtually everything Tony had ever said to her. Back tracking. Cross tracking. Forward tracking. Like the piece by piece composition of an enormous jigsaw puzzle in words and phrases, now indelibly imprinted on her memory. They wanted to catch Tony and lock him up for the rest of his life. They were extremely considerate to her but she knew after the first preliminary interview that despite all their niceness they did not really care anything about her feelings. They wanted her to see Tony through their eyes and to know him by their names. They wanted to impress on her the enormity and deviousness of his crimes and for her to become committed wholeheartedly to their cause. So her memory of events, initially so forthright and nervous, became increasingly more guarded and selective. No doubt they had carefully ransacked the white house for clues to his whereabouts, she considered, but they would never do the same to her mind. They knew it, too, because it showed after a while on their faces.

"You don't owe him anything, you know," Julie had smiled during one of their sessions. It was a smile just slightly tinted with exasperation. "He told you a lot of lies, didn't he?"

Donna had thought about this but remained largely intransigent. Tony might have misled her in some ways but it did not follow that he disliked her. Mummy always contended that white lies were legitimate. They protected the listener. The number of things he had explained to her, the silly jokes, the little acts of kindness – were *they* all lies? And every time one of the police team opened their mouths to convince her otherwise their words rang hollow with exaggeration.

"There was no butterfly factory, Donna," Julie had retorted. "After the robbery he just skulked in the house. He didn't dare go out anywhere except at night for fear of recognition. He was a thoroughly bad man."

That remark merely endorsed the reality of Tony's friendship, magnifying his visit to the Sports Day into an act of genuine nobility. Donna had nodded and smiled back, the image of Tony dented a bit in the solar plexus but structurally undamaged. Yet Tony had killed an innocent man, or at least been a party to the killing. This fact, together with the revelation of his criminal history which, courtesy of Julie, she gradually ingested certainly did perplex her. Despite all her natural efforts to seal her mind against the deluge of libels, a fine invisible trickle of corrosive poison was gradually seeping through. Even so she steadfastly refused to concede an inch to his pursuers. "I don't think a really bad man could have made so many beautiful creatures," Donna had smiled back with sudden inspiration.

On Tuesday they spent the day at the Gateshead Metro Centre, shopping with gran'ma. On Wednesday they all visited Pat and Ed at the old vicarage, played badminton on the lawn, and stayed for both lunch and tea. And on Thursday the four of them, only gran'ma deciding her varicose veins were not up to it, drove to the coast, along a thin rocky causeway onto an island where an ancient monastery stood. It was gran'dad's idea to take the route back through Sedgefield where he made her get out and inspect the Prime Minister's residence as if it was an historic monument but unoccupied, according to the uniformed policeman who stood by the gate. Donna thought it looked nice but nothing special.

Thursday was her one bad night. Propped up in bed, pencil case in hand, she had resolved to finish the Wulawait drawing but inventiveness utterly deserted her. Both her imagination and fingers seemed to have frozen in time. Even when she turned the page and attempted a brand new picture nothing happened. It felt as if the incomplete one somehow obstructed her way. Neither could she drop off to sleep. Her brain, like a hyperactive spider, spun out convoluted webs of thought. Eventually she sneaked downstairs and knelt on the floor outside the living room, listening to television voices, unsure about the effect of her intrusion on her grandparents if she crossed the threshold.

"...and the lease on the house was taken out by a man calling himself Alexander Brown," she heard. "He used forged identity papers and letters of reference. Here is an identikit picture of him based on..."

They were trawling over the story yet again. It was not the first time she had heard it, nor the second. The news bulletins kept getting an extra wind. Important people in high places were being held to account. Through the crack in the door Donna could see film footage. The images mostly matched the words. The airport. The warehouses. The vans. The river. Donna held her breath. The action was literally getting too close to home.

"Having navigated the Thames in the middle of the night the bullion would in all probability have been transferred to a seagoing vessel somewhere in the Thames Estuary. This is the theory anyway. All the known evidence points that way," concluded the narrator.

The film ended. A man in a suit with a large nose appeared sitting opposite two other people, one of whom she recognised. He addressed them in a flat peevish voice. "Detective Superintendent Crosby, let's begin with you. It's hard to know what's more bizarre in this whole sorry tale, isn't it? I mean if it hadn't been for a teenage girl recognising a butterfly ornament and raising the alarm, your men would still be chasing false leads in the Midlands."

"I don't see why that should follow," Crosby answered complacently. "The P.L.A. are extremely vigilant –"

"Vigilant!?" scoffed the interviewer. "Forty million pounds worth of gold floats down the river right under their noses and nobody turns a hair!? It sounds as if some laissez-faire smugglers charter has been declared to me! Why isn't all river traffic stopped and searched? Automatically?!"

"All river craft are monitored –"

"All of them?"

"Yes, of course. But they are only stopped and searched if there appears to be suspicious circumstances –"

"Suspicious circumstances! At least one known criminal – probably more – chugging merrily along in a boat in the dead of night, blithely passing through the barrage! What did the P.L.A think he was doing? Returning home late from a picnic at the Henley Regatta?!"

Donna pushed the door forward and apologetically offered her face round the frame. "I can't sleep," she whimpered. "Can I watch the telly for a bit with you?"

"Course, lassie," blinked gran'dad in surprise. "There's nothing much on, though. And we're going to bed soon. Ethel? Change the channel, will you?"

The screen went blank. Then an image appeared, like a film starting.

"Would you like another mug of cocoa, dear? I'm making some for us," offered gran'ma, leaving the room.

Donna slipped onto the sofa next to gran'dad and nodded her head. He put his arm round her and the title came up in block capitals.

"Angels with dirty faces?" recited Donna.

"Well done, lass. Not that you'll be seeing more 'an ten minutes."

"Gran'dad? What does it mean, theory?"

"Theory? It's like an idea. That hasn't been proved to be true just yet." He smiled mischievously. "I've got this theory you won't be awake for breakfast tomorrow. Get it?"

Donna giggled. The film was in black and white. Gran'ma returned with the drinks on a tray. Hot, milky and sweet. Nobody spoke. Nobody needed to. Donna sank back into her own thoughts as she sipped her drink.

"Hey ho! Hey ho!" sighed gran'dad at length.

"A penny for them, Donna?" asked gran'ma.

"Oh, I was just wondering," said Donna cautiously.

"Yes?"

"Can't even a very bad person do things that are good?"

Gran'ma and gran'dad seemed to exchange glances, as if uncertain who should reply. Then gran'dad collected the empty mugs and said, "They certainly can. And we've got it on the highest authority. Which ever of you is without sin cast the first stone. Come on now, Donna, back to bed."

*

A car horn honked impatiently behind, then another. The engine of the black cab purred on with total indifference, blocking the width of Mansfield Road.

"Goodbye. Good luck," said Julie hurrying to get back in. "Stay in touch, won't you?"

The three of them waved her into the distance before entering the house, Sarah volunteering to carry Donna's black case and carrier bags, eager to discover what goodies they might contain.

A sizeable chunk of Saturday remained. It had evidently been drizzling but now the sun threatened to break through. Donna handed out the gifts she had purchased in Gateshead and answered their questions. Sarah revealed that she had been swimming in the Gower and stripped off to reveal her back all tanned and sleek. Mummy produced an airmail letter from Katrina and proceeded to read in out loud while Donna studied the photographs which had accompanied it. After that Donna went upstairs to unpack. She was showing the neglected dolls that been unable to accompany her to Durham the glass butterfly case when Sarah walked in, ear-plugged to a shiny new walkman.

"What's that Sarah?" she asked. "I said what's –"

"It's a portable CD player. Here. Take a listen."

Donna manipulated the little pieces into her ears and instantly her head erupted with the fast furious music of a discoteque.

"Good sound? Yeah?"

"What?"

"I said 'good sound'?!"

"Fantastic! Where did you get it?"

"From Keith. I looked after his kids one night while he took mummy out to a show," explained Sarah. "Made their dinner and stuff. You can borrow it sometimes if you like."

"I thought you didn't like Keith?"

"Yeah. Well I don't that much," grinned Sarah impishly. "But at least he's going the right way about making me change my mind." And off she went.

Donna was still puzzling what to make of her sister's pronouncement when she chanced to gaze out of the windows. Something awful had happened in her absence. She spotted it almost at once and her heart lurched. The willow had been mutilated. Almost nothing remained of the foliage. The tree resembled a skeleton which has suffered multiple amputations of its noblest limbs. She bolted in a panic downstairs summoning her mummy to come and confirm the atrocity.

"Someone's pruned it," mummy explained. "It had grown far too misshapen and cumbersome."

"But why, mummy? It's cruel! It's wicked!" pleaded Donna. "There's nowhere for the birds to nest. It was so beautiful and now it'll just die."

"You'll be amazed at how quickly it will grow new branches," smiled mummy reassuringly. "By this time next year it's going to be more beautiful and stronger than ever and a much better sanctuary for the birds. You'll see. By the way, Abigail rang. She's invited you for tea tomorrow. Better ring her back. I've got the number."

The girls nattered away like long lost pals until Sarah intervened. She needed to phone Jeannie about the evening's social arrangements.

"Did you do any drawings in Durham?" asked mummy. "I'd love to see them."

Donna shook her head dejectedly, still inwardly perplexed by her failure of inspiration. Something obstructed it. Something needed doing to remove the blockage but she had no idea what it was.

Then, while mummy prepared supper, she was left to her own devices. It felt strange rediscovering the house, the smells, and clutter of domesticity. A vase of red and white carnations had been strategically placed in the living room. The cushion covers had been changed and on the sideboard amongst the silver framed photos she spotted a new one. Perched discreetly on the second row of the gallery with a slightly puzzled smile as if embarrassed about his intrusion, she recognised the man she had come to know as daddy.

"Can I go outside in the garden, mummy?"

"You don't need to ask, Donna. Of course you can!"

Donna walked into the ginnel and followed it cautiously round the corner. A small black and white cat she had never seen before eyed her suspiciously before arching it's body low to the ground and springing vertically upwards landing with feather light agility on top of Sidney's partition. The fence opposite on Tony's side had changed colour. By instinct she bent down to where the vent had become loosened but she knew already that it no longer existed. The metre wide slat of rotten fencing had been replaced. There was no longer a way through to the garden.

She came back and without asking permission passed straight out again by the front door. The white house when she reached it from the road looked no different. The hollow sockets of the windows. The pretentious wrought iron gate. The withered flowers and weeds in the wooden tubs. If it had not been for the estate agent's double-sided board declaring their intention to let the place again she could have fancied he was still there, studying his tide tables, waiting for the river to rise. As Sarah had indicated, it would be a difficult expectation to kill.

The idea may have come to her during the night. In any case she knew within minutes of waking up the next day what she needed to do. Fortunately a copy of the local paper had been acquired. Donna found it in the magazine pile and turned carefully to the local information section. Her index finger moved slowly down and along the timetable.

Yes. 1.23pm at Kew Bridge. Add on 15 minutes for Richmond Lock. A column of digits shunted up and down in her head then she had it – fixed. She ran back upstairs, found the Wulawait drawing and without a second's hesitation began to sketch. Sarah was not around unfortunately. She had been to a disco and slept over at Jeannie's.

"Well," thought Donna as she applied herself to the task, "if it's not today, Monday or Tuesday will do."

But shortly after noon the pallid, sleep-deprived face of Sarah showed up.

"Can you come with me down the road, Sarah?"

"What now? I've just got in! I need –"

"No. Later. About half-past one?"

"Why?"

"I'll tell you later."

So it was that at precisely 1.35 by the kitchen clock the sisters walked the four paces from their front door to the pavement, one holding a stationery box, the other wearing an expression of reluctant nonchalance. They turned right and after a few more paces stopped to speak to Sidney who was cradling the small black and white cat in his arms. He seemed pleased to see them. The girls each stroked the cat in turn then strolled on quickly towards the hump backed bridge, at which point they crossed the road.

Donna strained on tiptoes but could barely stretch her nose to the top ridge of the brick facia. She opened the stationery box and took out her picture together with a brown foolscap envelope.

"What do you want me to do?" asked Sarah with routine impatience.

"Just a second," said Donna. She read the message she had written on the back of the picture one more time: *dear toni sorry you did not have time to say goodby you are still my bestest frend love donna.* Then she folded it neatly and slipped it into the envelope which she licked and sealed.

"Can you lift me up now, Sarah?"

Sarah struggled to get a purchase on her sister's thighs and lower body but eventually succeeded and Donna's head soared high above the parapet. Beneath her the curve of greeny brown river, speckled with leaves and scraps of vegetable litter, all moving lugubriously towards the sea as the ebb got under way. She dropped the envelope, watched it complete a twisting somersault and smack the surface of the water. For a second it seemed to sink but almost immediately broke back up and gulped for air, latching onto a knot of floating vegetation. Her feet dangling in the air, the weight of her body now resting comfortably on Sarah's shoulders, Donna gazed after the little raft of debris as it swirled about at the mercy of the current and finally drifted round the bend out of sight.